THE SHADOW SIGILS

Book One in the Shadow Duology

Ky'erra Sylva

Ky'erra Sylva

For more information, or to book an event, contact :
(ksylva99@outlook.com)

Cover design by Elif Petek
Artwork design by BookCoverZone

ISBN - Paperback: 979-8-218-84076-1
ISBN - Ebook: 979-8-218-86023-3

First Edition: December 2025

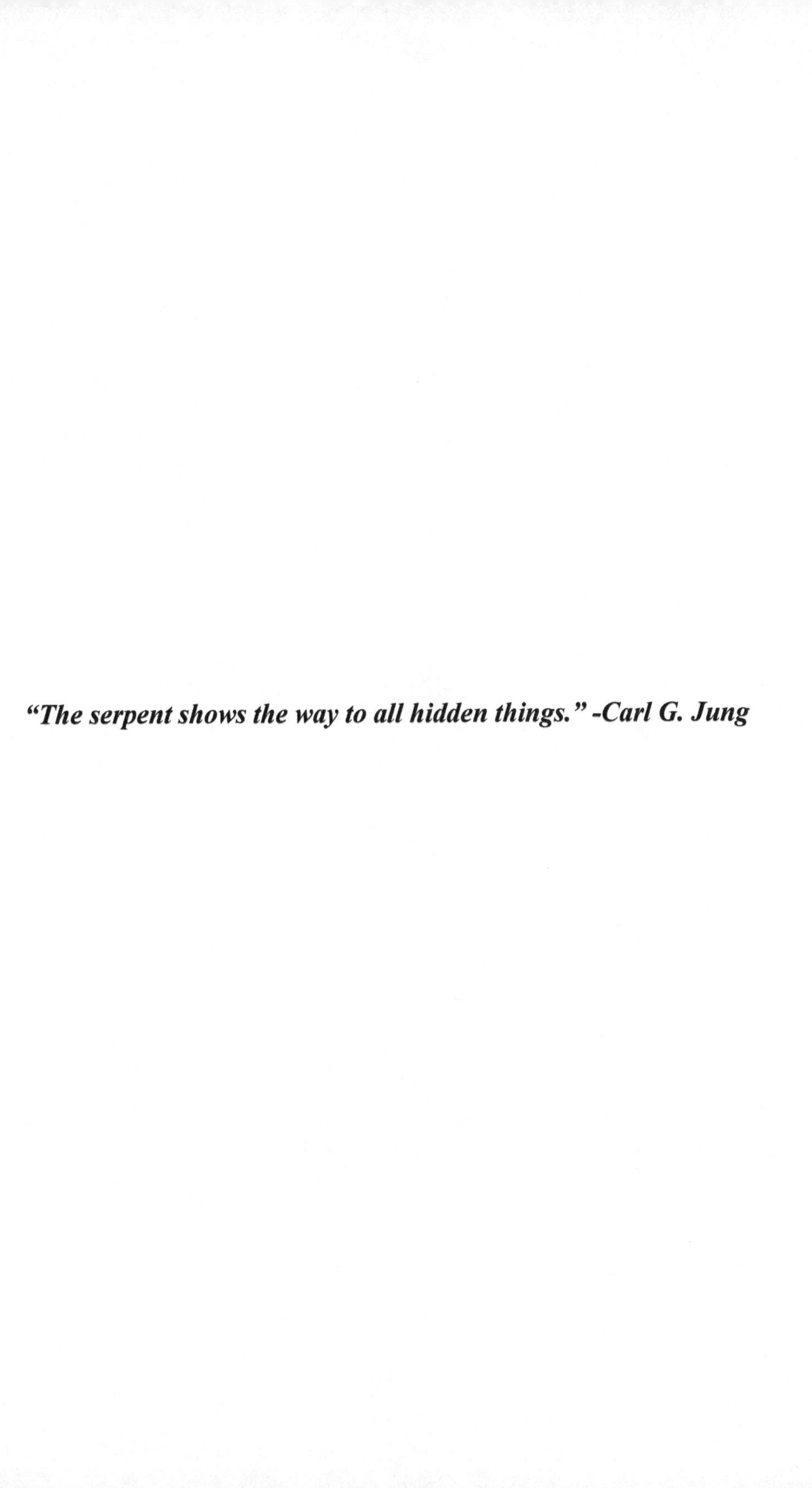

"The serpent shows the way to all hidden things." -Carl G. Jung

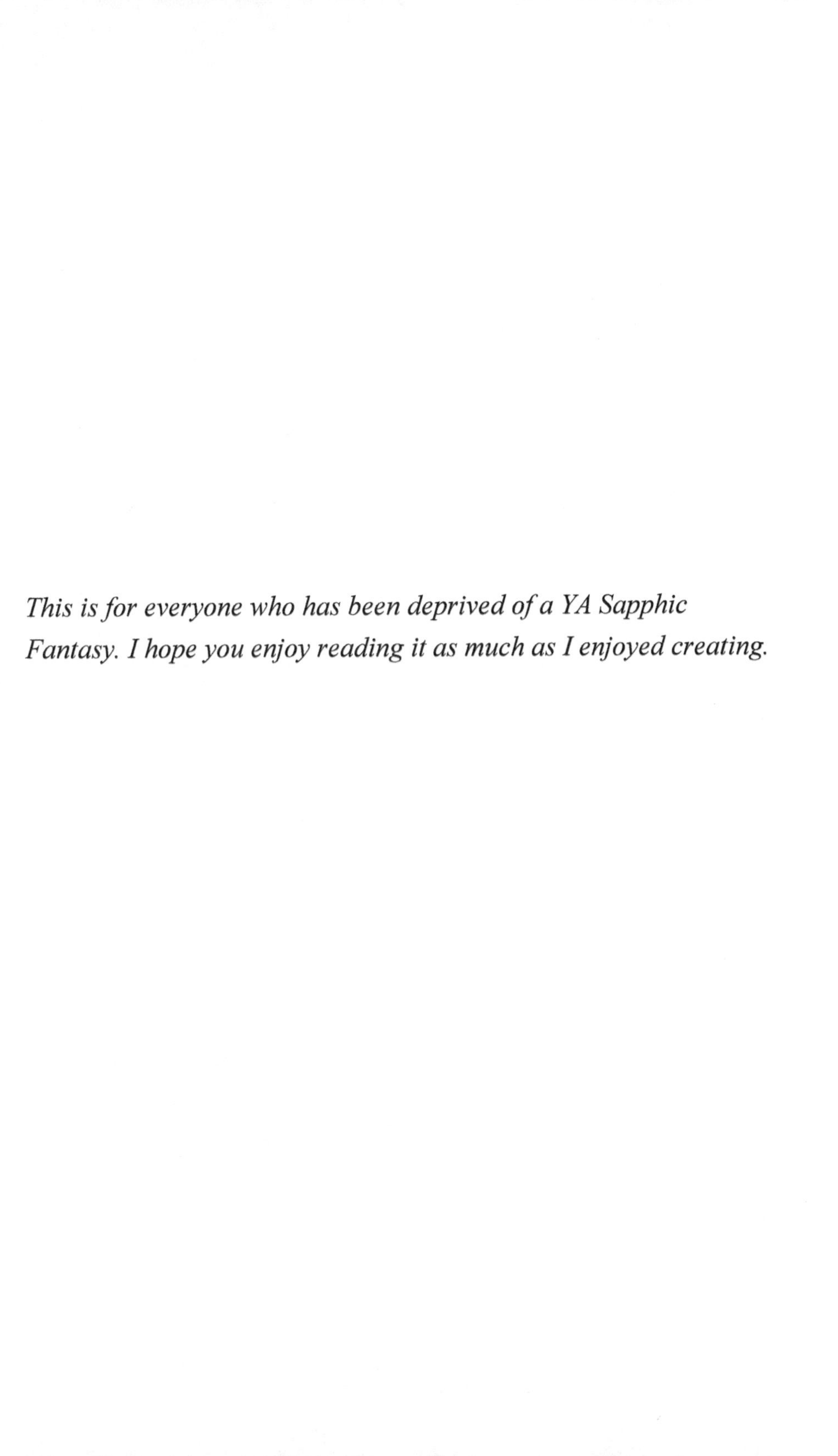

This is for everyone who has been deprived of a YA Sapphic Fantasy. I hope you enjoy reading it as much as I enjoyed creating.

Nethrala

Nightshade Syndicate
Ember Scorpion Clan
Ghost Orchid Clan
Crimson Widow Clan
Eclipsed Clan
Assassin Academy
Death Lotus Clan
Silver Veil Clan
Shadows Peak
Town
Obsidian Clan
Moon Clan
Shadowfang Clan
Silent Clan

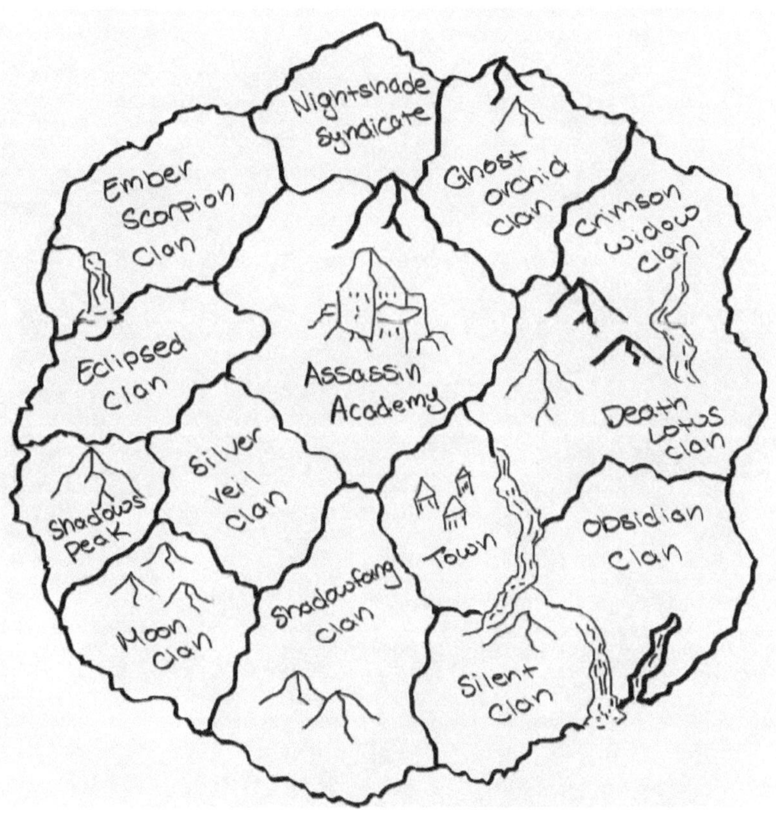

1

The moon hung low over Nethrala, its pale light casting a ghostly sheen over the ancient city of shadows. Narrow streets twisted like veins through the heart of the city, silent and lifeless, as if night itself had devoured all who once walked them. A hush blanketed the air, broken only by the whisper of leaves stirring in the unseen breeze.

Deep within the labyrinthine alleys, hidden in the folds of darkness, lay the stronghold of the ten assassin clans. Each clan dwelled in secrecy, their domains marked by sigils carved into unyielding stone—symbols of power, endurance, and silent wars fought in the dark. Masked sentinels stood at every threshold, their black-veiled faces betraying no emotion, their allegiance unquestionable.

Raven moved like a shadow among them. She was new to Nethrala, but she did not hesitate. She had come for one purpose.

Before her loomed the gates of the Assassin Academy—a bastion of power where the most elite assassins were honed. The sentinels stationed at the entrance, clad in obsidian armor, did not waver as she approached.

"State your business," one of them commanded, his voice cold as steel.

Raven halted, her light brown eyes gleaming with purpose. "I've come to challenge the prodigies," she declared, her tone steady, unwavering. "I seek to prove myself and claim the title of ruler over the ten clans."

The air between them thickened with tension. The sentinels exchanged a glance, a flicker of uncertainty passing between them. The outsider's arrival was unprecedented, and her boldness was unlike anything they had witnessed.

The left sentinel disappeared into the shadows, leaving Raven to stand beneath the Academy's imposing gate. Her pulse remained steady. Every fiber of her being was prepared for this.

Moments later, the sentinel returned, accompanied by a robed figure. His presence commanded instant deference.

"I am Counselor Zephyr," the elder said, his voice carrying the weight of time. "Your presence here is unprecedented, Raven. What makes you believe you have the right to make such a declaration?"

Raven met his gaze without faltering. In response, she tugged at her collar, revealing the head of a serpent birthmark against her skin.

Zephyr's expression shifted—flickering recognition, measured contemplation. Then, a slow nod.

"Very well," he murmured, though his voice carried an unspoken warning. "But understand this: the battle for rulership is not a mere contest. It is a trial written in blood. The traditions of the assassin clans run deeper than you can imagine."

Raven inclined her head. "I understand, Counselor Zephyr. And I accept the challenge."

Counselor Zephyr signaled the sentinels to open the massive gates with a single gesture. The heavy doors groaned as they swung inwards, revealing the inner sanctum of the Assassin Academy—a world of shadows, secrets, and silent warfare.

Raven studied her reflection, her fingers tracing the sharp angles of her jaw as she adjusted her uniform. Today marked the beginning of a new chapter, one she had no choice but to embrace. Arriving late last night, she had barely gotten any sleep after being issued her academy attire and shown to her dormitory.

Grateful for her status as one of the prodigies, she had the privilege of her own dorm room. The solitude suited her. With an overwhelming multitude of tasks awaiting her attention, the solitude of her room kept her from prying eyes and whispered suspicions.

She shifted her stance, taking in the uniform's details. The matte black hooded jacket fit snugly, allowing for full mobility. A detachable hood rested at her nape, ready to be pulled up at a moment's notice. Her slim-fit trousers, crafted from a silent, quick-drying material, whispered with each movement. Hidden inside deep pockets were an assortment of small tools—silent companions to any assassin.

Her boots were low-profile, sturdy yet unassuming, designed for stability on any terrain. A functional belt encircled her waist, concealing compartments that held essential tools. A discreet utility pouch at the back carried additional gear.

A clan insignia was supposed to mark her chest and back, blending seamlessly with the dark fabric—a symbol of allegiance amongst clans, and unity among assassins. But she had no allegiance, no clan. The absence of that insignia was a silent declaration.

This uniform was a far cry from what she had worn during her mother's training. Those had been secondhand garments—thin, worn, and barely suitable for winter. She had learned to survive in all conditions, but winter had shaped her most. The bitter cold had forced her to become something sharper, harder—something lethal.

Exhaling softly, she straightened. It was time.

She gathered her writing materials and stepped into the dimly lit corridor.

The whispers started immediately.

She felt their stares, the weight of their scrutiny pressing against her back. A deviation. An intrusion. A disruption to the academy's rigid traditions. She had blindsided them, forced her way into their world, and they resented her for it.

But she didn't care. This wasn't about them.

This was her mother's dying wish.

Her steps remained measured; her chin held high as she navigated the halls. She had already committed the academy's map to memory—every hallway, every blind spot, every hidden passage. Her greatest asset had always been her photographic memory. In this place, where failure meant death, no detail could escape her.

A voice cut through the silence.

"Hello."

Raven stopped.

A woman stood before her, smiling.

Her long chestnut hair cascaded in loose waves, catching the dim light and framing a face that seemed almost too perfect. High cheekbones, a softly curved jaw, and flawless skin made her presence striking. But it was her eyes that held Raven's attention—deep emerald, green, like the heart of an untouched forest. Intelligent. Assessing.

Too warm for an assassin.

Raven's breath hitched for the briefest moment before she controlled it.

She had not expected this.

"You're the new girl. The anomaly," the girl observed, curiosity gleaming in her gaze.

Raven didn't respond.

"I'm Valentina. We share our first class, and the headmaster assigned me to show you the ropes on your inaugural day. It appears you'll have no choice but to endure my company, oh silent one." A sly smile curved her lips before she spun on her heels, striding down the corridor.

Raven's eyes followed her retreating figure, drawn to the sigil stitched onto the back of her uniform—a black rose, its thorns twisting into the shape of a concealed dagger. She quickened her pace, falling into step beside Valentina.

"You belong to the Nightshade Clan," Raven noted.

Valentina hummed, flicking her gaze sideways. "Nightshade Syndicate."

Raven nodded, filing that distinction away.

They continued in silence, allowing Raven to absorb the essence of the school and cement the physical layout within her mental map. The halls twisted and turned like veins through a living beast, darkened corridors whispering secrets in their shadows.

The Assassin Academy was a fortress buried within a mountain range; its existence known only to the world's deadliest. Within the walls, killers were forged.

The entrance hall loomed ahead, vast and lined with ancient weapons and trophies from past graduates. A pair of immense iron doors stood as the gateway to this hidden world, their surface marred with deep, battle-worn etchings. Above them, blood-red letters formed a chilling decree:

"In shadows, we thrive."

Beyond that threshold, the academy unfolded like a labyrinth. Training halls branched off in every direction, each a crucible designed to hone a different deadly skill. Some bore obstacle courses designed to push agility to its limit, while others housed combat arenas where the air was thick with the echoes of past duels. Stealth corridors tested silence itself, their floors lined with pressure-sensitive tiles and hanging bells that punished the careless.

And then there was the Assassination Library.

A vault of forbidden knowledge. Ancient texts detailing poisons, anatomy, and the bloody history of their craft lay within its guarded walls. Rumors swirled that it contained the academy's darkest secrets—secrets that had sent even seasoned assassins to their graves.

Raven exhaled softly, her fingers brushing the cold iron of the academy's threshold. This was no ordinary school. This was a crucible, and she was about to be tested.

2

aven and Valentina entered the classroom, the space still empty of other students. Raven had left her quarters early to avoid the scrutinizing gazes of her peers, but to her surprise, Valentina had found her almost immediately.

"Join me over here," Valentina said, ascending the steps and settling into a seat.

The classroom followed a tiered design similar to a university lecture hall, with five descending rows leading to the professor's platform. A vast whiteboard stretched across one wall, and an unassuming desk sat slightly off-center, allowing the instructor to shift focus during individual work.

"There's no assigned seating?" Raven asked, noting the lack of structure.

Valentina shook her head, gesturing to the seat beside her. "Please, sit." her eyes glinted with warmth.

Raven studied her carefully. Valentina was undeniably beautiful, like a rose that concealed its thorns. The comparison unsettled her, though she couldn't pinpoint why.

"Very well." Raven climbed the steps and took the seat next

to her.

"So, Raven, isn't it?" Valentina leaned in slightly, voice laced with curiosity.

Raven turned to face her, giving her full attention without fully understanding why. The pull she felt toward Valentina gnawed at her, unbidden and unwanted.

"Why have they allowed you to challenge the prodigies?" Valentina asked, her voice smooth but edged with something sharper. "This isn't a privilege granted to just anyone. The Shadow Gauntlet is sacred, reserved for the chosen few. Each clan identifies its prodigies at an early age. Yet here you are—someone we've never seen, never heard of—emerging from nowhere to challenge our way of life."

Raven's expression remained impassive. "We've just met, Valentina. Your questions are rather audacious."

Before Valentina could respond, the classroom began filling with students. Some cast glances at Raven, curiosity and judgment evident in their expressions. News of her arrival had spread quickly.

Those bearing the Nightshade sigil bowed respectfully as they passed Valentina, a silent acknowledgment of her status. Though she stiffened at the gesture, she returned their bows with a graceful smile.

Raven observed carefully. She knew who Valentina was. She knew all of them—the prodigies of the academy—long before she arrived. Her mentor had ensured it.

But they didn't know that.

Valentina's pointed questions confirmed Raven's suspicion: they assumed she was an outsider, unfamiliar with their world and its hierarchy. They had no idea how much she already knew.

She intended to use that ignorance to her advantage.

Deciding to maintain her air of indifference, Raven refrained from mentioning the people who had bowed to Valentina. Instead, her attention shifted to the man who had just entered the room. His light brown hair was neatly combed back, his dark brown eyes sharp and assessing. A five o'clock shadow lined his jaw, and his athletic frame—standing at about 5'9—filled out the academy uniform.

Unlike the students, however, two sigils adorned his shoulders, marking both his faculty position and his allegiance.

Their gazes met. Raven held his stare, her expression a careful blend of boredom and mild disinterest. Intelligence had always come easily to her, setting Raven apart from her peers. The academy's curriculum hardly concerned her—she had little doubt that she already knew more than they could offer. Yet, she was there for a reason. To play her part. To fulfill her duty. To walk the path that had been laid before her.

The professor's voice cut through the silence. "I see we have a new student in our midst."

As if on command, every head in the room turned toward me—except for Valentina's.

"Introduce yourself," he continued.

Raven suppressed a sigh. Assassins were supposed to be secretive, yet here they were, engaging in such predictable customs. Rising from her seat, she gave a slight bow—just deep enough to be polite but laced with a hint of challenge.

"Raven."

The professor didn't react to her tone, his expression unreadable. "Do you belong to a clan, Raven?"

Raven tilted her head slightly, considering her response. "Technically, yes. Isn't it said that your clan is your blood, carried through generations? If that's the case, my clan is my mother's."

A flicker of curiosity crossed his face. Raven could sense it mirrored in the students around her, even at the edge of her vision. For the first time, Valentina turned to look at her.

"Do you know which clan she belonged to?" the professor asked.

Raven gave a single nod, her expression making it clear that she had no intention of elaborating. She would let them wonder. Let them dig. She knew they wouldn't find what they were looking for— not all of it, anyway. And by the time they did, it would already be too late.

The professor acknowledged her decision with a thoughtful hum before turning toward the board. Raven took her seat as he began to write.

"My name is Professor Murdoch. Welcome to Advanced Poisons."

He wasted no time diving into the intricacies of various toxins, explaining their origins, properties, and applications. Once the foundational principles were laid out, he shifted to something far more sinister—the manipulation of molecular structures to heighten their lethality. His message was clear: anything could be made deadlier with the right knowledge. The tools existed, waiting for mastery.

The class passed in a blur. Raven remained silent, absorbing every word while the professor refrained from acknowledging her further. Valentina, however, spoke twice. Each time, the room hushed, a testament to the influence she wielded—not just among her clan but within the academy itself. Her insights were sharp, commanding respect. It made Raven wonder: Was Valentina the favored contender in the Shadow Gauntlet? If so, would she be the one Raven would eventually have to eliminate?

As the session ended, students filed out, heading to their next courses. Yet, Raven and Valentina lingered.

Valentina turned to Raven, her gaze serious. "Is your next class Field Training?"

Raven gave a curt nod.

Valentina leaned in slightly, her voice low but urgent. "Listen carefully. Field Training is about survival. You'll be thrown into a simulator where the environment shifts unpredictably. You won't be alone; other students—shadow blades and prodigies—will all be there. And they're watching. They want to see what sets you apart." She paused. "Be ready, Raven. Training or not, expect a fight. Blood will be spilled."

Raven exhaled slowly, already bracing herself for the challenge ahead. She knew her skills would be tested, but this was sooner than expected. She had no time to deal with injuries, which meant she couldn't afford to hold back.

She pushed to her feet. "Lead the way," she said, motioning for Valentina to go first.

Valentina rose as well, her sharp gaze unreadable. "I'm in that class, too," she said. "And, like the rest, I'm curious about your abilities."

Raven studied her, searching for any trace of doubt, warning, or even a hint of hostility. But there was none. Just confidence. Was it because Valentina trusted her own strength? Or did she think Raven would hesitate when the time came?

A rare smile tugged at Raven's lips. "I understand."

They stepped out together, heading toward whatever trial awaited them.

3

Professor Zion addressed the assembled group of young assassins. "I'll be brief. Five of you have been selected for evaluation today. The rest of you, your role is just as crucial."

She paced before them, eyes scanning the disciplined line. "Your mission is simple: step into the simulator. Your primary objective—secure an egg and return it to your starting point, unscathed. If the egg breaks or you're 'killed,' you fail. You don't have to engage with everyone. If you can slip past unnoticed, all the better."

She shifted her gaze. "For those not being evaluated, your job is to protect the egg. If it's taken, you have two options—destroy it or eliminate the one carrying it. And as always, follow the honor code."

She gestured toward the opposite wall. "Collect any weapons you deem necessary. The sharper, the better."

The assassins bowed in acknowledgment and moved to arm themselves—except for Raven. Like the others, she carried the standard-issue pouch of knives and daggers, a gift from the school. That would be enough.

She used the moment to survey the room. It resembled an indoor arena, and the simulator sat in the middle. She couldn't tell how large the simulator was, nor what waited inside, but one thing was certain—whatever was created was real. Not an illusion. Not a game. The technology surpassed anything she had encountered before.

To the side of the simulator, a wooden seating area with three rows of benches allowed for spectating. A massive screen near the entrance ensured that those watching could monitor every movement inside.

The assassins regrouped in line, weapons in hand. One of them couldn't resist a taunt.

"No weapon? What, too skilled for one?"

Raven didn't spare them a glance. Her voice, edged with boredom, cut through the air. "I don't need one to beat you."

Professor Zion smirked. "I like the confidence, Raven. You're up first."

She pressed a button, and the simulator door swung open, revealing a dense forest bathed in dim light.

"The rest of you—get into position."

One by one, the remaining assassins disappeared into the simulation. Valentina was the last to step inside. Before vanishing, she turned to Raven with a smirk.

"You know, a smile wouldn't kill you, Raven. Just a thought."

Raven offered a casual shrug. "Have I not been friendly to you?"

Valentina smiled. "I'd like friendlier," she quipped before disappearing into the virtual realm.

Raven blinked, momentarily thrown by the possible implications of Valentina's words. Before her thoughts could settle, she shook her head, pulled her hood over her curls, and let the shadows consume half of her face.

As she entered the simulation, the soft, warm dirt shifted beneath her boots. The dense scent of earth filled her lungs, and the artificial wind rustled the trees overhead. Her black leather outfit melded seamlessly with the darkness, making her nearly invisible. She flexed her fingers, itching to reach for the dagger strapped to her waist beneath her jacket.

The woods remained eerily silent, save for the steady rhythm of her heartbeat. But she wasn't alone. The unseen eyes of her fellow assassins tracked her every move, waiting for the right moment to strike. Then, a bell chimed softly through the trees, its haunting echo signaling the start of the challenge.

Raven moved without hesitation, sprinting toward the far end of the woods. She knew the egg would be hidden there—alongside another assassin chosen to guard it. The others wouldn't attack until she had it; there was no honor in eliminating an opponent before they even reached their objective. That gave her a slim window to act.

Rather than taking the silent route, she deliberately made her presence known, crunching leaves and snapping twigs beneath her boots. If her enemies thought they had the advantage, they might make reckless moves—ones she could exploit.

As she neared her target, she pulled up short. The egg sat in a bed of soft leaves, untouched. Too easy. No guard in sight, no immediate traps. But Raven knew better.

Slowly, she drew two kunai knives, their hilts cool against her palms. With a practiced flick, she fastened thin wires to each, then hurled them toward opposite trees. The strings went taut between them, forming an invisible tripwire. If anything disturbed the tension—if so much as a breath of air shifted the line—she'd know a trap was set for her.

Once the kunai embedded securely in the trees, Raven knew it was safe to proceed. She crept forward cautiously, every muscle tense, senses sharpened to detect even the faintest disturbance. The simulated forest was designed to be deceptive, every shadow a potential ambush.

The egg rested in its makeshift cradle, untouched. With precise movements, she plucked it from its perch and secured it inside her empty back pouch.

She pivoted on her heel, launching into a sprint toward the safe zone. As if on cue, the ambush unfolded. Like ghosts slipping from the darkness, the assassins materialized from concealed corners, each one poised to challenge her.

The first to strike was Valentina. Silent as death, she emerged from the shadows, her all-black attire blending into the simulated night. She moved with the grace of a panther, attempting to surprise Raven from behind. But Raven was ready.

A flicker of motion in her peripheral vision was all the warning she needed. She whirled, dagger poised, intercepting Valentina's strike in a clash of steel. The battle was swift but brutal. Valentina was fast, but Raven was faster. With a calculated twist of her wrist, she disarmed her opponent, sending Valentina's weapon skidding across the forest floor. A sting flared across Raven's bicep—she hadn't emerged unscathed. The pain was sharp but ignored.

Valentina barely had time to recover before Raven's spinning butterfly kick struck her squarely in the face, sending her sprawling. One down.

Raven pressed forward, deflecting knives and daggers that sliced through the air toward her. Each projectile was expertly redirected, ensuring neither she nor the egg suffered harm.

A shadow moved above. Prodigy Whisper.

His name suited him well as he seemed to be as quiet as the wind. He dropped from the overhead ledge in an attempt to intercept Raven, his movements eerily quiet. Raven narrowly evaded his assault. Their duel was fast, a flurry of motion and steel. But speed alone wasn't enough. Raven's experience outmatched his agility. With a precise strike, she sent him reeling, eliminating him from the fight.

No time to pause. Another adversary emerged.

Prodigy Viper.

Her name alone was a warning. She specialized in poisons, and Raven knew better than to let even a single scratch mark her skin. The battle shifted from steel to deception—Viper's arsenal of concealed toxins was a threat far greater than brute strength.

Without hesitation, Viper launched a barrage of poisoned projectiles, each one expertly aimed. Raven met them with equal skill, deflecting each dart, each needle, each unseen danger with her dagger. Steel met toxin in a deadly symphony. The ground between them was soon littered with discarded weapons.

Then, without warning, Viper withdrew. She melted into the shadows, pausing only to give Raven the briefest of nods. Respect.

But Raven had no time to dwell on it.

The final obstacle stood ahead. A brute of an assassin, massive in size, a mountain compared to her. He wielded a serrated sword nearly the length of her body, his strikes designed to overwhelm.

Power against precision.

She danced around his attacks, each of his swings leaving deep gashes in the trees rather than her flesh. He was strong, but strength without speed meant little. With a final, well-timed strike, she sent him staggering. It was all the opening she needed.

Without hesitation, she sprinted past him toward the safe zone, the egg still secure in her pouch.

Raven continued her sprint, weaving through the maze of assassins determined to cut her down. Their attacks came swift and relentless, but they didn't expect her to be faster—deadlier. They underestimate her skill, her experience. Their mistake.

One by one, they fell, their movements sluggish compared to Raven's calculated precision. A dagger thrust—deflected. A blade swung toward her throat—sidestepped and countered with ruthless efficiency. Each confrontation was a fleeting moment, a step closer to her escape. She didn't stop. She didn't look back.

The safe zone was within reach. Her breath was steady, her resolve unshaken. No one could stop her.

She was closing in with every step. Her opponents, though skilled, were merely obstacles in her path. Raven's confidence grew with each encounter. They challenged her, but none were insurmountable.

The meadow ahead stretched wide, its short, lush grass damp beneath her boots. Her safe zone lay just beyond it, beckoning her forward. She slowed her pace, inhaling the crisp night air, her gaze lifting to the artificial moon. Its dim glow stirred memories of home—of relentless training, of discipline honed to perfection.

A blade flashed.

The steel caught the moonlight, casting an ominous glint across the grass. Instinct seized her before thought could. She twisted, narrowly evading the assassin's dagger as it sliced through the air where her throat had been a breath ago.

Prodigy Seraph was relentless. Attack after attack came, swift and unyielding, allowing Raven no room to breathe. She parried, dodged, countered—but each movement sent another jolt of pain through her wounded arm. Blood trickled down her fingers, hot and steady, a reminder that Valentina's strike had cost her more than she wanted to admit.

Her grip tightened on her dagger.

Seraph's rage was palpable, her strikes fueled by something deeper than mere competition. Why? Raven hadn't slighted her, hadn't sought her out. Was it because she dared challenge the prodigies without offering deference? Was it because she fought as though she belonged here?

All she had to do was show them. The mark on her skin—the symbol of a true prodigy. A single glance would silence their doubts. But no. She wouldn't grant them that satisfaction. They weren't worthy of knowing.

Seraph lunged.

Raven met her mid-stride, their blades clashing in a burst of steel and sparks. For a fleeting moment, their eyes locked, reflecting only disdain.

The pouch at Raven's hip held her prize—the egg. But her arm was weakening, her body screaming for relief. She couldn't afford to prolong this. Seraph was fast, dangerous, but she was also reckless.

Raven had trained for this. She understood precision, control, the art of conserving energy in battle. Seraph fought with fury, raw and untamed.

That was her mistake.

A shift of weight. A feint. A twist of the wrist.

Seraph's blade went flying, clattering uselessly onto the ground. Before she could react, Raven's leg swept beneath her, sending her sprawling into the dirt.

And just like that, it was over.

A swift, powerful punch to Seraph's face sent her crumpling to the ground, unconscious. Without hesitation, Raven bolted toward her safe zone, retrieving the egg from its pouch and cradling it as if it were a priceless artifact. Her heart pounded in her chest, the rush of battle still surging through her veins.

The moment she crossed the starting point, the bell tolled once more—her mission was complete. The egg remained uncracked, a testament to her precision and skill. She had succeeded. She had dominated. The training simulator powered down, plunging the room into silence.

As the simulation ended, the assassins reconvened, forming stiff lines. Some had emerged unscathed, favoring ranged tactics to avoid direct combat. Others bore the marks of their defeats—bruised jaws, split lips, and bloodied noses. The session had been humbling, especially for those who had dismissed Raven as an outsider. To their dismay, her only injury had come from Valentina's blade.

"Well," Professor Zion began, her voice edged with a stern satisfaction. "Raven has returned with the egg intact. In doing so, she has exposed many of you as mere novices—and yet, some of you are prodigies." Her gaze swept across the room, pinning each assassin in place. "I don't need to spell it out, but I'm sure you feel it. If today's performance repeats itself during the Shadow Gauntlet, she will emerge victorious… and you prodigies will meet your demise."

Though the prodigies maintained their blank expressions, the tension in their jaws betrayed their thoughts.

"Maybe I'm affording her too much praise," the professor

mused, shifting her attention to Raven. Meanwhile, Raven had already begun tending to her wound, securing a strip of fabric just above the gash to slow the bleeding. Unbothered by the professor's words, she resumed preparing for the next round.

Professor Zion pressed a button on her remote. With a sharp click, the simulator doors slid open, revealing a vast desert landscape. "It's time for the next evaluation," she announced. "Only the other prodigies will be evaluated moving forward. Whisper, you're up."

The assassins took their positions, battle-worn but resolute. The air thickened with quiet anticipation as Whisper entered the simulation. The evaluation began.

Lightning fast, a dagger streaked across the battlefield. Its foam-padded tip struck Whisper square in the back before he could react. A clean, unmistakable hit.

Whisper turned, blinking at the fallen dagger at his feet. Slowly, his gaze lifted—to find Raven perched atop a boulder, eyes cold and unreadable. Had the dagger been real, it would have pierced his heart. He would be dead.

The bell rang, signaling the end of the match. Whisper had failed before he had even reached the egg.

Subsequently, Prodigies Viper, Seraph, and Valentina faced their evaluations. Raven made quick work of Viper and Seraph. Emerging from the shadows, she intercepted them with precision, effortlessly sidestepping their attacks. Their arrogance cost them dearly—each strike she delivered was perfectly timed, incapacitating them within moments. Like Whisper, they had failed.

Valentina was the final participant. The wooded environment stretched around them once more, the air tense with expectation. But unlike with the others, Raven didn't attack immediately. Instead, she followed at a distance, her presence a silent threat weaving through the trees. From her vantage point above, she tracked Valentina's every move, watching as she maneuvered through the forest with calculated steps.

Viper and Seraph remained unconscious. That left only Raven

and Whisper as Valentina's true opponents.

The first challenge came swiftly. Shadow blades materialized, their sheer numbers overwhelming at first glance. Yet, Valentina showed no sign of panic. Perched on a tree branch, Raven observed, keenly studying her opponent's response. Valentina didn't just fight—she moved as though she were performing a dance, each motion flowing seamlessly into the next. No wasted effort. No hesitation. But despite her efficiency, there was something controlled about her strikes. She wasn't fighting with full force.

After subduing the shadow blades, Valentina retrieved the egg. Now, only Whisper stood in her way.

Their battle unfolded like a carefully rehearsed sequence, both combatants evenly matched. Whisper attacked first, but Valentina anticipated his every move, deflecting each strike with calculated ease. When he lunged, she pivoted effortlessly, delivering an uppercut that snapped his head back, followed by a swift left hook. Before he could regain his footing, she executed a fluid takedown, sending him crashing to the ground. Her dagger found its mark—a "fatal" strike to his chest.

Whisper groaned, a string of curses slipping past his lips.

Valentina only smirked, winking at him before breaking into a sprint toward the safety zone, the egg still in her grasp.

Fifty feet.

Raven moved.

She released two kunai, strings attached, embedding them into the ground just ahead of Valentina. The moment Valentina registered the trap, she leaped—but that was exactly what Raven had planned.

As soon as both of Valentina's feet left the ground, Raven launched herself from her perch. Their bodies collided mid-air, the impact knocking the wind out of Valentina. They hit the earth hard, a brutal crash that left Valentina gasping.

Raven recovered first, her dagger already in hand. With a simple flick of her wrist, she punctured the egg.

A sharp breath. A single tear trickled down Valentina's

cheek—whether from the loss, the impact, or the sheer struggle for air, Raven couldn't tell.

Raven stood, then reached down, grasping Valentina's arm to help her up. She placed one hand gently against Valentina's back, the other against her chest.

"Breathe. Slowly," she instructed.

Valentina complied, following the rhythm Raven set. But Raven didn't miss the tremor in her hands, the flicker of fear in her gaze.

She was on the edge of a panic attack.

Raven wasn't sure how to handle that. So she did the only thing she could—she stayed. Kept steady. Guided her through each breath until her trembling eased.

The bell tolled. The challenge was over.

Valentina had failed.

After Valentina regained her breath, she stepped away from Raven and let the egg fall to the ground. "You just bested all four prodigies today," she said, inhaling deeply as if still recovering from Raven's last attack. "Two of them are in medical. Your skills are undeniable."

Her gaze drifted to the shattered egg at her feet, disappointment flickering in her expression. She exhaled sharply before meeting Raven's eyes again. "This isn't the end. Next time, I won't go so easy on you."

Raven chuckled at the warning. She had no doubts about Valentina's determination—she had felt it in every strike. But Raven had no intention of losing, not now, not ever. Rather than responding, she turned on her heel and left the simulation arena, blending into the line of assassins.

Valentina followed a moment later.

Professor Zion stepped forward, surveying the aftermath before addressing the class. "Impressive work," she acknowledged, her gaze lingering on Raven for a moment longer. A silent nod of respect.

Raven met the professor's eyes and returned the nod, her expression unreadable.

"Dismissed."

The class dispersed.

4

As the day unfolded, Valentina remained by Raven's side, guiding her through the academy. She ensured Raven's wounded arm was properly bandaged, and Raven handed her an ice pack for the bruise forming on her face—the result of Raven's well-placed kick earlier that day. Though they only shared three classes, Valentina escorted her between each period, always lingering just long enough to smirk and toss out a mocking, "Be good," before slipping away to her own lessons. Each time, she returned promptly to collect her.

Reactions to Raven's presence in class were consistent—curiosity, envy, or wariness. No one voiced their thoughts, but their expressions spoke volumes. She was grateful that no one, aside from Valentina, attempted conversation. Feigning friendliness wasn't on her agenda. All she wanted was to get through the day unnoticed and begin her investigations.

Word of the training simulation had already spread. The fact that Raven had been the only student to pass while the other four prodigies were either injured or recovering had left a lasting impression. Professors and shadow blades regarded her with newfound respect, though they kept their distance. Her success might have earned their acknowledgment, but it also placed her under scrutiny.

She maintained her silence throughout the remaining classes, speaking only when absolutely necessary. Soon, the day came to an end.

Emerging from her final class, Raven found Valentina waiting in the hallway, leaning against the wall with the same casual confidence she had displayed all day.

"Are you hungry?" Valentina asked.

Raven shrugged, then winced as pain flared in her arm—another reminder of Valentina's earlier strike. "The day's over. Isn't your job of showing me around done?"

Valentina tilted her head slightly, her gaze flicking to Raven's bandaged arm before meeting her eyes again. "Maybe," she mused, her tone light, "but I wanted to show you where we eat. Figured you wouldn't want to wander in alone and feel overwhelmed."

Raven arched a brow. "I'm starting to think you just like being around me."

Valentina rolled her eyes, pushing off the wall and closing the distance between them. "The clans interact with each other," she explained, choosing to ignore Raven's remark. "We socialize, make allies, but usually, we sit with our own. I don't know how it'll be for you in the dining hall today. Maybe the groups will be mixed, maybe not. I don't want you to feel left out, looking around for a place to sit. And, well, people will be staring at you."

Raven nodded, feeling the weight of the sentiment. It wasn't surprising, yet it tugged at her heart to know that Valentina wanted to stay with her.

"Are we allowed to grab food and go?" she asked.

Valentina nodded. "Of course. No one is forcing you to stay there."

"Great," Raven replied. "I'm going to grab some food and

head to the back of the school. I heard it has amazing sunsets."

Valentina responded with a thoughtful hum. "How about this? You find a spot on the hill in the back, and I'll bring you some food."

Raven studied Valentina, her thoughts momentarily wandering. Trustworthy, yet an assassin. Deceit ran through their nature, but her clan was renowned for its honor. She dismissed the unease before it could take root.

"Are you going to try to poison me?" Raven asked.

Valentina chuckled. "Of course not. We're not allowed to kill other prodigies until the Shadow Gauntlet. Punishable by imprisonment and, ironically, death. Though there have been some pretty nasty fights."

Raven smiled. "I'm glad the law is the only thing preventing you from killing me."

Valentina nodded, smirking. "Honestly, count your blessings." With that, she turned and disappeared down the hallway.

Raven watched until Valentina was out of sight, then sighed. The reality of being here, carrying on her clan's legacy, settled over her like a weight. Her mother would have been proud. A tear slipped down her cheek before she wiped it away.

She moved through the empty hallways, undisturbed by shadow blades or eager prodigies. As she reached the back door, a hand seized her shoulder and spun her around.

Professor Zion stood before her. "Prodigy Raven, may I speak with you?"

Raven glanced past her, ensuring no one else was near. "Yes, in a source of knowledge bound tight with care when the moonlight spills through the window low."

Professor Zion nodded. "Very well. Enjoy the rest of your day." She turned and walked away.

Raven exhaled, then stepped outside. The golden sun bathed the open field, where winding pathways led to unknown destinations. A hundred meters ahead, the hill called to her.

She crossed the field with swift strides and ascended the peak, shrugging off her assassin jacket. It pooled behind her as she sat cross-legged, her black compression shirt clinging to her athletic frame. Her long, curly dark brown hair cascaded over her shoulders, resting against her back.

Hands on her knees, she inhaled deeply.

"I know a place that offers one of the most stunning sunsets I've ever seen," her mother had once said, voice warm and loving. *They had sat together in the grass outside their small woodland cottage, bathed in the fading light.*

Raven had been just eight years old when she first heard her mother's stories. She had listened, wide-eyed, hanging onto every word.

"Will we get to see it one day?" she had asked eagerly.

Her mother had smiled—soft, wistful. A smile that, even then, Raven had sensed held something unspoken.

"Yes, one day, you will."

Young Raven had beamed, thrilled at the thought of sharing something so precious with her mother. She had nestled against her, eyes fluttering shut, wrapped in the warmth of her embrace.

Her mother's touch had been a sanctuary, a refuge of warmth and safety.

Then, the memory shattered.

"Raven?"

Valentina's voice cut through the silence, pulling Raven back to the present. She blinked, disoriented for a moment, before looking up. Valentina stood before her, two bowls of food cradled in her hands.

"Are you okay?" Valentina asked, her voice tinged with concern.

Raven gave a slight nod, afraid that if she spoke, her voice would betray her.

Valentina didn't push. Instead, she lowered herself onto the grass beside Raven, setting the bowls between them. Without a word, she reached out and brushed a stray tear from Raven's cheek. The gesture was so unexpected, so gentle, that Raven found herself momentarily stunned.

Valentina offered her one of the bowls, and Raven accepted it, murmuring a quiet, "Thank you."

They ate in silence, watching as the sky bled from orange to violet. The sunset stretched over the horizon, a breathtaking expanse of shifting colors.

From the corner of her eye, Raven stole a glance at Valentina. The other girl seemed lost in thought, her brow slightly furrowed. It made Raven wonder. What was she thinking? What weighed on her mind?

She didn't ask.

Instead, she sat beside her, feeling an unfamiliar sense of ease. There was something about Valentina—something genuine. It wasn't just the way others looked at her, the respect they held for her. It was in her presence, in the way she carried herself.

It made Raven curious.

"I can feel you staring," Valentina said without looking away from the sky.

Raven hummed nonchalantly. "I was thinking."

Valentina finally turned to face her, eyes sharp yet unreadable. "About what?"

Raven studied her for a moment before answering. "Whether you're genuinely nice or if it's just an act."

Valentina chuckled, taking another bite of her food before replying. "I'd like to think I'm nice, but I wouldn't say I treat everyone the way I treated you today."

Raven lifted a brow. "And what do you mean by that?"

Valentina grinned, glancing down at her bowl. "Not everyone gets to share a meal and watch the sunset on their first day."

Raven smirked. "Ah, so this is a second-day special, then?"

Valentina laughed as she rose to her feet. "It's getting late. I need to check in with the elders about your first day." She hesitated briefly before adding, "You did well, Raven. Don't be a stranger."

Raven didn't respond immediately, only watching as

Valentina made her way down the hill, her steps fluid and unhurried. She exhaled, unaware that she had been holding her breath.

She turned back to the horizon. The sun had almost disappeared, leaving only a lingering trace of color before the sky surrendered to the night.

With a final glance at the darkening expanse, Raven finished her food and rose to her feet. She had a meeting to attend.

5

aven stepped into the dimly lit library, where most of the lights cast a soft glow over towering bookshelves. The scent of aged parchment and ink filled the air, and silence stretched between the aisles like an unspoken rule.

Approaching the librarian's desk, she greeted him with a small smile. "Hello, I was wondering if there's a closing time for the library?"

The librarian, engrossed in a book, looked up. His gaze flickered across the darkened surroundings before settling on her. After a thoughtful pause, he replied, "Officially, the library closes at ten. However, assassins thrive in the nighttime, and I don't like to limit knowledge. So, if you can get in, you can enjoy the library."

Raven chuckled appreciatively. "I like that," she said, glancing at the vast collection of books, where shadows stretched between the towering shelves. Above, a second floor loomed, lined with even more books.

"Do you happen to have private rooms for studying?" she asked, implying the need for solitude.

The librarian studied her for a moment before giving a slow nod. "All of this was covered in orientation."

Raven returned the nod. "Yeah, well, I just arrived last night, so I'm still learning some of the rules."

The librarian's eyes widened slightly. He straightened, setting his book down, and then, to Raven's surprise, he bowed. "My apologies, Prodigy Raven. We heard of your arrival, but I didn't recognize your face."

Raven lifted a hand, motioning for him to stop. "No trouble at all," she assured him.

He stood upright and gestured toward the second floor. "You'll find the private rooms up there, along with more books. If you need anything, please let me know."

"Thank you," Raven said sincerely. Her gaze drifted to the clan insignia stitched on his left shoulder—a lotus flower with black petals and concealed blades. The emblem of the Death Lotus Covenant.

She inclined her head. "It was nice meeting you. Thanks again."

With that, she turned and ascended the stairs.

At the top, she glanced up. Moonlight streamed through large windows in the ceiling, bathing the library in an ethereal glow. The stillness felt sacred. Following the soft illumination, her eyes landed on a door tucked away in the corner. Something instinctive pulled her toward it.

As she opened the door, she found someone waiting inside.

Professor Zion sat at a small table, a book open in front of her. At the sound of the door, she looked up, her face lighting up with a warm, knowing smile.

Raven stepped inside and closed the door behind her. "Hello, Professor."

Professor Zion stood and crossed the room in two strides, pulling Raven into a tight embrace. Raven responded immediately, burying herself in the familiar warmth.

She had known Professor Zion her whole life. She and her mother had been best friends. After her mother went into hiding, it was Zion who had taught Raven almost everything about the assassin world. She was their trusted informant, despite belonging to a different clan.

Pulling back slightly, Zion held Raven at arm's length, studying her with a soft, bittersweet expression.

"I feel like I haven't seen you in years, my pretty bird."

Raven smiled sadly. "Two years, to be exact. But who's counting?"

Zion chuckled, shaking her head before pulling Raven into another hug. "You look just like your mother." Then, her voice lowered with quiet sorrow. "I'm sorry to hear about her passing. I wanted to reach out to you, to come see you."

A lump formed in Raven's throat.

For the first time in a long while, she felt safe.

Losing her mother had left her unmoored, drowning in grief and uncertainty. For nearly a year, she had fought to make sense of her pain. To find direction. It had taken everything in her to finally step onto this path—to honor her mother's wishes and enter the Assassin Academy.

"I'm sorry I told you not to," Raven admitted. "I had so many feelings, so much anger. I needed to process everything alone."

Zion wiped a tear from Raven's cheek.

"But I'm ready now," Raven whispered. "I'm ready to do what needs to be done."

Professor Zion nodded. "Let's sit." She gestured to a chair opposite her, and Raven swiftly took a seat. Closing the book she had been reading, she met Raven's gaze. "First, how was your first day?"

Raven sighed dramatically, slumping into the chair as she stared at the ceiling. "I didn't think it would be so much," she admitted. "I'm used to you or Mom teaching me in the cottage or out in a field. Sitting in a room with a bunch of people and pretending I don't already know everything they're talking about? That's exhausting." She huffed, folding her arms. "Plus, everyone was staring at me all day." She pouted, emphasizing the last part as she glanced at the professor.

Professor Zion smiled. "Maybe they were staring because you're a pretty young lady."

Raven rolled her eyes but couldn't suppress a small smile. "Yeah, you would say that. It's like when Mom tells me I'm beautiful—you're both biased. It doesn't count."

Professor Zion chuckled, shaking her head. "Or maybe they were watching because you did exceptionally well in my class."

Raven scrunched up her nose in disbelief. "They were staring at me before that." She sat up and rolled her shoulder. "Plus, I got injured during that, remember?"

Professor Zion hummed in acknowledgment. "You did what was necessary."

Raven knew she was a skilled fighter—years of rigorous training with her mother and Professor Zion had shaped her into one. Some sessions had ended in tears, others in anger, but as she grew older, she understood the purpose: survival. Losing meant death. Soon, she would be the last of her clan, and she couldn't afford to die. Feigning an injury to mask her true abilities had hurt both her arm and her pride, but she knew it was necessary. If the other prodigies believed they stood a chance against her, they wouldn't question her background—or her true purpose.

Professor Zion laced her fingers together and rested them on the table. "Why did you take that injury from Valentina?" she asked. "You could have taken a hit to the face and called it a day."

Raven shrugged. "She seemed like the only one worthy of being able to say she left a mark on me."

Professor Zion nodded. "She's highly respected—favored to win the Shadow Gauntlet. She has a good heart, too. The other prodigies listen to her."

Raven smiled at the knowledge, recalling her earlier conversation with Valentina. "So, she's naturally kind."

"As kind as an assassin can be in this world," Professor Zion replied.

Raven exhaled, shifting in her chair. "So, what's the plan, exactly? I know I'm supposed to find information on the clan that got mine killed and expose them, but where do I start?"

Professor Zion slid the book she'd been reading across the table. Raven caught it with one hand and frowned at the cover. The book had no title. It was bound in real leather, and a three-dimensional spider was embossed into its surface. She traced her fingers along the spider's body, mesmerized.

"Where did you get this?" she asked, still trailing her fingers along the spider.

"That's… not important," Professor Zion said. "It belongs to the Crimson Widow clan."

Raven's eyes shot up. Her hand stilled on the spider's leg.

"Each clan keeps books to archive their history—the good and the bad," Professor Zion continued. "It's engraved in their traditions. If you're going to find the information and evidence you need, you'll have to find the rest of these books. One by one. Never have two at the same time, and never for too long. They'll notice."

Raven frowned and withdrew her hand, placing it in her lap. "How do we even know they recorded their betrayal?"

Professor Zion sighed. "We don't. But clans are their people. If they were ruthless enough to betray one clan, they've likely betrayed others, too. If they're planning a full takeover, they'll document it for their successors in case one of them falls. It's not a guarantee, but it's a solid place to start."

Raven nodded. "I'll go over it tonight. Thank you, Professor."

Professor Zion glanced at her watch and rose from her seat. "I need to go before they start wondering where I am. We'll meet again in three days."

Raven stood as well and, without hesitation, embraced her. She felt hug-deprived.

Professor Zion chuckled softly and squeezed her back. "Be

safe, little bird."

"I will."

As Professor Zion reached the door, she paused with her hand on the doorknob. "And Raven?"

Raven tilted her head.

"You don't have to call me 'Professor Zion' when we aren't in public."

A slow smile spread across Raven's lips. "Of course, Asha."

Asha smiled at Raven before slipping out the door, shutting it quietly behind her. Raven sighed and turned back to the book on the table. She doubted it would reveal much—Asha hadn't hinted at anything crucial—but she needed to start somewhere.

The pages were less like records and more like diary entries, filled with the writer's frustrations rather than hard facts. The Widow clan, it seemed, saw themselves as the architects of the assassin legacy, believing their influence kept the government from interfering in assassin affairs. Yet, despite their arrogance, they never managed to secure rulership. Time and again, the Crimson Widows produced prodigies, only to fall short when it mattered most. The writer's bitterness was palpable—each entry seethed with impatience for a Widow to take the throne.

Raven sighed, rubbing her tired eyes. "This is going to take forever if there are more books like this," she muttered.

She closed the book, slipping it into her waistband before stretching her stiff muscles. A quick glance at her watch made her groan—it was nearly midnight. She had been here for five hours.

When she opened the door to leave, she was met with darkness. The library had closed. The silence felt thick, pressing against her ears. She walked briskly to the entrance and reached for the door handle, only to find it locked.

Raven frowned. She pulled again. Nothing.

Jaw tightening in irritation, she reached into her pouch for her lock-picking tools. Just as she crouched down to work on the lock, the faint sound of approaching footsteps made her freeze.

Instinct took over. She dropped the tools, drawing her dagger in one swift motion as she spun around into a defensive stance.

The figure stopped a few feet away and… waved. Awkwardly.

Raven narrowed her eyes, trying to make out their face in the dim light.

Slowly, she straightened. "Emilia?"

The girl stepped closer, her lips stretching into a wide smile. Then, without warning, she lunged forward, throwing her arms around Raven.

Raven stiffened.

"Emilia?" she repeated, her voice laced with confusion.

Emilia pulled back just enough for Raven to see her face clearly. She was still smiling—beaming, really.

Raven stared at the girl she had once called her best friend. The one who had vanished from her life when they were twelve. The one who taught her how to read social cues and spoke endlessly about the prodigies. The girl who once harbored a crush on another Prodigy.

"Emilia," Raven murmured again, but this time, there was something else in her tone—something softer.

Emilia's smile faltered slightly, as if she heard it too. She reached out, fingertips brushing Raven's cheek, then leaned in until their foreheads touched.

"Ciao mia grazioso uccello," she whispered. *Hello, my pretty bird.*

Raven swallowed. "What are you doing here?"

Emilia pulled away, her hand dropping. "I go here."

Raven studied her. The girl she remembered had grown into a striking young woman—tan skin, piercing gray eyes, high cheekbones, and effortlessly sleek black hair. She had always been beautiful, but now there was a refined elegance about her.

Emilia stood there, letting Raven take her in. For a moment, neither of them spoke.

Then, Raven finally asked, "I meant… in the library."

Emilia's face lit up again. "Oh!" She clapped her hands

together. "I followed you here. I heard rumors about a prodigy sneaking in late last night. At first, I thought, 'No way, it couldn't be you—you never wanted to be part of this life.' But then..." She grinned. "It was you. So, I waited." She shrugged.

Raven still wasn't sure if she believed this was real. There had been so many nights when she thought about Emilia—wondered where she was, if she was safe, if she ever thought about Raven, too.

She remembered their first meeting, how Emilia had latched onto her with relentless enthusiasm. Raven, always distant, had tried to push her away, but Emilia never let her. And somewhere along the way, that irritation had turned into warmth.

For years, Emilia had been her safe place. Until she disappeared.

And now, here she was.

"You left me," Raven blurted, the weight of years pressing against her chest. The absence of Emilia had been a wound she learned to live with, but her mother's death tore it open again, leaving her utterly alone.

Emilia froze, startled by the rawness in Raven's voice. "I..." She hesitated, her gaze falling to the floor as her fingers curled into her sleeves. "I didn't have a choice. Mother said it was too dangerous. If we kept visiting, they would have come for you." She lifted her head, her dark eyes shimmering. "I would have risked everything to stay, but I couldn't put you in danger."

Raven clenched her jaw, her fists tightening at her sides. The Widow clan had taken too much from her. They just kept taking.

"Raven," Emilia whispered, placing a gentle hand on her shoulder. Her touch was hesitant, uncertain.

Tears burned in Raven's eyes before slipping down her cheeks. She wiped them away with the back of her hand, frustration bubbling inside her. "I hate them," she muttered, voice thick with grief. "They took everything."

Emilia's fingers cupped Raven's face, her thumbs sweeping away the stray tears. "Raven," she said softly, almost pleading.

"Where is your mother?"

The question shattered what little control Raven had left. Since arriving at this school—this place her mother once walked, among the clan that had stolen her life—Raven had forced herself to focus on the mission, to bury her pain. But now, in front of Emilia, the dam broke. A sob tore from her throat, then another, until she was trembling.

Without hesitation, Emilia pulled her into a tight embrace. No words were needed—she understood.

"How long?" she murmured.

"A year," Raven whispered against the fabric of Emilia's uniform, gripping it tightly as though she might disappear again.

Emilia hummed softly, her warmth anchoring Raven in place. After a long moment, she eased back, her voice quiet but steady. "You're not alone anymore. You have me... and you have my mom." She hesitated before adding, "This is going to destroy her."

Raven stilled, the words sinking in. She had missed Ms. Moretti—her mother's closest friend, a woman who had once felt like family. If soulmates existed outside of romance, her mother and Ms. Moretti would have been just that. The thought of seeing her again sent a sharp ache through Raven's chest.

She swallowed hard, wiping her face. "Will I see her soon?"

Emilia offered a small, reassuring smile. "Of course. We'll go this weekend."

Raven nodded. She trusted Emilia.

She turned toward the door, intending to retrieve her tools. But before she could take a step, Emilia moved past her, producing a small set of lock-picking tools—the standard issue for all academy students.

"Let me," she said, a knowing smirk tugging at her lips.

The unwritten rule was clear: break into anywhere without getting caught.

A ghost of a smile flickered across Raven's face. Maybe, just maybe, she wasn't as alone as she thought.

Emilia unlocked the door with practiced ease, pushing it open for Raven to exit. Raven stepped forward but hesitated just before crossing the threshold. Her fingers brushed Emilia's arm—a silent gesture, uncertain yet seeking.

Emilia's response was immediate. She covered Raven's hand with her own, her touch warm and reassuring. A gentle smile formed on her lips. "You'll never be alone again," she whispered, leaning in to press a soft kiss to Raven's cheek.

A flush spread across Raven's face. It had been so long since she'd last seen Emilia—long enough to nearly forget how effortlessly affectionate she could be. Despite herself, Raven grinned. "Thanks, Em." She cast a quick glance down the empty hallway, then turned back to find Emilia watching her intently, her expression unreadable.

Raven raised an eyebrow, silently questioning the look.

Emilia only smiled, waving a hand as if brushing away an unspoken thought. "I'll see you tomorrow, il mia grazioso uccello."

Then, with the same quiet grace as always, she turned and disappeared down the hall.

Raven lingered for a moment, the warmth of Emilia's touch still lingering on her skin. This reunion had been unexpected, but even more surprising was the promise that came with it—one she hadn't realized she needed.

6

Raven awoke to a persistent banging on her door. Instinctively, she lifted her wrist to check her watch. *0500 hours.* Groaning, she rolled out of bed and shuffled toward the door, silently cursing whoever thought it was a good idea to wake her at this hour.

She unlocked the door and swung it open, irritation written all over her face.

Leaning against the doorframe, Valentina stood in all her morning glory, her sharp gaze sweeping over Raven's figure with deliberate slowness.

"Good morning, Prodigy Raven."

Raven's annoyance wavered, giving way to surprise. She blinked, leaning slightly into the hallway, scanning for any sign of a hidden agenda. Nothing. Her focus returned to Valentina.

"Uh… good morning."

"May I come in?" Valentina asked smoothly.

Raven hesitated. "Why?" The question came out sharper than she intended, laced with the confusion of this unexpected visit—two hours before the usual start of the day.

For the briefest moment, something flickered across Valentina's face—hurt, maybe? But it was gone as quickly as it had appeared.

"Never mind," Valentina said, her voice almost too neutral. "I just came to deliver a—"

"No," Raven cut in, cringing at how abrupt she sounded. She cleared her throat, shifting on her feet. "I mean… no. Come in."

A slow smile curved Valentina's lips. She stepped inside with an easy confidence, her every movement deliberate, like she owned the space.

Raven shut the door, watching as Valentina made herself comfortable—on her bed, of all places. The room was bare, void of any personal touches that might betray more than Raven intended.

Silence settled between them until Valentina spoke. "We have a meeting at 0630."

Raven narrowed her eyes. "A meeting?"

Valentina nodded, propping herself up on her elbows. "A prodigy meeting. You'll meet the others, the Council, and"—she paused, holding Raven's gaze—"the Crown."

A quiet beat stretched between them as Raven processed the words.

The Crown.

The title alone carried weight. The current ruler of the clans, a shadowed figure who once stood where she did now—a prodigy—until he conquered the Shadow Gauntlet, eliminating every rival in his path.

She knew little about him. Her mother rarely spoke of him. Asha mentioned him in passing, always cryptic, always careful. The only thing Raven was certain of? He hailed from the Nightshade Syndicate, a dark-skinned man whose name was whispered more than it was spoken aloud.

A slow exhale left her lips. "Should I be worried?"

Valentina shook her head, dismissing the question. "They may ask questions," she explained. "But overall, I think it's just for them to familiarize themselves with you. Maybe gain an ally."

Raven scoffed. "An ally? With the prodigies? Valentina, we must kill one another in less than a year. Making friends with them is a waste of my time."

Valentina stared at Raven, her expression unreadable. Then, without another word, she pushed herself off the bed and walked toward the door.

Raven frowned, instinctively reaching out and grabbing her wrist. "Valentina?"

Valentina looked back at her with a sad smile, gently pulling her arm free. "I didn't know forming relationships with other prodigies would bother you that much." Her voice was quiet but carried a weight Raven couldn't quite place. Without waiting for a response, she turned, opened the door, and glanced over her shoulder. "The meeting is in the Grand Council Room. Please, do not be late."

Then she was gone, leaving Raven standing there, the lingering confusion settling in her chest.

Upon entering the Grand Council Room, Raven was met with silence. All eyes were already on her.

The elders, seated solemnly, rose in unison and bowed—a gesture of respect. Though unnecessary for a prodigy, Raven instinctively reciprocated. It was a habit drilled into her by her mother.

A flicker of surprise crossed the elders' faces before gratitude replaced it.

"Please," one of them spoke, "take a seat, Prodigy Raven."

Raven moved through the vast room, her footsteps echoing against the polished stone. She slid into an open seat beside Valentina, who kept her gaze fixed ahead, her jaw tight. Raven noticed but said nothing.

The elders sat down once more. "The crown will arrive shortly, and the meeting will commence," one of them announced. "Until then, Prodigy Raven, would you like to tell us something about yourself?"

Raven let her gaze drift across the elders, pausing momentarily on one face before continuing. "I didn't realize you were interested in such mundane things."

A chuckle broke the silence. "Only when it's called for."

She nodded, leaning back slightly. "My name is Raven. I'm seventeen years old. I—"

"You like to hit on girlfriends that aren't yours?"

The interruption came from across the table.

A prodigy—Onyx—leaned against the table, arms crossed over her chest, dark eyes sharp with irritation.

Valentina straightened beside her, frowning. "Calm yourself, Onyx."

Onyx ignored her. "Tell me," she demanded, tilting her head, "how do you know Emilia?"

Raven turned to her, expression blank. "Emilia?"

"Emilia Moretti," Onyx hissed.

Valentina shifted in her seat, finally glancing at Raven, intrigue flickering in her gaze.

Raven shrugged, the motion lazy, uninterested. "I met her in the library last night. Friendly girl."

Valentina studied Raven's face, searching for something—guilt, amusement, anything—but Raven remained impassive, exuding nothing but boredom.

Onyx, however, was not so easily deterred. "A colleague of mine saw you both leaving the library at the same time. After closing hours."

Raven hummed, tilting her head as if feigning interest. "Yes, I was improving my knowledge, and she was trying to gain a friend."

Onyx's expression darkened. "She has plenty."

"Clearly." Raven turned away, dismissing the conversation.

"Now, does anyone have questions that actually mean something? I didn't know I'd be dragged into a meeting just to deal with a jealous ex-girlfriend."

Onyx stiffened. "You mean *her* girlfriend."

Raven blinked, her expression all innocence. "What did I say?"

The council chamber fell silent as Onyx shoved off the table, shoulders tense, her cold blue eyes flashing with warning. She took a step toward Raven, but before she could close the distance, the heavy groan of the chamber doors filled the air.

Everyone turned.

The Crown entered.

In an instant, the room shifted. Chairs scraped against the polished stone floor as every member rose in unison, bowing in respect. The Crown acknowledged them with a mere wave of his hand before gesturing for them to sit.

As one, they obeyed.

"Thank you all for gathering on such short notice," he began, voice measured but carrying an unmistakable weight. "I have been informed that a new prodigy has been admitted into this school— without my approval and without a proper background check." His sharp gaze swept over the elders. "Anyone care to explain?"

Counselor Zephyr inhaled slowly before speaking. "I was the one who met Prodigy Raven at the gate that night and allowed her inside."

Raven's eyes flicked toward Zephyr. His composure was intact, but the slight tremor in his voice did not escape her notice. Subtle, but there. Her gaze lingered on the right shoulder of his robes, where the fiery scorpion emblem of the *Ember Scorpion Guild* curled its tail into a dagger—a mark of allegiance not easily ignored.

The Crown's expectant stare hardened. "Explain."

Zephyr took another breath. "She bears the mark. It was beyond my authority to deny her entry."

A wave of realization rippled through the chamber. The

council members turned toward Raven as one. Unfazed, she continued to stare at the wall as if the entire discussion were of no consequence to her.

Of course, they would question her. It was inevitable. But the very notion that she would show up without the mark was laughable.

"Show us," the Crown commanded.

At last, Raven turned her attention to him, her expression unreadable.

Then, she shook her head.

A flicker of surprise crossed his face. "Excuse me?"

Raven sighed and leaned forward, arms crossed over the table. "Honestly, I know very little about you, *Your Majesty*. I know you hail from Nightshade. You're likely in your late forties. You have no children of your own." She waved a hand dismissively. "Simple facts. Vague details." Her gaze sharpened. "Yet, you expect a young, underage girl to lift her shirt in front of you and everyone in this room?" She leaned back, her expression one of cold disinterest. "I think not."

Silence.

The Crown's lips pressed together, but he did not insist. Instead, his gaze turned to Zephyr.

"How did you see her mark?"

Raven tilted her head, amusement dancing in her eyes as she answered, "He took a peek in my shirt."

The chamber erupted into murmurs.

Counselor Zephyr turned crimson at her accusation, throwing his hands up in defense. "You can see the head of the snake on her shoulder!"

Raven smirked but didn't look at him. Instead, she turned her attention to the Crown. "He is correct. My mark extends to the top of my shoulder." She shifted her gaze to the green-eyed girl. "Valentina, you are of Nightshade. Who better to confirm my claim than a possible heir of the same clan? Come. See for yourself."

Valentina hesitated, her fingers tightening around the armrest of her chair. A glance from the Crown was all she needed before rising.

Raven met her eyes steadily, then began unzipping her uniform coat, deliberately shrugging it off her shoulders. Valentina's face remained unreadable, but the subtle rise and fall of her chest betrayed her nervousness.

Raven tilted her head to the right, silently giving permission. For a long second, Valentina hesitated, then reached forward and peeled back the collar of Raven's shirt. Her breath brushed against Raven's skin, and the light touch of her fingers sent a chill down Raven's spine. She tensed—just briefly—before forcing herself to relax. If Valentina noticed, she gave no sign.

After a moment, Valentina released the fabric and straightened. "She bears the mark, Your Majesty."

The Crown nodded. "It seems there is more to discuss than we expected. Take your seat, Valentina."

Valentina sat stiffly, gripping the armrests, her knuckles white. Raven turned back to the table, her gaze flicking toward Valentina's rigid posture.

The Crown exhaled, then leaned forward. "Let us start over. My name is Pierre. Yes, I am from the Nightshade Clan. I won my shadow gauntlet years ago and have ruled the elev—" His voice faltered, and he quickly corrected himself. "—ten clans ever since."

Raven caught the slip but said nothing.

Pierre gestured toward the individuals at his left. "These are the prodigies. Introduce yourselves."

The first to rise was a young man with sharp features and an air of quiet authority. "Whisper. Ghost Orchid Clan." He gave a curt bow, his gaze briefly flicking toward Valentina before he sat down.

Next was a woman with a smirk that didn't quite reach her eyes. "Viper. Silent Clan." She nodded toward Raven, who returned the gesture.

One by one, the others followed:

"Seraph of the Death Lotus Clan."

"Onyx of the Obsidian Clan."

"Nikolai of the Ember Scorpion Guild."

"Frost of the Eclipsed Clan."

"Kenji of the Moon Clan."

"Tariq of the Silver Veil Clan."

Then the last one spoke.

"I am Phantom of the Crimson Widow Clan."

His voice was smooth, but Raven barely contained the disgust curling in her stomach. The Crimson Widow Clan.

She forced a tight smile and turned her attention to the elders, waiting for the next round of introductions.

7

aven sat through her first class, her mind preoccupied with the meeting. Valentina had assured her it wasn't meant to be hostile, yet she couldn't shake the feeling that they intended to catch her off guard. Pierre, the ruler, carried himself with competence, but there was something in his gaze that unsettled her. She had little personal knowledge of him, so she resisted making quick judgments—though the reactions of others during the meeting spoke volumes.

The weight of the discussion still pressed on her as she and Valentina arrived late to class. Unlike before, they took separate seats—Raven choosing one closer to the professor, hoping to avoid drawing attention. Valentina, however, sat where they had on the first day.

Raven sensed Valentina's displeasure but couldn't pinpoint the reason. Between her studies, training, and mission preparations, she had little time to untangle the complexities of interpersonal relationships. There were journals to find, mysteries surrounding the assassins to solve, and a greater understanding of this world she had stepped into to gain. She sighed, leaning back in her chair, her mind returning to the journals and where she should begin searching.

The scrape of chairs against the floor signaled the end of class, pulling her from her thoughts. Without hesitation, Raven stood and made her way to the door, expecting that Valentina might prefer to walk alone.

"Hey, you," Emilia's voice greeted her just as she stepped into the hallway.

Raven's lips curled into a smile. Somehow, Emilia had a way of making everything else fade into the background. "Hey," she replied.

"What's your next class?" Emilia asked as they fell into step together.

"Training with Professor Zion."

Emilia nodded, her eyes twinkling with the unspoken understanding of their shared secret. "How's your morning been?"

Raven shrugged. "I had a prodigy meeting."

"A prodigy meeting?" Emilia's voice held curiosity. "How did that go?"

Raven hesitated, biting her lower lip. "Well... I'll be joining your clan."

Emilia came to an abrupt halt, forcing Raven to stop and meet her gaze. "You're *what*? How?" Her voice carried a mix of shock and confusion.

Raven pressed her lips together, choosing her words carefully. She could feel unseen eyes on them, unsure of who might be listening. "I told them about my adoptive mother—how she was part of the Silent Clan. I expressed my desire to join because she always spoke so highly of it."

Emilia continued to stare at her, the perplexity lingering. But after a moment, she nodded. "I have a lot of questions."

Raven offered a reassuring smile. "And you'll get all the answers. But first, I have something to ask."

Emilia nodded, prompting Raven to continue.

"You are the heir to your clan, correct?"

Another nod.

"And Viper is the prodigy of your clan?"

"Yes."

Raven leaned forward. "Who outranks who?"

Emilia looked up at the ceiling as if sorting through her thoughts. "It's a strange system," she admitted, shifting her gaze back to Raven. "The clan ruler holds the highest authority. Then the prodigy, then the heir."

Raven arched a brow. "The prodigy ranks above the heir?"

"They have to," Emilia said. "Prodigies are chosen because there's a chance they'll lead the clans. We respect them as if they already do. The heir is next in line to rule their individual clan, but by the time they take over, their clan's prodigy has either ascended to the throne or..." She hesitated. "Well, they don't live long enough to matter."

Raven caught the brief flicker of something unreadable in Emilia's expression. Discomfort? Grief? The attempt at neutral wording didn't hide the brutal truth.

"I'm surprised the prodigy doesn't outrank the ruler," Raven mused.

Emilia shrugged. "Prodigies come and go."

The casual remark made Raven flinch. Respected, yet disposable. A system built on necessary loss.

Emilia placed a hand on Raven's shoulder, as if sensing her unease.

Raven inhaled slowly. It made sense. Stability was key. The prodigies were powerful, but ruling required more than power—it needed continuity. Letting prodigies govern would only create instability, as one generation fell and another rose. The system ensured leadership remained constant, while the prodigies fought, trained, and survived long enough to—

A deliberate cough interrupted her thoughts.

Both Raven and Emilia turned to see Onyx standing before

them, arms crossed over her chest, blue eyes narrowed at Emilia's hand resting on Raven's shoulder.

A slow smile crept onto Raven's lips. She was well aware of Emilia and Onyx's relationship, but Onyx's open hostility amused her. It was possessive, even territorial. And something about that entertained her.

"Hello," Raven greeted, voice polite but teasing.

Emilia hesitated. "Hey, babe," she replied, confusion lacing her words.

Onyx's gaze flicked between them. "I see you two have gotten quite familiar since last night."

Emilia's jaw tightened. "I just found out she joined my clan. As heir, it's my duty to ensure she's settled, understands her place, and knows she falls under our protection now." There was an unmistakable warning in her voice, one both Raven and Onyx caught.

Raven grinned. "Thank you, dearest Emilia," she said, taking Emilia's hand and pressing a kiss against her knuckles. "I appreciate your generosity."

Emilia narrowed her eyes, sensing the deliberate taunt. But the slight twitch of her lips betrayed her amusement.

Onyx took a sharp step forward, a low growl escaping her throat.

Emilia instantly positioned herself between them. "Back off, Onyx," she ordered, voice firm.

The tension stretched, thick and heavy, until a new voice cut through it.

"Raven."

Valentina's tone was sharp, drawing all attention toward her as she stepped forward.

"You're late to class."

Raven slipped past Emilia and Onyx, barely sparing them a glance. "I'll see you later," she muttered to Emilia before striding toward Valentina. As she left, she could still hear the argument continuing behind her, but she didn't stop. Emilia would have words with her later, she was sure of it. A smirk tugged at her lips as she turned the corner with Valentina, leaving the chaos behind.

Valentina walked beside her in silence, her gaze fixed ahead. Raven wasn't used to quiet from her—not this kind. Something about it felt… wrong.

"You're upset with me," Raven stated.

Valentina didn't respond.

Raven sighed, stepping in front of her and catching her wrist, bringing them both to a halt. "Valentina."

Finally, Valentina looked up to face her, her expression unreadable.

"What have I done to make you hate me?" Raven asked, voice softer now.

Valentina's jaw tightened. "I do not hate you," she said at last. "I was only respecting your wishes. You don't want to form bonds with a prodigy, and I didn't want to force that burden on you."

Raven studied her, searching for any sign of emotion beyond the carefully maintained calm. It was there, just beneath the surface— a flicker of something wounded in her eyes.

"You didn't count, Valentina," Raven murmured.

Valentina's expression barely shifted, but something in her eyes sharpened. "I am a prodigy, Raven."

Raven dropped her gaze, grasping for the right words. *Find your words.*

She was no good at this. Emilia always had the right things to say. Asha knew how to make people feel seen. Even Ms. Moretti and her mother had guided conversations like artists shaping clay. But Raven? Raven had always been an observer, not a speaker.

Valentina, though… Valentina was different. Maybe because she was the first person Raven had met after so much loneliness . Or maybe it was just something about her—something that made it impossible not to care.

She looked up and found Valentina watching her, waiting.

Raven sighed and stepped closer, cutting the space between

them. Valentina stiffened.

"I've been alone for a long time," Raven admitted. "When my mother died, I had a choice—come here or be free. And I don't..." She frowned, struggling against the words. "I don't know how to talk to people. I don't like expressing my emotions, and I don't like getting close to people. Death hangs over us like a dark cloud, and our days are counting down."

Valentina held her gaze. "And what do you do when death hangs over you like a dark cloud? When you could die in just a few months?"

Raven searched her face, but no answer came. "I don't know."

Valentina stepped closer. "Live," she whispered.

The kiss was soft—brief but electric. Raven froze for a heartbeat before leaning into it, warmth flooding through her.

Then, just as quickly, Valentina pulled back, her composure fracturing as uncertainty flickered across her face. "I'm sorry," she said hastily. "We just met yesterday and I—"

Raven smiled—small, but real. "No need to apologize," she said, voice quiet. "Come on. We're late."

Raven completed all her classes for the day and returned to her room, exhaustion settling deep in her bones. With a sigh, she dropped her bag by the door and collapsed onto her bed, staring up at the ceiling. The weight of the past two days pressed on her—new alliances, unexpected emotions, and the lingering whispers of her past.

Becoming a member of Emilia's clan brought a measure of security. Finally, the questions surrounding her origins and affiliation were answered, yet an unsettling feeling remained.

Shedding her school uniform, Raven changed into a tank top and boy shorts, tying her curls into a messy ponytail. A few strands fell loose, framing her face as she sat on the edge of the bed. Her gaze flickered to the door before she slid off the mattress, moving with quiet precision—three paces forward, five to the right. Kneeling, she pulled up the loose floorboard, revealing a hidden compartment.

The Crimson Widow journal lay inside.

She retrieved it, brushing her fingers over the worn cover before sealing the hiding spot again. Maybe this time, it would offer something—anything—beyond cryptic bitterness.

Settling into her chair, she flipped through the pages, her eyes tracing the jagged script. Hours passed in silent study, but the journal remained as elusive as ever, filled with venom but little guidance.

Raven exhaled, rubbing her temples before leaning back. Her thoughts drifted unbidden to Valentina. Their unexpected kiss replayed in her mind. It had been impulsive, electric—and confusing. They had only known each other for two days, yet Valentina stirred something unnameable in her.

A knock at the door pulled her from her thoughts.

Raven stood, smoothing down her top before cracking the door open. Emilia stood on the other side, dressed in pajama pants and a short-sleeved shirt, the Silent Clan's sigil embroidered on the left side of her chest.

A smile tugged at Raven's lips, as it always did in Emilia's presence.

Emilia grinned, stepping forward and wrapping her arms around Raven in a warm embrace. "Ciao, mio grazioso Uccello," she purred, pressing a soft kiss to Raven's cheek before pulling away.

Raven felt heat rise to her face but ignored it. "What brings you here so late?"

Emilia stepped inside, nudging the door shut with her foot before settling onto Raven's bed. She scooted back until she was nestled against the pillows, her expression relaxed yet unreadable.

"Well," she began, stretching her arms over her head, "I didn't get to see you much today, and we still have things to talk about. Plus, my best friend is finally here at school. Do you think I'm not going to take advantage of that?"

Raven chuckled, shaking her head as she joined Emilia on the bed. As soon as she sat down, Emilia rested her head on Raven's shoulder and reached for her hand, threading their fingers together.

"I missed you," Emilia admitted, voice barely above a whisper.

Raven's grip tightened just slightly. "And I you."

They sat in silence for a while, savoring each other's presence, readjusting to being in the same space again. The quiet between them was familiar, almost comforting. Then Emilia spoke.

"You know you got me in a lot of trouble today."

Raven smirked, the memory of pushing Onyx's buttons flashing through her mind. "Your girlfriend is really possessive."

Emilia chuckled. "Apparently, so are you."

Raven shrugged, careful not to disturb Emilia's position. "You were mine first."

Emilia sat up, her fingers still laced with Raven's. She met Raven's gaze, her expression softer now. "I will always be yours. So please, play nice?"

Raven held Emilia's eyes for a long moment before looking away. She shifted off the bed, running a hand through her dark curls as she walked to her desk. "I will have to kill her one day, Em." She sighed, staring blankly at the wall. "Why couldn't you love someone else?"

Emilia's breath hitched, but she recovered quickly. "I did," she whispered, so softly it seemed like a thought rather than spoken words.

Raven heard it. But for Emilia's sake, she let the words slip past without acknowledgment.

"I understand what you must do as a prodigy," Emilia said, getting off the bed and walking over to her. "I just want you to be cordial until that day comes." She reached out, tucking a stray curl behind Raven's ear, her touch lingering. "For me?"

Raven let out a slow breath and met Emilia's gaze again. "I'll try."

Emilia smiled, her arms wrapping around Raven's shoulders. "Thank you." She kissed the top of Raven's head before shifting her attention to the open book on the desk. Her fingers skimmed over the pages, curiosity flashing in her eyes.

"What is it?" Raven asked, watching her carefully.

Emilia picked up the book, flipping through the pages with increasing urgency. Her brows knit together as if trying to place something. "I've seen this before, but a different version."

Raven straightened. "Where?"

Emilia closed the book, her fingers tracing the Widow emblem on the cover. She hesitated before speaking. "My mother had one. I found her reading it one day. She said it was to help you and Ms. Norris." A crease formed between her brows as a memory surfaced. "Actually, after that, she told me we couldn't visit you guys anymore."

A sharp silence settled between them.

Raven hummed in thought, her gaze fixed on the book. Had Ms. Moretti been searching for evidence against the Widow clan? Had she uncovered something dangerous?

"Do you know where it is now?" Raven asked.

Emilia shook her head. "I never saw it again. My mother told me never to speak of it."

Raven exhaled and turned toward the hidden compartment in her room. She counted her steps, stopping precisely in front of it. She knelt, placed the book back in its resting place, and shut it away.

"I'm afraid I must say the same thing," she murmured.

Emilia sat on the edge of the bed, watching her carefully. "What is it?"

Raven joined her. "Asha believes the journals will reveal the Crimson Widow's role in my clan's demise. I have to find and study them one by one before I can accuse the clan—and eliminate whoever I need to."

Emilia nodded, absorbing the weight of her words. "We're in

for the fight of our lives, aren't we?"

Raven didn't hesitate. "Yes."

She had always known her prodigy status wouldn't protect her forever.

This was what she had been training for.

8

sha gestured toward the frozen lake, her voice steady. *"To become strong, little bird, you must face your fears."*

Raven glanced at her mother, who sat cross-legged in the snow a few feet away, her breath misting in the crisp Vardelundian air. The winter was brutal, the cold unrelenting, yet her mother remained still, unfazed by the ice beneath her. Strength radiated from her in a way Raven longed to emulate.

Taking a slow breath, Raven slipped off her shoes. The snow bit at her bare feet instantly, sharp and unforgiving. She hissed through clenched teeth, but she didn't step back. Pain was temporary. Strength was earned.

She moved forward, the ice crackling faintly beneath her weight. At the river's edge, she hesitated. Shards of ice drifted on the water's surface, a warning of the cold's merciless grip. The thought of the frigid water wrapping around her made her stomach clench, but retreating wasn't an option.

Her mother's gaze held her, silent but steady. Asha remained beside her, waiting.

Raven inhaled deeply, forcing the tremor from her limbs.

Before her body could second-guess her mind, she plunged forward. The icy water consumed her instantly, a sharp, breathtaking shock that stole the air from her lungs.

For a moment, she didn't move. Cold enveloped her, pressing against her ribs, her limbs. Then instinct took over, and she kicked upward, breaking the surface with a gasp.

The wind lashed against her wet skin, but beneath the sting of the cold, something else burned—pride.

Emerging from the water, Raven spotted her mother standing beside Asha, concern carved into their faces. Her body trembled, teeth chattering uncontrollably as she fought against the numbing cold, swimming toward them. She didn't make it.

The icy grip of the lake dragged her under again. Darkness blurred her thoughts.

When she came to, warmth surrounded her. The crackling fire cast flickering shadows on the cave walls, and layers of blankets cocooned her shivering form. A steady weight rested against her— her mother, arms wrapped tightly around her.

"She's pushing herself too hard," her mother's voice, hushed and urgent, reached her through the haze.

"She is stronger than you think, Nova," Asha countered, her tone firm. "She has outperformed many prodigies back home."

Nova sighed, her hold tightening protectively. "I just don't want her to get hurt. She's all I have."

"She is the last of your clan," Asha reminded her. "She must be strong."

Raven lay still, letting their words sink in. Disappointment coiled in her chest. Had she failed them? She had trained relentlessly, endured every hardship thrown at her. Yet, it wasn't enough.

That night, after they had fallen asleep, she slipped away, returning to the lake's edge. The wind howled, the water an obsidian abyss of frigid torment. Steeling herself, she stepped in. Again. And again. Until her skin no longer burned from the cold. Until she could move without feeling the ice clawing at her bones.

She pushed too far.

Collapsing onto the snow, exhaustion consumed her. The last thing she saw was the distant glow of torchlight, her mother's voice calling her name. Then darkness.

She resurfaced to warmth once more.

A gentle shake stirred her awake. The scent of morning drifted through the air.

"Let's grab breakfast before we head out," Emilia's voice cut through the remnants of her dream.

Raven blinked groggily. "Head out? It's Saturday," she mumbled, stretching—only to wince as stiffness shot through her limbs.

Emilia chuckled. "Yes, I told you I'd take you home, remember? I need to freshen up first. Meet me in the cafeteria."

Raven nodded slowly, still shaking off sleep. "We have to grab Prodigy Viper, too—she's supposed to introduce me to your mother." She let out a dry chuckle.

Emilia nodded, stepping toward the door. As she pulled it open, she froze, then quickly dipped her head in a respectful bow.

"Oh—morning, Prodigy Valentina."

"Morning, Emilia," came the slow, measured response from beyond the doorway.

Emilia turned back to Raven and waved goodbye before disappearing out the door. The moment she was gone, Valentina stepped into the room, her gaze fixed on Raven with a raised eyebrow.

She moved toward the bed, settling at its edge. "I didn't know you two were so close," she remarked, the unspoken question hanging between them.

Raven met her eyes but said nothing. A single kiss wasn't reason enough for her to start unraveling her past, not when the truth was something she couldn't afford to share.

Valentina hummed in response to the silence, her gaze drifting across the room before settling on the large window. The sunlight poured in, casting sharp shadows along the floor.

Raven stood and headed to the bathroom, tossing over her shoulder, "Give me a moment."

Valentina's faint "Yeah" followed her as she closed the door. In front of the mirror, Raven brushed her teeth and ran a hand through her thick curls, shaking them loose. The familiar ritual steadied her.

By the time she stepped back out, Valentina was still sitting in silence, watching as Raven moved toward her closet. She hesitated before pulling it open. Inside, the uniforms were neatly hung, their crisp edges reminding her of routine and restrictions. Choosing anything else would mean attracting attention she didn't want. With a sigh, she grabbed a fresh uniform and began changing—forgetting, for a moment, that she wasn't alone.

When she turned back, Valentina was staring at the floor, a faint pink hue dusting her cheeks.

"Valentina?" Raven called, puzzled.

"Hmm?" Valentina still avoided her gaze.

Raven frowned. "Are you alright?"

Clearing her throat, Valentina looked up. "Yeah, sorry." She ran a hand through her hair, still refusing to meet Raven's eyes. "I came to ask if you wanted to get breakfast. And if you had any plans this weekend."

Fastening the straps on her shoes, Raven secured her dagger to her left leg, then reached for the sword the guild had gifted her. She strapped it across her back, feeling its familiar weight.

"I'm meeting Emilia there," she answered. "I'd like it if you joined us. After that, Viper, Emilia, and I leave for the clan so I can meet the head and officially join."

Valentina nodded in understanding. "Why are you arming yourself like we're heading into battle?"

Raven met her gaze, adjusting the last of her straps. "Because we leave school today and re-enter the real world. I don't plan on being caught empty-handed."

Valentina's expression shifted. "Everyone knows you're a prodigy now. Word spreads fast. No one would be dumb enough to attack you on Nethrala unless they want to deal with the consequences."

Raven only shrugged. She wasn't about to gamble her life on other people's fear.

"I'd rather be safe than sorry," Raven replied, offering a tight smile. Survival had been ingrained in her from birth—an ever-present fear that someone might come for her family. Despite bearing the prodigy mark, she remained an anomaly in the assassin world, never willing to be caught off guard.

"Will you join us for breakfast?"

Valentina smiled and nodded. "After you." She rose to her feet, her movements fluid yet deliberate.

Raven opened the door, letting Valentina step through before following her into the hall. They walked in comfortable silence, though Raven couldn't shake the curiosity gnawing at her. Did Valentina enjoy these quiet moments, or was something weighing on her mind? The question hovered on the tip of her tongue, but she refrained from asking. She had no desire to get tangled in discussions about feelings—especially when they might lead to Emilia.

When they reached the cafeteria, Raven stopped short, momentarily breathless at the sight before her.

The vast room radiated an air of clandestine elegance, an unexpected contrast to its mundane function. Dark, polished marble floors gleamed beneath the glow of suspended lanterns. Towering obsidian pillars reached toward a vaulted ceiling, their surfaces etched with shimmering sigils. These symbols, meticulously arranged along the walls, represented the academy's deadliest skills, each pulsating with an eerie, otherworldly luminescence.

At the heart of the room stretched a sprawling dining area where young recruits and seasoned assassins alike gathered. Sleek ebony tables, flanked by high-backed obsidian chairs, formed rigid rows—both intimidating and orderly. Hooded figures moved in silence, their dark attire blending seamlessly into the dimly lit space. Conversations remained hushed, spoken only in murmurs, while the scent of exotic spices and rare herbs drifted from the shadowed entrance of the kitchen.

Valentina chuckled at Raven's reaction and, with a mischievous glint in her eyes, took her hand, pulling her toward the food selection. Raven hesitated, overwhelmed by the choices before settling on a simple plate: fresh fruit, tea, and a slice of bread with jam.

Valentina, on the other hand, selected huevos rancheros, her fork already poised as they turned to find a place to sit.

A familiar voice called out.

"Over here!"

Emilia waved them over, her presence commanding even in the sea of assassins. Beside her sat Onyx, who leveled a cold glare at Raven as she approached.

Ignoring the hostility, Raven took a seat across from Emilia. Valentina slid in beside her, her warmth a stark contrast to the icy tension crackling across the table.

Emilia inclined her head slightly in greeting—a natural gesture of respect. "Lovely of you to join us, Prodigy Valentina."

Valentina returned the sentiment with a polite smile. "Thank you for allowing me to come."

They began eating, but Raven found herself locked in an unspoken battle with Onyx. Their gazes clashed, sharp and unwavering.

Raven held nothing personal against Onyx—except for the woman's relentless attempts to stake a claim on Emilia. But she knew Onyx's hatred ran far deeper. The assassin despised her presence, though she never truly understand why Raven was in Emilia's life.

And she never would.

Raven turned to Emilia, finding her already looking at her with a pointed expression—a silent reminder to be nice.

"Hello, Emilia," Raven greeted with mock innocence, feigning ignorance.

"Il mia grazioso uccello," Emilia responded with a smile.

Raven noticed Onyx's face scrunch in confusion. She doesn't speak Italian. A small smirk tugged at Raven's lips.

As expected, Onyx asked, "What did you just call her?"

Emilia shrugged as if it didn't matter. "Nothing important." Then, without missing a beat, she turned to Raven. "After we eat, we must leave."

Raven nodded and began eating.

Onyx, however, remained still, her gaze fixed on Raven. "Where are you going?"

Raven met her eyes and took a slow, deliberate bite, waiting for Emilia to answer.

"She's coming home with me," Emilia said casually.

Onyx's jaw tightened.

Valentina, silent, observed the exchange. Raven wasn't sure if Valentina was uncomfortable with the growing tension, but if she was, she didn't show it.

Raven had always admired Emilia's vagueness—how she shared just enough to intrigue but never enough to satisfy. It was a skill honed since childhood, an unspoken rule among assassins: never waste time explaining yourself. Watching Emilia use the same tactic on her girlfriend was amusing, especially since it clearly infuriated Onyx.

Is Emilia usually open with her? Raven wondered. Or is she vague only when it comes to me?

Onyx's voice was strained when she asked, "Why?"

Valentina spoke this time. "Raven is part of Emilia's clan now. She must report back and meet the head."

"With Viper," she added.

Raven and Emilia exchanged glances. "With Viper," they echoed in unison.

Onyx exhaled sharply and returned to her food, stabbing at it with more force than necessary. Raven ignored her, cupping her tea and blowing gently to cool it down. After a few breaths, she took a sip and nearly melted at the taste.

"Em," Raven called softly.

Emilia looked up.

"Try this." Raven's lips curled into a smile.

Without hesitation, Emilia accepted the cup and took a sip. Her eyes closed briefly, and she sighed. "This reminds me of when we—" She stopped abruptly, realizing she had almost revealed something she shouldn't.

She quickly handed the tea back to Raven.

Before Raven could take it, Onyx's hand lashed out, knocking the cup from her grasp.

The ceramic hit the table with a sharp clatter before shattering against the floor. Tea spilled over the edge, dripping onto the ground. The cafeteria fell silent.

Valentina calmly grabbed a napkin, wiped the edge of the table, and placed it on her finished plate as if nothing had happened.

Raven slowly lifted her gaze to Onyx, whose expression was unreadable.

"Babe," Emilia hissed.

Onyx ignored her, her glare locked onto Raven.

Raven's voice was cool. "Is there a problem, Prodigy Onyx?"

Onyx's jaw clenched. "Yes. You."

A charged silence stretched between them.

Then, Raven pushed her chair back and stood. "I'll go get napkins to clean up your mess."

Onyx snapped. One moment she was still; the next, she lunged across the table, arms reaching for Raven.

But Raven was faster.

She sidestepped at the last second, sending Onyx crashing to the floor. Onyx twisted mid-fall, landing in a crouch.

Raven barely had time to turn before Onyx attacked again.

The first clash was a blur—lightning-fast strikes, evasion, counterattacks. No weapons were drawn; that would mean risking a fatal injury before the gauntlet. Instead, fists and feet flew, knocking over tables and chairs as they wove through the chaos.

Onyx fought recklessly, fueled by jealousy and rage. Her strikes were fast but undisciplined.

Raven, however, was calm, precise, and calculating. She read Onyx's movements like an open book, dodging, countering, and exploiting every mistake.

Then, Onyx's wild swing nearly struck Valentina.

Raven's fingers snapped around Onyx's wrist just in time. With a sharp twist, she spun Onyx around and slammed a foot into her abdomen.

Onyx flew backward.

For the first time, a flicker of real anger flared in Raven's chest. It surprised her.

The fight had started as a game. A way to rattle Onyx.

But now? Now, it felt personal.

And she wasn't sure why.

Raven's controlled fury intensified. Onyx pushed herself up and launched another attack, but Raven countered with swift, punishing blows. The fight escalated, and the cafeteria, once buzzing with excitement, fell into uneasy silence.

At first, the onlookers had been entertained by the spectacle, but now, they exchanged wary glances as Raven's strikes grew more aggressive. Onyx, battered and struggling for breath, barely remained on her feet. It wasn't just a sparring match anymore—it was turning into something far more dangerous.

"Stop, Raven! That's enough!"

Emilia's voice cut through the tension, sharp with urgency. She stepped forward, her expression tight with concern. Raven hesitated, her breath heavy, fists clenched. The fire in her eyes flickered as Emilia's presence forced its way into her consciousness.

Onyx collapsed onto the floor, gasping. No one moved. No one had dared to step between the two prodigies mid-fight, but now, the cafeteria held its breath, waiting for what came next.

Emilia took control, her gaze shifting between Raven and Onyx. "Enough," she said, her voice firm, brooking no argument. She knelt beside Onyx, assessing her injuries. "We need to talk."

Raven, still catching her breath, stepped back, allowing Emilia to help Onyx up. Ignoring the hushed murmurs around her, Raven turned her attention to Valentina.

"Are you okay?" she asked, her voice softer now, laced with concern.

Valentina met her gaze and smiled, unshaken despite the chaos that had just unfolded. "Thank you for keeping me out of it."

Relief settled in Raven's chest, and for the first time since the fight began, she exhaled.

"Always."

9

The car ride to the Silent Clan's domain was steeped in silence. From the front seat, Viper kept a vigilant watch through the dark-tinted windows, her posture rigid with caution. Emilia sat beside Raven, her gaze fixed ahead, but the stillness between them carried weight. Raven wasn't sure if Emilia resented her, but the possibility gnawed at her.

A sigh escaped her lips as she turned her attention to the passing scenery. *I was just being nice*, she told herself, though deep down, she knew she had deliberately tested Onyx's temper. She couldn't help but feel that her lack of self-control wasn't entirely her fault.

The landscape shifted—trees thickened, closing in around them, until they reached a towering dirt wall. Raven's gaze lifted as a sigil came into view through the front windshield: a sleek, silver viper coiled around crossed daggers. The emblem parted down the middle, granting them entry. The SUV eased forward before rolling to a stop.

"Welcome to Silent Clan," Viper announced as she stepped out.

Raven followed suit, her boots crunching against the gravel. The driver remained silent, but his gaze lingered on her with suspicion. Ignoring the scrutiny, she trailed behind Viper and Emilia as they ascended the stone steps leading out of the underground garage and into the mansion's grand corridor.

The interior was breathtaking. Vines clung to the walls, seamlessly blending nature with architecture. Beneath their feet, polished marble gleamed, reflecting the dim glow of the chandeliers. At the heart of the corridor, an enormous Silent Clan sigil was embedded into the floor. Twin staircases spiraled upward to the upper levels.

As they climbed, Raven ran her fingers along the cool, ornate railings, admiring the craftsmanship. She was so absorbed in the details that she barely noticed when Emilia abruptly stopped. Raven bumped into her, pulling back immediately.

"Sorry," she muttered.

Emilia turned to face her, her expression unreadable. Before Raven could decipher the look, Viper knocked on a nearby door. A soft, measured voice responded from within.

"Come in."

Viper pushed open the door, revealing a study lined with towering bookshelves. Two plush couches faced each other, a coffee table nestled between them. A dark green reading chair sat in the corner beside a tall lamp, its glow casting a warm halo over the space. But Raven's attention was drawn upward—to the chandelier suspended overhead, its light dancing across the room.

At the far end of the study, Ms. Moretti traced her fingers along the spines of the books, her back to them. "What brings you two home this weekend?" she asked without turning around.

"We have a new addition to the clan," Viper explained. "King Pierre wanted her introduced immediately and placed within our ranks."

Ms. Moretti hummed in acknowledgment as she plucked a book from the shelf. When she turned to face them, her sharp gaze landed on Raven—and froze.

A beat of silence passed.

Emilia cleared her throat, redirecting her mother's attention. "She's a prodigy who recently enrolled in the school. Her adoptive mother was part of this clan, and she wishes to join. The council approved her request."

Ms. Moretti's eyes lingered on Raven before shifting back to Emilia and Viper. Finally, she nodded. "Very well. We will initiate her tomorrow. I'd like to take today to get to know her."

Viper and Emilia bowed before turning to leave. Just as Emilia exited, she cast a fleeting glance at Raven.

She's mad at me.

The door clicked shut, leaving Raven alone with Ms. Moretti. For a moment, they simply stood there, staring at each other. Then, in an instant, Ms. Moretti moved.

She stepped around the desk, her arms opening wide.

Raven didn't hesitate. She rushed forward, throwing herself into the embrace, wrapping her arms tightly around Ms. Moretti as tears stung her eyes.

Ms. Moretti held her just as fiercely, her own tears dampening Raven's shoulder. "I've missed you," Raven whispered.

"I've missed you too, my sweet girl." Ms. Moretti ran a soothing hand down Raven's back before pulling away to look at her.

Then her gaze hardened. "Where is your mother? How did she let you come here?" A pause. "You didn't run away, did you?"

Raven gave a sad smile, meeting Ms. Moretti's piercing green eyes. "Mother has passed."

The air in the room shifted.

Ms. Moretti's grip on Raven loosened as she stepped back. Her face tensed—eyes searching, fingers curling against the desk as if for support. "How?"

Raven inhaled sharply. "She said the chemicals from the night of the setup finally wore her body down. She couldn't fight it anymore." The words tasted bitter on her tongue. A lump formed in her throat. "She passed in my arms."

The silence that followed was suffocating.

Then, with a sharp inhale, Ms. Moretti turned and, with a furious motion, swept the flower vase from her desk.

The crash shattered the air.

Water splattered onto the books, glass shards scattering across the floor. Ms. Moretti's face crumpled as a raw, anguished scream tore from her throat.

She collapsed.

Raven was at her side in an instant, reaching for her just as the door burst open.

Emilia stood there, alarm flashing across her face.

Raven pulled Ms. Moretti into a tight embrace. Emilia, whispering something under her breath, swiftly shut the door and locked it. She knelt beside them, and Ms. Moretti, still sobbing, wrapped them both in her arms.

Together, they sat silently on the floor, grief pressing heavily on them. Emilia hadn't had the chance to mourn at school, forced to pretend she had only just met Raven. Ms. Moretti had never allowed herself to believe her best friend was truly gone—until now. And Raven, who had never stopped grieving, finally let herself feel the emotions she had buried. For the first time in years, she lowered her guard, knowing she was safe with the only people who mattered.

Eventually, they wiped away their tears and moved to the sofas. Though sorrow lingered between them, they found solace in each other's presence.

"So," Ms. Moretti said as she settled onto the couch, her voice laced with sadness. Raven and Emilia sat across from her. "How exactly did you convince them to let you join my clan? And what adoptive mother?"

Raven quickly recounted the events of the council meeting and the fabricated story she had given. "I thought it was a good idea—this way, no one questions why Emilia, and I are so close or why I keep visiting you. Plus, everyone was more comfortable when I aligned myself with a clan."

Ms. Moretti nodded, studying Raven closely. A small smile touched her lips. "You've grown into a beautiful young woman. You look like your mother."

Raven gave a sad smile. "Thank you."

A poignant silence filled the room. Then Raven spoke again. "Ms. Moretti."

"Yes, dear?"

"Asha gave me a book with a widow's emblem. She said it holds the key to uncovering the truth and exposing the Crimson Widow Clan. But the book I have is empty. I need to find another one. Do you know where I can find it?"

Ms. Moretti was quiet for a long time, her gaze distant. When she finally exhaled, her expression was grim. "I do know where one is. And part of me wants to tell you to forget about this—it's too dangerous. But I also want them to pay for what they did to her." She ran a hand through her hair, then turned her gaze back to Raven. "Besides, I know you wouldn't listen to me anyway."

Raven tilted her head, watching Ms. Moretti. "I'll always listen to your advice. But I can't let fear dictate my life. One day, I may face death in the Shadow Gauntlet. I have to live my life on my own terms."

Ms. Moretti and Emilia exchanged knowing looks before chuckling, as if Raven had just told a joke.

Raven frowned. "What's so funny?"

"We just know you're not losing the Shadow Gauntlet," Ms. Moretti said, waving her hand dismissively.

Her expression turned serious again. "I'll tell you where the book is, but you have to be careful. There are four of them, and the last one I found had clues about the others. They're hidden in dangerous places. The more you search, the more you risk exposure— revealing who you truly are."

Raven nodded, already aware this wouldn't be easy. "Where is it?" She hesitated. "And please don't tell me it's inside the Crimson

Widow Clan's home."

Ms. Moretti shook her head. "Of course not."

Raven sighed in relief.

"It's beneath it."

Raven groaned and flopped onto the couch, staring at the ceiling. Silence filled the room as she considered her next move. Would she even survive long enough to face the Shadow Gauntlet? Or would she emerge victorious, only to be burdened by another battle?

"Do we have a plan?" she asked finally.

"I have an idea," Emilia spoke up, drawing Raven's attention. "You might not like it."

Raven gestured for her to continue.

"Next week is the memorial. Every year, we honor the fallen from the Shadowfang Clan," Emilia explained. She hesitated, gauging Raven's reaction. Seeing none, she continued. "During that time, all the clans leave their homes. It reminds us of our vulnerability, urging us to keep our guard on every mission."

"To remind ourselves not to trust everyone," Ms. Moretti murmured, her mind seemingly elsewhere.

"Exactly," Emilia agreed. "Since everyone will be away, it's the perfect time for you to sneak into the Crimson Widow hideout and retrieve the book."

Raven hesitated, lowering her gaze. "Would I have to leave immediately?"

She had spent years grieving alone. A part of her longed to be among her people—to hear their stories of her fallen clan, to mourn together.

Emilia nodded sympathetically. "Yes."

Raven clenched her fists. She knew what she had to do. Assassins weren't supposed to let emotions cloud their judgment. Justice for her clan came first.

"Very well," she said, her voice firm.

"I'll get a layout of the Crimson Widow compound," Ms.

Moretti added. "We'll plan every detail. I won't lose you, too."

Raven offered a weary smile. "I'm tired."

"For now, you'll stay in Emilia's room," Ms. Moretti said. "The next time you visit, we'll have your room ready. Emilia, help her settle in."

"Yes, Mother," Emilia said, rising to guide Raven to her room.

Just before leaving, Ms. Moretti called out, "Raven."

She turned to face the woman who had been a constant in her life.

"I'm sorry we weren't there for you."

Raven's heart clenched, but she mustered a small, sad smile. "As am I."

10

Raven's eyes fluttered open, adjusting to the warm glow of sunlight filtering through the trees. The golden hues of twilight suggested she had been in deep slumber, the day slipping away without her notice.

A familiar figure sat in the window seat, bathed in the fading light—Emilia. Lost in contemplation, her gaze remained fixed on the horizon.

Yawning slightly, Raven pushed herself upright. The movement caught Emilia's attention, and she turned, her expression softening.

"You were pretty tired, huh?" Emilia observed.

Raven stretched her arms, exhaling slowly. "Yeah… I didn't mean to sleep so long. Today drained me."

Emilia studied her for a moment before returning her gaze to the sunset.

Raven hesitated, biting her lower lip. "Are you upset with me? About what happened with Onyx?"

Silence stretched between them before Emilia finally spoke.

"Onyx and I broke up." The words were calm, almost detached.

Raven inhaled sharply. "I'm sorry."

Emilia shook her head. "It's not your fault." She paused before adding, "I didn't like how she treated you. It made me angry. And the fight… that was the last straw."

Raven swallowed, guilt settling in her chest.

"I've spent my whole life feeling helpless when it comes to you," Emilia continued, her voice quieter now. "But I'm older now, stronger. I refuse to let anyone hurt you—not even someone I care about."

Raven reached for Emilia's hand, squeezing it gently. Emilia let herself be pulled closer, but Raven didn't say anything. She simply raised a finger, silently asking her to turn around.

Emilia complied, and Raven wrapped her arms around her waist, holding her close. Leaning back, Emilia rested against Raven's chest, her head settling against her shoulder. They sat like that in quiet understanding, watching as the sun dipped below the horizon.

This embrace had always been their safe haven, a place where words weren't needed.

And yet, Raven's mind swirled with unspoken truths. She wanted to tell Emilia about her kiss with Valentina. She told her everything—didn't she? But with Onyx now out of the picture, guilt held her back.

"Let's train," Emilia suddenly said.

Raven blinked. "Now?"

Emilia rested her hands over Raven's. "Yes. I want to see if you've still got it."

Raven bit back a retort. Was beating Onyx half to death not enough proof?

"Fine," she relented, slipping out of Emilia's arms. "But swords. I don't like hand-to-hand."

Emilia frowned, turning to face her. "Since when?"

Raven hesitated. "Since mercy became lost on me," she murmured, almost ashamed.

Emilia studied her, confusion flickering in her eyes. But Raven gave her no chance to ask further. Instead, she grabbed the sword she had left beside the bed and tossed Emilia a grin.

"Come on. I've been dying to test this out."

A slow smirk spread across Emilia's face. "You're going down, Prodigy Raven." She mocked with a bow.

The tension in the room shifted, but the unspoken truths still lingered.

Raven and Emilia clashed, their swords ringing like thunder in the still night. Each strike sent sparks flying, steel grinding against steel in a brutal dance of precision. Moonlight spilled through shattered windows, carving silver lines across the battlefield.

Raven's cloak whipped around her as she parried Emilia's lightning-fast strikes. They moved in perfect counterpoint—attack, evade, counter—like two parts of the same deadly symphony. Silence filled the space between them, broken only by the whisper of fabric and the ragged edge of their breathing.

A smirk ghosted across Raven's lips—an unspoken acknowledgment of the bond they shared. But friendship had no place here.

Emilia struck first, a flurry of relentless blows. Raven matched her, her blade an extension of her will. Sparks flashed in chaotic bursts, illuminating the fortress walls. The stone trembled under the force of their fight, as if bearing witness to something inevitable.

A feint. A shift in shadows. In the blink of an eye, Raven turned the tide. Her sword arched through the air, striking Emilia's weapon from her grasp. The blade clattered to the stone floor, leaving only silence.

Raven didn't lower her guard. She stepped forward, blade poised at Emilia's throat. The moonlight caught on the edge of the steel, a lethal promise. Yet Emilia, though disarmed, held her gaze without fear.

For a moment, they stood frozen, the past and present colliding in the space between them.

Then Raven exhaled, her fingers flexing around the hilt before she finally lowered her sword. The rasp of metal sliding into its sheath cut through the quiet like the final note of a song.

Without a word, she extended a hand. Emilia hesitated, then clasped it. Instead of shaking, she pulled Raven into a sudden, fierce embrace.

Raven stiffened, startled—but then she let out a quiet laugh, wrapping her arms around Emilia in return.

"I've missed you," Emilia murmured against her shoulder.

Raven sighed, pressing her forehead against Emilia's. "I've missed you too. Mother would be so happy I found you again."

A warmth flickered in Emilia's eyes before she smiled and grabbed Raven's hand, pulling her toward the hallway. They walked in silence, the dimly lit corridors winding like a maze. Raven memorized every twist and turn, her mind mapping the path.

At last, they emerged into a spacious kitchen. Ms. Moretti and Viper leaned against the island, laughter cutting through the air. As soon as the girls entered, the conversation stopped, all eyes shifting toward them.

"What have you two been up to?" Ms. Moretti asked, taking a slow sip of her drink.

"Training," Emilia said, grinning as she released Raven's hand and made her way to the fridge for a bottle of water.

Viper smirked. "Then why do you look like you ran through a storm, and Raven looks like she just took a stroll in the garden?"

Emilia groaned, downing half her water in response. The answer was obvious. Raven had simply been better.

"How have you enjoyed the house so far?" Viper asked, turning to Raven.

Raven joined the others, making the small group shift slightly to face her. "It's great—huge. I wasn't expecting this. I also thought there would be more people around."

Viper nodded. "Many are out on missions, or they're still at school, avoiding coming home for the weekend."

Raven reached for Emilia's water bottle, snatching it before the girl could react. She took a sip, her lips quirking into a smirk as Emilia glared at her, though a glint of amusement flickered in her eyes.

"Will my initiation just be the four of us?" Raven asked.

"No," Ms. Moretti chimed in. "A few more will be guarding the house. I'm sorry that more people couldn't be here."

Raven glanced at Emilia, who was staring at her stolen water bottle, before shifting her gaze back to Ms. Moretti. "No, I like a more intimate setting," she said, sliding the bottle back toward Emilia. Her best friend caught it and chugged the rest, grinning.

"What should we do in the meantime?" Emilia asked, walking to the trashcan to toss the empty bottle.

Viper ran her fingers through her red hair, her lips curling into a smile. "How about we make dinner and play a board game?"

The idea hung in the air for a moment. Nethrala was isolated from the world, its location far off the mainland. Strangers who stumbled upon it had only two choices: stay, learn the way of the assassin, and join a clan—or die. The guild couldn't risk outsiders exposing them. Modern technology was scarce, its use restricted for fear of being traced. Life here was simple: training, missions, school, hunting, and the occasional board game.

Ms. Moretti clapped her hands together, her smile warm. "I think that's a wonderful idea, Viper. What do you girls say?" She turned to Emilia and Raven.

Emilia beamed. "Only if we can have arancini, focaccia, and fettuccine alfredo."

Ms. Moretti sighed, shaking her head. "Is that all?"

Emilia just grinned.

Viper chuckled, and Raven found herself staring at the playful exchange between mother and daughter. A familiar ache pressed against her chest. She had missed them—more than she had realized. Watching them now reminded her of the days at the cottage, when Emilia would beg for extra food, and Raven's mother would laugh, giving the girl anything she wanted. Ms. Moretti would shake her head, pretending to disapprove, but Emilia always got her way. Raven would hug her, giggling, and her mother would smile, indulging Emilia like a second daughter.

The memory came suddenly, and with it, a sharp pang of grief.

Raven turned away, blinking rapidly. Her throat tightened. She had been teetering on the edge of her emotions since reuniting with Emilia, and it unsettled her. Emilia always brought out her softer side, pulling her back into a world where emotions mattered. Raven had fought against that for years—had hated the vulnerability it demanded. But she had grown to love Emilia, and she didn't want to shut her out.

Not now.

But with Viper watching, she couldn't let the emotions show.

"I think that sounds good. I'll wait in the main room," she murmured, voice barely above a whisper. Before anyone could respond, she turned on her heel, walking quickly toward the main room. Her boots echoed against the marble floor.

A hand caught her wrist before she made it far. The touch was familiar. She didn't need to turn to know it was Emilia.

"What's wrong, Raven?" Emilia's voice was quiet but firm, her brows furrowed in concern.

Raven forced a small smile. She shook her head, unwilling to speak.

Emilia studied her, then sighed. "I'm going upstairs to shower and change. You should, too. I have clothes you can borrow until we get you your own."

Raven nodded, allowing Emilia to lead her to the room. Inside, Emilia grabbed a large shirt and a sweatshirt, tossing them toward Raven. She caught them without looking, her gaze fixed on the darkened window. The silence of the house, the trees swaying beyond the glass—it all reminded her of home.

Her next words slipped out before she could stop them.

"Valentina and I kissed."

The weight of the confession settled between them. She wasn't sure why she had said it. Maybe it was the raw emotions swirling in her chest. Maybe she missed the girl she used to be before her mother died.

Either way, the words were out now.

And there was no taking them back.

There was no response to her announcement, so she turned around. Emilia stood in the bathroom doorway; her expression unreadable. Raven pursed her lips, unsettled by the silence. She could usually tell what Emilia was thinking, but this time was different.

"Do you like her?" Emilia asked, her gaze locked onto Raven's.

Raven's brow furrowed. *Do I like her? I don't even know her. But she's strong, sweet... beautiful.*

"She's a prodigy," Raven answered simply.

"That's not what I asked," Emilia pressed.

Raven sighed and looked up at the ceiling. Feelings had never been her strong suit. Relationships, even less so. She had always been grateful for Emilia's friendship, though she suspected it was only because the Italian had been too stubborn to let her push her away.

"I don't know," Raven admitted. "I've never really thought about what it means to like someone. She's nice." She glanced at Emilia, hoping for guidance.

Emilia's sharp expression softened at Raven's uncertainty. She stepped forward, draping an arm over her shoulder and pulling her close. "You don't have to figure it out now. Just get to know her. Valentina is a wonderful person. Everyone respects her, and—let's be honest—she's gorgeous. Count yourself lucky. Plenty of people wish they had kissed her instead." She chuckled.

Raven smiled, pressing a quick kiss to Emilia's forehead.

"Thank you."

Emilia grinned, releasing her and disappearing into the bathroom. Raven listened to the sound of the shower running before gathering her own things. Once Emilia was done, Raven took a quick shower and changed into comfortable clothes. Together, they headed downstairs to join Viper and Ms. Moretti.

In the kitchen, Ms. Moretti was finishing up the meal with Viper's help. She glanced at the two girls and instructed them to prepare the living room.

Emilia hurried ahead, and Raven followed. The dim lighting cast a soft glow over the room as Emilia knelt by the fireplace, stacking logs to start a fire. She motioned toward the closet.

"Grab the floor pillows and blankets," she instructed.

Raven nodded, pulling them out and spreading them across the floor. A small smile tugged at her lips. She never thought she could feel this content again. It reminded her of better times. *Mom would be happy to know I found Ms. Moretti. She'd be happy to know her best friend took me in.*

Once everything was set, Ms. Moretti and Viper returned, carrying dishes of steaming food. They placed the trays in the center of the makeshift seating area.

"I hope you enjoy the meal, Raven. I'm not much of a cook," Ms. Moretti said, amusement glinting in her eyes.

Raven gave her a knowing look. "I doubt that." Every time she and Emilia had come to the cottage, she ended up cooking for the entire trip. Raven shook her head fondly. Ms. Moretti always said she just wanted to take care of them.

Ms. Moretti chuckled but said nothing as they settled in to eat. The first few minutes passed in comfortable silence, everyone focused on their food. Raven had slept through lunch, and hunger gnawed at her stomach. She was grateful Emilia had made sure her favorite dishes were on the table.

Midway through the meal, Ms. Moretti suddenly set her plate down, her eyes widening. Without a word, she hurried out of the room.

Raven, Emilia, and Viper exchanged puzzled glances.

"Mom?" Emilia called between bites. "Are you okay?"

A moment later, Ms. Moretti returned, carrying a tray of hot tea. She placed it in the center and gave Emilia a pointed look. "Please, don't talk with your mouth full."

Emilia shrugged, reaching for a cup. The others followed suit, finishing their meal while sipping the steaming tea. Raven exhaled slowly, warmth settling in her chest. For the first time in a long while, she felt happy.

11

Viper, Emilia, and Raven walked back to school in their uniforms, Raven now bearing the Silent Clan's sigil on the back of her jacket. Her initiation had been brief and unnerving.

At the clan mansion, members had gathered in the backyard, standing before her and Ms. Moretti. The clan leader introduced Raven, revealing that she was the daughter of a former member who had deserted in an attempt to start a new life and keep her child safe. But, as was the fate of all who abandoned the clan, she had perished.

No one looked surprised. No one questioned it.

Ms. Moretti proceeded with the initiation. Raven swore loyalty and allegiance to the Silent Clan, sealing her vow in the same way all members did—by licking the blood of Ms. Moretti, Emilia, and Viper from a knife they each used to slice their palms. The metallic tang had lingered on her tongue, and though she despised every second of it, she hadn't hesitated.

The clan members clapped, welcoming her as one of their own. And just like that, it was done.

Now, as they arrived at the academy gates, Viper turned to Raven and extended a hand. "I must go," she announced. "It was nice spending time with you."

Raven shook her hand firmly. "It was nice getting to know you. You're a very skilled game player."

Viper grinned and took a step back. "Can't have you beating me in everything now, can I?"

Raven and Emilia chuckled as Viper disappeared down the corridor.

"I, too, must go," Emilia said, giving Raven a quick hug before leaving just as abruptly, offering no explanation.

Raven watched her disappear before turning toward the library. Her love for reading drew her back—especially now, when she still hadn't explored the full range of books housed in an assassin school.

Stepping inside, she inhaled the familiar scent of parchment and ink. The quiet atmosphere mirrored her first visit, though she had yet to figure out how other students spent their free time or what additional amenities the academy offered. The sparse crowd suited her just fine.

She wandered through the aisles, fingers trailing along the spines of untouched books. The fiction section brought a rare smile to her face. Just as she reached for a title, someone cleared their throat.

She turned.

Valentina stood at the end of the aisle, a subtle smile playing on her lips.

Raven lowered her hand from the shelf. "Hello."

"I have news for you," Valentina said, approaching with the same effortless grace she always carried.

Suppressing a sigh, Raven returned her smile but couldn't help teasing, "Every time I see you, it's either because you have news or because you're escorting me somewhere."

Valentina pursed her lips, feigning contemplation. Then, her smile returned. "Maybe I just like being the one to tell you things. Maybe I just like being around you."

Raven huffed a quiet chuckle. "Alright, what's the news?"

The warmth in Valentina's expression faded. "We leave for a mission tonight."

Raven tilted her head. "A mission?"

Valentina gave a single nod.

Raven frowned. "And what if I hadn't returned by tonight?"

Valentina shrugged, the gesture deliberate and unbothered. "You would have."

Raven studied her, unsettled by the cryptic response. Valentina's gaze never wavered.

"You're an enigma," Raven said bluntly.

Valentina's smile returned gracefully, acknowledging the observation. "How so?"

Raven shrugged, her gaze sharp. "You're so cryptic."

"You're one to talk," Valentina snorted, her smile unfaltering.

Raven narrowed her eyes, studying Valentina's face. "You never ask me questions and seem content with how little you know about me. But when I think about it, it feels like you act that way because you already know more than you let on."

Valentina bit her lower lip, her expressive eyes flickering with thought. "I trust you'll tell me what you wish to share when you feel comfortable, so there's no need to pry," she said evenly.

Raven wondered if Valentina harbored unspoken questions— if she ever felt the urge to unravel more about her. *Why do I care?*

As Raven watched, Valentina turned her attention to the bookshelf, running her fingers along the spines before pulling one free. Raven found herself studying the contours of her jawline, the delicate slope of her nose, and the fullness of her lips. The sunlight caught Valentina's green eyes, transforming them into shimmering emeralds. Her dark hair, tied back in a sleek ponytail, framed her face. Raven's heart fluttered, and she scowled.

"You're staring," Valentina teased, her voice light as she flipped open the book.

Raven's face heated. She tore her gaze away and focused on the books before her, feigning interest. They fell into silence, each pretending to browse but finding themselves more preoccupied with the other's presence than the words on the pages.

Later, Raven and Valentina sat atop the hill, their food laid out before them as they waited for the sun to set. Raven had invited her after leaving the library, and Valentina had readily agreed. They had parted briefly to return to their rooms—Raven had taken the opportunity to change out of her school uniform and into her mission attire.

The uniform mirrored the academy's standard design, but it was all black, accented with additional accessories. Without clan sigils, it ensured anonymity, preventing targets from identifying which factions were involved. The League thrived on secrecy, and these precautions safeguarded its operatives.

Now, seated beside Valentina, Raven struggled for words. The invitation had been impulsive, yet it felt oddly significant. She had always reserved sunsets for herself and her mother—sharing this moment with someone else unsettled her.

She attempted to distract herself by reading, but her mind refused to cooperate. Images of Valentina intruded persistently. It frustrated her. Even now, sitting in comfortable silence, she felt that peculiar sensation in her stomach—the same one she had tried so hard to ignore.

She finished the last bite of her meal and set the container aside, resisting the urge to steal another glance at Valentina. But the girl had an uncanny ability to sense her gaze, making Raven feel exposed in a way she wasn't used to. Instead, she removed her sword and rested it beside her before reclining on the grass, eyes fixed on the darkening sky as the sun dipped below the horizon.

Valentina set her food down on the opposite side, glancing over her shoulder at Raven. "I kissed you," she said, her voice low.

Raven met Valentina's gaze, unbothered. "I know. I was there."

Valentina rolled her eyes, turning her attention back to the sky. "I was going to tell you I think I like you, but never mind."

Raven heard the smile in Valentina's voice, prompting a response that teetered between jest and sincerity. "Well, if you didn't like me, that would make your actions kind of creepy."

Valentina turned back to her mockingly, feigning hurt. Raven's lips twitched into a soft smile. In Valentina's presence, the burden of her mission at the academy momentarily eased—the weight of uncovering the secrets of another clan and bringing justice to her mother's people felt lighter, more distant.

Raven reached upward, meaning to brush her fingers against Valentina's cheek, but the distance between them made it awkward. Before she could lower her hand, Valentina met it halfway, closing her eyes as she leaned into the touch. Raven gently rubbed her thumb along Valentina's cheek before pulling her closer.

Valentina's eyes remained closed as their lips met—soft, searching, hesitant. A heartbeat skipped in Raven's chest as their lips parted, their foreheads pressing together. For a moment, their eyes locked, neither daring to move.

"That was nice," Valentina murmured.

Raven hummed in agreement. "Lay with me," she whispered.

Valentina shifted, resting her head against Raven's chest, their legs tangling naturally. Raven wrapped an arm around Valentina's waist, pulling her close. The world around them faded into the enchanting hues of the sunset, the cool breeze lulling them into a quiet serenity.

The reality of their impending departure loomed, a quiet dread neither of them spoke aloud.

Valentina traced slow, absentminded circles along the fabric of Raven's shirt. The intimate gesture sent warmth through Raven's chest, her eyes fluttering shut. She knew the truth—she liked Valentina. But the fear of losing another connection held her back. Emilia, Asha, Ms. Moretti—she had lost before, and she wasn't sure she could endure it again.

As darkness enshrouded them, Valentina reluctantly pulled away. She gathered her discarded trash and rose from her seat, her movements slower than before. Raven followed suit, securing her sword and belongings.

The return walk was quiet, but not in an uncomfortable way. The occasional brush of Valentina's fingers against Raven's sent warmth through her, and before she could overthink it, she nudged the green-eyed assassin in return.

At the school entrance, they discarded their trash. Raven trailed Valentina toward their designated meeting point for the mission debrief. The brisk pace kept them from lingering, but just before they entered, Valentina suddenly reached for Raven's hand, stopping her in her tracks.

Raven arched a brow.

Without a word, Valentina tugged her closer and pressed a swift, unexpected kiss to her lips.

A surprised laugh escaped Raven as warmth rushed to her cheeks. Valentina's face mirrored the reaction, a faint blush coloring her skin.

"I'm sorry, I had to," Valentina confessed.

"You never have to apologize," Raven murmured.

Their fingers remained lightly entwined for a fleeting moment before Valentina pulled away, leading them inside.

12

Raven, Frost, and Whisper crouched low in the shadows, their bodies blending seamlessly with the inky darkness of the underbrush. A handful of guards patrolled the warehouse perimeter, their sharp eyes scanning for any sign of movement. The mission was clear yet fraught with peril—eliminate the intruders who had breached Nethrala and rescue their fellow assassin before they could resort to self-termination, the last resort to protect the guild's secrets.

From their concealed vantage point, Raven tracked the movements of Team Two—Viper, Seraph, Nikolai, and Phantom—as they darted across the open field toward the warehouse. The structure, draped in vines and moss, pulsed with a dim glow from its high-set windows, an ominous sign of their captured ally within. Silent and efficient, Team Two eliminated the guards on their side of the wall before vanishing back into the shadows.

On the opposite side, Team Three—Valentina, Onyx, Kenji, and Tariq—moved in unison, their approach just as swift. Raven watched as Valentina dispatched a guard with one clean strike, wiping her blade before sheathing it in a single fluid motion.

With both teams in position at the warehouse doors, Raven signaled to Frost and Whisper. Without hesitation, they sprinted across the field, making for the rear of the structure. Raven leapt first, grasping the window ledge and pulling herself up with practiced ease. The windows were opaque, revealing only shifting shadows within, but she didn't slow. Silently, she scaled the roof, her movements precise, her footsteps barely a whisper against the metal surface.

A muffled grunt made her glance back. Frost winced, rubbing her shin where she had misjudged a step. Beside her, Whisper crouched in silent amusement. Raven narrowed her eyes but said nothing.

They crept toward the skylight, peering into the dimly lit warehouse below. Stacks of crates and supply boxes provided ample cover, but the real challenge lay in making their descent unnoticed. Raven signaled to the others that she would go first. With a final check of her weapons—a dagger strapped to her left leg, a sword secured to her back—she drew up her mask and adjusted her hood, ensuring only the stark black of her uniform was visible. Then, she leapt.

Her landing was soundless. She barely had time to assess her surroundings before she caught movement to her right. A guard stood just feet away, his back to her as he scanned the shadows. His hand rested on a firearm, his head swiveling from side to side in routine vigilance.

He began to turn.

Raven struck before he could react, unsheathing her dagger in one fluid motion and slicing a clean line across his throat. He gasped, eyes wide with shock, as she eased his body down without a sound. Quick and efficient, she stripped him of his weapon, unloaded it, and stashed the magazine among the empty crates. One less threat.

Scanning the room, she saw no immediate danger. With a sharp flick of her fingers, she signaled to Frost and Whisper. They descended just as smoothly, their landings barely stirring the dust.

Now, the true mission began. As the designated distraction, Raven would draw attention while the others secured their comrade and eliminated any opposition.

Failure was not an option.

After wiping her dagger clean on the fallen adversary's shirt, Raven sheathed it and moved swiftly through the labyrinth of crates, her steps soundless against the cold floor. Frost and Whisper flanked her from the shadows, each a ghost among the shifting darkness that betrayed the presence of their enemies.

Their target loomed ahead. Without hesitation, Raven stepped into the open while her companions remained concealed.

"Hello," she announced, her voice carrying through the tense silence.

Every guard in the room froze, weapons snapping into position, all trained on her chest. Unfazed, Raven smiled.

The man at the center of the chaos exuded authority. His suit was immaculate, not a wrinkle in sight, a stark contrast to the bloodied handkerchief he toyed with between bruised knuckles. Seated before him was a prisoner—bound, beaten, and eerily silent. Whether the captive was too weak to fight or simply too terrified remained unclear.

The leader's gaze sharpened. "And you are?"

Raven caught the flicker of curiosity behind his guarded expression. She tilted her head slightly, her face still hidden behind her veil.

"Just a little bird."

A flicker of amusement ghosted across the man's face, but his hand twitched—a subtle motion, a precursor to an order. Before he could speak, a small metal canister rolled between them.

Both locked eyes for a fraction of a second before the canister hissed, spewing thick clouds of smoke into the air.
Raven vanished into the swirling fog.

"Find her!" The leader's voice rose in fury. "And whoever is helping her!"

Doors slammed open. The sharp staccato of gunfire erupted, followed by shouts and the unmistakable thuds of bodies hitting the ground. Navigating the disorienting haze, Raven crouched low, one hand slicing through the smoke to clear her vision. Her fingers brushed against something—someone.

She looked up into a bruised face, one eye swollen, blood streaking down from a busted nose.

A prisoner. The prisoner.

Without hesitation, Raven's dagger made quick work of the restraints.

"Thank you," the woman rasped, her voice raw.

"Name?" Raven asked.

"Ella."

Raven nodded. The smoke had begun to thin. Open doors signaled approaching reinforcements, and she had no intention of being there when they arrived.

She pulled down her mask just enough for Ella to see the firm set of her jaw.

"Follow me. Stay close. No questions."

Ella didn't hesitate.

Through the lingering haze, Raven led her toward an exit—a narrow doorway spilling into the open night. Shadows swallowed them as they ran, their breath measured, their footfalls calculated.

The moment they reached the tree line, familiar figures emerged from the undergrowth—some bloodied, others breathless, but all accounted for.

Phantom stepped forward, scanning Ella with a keen eye before speaking. "Are you okay?"

Ella nodded, pressing a reassuring hand to his shoulder.

Phantom exhaled sharply. "We need to go."

No one argued.

Then, the darkness shifted.

A dozen lights snapped on, six ahead, six behind.

No words were needed. Every prodigy understood—this mission wasn't over.

Raven pulled up her mask, her expression hardening with determination. "Protect the egg." The command sliced through the tension as she unsheathed her sword.

Viper lowered her mask, concerned flickering in her eyes. "You're planning to face them alone?"

Raven shrugged, the motion almost lazy. "Could use a challenge. You lot are getting dull."

Viper rolled her eyes, though a smirk tugged at the corner of her lips as she secured her mask again.

"Rendezvous at the checkpoint," Valentina instructed, her tone leaving no room for argument. "We stick to the plan. Protect the egg. Viper and Frost take point. Onyx and Nikolai, you're on my right. Kenji and Whisper, left flank. Tariq and Seraph, hold the rear. Phantom and I will stay with Ella in the middle. Everyone clear?"

Silent nods spread through the group as they moved with well-practiced precision. Valentina's command was unquestioned, her presence a steadying force.

Raven and Valentina exchanged a final glance. A subtle wink from Raven—a shared understanding, unspoken but acknowledged. Then, without hesitation, she turned and strode toward the approaching lights, pulse thrumming in anticipation.

The oncoming figures moved with practiced efficiency. Armed, trained, and heading straight for them. Raven veered away from the direct path, melting into the shadows, letting the night swallow her. Combat was inevitable, but brute force wasn't the answer. Disarming or isolating—those were the smarter choices.

A sharp whistle cut through the air. Her muscles tensed. The lights shifted, searching, closing in. Instead of engaging, she pivoted, slipping through the warehouse's open door. Inside, the air was thick with dust, the scent of oil and metal lingering. Crates stacked high formed a labyrinth of cover, but also a dead end if she wasn't careful.

She stilled, listening. Footsteps. Close. Too close. They were splitting up—a smart move. But they were in her territory now. And if they truly understood who they were up against, they would have turned back the moment they set foot inside.

A grin ghosted across her lips as she pressed herself into the shadows, watching, waiting.

Ducking unnecessarily but with purpose, she aimed to minimize her presence. The dim lights flickered, casting shifting shadows from crates and moving figures. Every breath was measured, every movement calculated.

A lone guard turned into a dead end. Raven struck the moment his back was to her. With a fluid arc, her sword sliced through his wrist before sweeping upward in a clean motion to open his throat. His body went slack, and she lunged forward, catching his head before he collapsed.

No time to hesitate.

Raven slipped through a narrow opening, navigating unseen to the other side. A sharp turn brought her face-to-face with two adversaries. They barely had time to react. Her blade drove into the first man's firing arm before she tackled the second, sending them both crashing to the ground. The impact jolted the sword from her grasp—too cumbersome for close quarters.

The man kicked Raven off, and she rolled to her feet, yanking the dagger from her thigh holster. The first man reached for his gun, but Raven hurled the blade straight into his eye. He let out a strangled curse, hands clawing at the embedded weapon.

The second adversary, his dominant arm disabled, struggled to switch his gun. Not fast enough. Raven surged forward, her knee slamming into his chest. He stumbled back, gasping for breath. Without hesitation, Raven wrenched the dagger from the first man's skull and buried it deep in the second mans heart. His body convulsed before falling still.

Shouts echoed—reinforcements.

Raven snatched the fallen gun, turned, and fired a single

shot. The bullet struck clean between her enemy's eyes. His head snapped back before his body crumpled.

Silence stretched for a breath.

Then, the sound of cocked weapons.

Raven grabbed her sword and pivoted—too late. Three figures had her surrounded. Two in front, one behind.

"Drop the sword," the woman ordered.

Raven met her gaze, then let her blade fall. It hit the ground with a dull clink.

"On your knees."

Raven obeyed, lowering myself slowly, never breaking eye contact. The woman shifted slightly, gun raised.

"Grab h—"

Her words cut off in a gurgle. Blood bubbled from her lips before she collapsed forward. A knife protruded from the back of her neck.

The others barely had time to register what happened before Valentina dropped from above, her movements a blur. Another fell to her strike.

Raven twisted on her knees, yanking her dagger free and ramming it into the thigh of the man behind her. He howled in pain, swinging the buttstock of his rifle toward her head.

Raven flipped, hooking her legs around his neck and using his momentum against him. He hit the ground, stunned. Her blade followed—slicing deep into his throat. A strangled gurgle, a final twitch, then nothing.

Raven gracefully disentangled her legs from his neck, rising to her feet. She met Valentina's gaze, their silent exchange thick with unspoken understanding.

"What are you doing here?" Raven lowered her mask, her voice steady but edged with surprise.

Valentina stepped closer, mirroring her gesture by revealing her own face. She pulled Raven into a firm embrace, exhaling a quiet sigh. "I was worried. I'm sorry."

A chuckle escaped Raven's lips as she returned the embrace, her grip tightening briefly before releasing. "I had a plan."

Valentina's forehead brushed against hers, a smile playing on her lips. "I'm sure you did, but that was too close for my liking. I'd be very upset if someone took you from this world before I could get to know you better."

Raven's heart gave a traitorous flutter. "Like a date?"

"Yes, like a date." Valentina's gaze held hers, unwavering. "But more than that. From now on, we're a team."

Raven hesitated, the weight of the words settling over her. She retrieved her sword, cleaning it on the fallen adversaries with practiced efficiency. As she gathered her dagger, she mulled over Valentina's request.

Finally, she turned to Valentina, expression unreadable. "A team."

Their masks came back up in silent agreement. Moving in sync, they slipped from the warehouse, their bodies low as they scanned the terrain. The open field was eerily quiet. Satisfied, they sprinted across it, slipping into the cover of the trees. Only when the distant checkpoint loomed ahead did they slow.

Stepping out of the woods, they took in the scene before them. Bodies littered the ground—evidence of the prodigies' efficiency. But one figure remained. A bound and battered man.

As Raven and Valentina approached, the prodigies shifted into defensive positions.

Raven's hand instinctively went to her sword, but Valentina smacked her arm lightly.

"I'm only teasing," Raven grinned, sliding the weapon back into its sheath.

The prodigies exchanged amused glances but stood firm. As they parted, they revealed their captive—his face swollen with bruises, his eyes burning with defiance.

Raven knelt before him, resting her hands on her knees. Their gazes locked. Slowly, she reached forward and removed the gag.

A subtle movement from Frost caught her attention. He had shifted, tense, ready to intervene. Before he could, Valentina placed a firm hand on his forearm, stilling him.

Raven refocused on the man. "Your men told me you came here to uncover the guild's secrets," she began, her voice smooth, deliberate. "To find our weaknesses. To turn some of us to your cause. Then you'd report back to your government so they could eliminate us."

It was a lie. But the man didn't know that.

His jaw clenched. "My men would never betray our mission. And neither will I."

Raven watched him closely. A twitch at the corner of his lip. The way his jaw worked. A bead of sweat formed on his brow.

She hummed, tilting her head. "You already have."

A flick of her wrist, and her sword was at his throat.

"Thank you for your cooperation."

Panic flashed across his face. "Wait!"

Raven said nothing, only angling her blade ever so slightly. The man swallowed hard. "Alright! Yes, we were sent to infiltrate, gather intelligence, and attempt recruitment. I don't know what happens after that, but we thought—we believed—we were doing the right thing."

Raven exhaled a slow, humorless laugh. Her grip tightened on the hilt.

"A noble cause," she echoed, her voice dripping with disdain. Then, in one fluid motion, she drove her sword into his leg.

His scream split the air.

She leaned in, her lips close to his ear as his body trembled in agony. "Governments that seek us out never have a good cause," she whispered. "They'll erase you. Pretend you never existed."

She pulled the blade free with a sickening slide, stepping back as he sobbed into the dirt. Wiping her sword on her pants, she sheathed it with a sharp click.

"Though," she mused, "maybe they're nicer than I am."

She stuffed the gag back into his mouth and looked to the prodigies. Their nods of approval met her, though unease lingered in their eyes. A reminder. No matter how skilled they were, no matter the alliances forged—one day, they would be forced to turn against her.

One day, they would have to try to kill her.

Raven searched Valentina's face for judgment. For hesitation. But all she found was warmth. And something else—something she couldn't name.

Valentina looked away first, turning to Ella.

"How are you?"

Ella inclined her head, her voice steady despite the wear of battle. "I am better. Thank you all for saving me. My clan will always be open to you."

"We are honored," Valentina said, bowing with respect.

The others followed suit, even Raven—though something inside her twisted at the realization.

Crimson Widow Clan.

I should've let her die.

13

The prodigies, accompanied by their captive and the head of the Crimson Widow Clan, returned to the school grounds, where the Crown and the elders awaited them. King Pierre stood at the center, a few feet ahead of the elders, his hands clasped behind his back. A smile played on his lips, but it never quite reached his eyes.

The prodigies bowed in unison before Phantom unceremoniously tossed the captive at the king's feet. The man grunted as he hit the ground but quickly shifted to sit without aggravating his injured leg. His hands were bound, and a gag silenced him, leaving him with no choice but to await his fate.

King Pierre's gaze flickered from the captive to the prodigies. "Well done," he said, his voice calm yet authoritative. Then, his attention shifted. "Ella." He extended his hands toward her.

Ella stepped forward, her battered face lighting up with a grateful smile as she took his hands. "Thank you for sending them," she said, her voice hoarse.

Pierre's fingers tightened slightly over hers. "I was worried about you, my dear friend. I am glad you are safe."

Ella nodded, then turned to the captive, her expression darkening. "Their attack was too well-planned. It's almost as if they knew the layout of our land."

A flicker of concern crossed the king's features. "A traitor?"

She exhaled sharply. "That's what I'm thinking. And who's to say we got them all? Someone could have been waiting in the shadows and slipped away."

Pierre released her hands and approached the captive, studying him with cold scrutiny. "We'll get answers." He flicked his wrist, a silent command.

Two elders stepped forward, their robes shifting like liquid shadows as they seized the captive. Without a word, they vanished into the night.

The king turned back to the prodigies. "You are dismissed."

He paused. "Valentina."

Valentina met his gaze.

"I want a full debrief in the morning."

She bowed. "Of course, my king."

Satisfied, Pierre turned to Ella. "Come with me."

As they walked away, the prodigies lingered, an unspoken weight settling over them. Their mission had been a success—but at what cost?

Slowly, they dispersed. Raven remained behind, watching as the king and the leader of the Crimson Widow Clan disappeared down the dimly lit pathway, their conversation low but intent.

Valentina stepped up beside her. "Why are you watching them?"

Raven shrugged, feigning indifference. "I didn't know they were such close friends. They're from different clans."

Valentina nodded knowingly. "They have been for years. The king tries to maintain ties with all the clan heads, but it's clear those two share something deeper."

Raven hummed in thought. There was something about the king she wanted to understand—but prying too much could be dangerous.

Lowering her mask and hood, she turned to Valentina. "I'm going to shower and change. Want to hang out after?"

Valentina hesitated. "It's pretty late."

Suppressing her disappointment, Raven forced a small nod. "Yeah, I guess you're right. We do have class in a few hours."

Valentina studied her for a long moment before finally removing her mask and hood as well. "Actually, we have today off since we were on a mission. They give us time to recover and clear our heads."

"Oh." Raven kept her expression neutral, though a nagging thought crept in. *So she doesn't want to hang out with me.*

A small smile tugged at Valentina's lips, breaking the tension. "I'll meet you at your room in a bit. We can go to the movie room."

Raven's face lit up, the uncertainty vanishing. "Sounds good."

Before she could react, Valentina leaned in, pressed a quick kiss to her lips, and darted off.

As Raven watched her disappear down the hall, her gaze flickered back to where the Crown had vanished. Her curiosity burned stronger than ever. I need to know more. But she forced the thought away. Tonight wasn't the time.

Valentina kept her promise, arriving outside Raven's door at the agreed time. They walked side by side through the academy's dimly lit halls, the silence between them comfortable.

Then Valentina stopped in front of a set of double doors.

"Here?" Raven glanced between the doors and Valentina.

Valentina nodded, pushing one open. "After you, oh stoic one."

Raven chuckled, recalling the nickname from their first encounter, and stepped inside.

The movie room was more impressive than she'd imagined. The walls were lined with built-in shelves stocked with snacks—candies, chips, popcorn, and a variety of drinks. Plush reclining seats, large enough to fit two, were draped with folded blankets and pillows. A massive projector screen dominated the front wall, while the projector itself hung from the ceiling at the back. The space had a sleek color scheme of black, gray, and white, and the dimmed lights gave the room a relaxed ambiance.

But one detail was off. Someone was already there.

Valentina frowned. "I'm sorry. I thought it would be empty. Most people are asleep by now because of school."

As they hesitated in the doorway, the person in front turned around.

Raven's face broke into a smile, immediately recognizing Emilia.

Emilia's eyes widened, and she jumped from her seat, rushing toward Raven before pulling her into a tight hug.

"Oh my gosh," Emilia breathed, pulling back just enough to scan Raven's face. "They told me the prodigies were sent on a mission, and I was so worried. I couldn't sleep. I've been here for hours. Do you know how tired I am?"

Raven laughed. "I'm guessing very."

Emilia threw her hands up dramatically. "Super." Then, without hesitation, she hugged Raven again. "I'm just glad you made it back in one piece."

Raven smirked. "Your lack of faith in me wounds me."

Emilia scoffed, pulling back just enough to smack Raven's arm. "You know I believe in you. But missions can take a turn for the worse."

Raven's expression sobered. She knew that all too well—especially when a Crimson Widow was involved.

Then Emilia turned toward Valentina and gave her a respectful bow. "Prodigy Valentina."

"Emilia," Valentina replied coolly, her expression unreadable.

Emilia's gaze flickered between Raven and Valentina, realization dawning in her eyes. Stretching with a feigned yawn, she smirked. "You know, I'm truly exhausted. You two enjoy your night. I'm heading to bed." Leaning over, she pressed a habitual peck on Raven's cheek and murmured, "Ciao, il mia uccellino." With a casual wave to Valentina, she gracefully exited the room.

Valentina watched her leave, her expression hard to decipher. Then, turning to Raven, she said, "I'm going to pick a movie. Feel free to get snacks."

As Valentina moved to choose a spot, Raven approached the snack table. The assortment of treats should have been an easy choice, but hesitation gripped her. Her mother had always forbidden sweets, fearing they would interfere with her training. Now, for the first time, she stood before an array of choices—each one a silent rebellion.

You deserve this, she told herself. *And if not for you, then at least for Valentina.*

Biting her lip, she finally sighed and grabbed some chocolate, fruit-flavored candy, popcorn, and juice.

She approached Valentina, clearing her throat. Valentina glanced away from the screen, her eyes widening slightly in surprise. Without hesitation, she rose and helped Raven balance the assortment, arranging them neatly between them.

Raven let out a breath of relief, grateful nothing had slipped from her grasp. She settled beside Valentina, pulling the blanket over both of them. A small, fleeting smile crossed Valentina's lips before she pressed play.

As the lights dimmed, a cozy ambiance settled around them. They reclined, their attention fixed on the screen as action, emotion, and humor wove seamlessly together. Laughter and occasional startled reactions broke the silence. The night stretched on, each passing moment easing the tension between them.

Midway through the film, Raven broke the silence.

"I didn't know there were TVs on the island."

Valentina nodded, her gaze still on the screen. "Every clan house has one for surveillance, and the school has two—one for security and one for movies. The system is monitored to ensure no one tries to locate us or send messages outside. The IP address is encrypted. If anyone attempts to hack in, they won't get far."

Raven absorbed the information, nodding slowly, her attention returning to the screen. However, a shift in the air made her glance sideways. Valentina was watching her.

"Yes?" Raven asked, tossing a handful of popcorn into her mouth.

Valentina hesitated. "Can I ask you something?"

Raven turned to her fully, waiting.

"You and Emilia," Valentina began carefully.

Raven chewed her popcorn, keeping her expression neutral. "Is there a question somewhere in there?"

Valentina faltered. "Do you like her? Does she like you?" She exhaled sharply, her words tumbling out in a rush. "She broke up with Onyx, then you two spent the weekend together. And clearly, she feels comfortable enough to be affectionate with you—"

Raven reached for Valentina's hand, stilling her nervous rambling. "There's nothing going on with Emilia and me," she said gently. "We just—"

She hesitated. The truth knotted inside her, tangled with uncertainties. She knew she liked Valentina—but how much did she really know about her? How deeply could she trust her? And with Valentina's proximity to the crown, that trust became even more complicated.

The realization hit hard: if the crown had played a role in her clan's destruction, then at some point, she might have to face it—face him—too.

A storm of emotions swirled in Raven's chest. She let go of Valentina's hand, blinking back the sting of tears. "I want to trust you," she admitted. "I want this relationship to be built on honesty. But I don't know if I can." Her voice wavered. "There aren't many people I can rely on in this world, and I don't want you to be just another one of them. But I don't know enough about you. How can I be sure you won't betray me?"

Valentina said nothing for a long moment, her gaze lingering on Raven's face.

Raven had spent her life navigating solitude, and it showed. It was etched in the way she carried herself, the way she spoke, the way she hesitated to let anyone in.

And Valentina, perhaps for the first time, truly saw it.

Raven had endured an entire year in solitude. The prevailing belief was that her mother had forsaken their clan, an act that condemned Raven to an existence on the fringes—an outcast in a world that had abandoned her.

She forcefully wiped away her tears, a rare display of vulnerability. Only Asha, Emilia, and Ms. Moretti had ever witnessed such moments. Disgusted with herself for showing weakness, she gritted her teeth, silently commanding herself to regain composure.

"Did you say relationship?" Valentina's voice cut through the tension.

Raven blinked at her through tear-blurred eyes, a disbelieving chuckle escaping her lips. "I guess I did."

Valentina smiled, warm yet enigmatic. "If you agree to be my girlfriend, I'll tell you everything about myself tonight."

Raven frowned, wiping away the last traces of moisture from her face. "Isn't that a form of blackmail?"

Valentina shrugged. "We're assassins. Seems like a fitting way to start a relationship." She grinned, her teeth gleaming under the dim light.

Despite herself, Raven shook her head, a reluctant smile playing on her lips. "You want to be my girlfriend after four days?"

Valentina's smile widened, and she gave a confident nod.

"Would I have to spill my entire life story tonight too?"

Valentina shook her head. "You'll tell me when you're ready. I trust you. I have no problem earning your trust. I can only imagine what you've been through."

Raven exhaled, nodding. A flicker of gratitude passed through her. "Okay. Let's hear it."

Valentina shifted, turning her full attention toward Raven, momentarily forgetting the movie playing on the screen. With a casual brush of her hands against her shirt, she sat up straight, preparing to unravel the chapters of her past.

"When I was younger, they told me I was a prodigy. I didn't understand what it meant at the time."

She lifted her left arm, revealing the dark, coiling serpent birthmark wrapping around her forearm. Her expression flickered between vulnerability and disdain.

"Because of this stupid birthmark, I was fated to die young. Never to grow old, never to fall in love, never to have a real life." She scoffed, yanking her sleeve down as if the very sight of it disgusted her. "My whole life has been about training to kill and then dying in the end. But they tell you it's an honor. That you're one of the chosen ones."

Her voice hardened. "I say we're cursed."

She locked eyes with Raven. "You, me, Whisper, Viper, and Seraph—we're semi-lucky. Since we were firstborns, the Shadow Gauntlet doesn't start for us until we turn eighteen. Onyx, Phantom, and Frost will be seventeen when it begins. Kenji and Tariq, sixteen. Nikolai will still be thirteen. We have years on them."

Raven bit her lower lip. The rules dictated that the Shadow Gauntlet had to commence once the first group of prodigies reached eighteen, but she had never considered the age gaps between them. She had assumed they were all close in age. But they weren't.

And for some of them, that difference could mean life or death.

"They should've held the Shadow Gauntlet when the last prodigies turned eighteen," Raven said.

Valentina nodded, running a hand through her hair. "It's just not fair. But we can't say that out loud. Every prodigy is expected to be grateful, to act like a leader, just in case they win the Gauntlet and end up ruling the clans. They have to trust you, or at least believe they can. Not that it really matters—the king has the final say. If he decides you're unfit, he can challenge you to a fight to the death."

Raven blinked. "Repeat that."

Valentina pursed her lips. "I forgot you're still catching up. If you win the Shadow Gauntlet, great. But if the king or queen doesn't think you're fit to rule—or just doesn't want to step down—they can challenge you. If they win, the clans wait for the next batch of prodigies."

"When was the last time that happened?"

Valentina shrugged. "Never."

Raven nodded, but unease settled in her gut. If the king was a traitor and found out who she really was, even winning the Gauntlet wouldn't protect her. He could challenge her himself—to silence her before she exposed him. If he was a traitor, he had to die. The only question was when.

She forced herself to push the thought aside. "Tell me more about yourself."

Valentina chewed her lower lip. "I like the color blue. I hate olives. My mother is my best friend. My dad died when I was young."

Raven's expression darkened. "I'm sorry."

Valentina gave a hollow smile. "It's okay. He was sent on a mission with the Shadowfangs—our eleventh clan. Like them, he never came back."

"The Shadowfangs?" Raven asked, feigning confusion.

Valentina's gaze flickered to the movie screen. "Yeah. We used to have eleven clans, not ten. But they were wiped out on a mission that went wrong. We're holding a memorial in a few days." She hesitated, then lowered her voice. "I don't know. Something about it never sat right with me. My mother told me not to ask questions, but… it just feels wrong. We didn't even get to give them an assassin's burial."

Raven stayed silent.

"Anyway," Valentina sighed. "Please don't repeat any of this. I'd be in trouble for even saying it. It's exhausting, you know? Pretending to be okay. Pretending I want this. I don't. I don't want to rule the clans. I don't even trust half our people. But I have to smile and act like I do. For my own survival."

Raven nodded. She understood Valentina more than she wanted to admit. The weight of expectations. The suffocating confinement of destiny. The knowledge that her future was dictated by something as arbitrary as a birthmark.

"I understand you," she murmured. And in the dim glow of the screen, for the first time, she knew Valentina understood her too.

14

aven had her feet propped up on the arm of the couch she lay on, her head cradled in Emilia's lap. In quiet anticipation of Asha's arrival, they hoped Ms. Moretti had given her the information Raven needed to enter the Crimson Widow territory and find the book. Ella's open invitation was an option, yet the risk of becoming the prime suspect if the book disappeared made Raven hesitate.

Emilia sighed. "Lei dov'è?" *Where is she?*

Raven playfully wiggled her feet. "Considering we broke into her office and she's not expecting us, I don't think she's in a rush to get here."

Emilia rolled her eyes but said nothing. Raven smirked. Some things never changed. Emilia had been impatient since childhood, while Raven had always met it with quiet endurance. Their friendship had weathered every test, and even now, Emilia's exasperation brought a comforting sense of familiarity.

"So, you and Valentina," Emilia said, her voice taking on a teasing lilt.

Raven groaned and turned her head toward Asha's desk.

"Come on," Emilia prodded. "Tell me what you're feeling. Do you like her? Did you guys kiss again? Do you trust her?"

"Enough," Raven said, sharper than intended.

Emilia fell silent for a beat.

"I do like her," Raven admitted. "More than I should. More than what's safe."

Emilia's fingers moved gently through Raven's hair, the soothing motion grounding her.

"I learned a lot about her. We have more in common than I realized."

"And yet, you're still holding back."

Raven shrugged. "I need to know where she stands with the crown before I can tell her anything."

Emilia's hand stilled. "Why do you care about her relationship with the crown?"

Raven hesitated.

"Raven."

She exhaled slowly. "I think King Pierre was involved in setting up my clan. I don't have proof, but his closeness with the Widow Clan's leader makes me suspicious. And Valentina told me something… The current ruler has the right to challenge whoever wins the Shadow Gauntlet. That makes me wonder if he intends to keep his throne at all costs. If that's the case, why wipe out my clan?"

"You think that no matter who wins, King Pierre will challenge them and kill them?" Emilia asked.

Raven sat up, locking eyes with her. "It's just a theory. I need more answers."

Emilia chewed on her lower lip. "I'll see what I can find out as heir."

A small, genuine smile touched Raven's lips. "Thank you. I know it's dangerous."

Emilia shrugged. "What are they going to do, try and kill me?"

"Probably," Raven deadpanned.

"Probably," Emilia echoed, then brightened. "But you'd kill them before they even laid a finger on me."

"Obviously."

Raven suddenly tensed, her senses sharpening as unease prickled her skin. Her gaze snapped toward the door. "She's coming."

Emilia sprang up. "Can we attack her?"

Raven tilted her head. "Why?"

Emilia was already slipping into the shadows. "For old times' sake."

Suppressing a chuckle, Raven doused the light in Asha's office before ducking behind the desk. The office was spacious but left little room for concealment. A swivel chair sat behind the large wooden desk, flanked by two visitor chairs. A window behind the desk overlooked the training grounds, its blinds drawn against prying eyes. A well-worn rug covered the floor between two sofas, a table nestled between them. A few paintings adorned the walls, and on the desk, a photograph of Asha's graduating class sat in a simple frame.

Raven's gaze caught on a familiar face in the picture—her mother, standing beside Asha and Ms. Moretti, her smile radiant.

Shaking off the bittersweet memory, Raven pressed herself lower, angling her view toward the door.

Asha entered swiftly, flipping on the light just as Emilia lunged.

Asha dodged the initial strike, her reflexes razor-sharp, but Raven moved in sync. Knocking on the desk to steal Asha's focus, she drove a kick into her chest.

Asha stumbled backward. Emilia swept her legs, sending her crashing to the ground.

Asha recovered quickly, landing a precise kick to Emilia's shin before seizing her by the neck. She braced a foot against Emilia's hip and rolled forward, shifting her weight to pin her down. Just as Asha aimed a strike, Raven intervened, kicking her wrist to knock the blow off-course before delivering a sharp strike to her cheek.

Emilia twisted free as Raven locked Asha's arms, securing her legs in a tight hold. Emilia pressed a blade to her throat.

Asha smirked. "You've both grown, haven't you?"

Emilia nicked her throat just enough to draw blood. "You're getting old, Asha." She wiped her blade clean and sheathed it with a playful smile.

Raven released Asha, and they all rose to their feet. Asha, with a smear of blood on her neck, glanced at Emilia, who maintained her smile, before shifting her gaze to Raven. Raven met her stare with an unreadable expression.

Shaking her head in amusement, Asha pulled them both into a brief embrace. "Gods, I've missed you two together."

They settled onto the couch as Asha leaned back, exhaling. "Is it safe?" Emilia asked.

Asha nodded. "The staff rooms are designed to prevent eavesdropping or bugs. We discuss too many important matters with the king, and if we always gathered in the same room, it'd be obvious when something significant was happening." She waved a hand dismissively. "We're safe here. Speak freely."

Raven stood, retrieving the Crimson Widow journal from Asha's desk and setting it on the table between them.

"Find anything interesting?" Asha asked.

"No. Just confirmation that the Crimson Widow Clan is a shadow of what it once was," Raven remarked, leaning back against the couch.

Asha smirked. "Yeah, I gathered that too." She glanced at the covered window, then refocused on them. "So, you're going to break into Crimson Widow territory?"

Raven nodded. "During the ceremony, when everyone is honoring the fallen."

Asha's gaze flickered to Emilia—just for a moment, but Raven caught it. "You don't want to be with them while they remember your clan?"

Raven lowered her eyes. "I was advised against it. Every second matters. And... it just doesn't feel right." She flexed her fingers, as if testing her own words. "I didn't know them the way everyone else did. The only one I'd truly grieve is my mother. And I can't let them see me like that. Too many questions. Too many eyes. My absence won't be unusual."

Asha tilted her head, considering. "You're a prodigy, Raven. They'll expect you there."

Raven lifted her chin, resolute. "I'll make an appearance. Just long enough to confirm the ones in charge are present. Then, I'll slip out. Emilia will stay behind in case Valentina comes looking for me."

Asha's lips thinned. "So you're going in alone?"

Raven nodded. "It's the best way. No one else is at risk."

Asha exhaled sharply. "And if something happens to you?"

Raven smiled, a glint of confidence in her eyes. "Then we better hope I had the world's best teacher."

Asha dragged a hand down her face. "I don't like this, Raven. We lost your mother. I don't want to lose you too."

Raven leaned forward, squeezing Asha's hands. "Trust me."

Asha turned to Emilia. "And you? You're okay with this?"

Emilia bit her lip. "Worried? Always. But if anyone can do this, it's her."

Raven frowned slightly. There was something unspoken in Emilia's tone. A quiet certainty that didn't sit right. She held Emilia's gaze, but Emilia only nodded toward Asha.

After a moment, Asha sighed. "Alright."

She stood and flipped over her chair, peeling a map from the bottom before setting it flat on the table. They leaned in.

It detailed the Crimson Widow mansion—from the front gate to where the woods crept behind the estate. Raven studied every corridor, committing it to memory.

She tapped a small box at the back of the house. "What's this?"

Asha shrugged. "A shed. A fallback for when the armory is blocked."

Nodding, Raven traced the map with her fingers, eyes flicking over potential routes.

Asha clapped her hands, and the room plunged into darkness.

Raven's muscles tensed. Too fast. Too quiet.

The silence was oppressive, pressing in like a physical force. Her heartbeat kicked up a notch as her senses sharpened, her body already bracing for a fight.

Asha switched on the UV light, revealing a hidden layout beneath the map—a blueprint etched in simplicity. A large central structure was flanked by two smaller ones, forming the foundation of the house. Raven's eyes narrowed as she spotted stairs within the central structure. She tilted her head, intrigued.

"Dim the light slightly," Raven requested.

Asha nodded and adjusted the brightness. As the glow softened, the map revealed another set of stairs leading to a concealed room hidden behind the library's doorway. Raven felt a rush of validation—she had suspected a secret compartment, and here was the proof.

"Is that...?" Emilia trailed off, eyes locked on the map.

Raven nodded. "It is."

"Now, as bright as it can go," Raven instructed.

Asha complied, and Raven gently adjusted her hand, tracing the now-visible path of another set of stairs. This one began beneath the house, winding through the underground, and ended at the shed. A slow smile spread across her lips.

Asha switched off the UV light, plunging them back into darkness. A hush settled over the room, tension thick in the air. Then, with a sharp clap of her hands, Asha turned the lights back on.

"That's it," Raven declared, pointing to the shed. "That's my way in. It's isolated in the woods, so I won't have to go through the main building. Once I'm done, I can slip away unseen."

Emilia pressed her lips together, thoughtful. "The problem is, if their shed is anything like ours, it'll be heavily secured. Different clans use different security measures—guard dogs, cameras, lasers, high-tech locks. If this leads to their underground chambers and that book, I'd bet their security is next-level."

Asha hummed in agreement as Raven studied the map again. The risks were high, but the hope of finding proof kept her grounded.

"So, the house itself?" Raven asked.

"I said 'next-level,' not 'impossible'. I have a suggestion, but you won't like it," Emilia admitted.

Raven smirked. "That's twice on this mission you've said that."

Emilia chuckled. "Yeah, well, I want to make sure you know I'm not sugarcoating it."

"Alright, spill."

Emilia hesitated, glancing between Asha and Raven. "Someone might know how to get inside the Crimson Widow Clan's tunnels—someone who's been inside every clan's house."

Raven stiffened, bracing herself. She already hated where this was going.

"Valentina," Emilia said.

"No." The rejection was immediate.

"Listen—"

"No."

Emilia rolled her eyes and crossed her arms. "The prodigies are required to attend political events with the King. He chooses which ones, but all of them—except you—have set foot in the other clans' houses and met their leaders. Valentina, being from the King's clan, gets extra privileges. She might know security details she's not supposed to."

Asha arched a brow. "And how do you know she does?"

Emilia shrugged. "I hear things. As heir, I know she has access to our codes, and no one suspects her of betrayal because, well, she has no reason to?"

Or does she? Raven thought, but kept it to herself. Valentina had shared a secret with her—one Raven couldn't expose.

"So you're asking me to just walk up to her and say, 'Hey Valentina, do you happen to have the Crimson Widow security codes? I think they killed my clan, and I need proof'?"

Emilia opened her mouth.

"No," Asha cut in sharply.

Emilia shut her mouth, scowling.

That was exactly what she expected me to do.

Asha sighed, rubbing her temples. "How close are you with Valentina?"

Raven hesitated, suddenly finding interest in her fingers. "Well… she's kind of… my girlfriend now?"

Emilia and Asha whipped their heads toward her.

"Wait, what?" Emilia blurted.

Asha held up a hand to silence Emilia. "Okay, so she likes you, and you like her. That means there has to be trust. A relationship built on lies won't last." Her words carried the weight of advice, though she masked it as strategy. "Tell her the truth."

Emilia threw her hands up. "I just—"

Asha shot her a look that silenced her.

"Tell her the truth," Asha repeated, "and if she helps you, it's because she cares. Or because, as the future leader, she knows the risk of the Crimson Widow Clan being traitors. She can't let that risk happen."

Raven exhaled sharply. "And if she doesn't help? If she tries to expose me?"

"You kill her."

Silence stretched between them. Raven searched Asha's face, hoping for hesitation, a trace of doubt—anything that would suggest she wasn't serious. But Asha held her gaze, unwavering.

Raven's chest tightened. The thought of Valentina dead sent an ache through her she couldn't explain. Her fingers curled into fists. "Prodigies can't kill prodigies before the Shadow Gauntlet," she whispered.

Asha leaned forward, resting a hand on Raven's arm. The touch was gentle, almost motherly. Raven's eyes burned, blurring with tears she didn't expect. *Why am I crying? Over Valentina? Over killing her? Over the fear that she'll reject me?*

"Love is never easy," Asha said. "Especially in our world. If you truly want to be with her, tell her the truth now, before it's too late."

A tear slipped down Raven's cheek. "You're not just telling me to be honest. You're telling me to kill her if she doesn't accept it."

Asha didn't answer. Instead, she turned to Emilia.

Emilia scooted closer, wrapping her arms around Raven's waist. "I wish I could give you better advice," she murmured, resting her chin on Raven's shoulder. "But Asha is right. If Valentina turns against you, we can't afford to let her walk away. She'd put us all in danger. If it comes to that, we'll make it look like an accident. Frame someone. Whatever it takes."

Raven's stomach twisted.

Emilia sighed. "But I don't think it'll come to that." She smirked. "I've seen the way she looks at you. The way she subtly glares at me when she thinks no one's watching. She likes you. If you told her you planned to burn the entire League to the ground, she'd probably help you."

A weak chuckle escaped Raven's lips as she wiped at her tears. "You really think so?"

"I know so."

Asha cupped Raven's face, her thumbs brushing away the last of the tears. Emilia squeezed her waist gently. Raven had only cried a few times in her life, and every time, Asha and Emilia treated it like something sacred—never a sign of weakness, only proof that she was still human.

She closed her eyes, leaning into Asha's hands. *The decision is coming. And when it does, I have to be ready.*

15

Vipers voice betrayed a slight quiver as she asked, "How do we know this is going to work?"

Asha shrugged, offering no further reassurance.

Raven scanned the assembled prodigies and shadow blades. Some outwardly appeared calm, while others couldn't hide their nervous energy—fingers twitching, weight shifting from foot to foot. Beneath their composed facades, the tension was undeniable.

"All you have to do is jump from this building. When the time comes, open your arms and let the wings expand, gliding to safety. Aim for the mattress with the red X," Asha instructed.

Murmurs rippled through the group. A few trainees cast uneasy glances at one another, clearly hoping to dissuade Asha from the plan.

Raven, blocking out the chatter, focused on inspecting her glider suit. She ran a hand down her right sleeve, frowning as her fingers found a series of tiny holes. Quickly, she extended her arm, testing the material. The damage wasn't catastrophic—but it was enough to weaken the fabric. Turning to her left wing, she examined its structure, it was fine.

"Hey," Raven called out, still assessing the damage. "Has anyone checked their wings? One of mine are compromised."

The group immediately followed suit. Within moments, murmurs of concern escalated into outright alarm as others discovered similar flaws.

Asha stepped forward to investigate. Raven barely registered her presence—her gaze was scanning the crowd. Something was off.

"Where's Valentina?"

A sharp pang of unease gripped her. Her eyes darted over the assembled trainees until she landed on Viper, who had gone pale.

"She already jumped."

Time ground to a halt.

Raven sprinted to the edge, heart hammering. Below, Valentina was plummeting, arms outstretched, waiting for her wings to catch the wind. The glider failed. She kept falling.

Without thinking, Raven lunged off the ledge.

Wind roared past her ears as the ground hurtled closer. Everything else—the shouts above, the sky, Asha—ceased to exist. Only Valentina mattered.

She flattened herself against the wind, streamlining her body. But something was off—her trajectory. She was veering too far left— a miscalculation. She adjusted, lifting her left arm, letting the wind tilt her back on course.

The air was brutal, tearing at her face, drying her eyes, and making it impossible to breathe. Valentina was just beyond reach— too far.

No.

Raven extended her arm again, allowing the wind to jolt her forward. Her fingers grazed Valentina's wrist. A second later, their hands locked.

Momentum carried them sideways, veering toward the mattress below.

The impact was hard—but not deadly.

Valentina clung to her, breath ragged, trembling against Raven's chest. Slowly, Raven began running her hand up and down Valentina's back in steady, soothing motions, matching her breathing to calm her.

For a while, neither of them spoke.

Then, in a near whisper:

"Thank you."

Raven said nothing.

A rush of footsteps broke the silence.

"Raven! Valentina!" Asha's voice rang out as the others reached them. Viper pulled Raven up, while Whisper helped Valentina to her feet.

Asha stepped closer, guilt evident in her posture. "I'm sorry. No one has used these in a while, and there were no reports of damage. I should have checked myself. That was—"

"Reckless," Raven cut in, her voice sharp.

Asha flinched.

Raven had always trusted her. Even when her training pushed them to the brink, even when it cost them blood and bruises, she had never questioned Asha's methods. But this? This was different. Valentina could have died.

The anger came swift, potent—dangerous. For one fleeting second, Raven envisioned what it would be like to make Asha pay for her mistake. The thought scared her.

She took a breath.

Then another.

She let it go.

"I should have checked my equipment," Valentina admitted, breaking the heavy silence that hung over the training field. "We're always supposed to check our gear before a mission, and I didn't. I was too eager to try the suit, and it almost cost me my life—and Raven's. For that, I apologize."

Raven remained silent as she stepped out of her glider suit. With a measured expression, she walked over and held it out to Asha. The instructor accepted it without a word.

"Dismissed," Asha announced to the class.

One by one, the students began removing their suits and handing them over. Raven turned on her heel, eager to leave before her anger consumed her. She was halfway across the field when a hand caught her arm.

"Raven," Valentina whispered.

The tension drained from Raven's body the moment their eyes met. The fire inside her cooled, replaced by a warmth she hadn't expected.

"Yes?"

"Don't be upset with Professor Zion or me," Valentina pleaded. "Accidents happen."

A sad smile flickered across Raven's lips. "I'm not upset with you. And I don't care if accidents happen—if it means losing you. She should have been more responsible as an instructor." The words came out harsher than intended. She knew it wasn't fair to blame Asha, but last night's conversation still lingered in her mind.

Valentina nodded. "I won't argue with you, but if you blame her, then you have to blame me, too. I should have been more responsible as an assassin."

Raven scoffed, unwilling to place any blame on Valentina. "Even if—"

"Valentina!"

A familiar voice cut through the moment, and both women turned. Whisper approached them at a jog, slowing as he neared. He gave Raven a small nod before turning his full attention to Valentina.

"How are you feeling?" he asked.

Valentina smiled and shrugged, feigning indifference. "I'm fine, Whispy. Not even a scratch."

Raven saw through the act. The fall had shaken Valentina more than she let on.

Whisper hesitated before clearing his throat. "I was wondering if you'd like to get dinner sometime. Maybe catch up?"

Valentina blinked. "Catch up?"

Whisper glanced down, his nervousness apparent. "Yeah. I know things didn't work out between us before, but we're older now. I was hoping we could give it another try." His voice dropped slightly. "We might die in a few months. I don't want to live with regrets."

Raven's mind drifted back to her second-ever class with Valentina. Professor Zion had assigned them a test: steal an egg from one another. From her perch in a tree, Raven had observed every move Valentina made. She had been flawless—calculated, swift, untouchable. Then came Whisper.

Their fight had looked different from the others. It was as if they knew each other's rhythms, like dancers in a routine they had long since mastered. Valentina had dodged every one of Whisper's attacks, responding with precise, effortless counters. She had won, and the cocky wink she'd thrown his way had lingered in Raven's mind.

Now, standing before them, Whisper looked desperate.

Valentina exhaled softly and shook her head. "I'm in a relationship."

Whisper frowned. "With who?"

Valentina's gaze shifted to Raven.

Raven didn't move.

Whisper followed Valentina's line of sight, meeting Raven's cold stare. He swallowed, shifting uncomfortably. Then, as if grasping for control, he squared his shoulders.

"What if I fought her for you?"

Valentina's expression darkened. "There's nothing to fight over, Whispy. I am hers."

A muscle in Whisper's jaw twitched. He looked between them, his eyes lingering on Valentina as if trying to find something—hope, doubt, anything. When he found nothing, his shoulders tensed.

Raven tilted her head slightly. The challenge was bold, but it irritated her more than it impressed her.

Whisper reached for his blade.

A smirk tugged at Raven's lips. If he wanted a fight, she was more than happy to oblige.

Before either could move, Valentina stepped between them, drawing her own dagger.

"Enough, Whisper," she said firmly. "I like Raven."

"You don't even know her," Whisper argued. "You've known me your whole life."

"And yet, you still weren't enough," Raven murmured, her tone laced with amusement.

Whisper's eyes darkened. He took a step forward, fists clenched, but Valentina didn't waver.

"Don't," she warned. Her grip on the dagger was tight, her knuckles white.

Raven didn't bother drawing her own blade. She didn't need to.

A moment of silence stretched between them. Finally, Whisper exhaled and took a step back, his hands raised in surrender. "I'm sorry for upsetting you both," he muttered. "I understand when I'm not wanted."

"Not fast enough," Raven whispered with a mocking smile.

Whisper's jaw tightened, but he said nothing. He turned and walked away, shoulders hunched.

Valentina sheathed her dagger and turned to Raven, who was already watching her.

Valentina stepped closer and placed a hand against Raven's stomach. "You like provoking people, don't you?" she mused, leaning in.

Raven smirked. "What are they going to do? Fight me?"

She kissed Valentina lightly.

Valentina sighed, slipping her arms around Raven's waist. "You're impossible," she murmured against her lips.

Raven cupped Valentina's face gently, holding her close.

Breaking the kiss, she rested her forehead against Valentina's. "I want to tell you more about myself."

Valentina raised an eyebrow. "More? But I already know so much."

Raven rolled her eyes. "I'm serious. There are things I need you to know." She hesitated. "Whisper was right. We can't build something real if you're in the dark."

Valentina searched her eyes, but Raven gave nothing away.

"Meet me in my room after dinner," Raven said.

"Okay," Valentina agreed.

Raven studied her for a moment longer, then smiled.

Raven lay on the floor, reading a book she had pulled from the library, while Emilia sat at the edge of the bed, pencil in hand, sketching. Every so often, Raven felt Emilia's gaze flicker toward her, but she said nothing. It had been years since Emilia had last given her a drawing, and she wanted to keep this one.

Emilia was a skilled artist, her work astonishingly lifelike despite being solely in black and white. She never added color, but her shading was so precise that her sketches resembled photographs. A light knock on the door interrupted their quiet routine. Raven closed her book and rose to her feet, a smile forming as she opened the door. Valentina stood there, greeting her with a quick peck on the lips before stepping inside.

Valentina halted upon noticing Emilia, who was still absorbed in her drawing. She didn't even acknowledge Valentina's presence. Raven smirked—Emilia in the zone meant all social conventions ceased to exist.

Raven cleared her throat. "Em."

Emilia sighed, clearly annoyed, but set her sketchbook aside. "What?"

"We have a guest," Raven said, her tone carrying a hint of warning.

Emilia stood and gave an exaggerated, mocking bow. "Prodigies."

Raven rolled her eyes and gave her a playful shove, sending Emilia tumbling back onto the bed with a chuckle. She made herself comfortable, arranging the pillows as if she owned the place.
Raven turned back to Valentina. "Pull up a chair."

Valentina dragged the desk chair forward, settling in with an unreadable expression as her gaze shifted between Raven and Emilia. "So," Valentina started, her curiosity evident. "What is she doing here?"

Raven hesitated before glancing at Emilia, who merely shrugged. "She's…" Raven searched for the right words. "Part of the story."

Valentina arched an eyebrow.

Raven clapped her hands together. "Where should I begin?"

"The beginning?" Emilia offered dryly, prompting another eye roll from Raven.

"Is the beginning okay with you?" Raven asked Valentina.

Valentina nodded, leaning forward in anticipation.

Raven took a deep breath. "My name is Raven Norris. I am the daughter of Nova Norris, the—"

"The head of the Eleventh Clan," Valentina gasped. "Wait."

Raven held up a hand. "Let me finish, love."

Valentina pressed her lips together and nodded, inching closer, her eyes shining with curiosity.

"When I was little, my mother used to tell me stories about our clan's history. The one that stayed with me was about the last mission.

"King Pierre gave them an assignment—dangerous, urgent. Someone had discovered our island. Not just the island but the clans, the work the assassins did for the United Nations. It required all hands. My mother was pregnant with me then, so she went as overwatch.

"But it was a setup.

"The building they infiltrated wasn't just aware of them. They were waiting. One by one, my people died. My mother tried to intervene, but Asha—Professor Zion—stopped her. Asha had sensed something was wrong and arrived early to warn them, but she was too late.

"The Crimson Widow Clan was the one that provided the intel to King Pierre. The mission was originally theirs, but conveniently, members of their clan had all fallen ill—at least, that's what they claimed. But after my people were slaughtered, the Widow Clan miraculously recovered overnight. No investigation, no consequences."

Valentina chewed her lip. "But how do you know they weren't the ones meant to be set up?"

"My mother thought the same thing at first, but Asha was in Nethrala when she ran into members of the Crimson Widow Clan. They didn't see her, but she saw them. None of them looked sick. And after the mission, the Widow Clan acted as if they had been blessed by fate for avoiding it."

Valentina leaned back, deep in thought, before her gaze drifted toward Emilia.

Raven exhaled, already anticipating her question.

"Emilia?" Valentina asked.

Raven turned just in time to catch Emilia's smug smile. She knew exactly what Valentina was thinking.

Raven pursed her lips. "Let me finish."

Valentina gestured for her to continue.

"Asha convinced my mother to go into hiding. They pieced together the betrayal, but by then, it was too late. I was born a prodigy. My mother knew we could never return.

"Ms. Moretti, Emilia's mom, was my mother's best friend. She found out we were alive and visited with Emilia. That's how we met."

Emilia grinned. "She loved me instantly."

Raven scoffed. "I wanted nothing to do with her. She was persistent, though, wouldn't let me ignore her." A small smile tugged at her lips. "She grew on me.

"For a long time, those four people—my mother, Asha, Ms. Moretti, and Emilia—were my entire world. The only people I trusted.

"But then Emilia stopped visiting.

"I was twelve. I fell into depression for months. My mother and Asha tried to pull me out of it, but even my mother was heartbroken. I always believed Ms. Moretti was her soulmate.

"When my mother died, Asha begged me to return. To expose the Crimson Widow Clan. But I couldn't. I couldn't face them knowing what they had done. I couldn't pretend.

"Asha and my mother always told me it was my destiny to lead the clans. To rule them. I knew it was because I was a prodigy; it was expected of all of us. But whenever I questioned it, they only shook their heads and said, 'One day, you will understand.'"

Raven exhaled, jaw clenched as she continued. "I told Asha I wanted no part of it. I didn't want to carry the burden of a prodigy, and I wanted nothing to do with the Crimson Widow Clan. I needed space—to be alone. She let me go. I spent years traveling, isolating myself, trying to make sense of everything. But no matter how far I ran, one truth always found me: I wanted revenge."

Her fingers curled into fists. "They took everything. They made sure I was alone. And in the end, they killed my mother."

A heavy silence filled the room. Then Raven drew a sharp breath and continued, "So, I returned with a mission—to expose them and end their line. What I didn't expect was King Pierre."

She shook her head. "At first, he was just a name, a passing thought in the grand scheme of my plan. He commanded the clans. That was all. But then I saw him with the Crimson Widow Clan's head. And I understood. He wasn't just overseeing them—he was protecting them."

Valentina stood, pacing as if trying to piece everything together. "So what you said at the prodigy meeting—it was all a lie? You only wanted to be placed in Emilia's clan so King Pierre couldn't track who you really were."

"Not exactly," Raven admitted. "Emilia made it obvious she wasn't going to pretend we didn't know each other. With how close we already appeared, too many questions would arise. So, I made sure we were in the same clan. It gave me access to her, to Ms. Moretti, and to the information I needed—without suspicion."

Valentina's eyes narrowed. "And King Pierre? Why would he be involved? What does he gain from wiping out your clan?"

Raven exhaled. "That's the missing piece. I don't know exactly why my clan had to die. But I think Pierre doesn't plan on giving up the crown. My theory? After one of us wins the Shadow Gauntlet, he'll deem them unfit and challenge them. That way, even if you win, you still lose."

Valentina slowly sat back down, folding her hands in her lap. She studied Raven carefully. "You've kept this secret for a long time. Why tell me now?"

Raven glanced at Emilia, who shifted closer on the bed.

"She trusts you," Emilia said. "And I believe you could help us. Help expose the Widow Clan. Maybe even King Pierre. But if you don't believe us—" Emilia's voice dropped slightly. "I won't let you put her life in danger."

Valentina's gaze hardened. "Would you kill me?" she asked Raven directly. "Would you let her kill me?"

Raven's throat tightened. The answer should have been simple. Yes. If it meant protecting Asha, Emilia, and Ms. Moretti, she would do whatever it took.

But the thought of hurting Valentina made her stomach churn. "I—" She hesitated. She didn't need to answer. Valentina had already read the truth in her silence.

After a long pause, Valentina nodded, as if coming to a decision. "My father died helping the Eleventh Clan," she said quietly. "I had my suspicions. But my mother told me to leave it alone. She didn't want me making enemies."

She exhaled sharply. "But if this mission can reveal the truth—if it can bring justice to my father's death—then count me in."

She turned to Raven, a ghost of a smile playing on her lips. "Besides, we're a team. Remember?"

For the first time that night, Raven felt the corners of her lips tug upward.

"A team," she confirmed.

16

aven sat on her bed, leaning forward with her elbows on her knees, staring at the floor. The weight of the impending ceremony pressed heavily against her chest, the sorrow threatening to suffocate her. She had tried to push the memories away, to bury them under layers of forced strength, but today, they clawed their way to the surface. The whispers of her mother's legacy, the stories others told about her, the grief she never allowed herself to fully acknowledge—all of it felt like too much to bear.

A knock at the door pulled her from her thoughts. She inhaled sharply but didn't move. She already knew who it was.

Emilia had told Valentina about the plan, but Valentina refused to stay at the memorial while Raven faced potential danger. They had crafted a lie—pretending to spend time together to lift Valentina's spirits—and Emilia had agreed to cover for them.

Finally, Raven forced herself to stand. One breath. One step. She crossed the room, hesitated at the door, and then opened it.

Emilia stood there, a sad smile tugging at her lips. Before Raven could say a word, Emilia stepped inside and wrapped her arms around her.

Raven exhaled shakily and clung to her, burying her face in Emilia's shoulder. For just a moment, she allowed herself to be held, to be weak.

When Emilia finally pulled back, she reached for Raven's uniform, fingers brushing over the sigil stitched into the fabric.

"I have something for you," she said, pulling out a small cloth emblem and pressing it into Raven's hand.

Raven blinked. The sigil of her clan. Her fingers trembled as she traced its edges. It was soft, worn—something that had been kept safe for a long time.

A lump formed in her throat. She didn't trust herself to speak, so instead, she leaned forward and pressed a kiss to Emilia's cheek. "Thank you," she murmured.

Emilia smiled, her voice gentle. "Of course, il mia grazioso uccello. Now, let's go."

Raven and Emilia stepped out of the room, their footsteps echoing softly as they made their way toward the front of the academy. Without a word, Raven reached behind her and unstrapped the sword from her back, holding it low at her side. She didn't want to bring it into the memorial—not with so many eyes, not with what it might signal. But walking into Crimson Widow territory completely unarmed? That wasn't an option either. She'd leave it in the clan car for now. Retrieve it later. Quietly.

The front of the school came into view. Viper was already there, leaning against the car like she had all the time in the world. Emilia moved ahead smoothly, a natural diversion, while Raven took the moment to pop the trunk and slide the sword inside. She closed it without a sound and stepped into place beside the others.

"Ready?" Viper asked, her eyes flicking between them.

A series of silent nods followed. No one spoke as they climbed into the car.

The ride unfolded in near-total silence. Each of them stared out their own window, absorbed in thoughts too heavy to share aloud. Halfway through the drive, Emilia reached across the seat and laced her fingers through Raven's. Raven squeezed gently, grounding her without breaking her gaze from the glass. No words were exchanged—none were needed.

Outside, the skies had turned gray. The change wasn't lost on Raven. Nethrala had been warm and sunlit for weeks, but now, on the one day grief was meant to be acknowledged, the clouds gathered like a warning. It was as if the world itself wanted to strip away the mask she wore, force her to face what she kept buried. Still, she held firm. Some truths were safer left hidden.

When the car came to a halt, Emilia let go of her hand. They stepped out into the murmuring crowd. Emilia approached the driver with a quiet request to keep the vehicle unlocked—just in case she needed to grab something later without the hassle of finding him. He gave a small nod, and Emilia returned to the others.

"I think we should find my mom, see if she needs anything," Emilia said, her voice low but clear.

Raven and Viper both nodded, eyes scanning the mass of mourners.

"There," Viper said, pointing subtly before taking the lead.

They moved together through the crowd, slipping between groups of people offering hushed prayers and respectful bows. The atmosphere was heavy, reverent. As they neared Ms. Moretti, she turned to greet them with a smile that tried to be warm—but didn't quite make it.

Viper's brow furrowed. "May I hug you?"

A soft chuckle escaped Ms. Moretti as she opened her arms. The embrace was short, but the tears glistening in her eyes lingered. Raven had to look away, jaw tight, chest tightening.

When Viper stepped back, offering a small bow before retreating, Emilia stepped in. She wrapped her arms around her mother, and Ms. Moretti pulled her close—silent strength in the way she held her.

Raven didn't join them. Instead, she let her gaze drift, skimming over unfamiliar faces until it landed on one that made her freeze.

Asha.

Even at a distance, Raven saw it. The way Asha's expression barely held together. The sheen in her eyes, the tremble in her lips— she was on the edge.

Raven's breath hitched.

She turned away.

She couldn't endure this. Not right now.

Stepping away from the mother-daughter duo, Raven drifted through the crowd with no real destination—only the need to escape the weight of sorrow pressing down on her. The air was thick with grief, a reminder of wounds that never fully healed. She kept moving, weaving through bodies, until the crowd thinned, revealing a Shadowfang Clan shrine.

At its center was a large image of her mother.

A chill ran down her spine.

It had been so long since she had seen her mother's face in a way that resonated with the warmth of her childhood. The last memory she clung to was different—her mother dying in her arms, her life slipping away like sand through Raven's fingers. Now, this image before her, vibrant and full of life, felt like a cruel reminder of what was lost.

Her fists clenched, nails digging into her palms. She gritted her teeth as a surge of emotions twisted through her—anger, grief, the overwhelming urge to scream or draw her sword and carve her fury into the Widow Clan's legacy.

A hand slipped into hers, steady and familiar.

Raven exhaled sharply, some of the tension unraveling as she recognized the warmth of Valentina's touch.

"Not here, my love," Valentina whispered, her breath soft against Raven's ear. She rested her chin on Raven's shoulder, grounding her.

Raven turned to face her, finding solace in those warm green eyes. The perfect shade of green.

Foreheads touching, they shared a moment of quiet amidst the restless storm.

"I can't stay here," Raven confessed, her voice barely above a whisper.

"I know," Valentina replied. She pulled back, offering a small, knowing smile—one that didn't quite reach her eyes.

Raven scanned the crowd, ensuring no one paid them any attention. "Have you seen her?" she asked, lowering her voice.

Valentina nodded. "I saw her. And Prodigy Phantom. But before we leave, we need eyes on the heir. We need to be sure everyone is here."

"What does the heir look like?"

"Smooth mocha-colored skin, locs, brown eyes. Fit, about five-seven."

Raven swept her gaze across the gathering, but the description didn't match anyone in her immediate line of sight. She turned back to Valentina. "I'll check in with Ms. Moretti and Emilia. If they spot her, they'll alert me, and we can move. If you see her first, come find me."

Valentina nodded, offering a quick peck on Raven's lips before disappearing into the crowd.

Raven cast one last glance at the shrine before turning away, slipping back into the shifting mass of people.

When she reached Ms. Moretti, the woman was engaged in conversation. Raven's gaze flicked to Emilia, who stood a few feet away, talking to Onyx. The tension between them was obvious. Emilia looked irritated; Onyx, on the other hand, wore the expression of someone asking for another chance.

Raven approached, angling herself so that her back was to Onyx as she leaned in close to Emilia.

"I need you to let me know the second you see the Crimson Widow heir. After that, we move."

Emilia nodded, her sharp blue eyes serious. "Got it."

Raven turned slightly, locking eyes with Onyx. The other woman appeared composed, but Raven noticed the subtle clenching of her jaw.

Smirking, Raven pressed a light kiss to Emilia's temple, watching Onyx from the corner of her eye. The twitch of her fingers, the way her expression remained carefully neutral—it was all too easy to read.

Raven finally acknowledged her with a slight bow. "Onyx."

Onyx returned the gesture stiffly.

Satisfied, Raven squeezed Emilia's hand once before turning and walking away, leaving the two to finish whatever conversation had been cut short.

Returning to Ms. Moretti, who was no longer engaged in conversation, Raven found her standing with her hands clasped in front of her, waiting. When Raven approached, neither of them smiled. There was no need for pretenses. Raven didn't want to pretend to be happy, and Ms. Moretti had no reason to force one.

Over the years, Ms. Moretti had mourned her best friend in front of the world while knowing she was alive. Now, Raven stood before her, the child of the woman she had lost for a second time. And yet, they couldn't grieve together openly.

"It is hard to look at you, little bird," Ms. Moretti admitted, her voice softer than before. "You remind me of her, and it hurts me to know she's not here anymore."

Raven chewed on the inside of her lip. A lump formed in her throat, but she swallowed it down. "I love you. She loved you. She would be so thankful to know that I was with you now." She looked away, her gaze unfocused. "It is taking everything in me not to fall into your arms and cry."

Ms. Moretti let out a bitter chuckle. "I know the feeling."

For a moment, they stood there in unspoken grief, the weight of memories pressing down on both of them.

Raven exhaled, forcing herself to focus. "I need you to let me know when you see the Crimson Widow Clan's heir. When we have confirmation, Valentina and I will head out."

Ms. Moretti frowned. "Valentina?"

Raven nodded. "She knows the security codes, she knows who I am, plus she's my girlfriend."

Something flickered across Ms. Moretti's face—first surprise, then something warmer, like nostalgia. "Valentina is a sweetheart. I tried to get Emilia to date her when they were younger, but she was in love with—" She trailed off, shaking her head. "Anyway, she ended up with Onyx."

Raven snorted. "She chose Onyx over Valentina?"

Ms. Moretti waved a hand dismissively. "Please don't remind me."

Despite herself, Raven smirked. She turned back toward the event, scanning the room for potential threats. Out of the corner of her eye, she caught Emilia stepping up beside her.

"What are you guys talking about?" Emilia asked.

"Your poor taste in women," Raven said nonchalantly, her gaze lingering on the crowd before settling back on Emilia.

Emilia studied Raven's face, searching for something unspoken. Raven raised an eyebrow. "What?"

Emilia exhaled sharply and waved her off. "I don't see the heir."

Raven groaned. "We're wasting time." She scanned the crowd and quickly spotted Valentina pushing her way toward them.

Valentina approached, giving a small bow to Ms. Moretti, who returned the gesture. "She's here."

Raven exhaled, steeling herself. When she opened her eyes, all three women were watching her, their expressions unreadable.

"I'll be back," she said with quiet confidence.

Emilia and Ms. Moretti remained still, their stern faces betraying no emotion. Yet Raven caught the glistening in their eyes.

"I'm not hugging you until you return," Emilia declared.

Raven rolled her eyes. "Have a little faith in me."

Valentina took Raven's hand, her grip firm and reassuring. "I won't let anything happen to her," she promised, her voice unwavering as she met Emilia's gaze.

Raven offered Valentina a soft smile but couldn't shake the feeling that they were all being overly dramatic. It was a simple in-and-out mission. They had accounted for every detail. As long as she didn't trip an alarm, they'd be gone before the Widow Clan even realized they were there.

Still, she understood why the others were hesitant. To them, she wasn't just another fighter—she was the last remnant of her mother's legacy, the last of her clan, the last tangible piece of their forbidden past. And she was walking straight into the heart of the very people who had taken everything from her.

"I love you guys," Raven said, squeezing Valentina's hand. "I'll see you soon."

As they moved through the shifting crowd, people pressed toward the shrine and stage, but Raven and Valentina moved in the opposite direction. Raven needed her swords. The mission awaited.

Then, suddenly, someone stepped in front of her.

Raven stopped short, Valentina nearly colliding into her.

A woman stood before them, offering a respectful bow.

"Mom?" Valentina whispered, stepping out from behind Raven.

The woman smiled warmly. "I've been looking for you. The King is about to speak, and I wanted to pay tribute to your father."

Valentina's expression turned solemn. "I can't stay."

Her mother frowned. "What do you mean?"

Valentina hesitated before exhaling deeply. "It's too much. Seeing his picture, hearing his name… it aches." Her voice wavered, and unshed tears shimmered in her eyes. "I don't want to leave you alone, but I need to breathe. I don't want to remember that he's gone."

Her mother stepped closer, cupping Valentina's face gently. "I understand, sweetie."

Her gaze shifted to Raven, then down to their joined hands. "So, you're the infamous new Prodigy."

Raven lifted a hand in a shy wave. Up close, she could see the striking resemblance between Valentina and her mother—the same piercing green eyes, the same sharp features. Only time had added silver to her hair and lines to her face.

The woman extended her hand. "Camilla Gonzales."

Raven took it. "Nice to meet you, Ms. Gonzales."

"Just Camilla, please." She turned back to Valentina. "Go, darling. Grieve in your own way."

Valentina's lips trembled, but she managed a grateful smile. She leaned in and pressed a kiss to her mother's cheek. "Te amo."

17

Raven and Valentina moved through the dense trees, the Crimson Widow Clan mansion's imposing silhouette visible in the distance. They didn't need to get too close, but Raven kept her gaze sharp, scanning the area for the storage facility. It wouldn't be in plain sight—that much she was sure of—but she held onto the hope that she could find it nonetheless.

Valentina followed closely, her presence a silent reassurance. Though Raven remained alert, she knew that if danger lurked nearby, Valentina would sense it first. The unspoken trust between them allowed her to focus entirely on the task at hand.

Raven halted abruptly, throwing out an arm to stop Valentina. "It's here," she said, gesturing toward an unremarkable stretch of trees. Her memory had never failed her before. She half-expected Valentina to question her claim, but instead, Valentina nodded.

"I never came in from this side," Valentina admitted, stepping toward a sturdy tree trunk slightly to the left. "But if you're right, then the security box should be here."

She ran a gloved hand along the bark before pressing against a specific spot. A moment later, a concealed black panel slid into view, blue numbers glowing against the darkness. She entered a sequence, and the air shimmered before them.

Raven inhaled sharply as the storage building materialized. What she had expected to be a simple supply shed was instead a sleek, modern structure with tiled walls, a reinforced metal door, and one-way glass windows. A secure armory, hidden in plain sight—ingenious.

"We have the technology," Valentina said, almost amused as she stepped toward the front of the building, fingers skimming the smooth tiles. "We just don't always use it."

Raven tore her gaze from the facility and turned her attention back to the mansion, taking on the role of lookout. The storage building was positioned at a safe distance—far enough that even if someone inside the mansion glanced out a window, they wouldn't notice the sudden appearance of the structure.

A sharp beep, followed by the click of a lock releasing, made her turn. Valentina stood at the now-unlocked door, scanning their surroundings one last time before stepping back instead of entering. Raven frowned slightly. "What's wrong?"

Valentina didn't answer immediately, her stance cautious. "Just making sure we're not walking into a trap."

Raven's pulse quickened. If Valentina was hesitating, there was a reason. Time was running out, and standing still was just as dangerous as moving forward.

Raven took a deep breath as she stepped closer to Valentina. "Shall we?"

Valentina hesitated, glancing over her shoulder before facing Raven again. "The code should've disabled the security system."

Raven caught the hesitation in her voice. "Should have?"

Valentina exhaled, fidgeting with the hem of her sleeve. "I haven't been here in a while. What if the system changed? What if we step inside, and a silent alert goes off?" She swallowed hard. "What if they show up and kill you?"

Raven arched a brow. "Us."

Valentina only shrugged, her nerves evident. "I care more about watching you die than my own life being taken."

Raven studied her for a moment before extending a hand. "Then let's make sure neither of those things happen. In and out."

Valentina nodded, clasping Raven's hand. Together, they stepped inside. The door slid shut behind them with an eerie finality.

The room was compact, lined with an array of weapons displayed on the walls. Though confined, both knew this was only a facade—there was a hidden entrance somewhere.

Raven crouched, running her fingers along the floor, searching for subtle scuff marks.

"Wait."

She looked up to see Valentina standing near an oddly placed weapon, her fingers hovering over the hilt. A flicker of mischief crossed her face.

Without another word, Valentina grasped the weapon and slid it. It moved halfway before stopping. A low, mechanical hum resonated through the walls as the largest weapon rack split apart, revealing a hidden passage.

Raven was already moving before Valentina released the fake weapon. She descended the staircase, Valentina on her heels.

The passage was dimly lit, the air thick with dust and cobwebs. The stairs stretched longer than expected, each evenly spaced, their footsteps muffled by the compact earth beneath them.

"How long is this staircase?" Valentina muttered under her breath.

Just as Raven considered asking the same, a faint glow emerged from the bottom.

They stepped into a cavern illuminated by candlelight, positioned at each corner to cast eerie shadows along the walls. In the center stood a podium, crafted from packed dirt. Resting atop it was the book.

On the far side of the cave, another set of stairs ascended back toward the mansion. But that was not an option.

Raven exhaled sharply. "Traps?"

Valentina surveyed the area, her gaze lingering on the ground before shrugging. "Maybe. But if there are, I don't know how to disable them."

Raven clicked her tongue. "So, we either trigger an alarm—if we haven't already—and get out of here fast, or…"

Valentina smirked. "Exactly."

Raven sighed, rolling her shoulders. "If we trip anything, we can't take the book."

Valentina's brow furrowed. "Then how do you find the others?"

Raven tapped her temple. "Photographic memory. I just need to scan the pages, commit them to memory. I'll decode it later."

Valentina took a breath and gestured toward the podium.

Raven licked her lips, bracing herself. The beginning of the end.

She stepped forward.

Nothing happened.

No alarms. No movement. No sounds.

She paused, heart hammering, ears straining for the faintest disturbance.

Still nothing.

Raven allowed herself a slow, measured breath. Then, she reached for the book.

Raven reached forward and picked up the book, a smile forming on her face. But something felt off. A nagging unease settled in her chest, as if she had done something wrong. She glanced at Valentina, who was carefully examining the room, her movements deliberate. Raven appreciated the caution.

Instead of tucking the book under her arm, she opened it, flipping through the pages. She wasn't sure why she felt the need to do this, but a shiver ran down her spine. It could have been paranoia— neither she nor Valentina had found anything suspicious—but she had learned to trust her instincts. Her mother always said they were never wrong.

As she scanned the pages, she stopped midway. Two pages were glued together, concealing a pocket. Her fingers traced the edges before carefully peeling them apart. Inside, she found a slip of paper covered in unfamiliar symbols and coordinates.

Her pulse quickened. She didn't understand their meaning, but their concealment told her they were important. She studied the markings, committing everything she could to memory, before carefully slipping the paper back into its hidden compartment. There wasn't time to decipher it now. Some of the text caught her eye— cryptic phrases that felt significant—but she would have to come back later to analyze them properly.

Satisfied, she closed the book and returned it to its place.

Valentina, leaning against the wall, arms crossed, watched her.

"Done?" she asked, pushing off from the wall.

Raven nodded, moving toward the tunnel they had come through. But she hesitated. The darkness ahead seemed heavier now, pressing in from all sides. She squinted into the shadows, even though she knew no one was there.

A sigh escaped her lips. Something about the tunnel felt wrong. Unwelcoming.

She turned to Valentina, who arched a brow in silent question.

"We need to leave through the other tunnel."

Valentina frowned. "The other tunnel? The one that leads into the house?"

Raven hesitated, glancing back the way they came. "I don't think it's wise to leave the way we entered. I can't explain it, but something tells me we should take the other route."

Valentina studied her, searching her expression for doubt or uncertainty. Finally, she nodded. "I trust you."

They moved toward the tunnel, their steps light but purposeful. The passage was as dark as the first, and Raven's senses were on high alert. Every few paces, she paused to listen, unwilling to be caught off guard. But the tunnel remained eerily silent. The only reassurance of Valentina's presence came when their hands brushed briefly in the darkness.

When they reached the top, Raven pressed her palms flat against the wooden door and leaned in, straining to hear anything beyond it. No sound. No vibrations. No movement.

Slowly, she pushed the entrance open, feeling Valentina shift behind her. A quick glance over her shoulder revealed Valentina had drawn her sword, her muscles coiled and ready.

They stepped into a dimly lit office. Though the overhead lights were off, sunlight streamed through the windows, illuminating the room in a pale glow. Raven moved toward the nearest window, parting the blinds just enough to peek outside. Behind her, she heard the quiet rasp of Valentina sheathing her sword.

The window faced the storage area. A strategic placement, Raven noted—whoever worked here had a clear vantage point of both entrances. However, the dense trees obscured direct visibility of the building itself.

Valentina moved beside her and peered out as well. "There are people over there."

Raven squinted, trying to see what Valentina had noticed. "How can you tell?"

"The trees," Valentina whispered. "The smaller ones are swaying, but there's no wind. Someone's moving through them. We need to go, now, before they check the house."

Raven lingered a moment longer before nodding. "Lead the way."

Valentina moved swiftly, repeating Raven's earlier caution as she pressed her ear to the door before slowly turning the knob. She cracked it open, checked the hallway, then stepped out, Raven following closely behind.

As they maneuvered through the mansion, Raven observed how confidently Valentina moved. It was as if she knew the layout by heart. Had she been here before? The thought nagged at her. Did all the prodigies grow up together? Did they have playdates, form friendships before the weight of expectation forced them apart? Or had they been isolated from the start, knowing they'd one day be forced to kill one another?

Eventually, Valentina opened another door and ushered Raven inside.

The room was dark—walls, bedding, and furniture all varying shades of black and deep purple. The bed sat against the wall, flanked by two dressers and a study desk. Posters and framed pictures adorned the walls.

Raven's gaze caught on one photo. It was a group picture of the prodigies as children, their smiles wide and carefree. A school photo, perhaps, but Raven recognized the setting—it had been taken at one of the clan sanctuaries.

A soft creak made her turn. Valentina was at the window, peering outside. She nodded to herself, then turned back to Raven with a glint in her eye.

Raven frowned. "You're not seriously thinking—"

"This is our way out," Valentina interrupted. "We land, jog into the woods, and we're gone. No security cameras, no alarm systems."

Raven folded her arms. "How do you know?"

Valentina smirked and swung one leg over the windowsill, half-sitting on the ledge. "Because we used to sneak out. All of us. We were prodigies, but we were also kids. Sometimes, we just wanted to escape—to forget the expectations, the training, the perfection."

Without hesitation, Valentina jumped.

Raven rushed to the window, her heart lurching—but Valentina had landed in a crouch, rolling to absorb the impact. She stood and looked up with a grin, holding out her arms.

"Come on, I'll catch you."

Raven rolled her eyes but couldn't suppress her smile. She was becoming increasingly aware of how much she liked Valentina.

She swung her legs over the ledge, balancing on the windowsill. Adjusting her stance, she leapt—

Valentina caught her, but the force sent them both tumbling onto the grass.

Laughter bubbled from Raven's lips as she propped herself up on her elbows. "Nice catch."

Valentina grinned, giving her a playful shove. Raven let herself fall back dramatically before rolling onto her feet, her smile lingering. She extended a hand to Valentina.

Valentina took it. "Let's get out of here."

Raven nodded, and together, they sprinted into the woods.

18

Emilia stared at Raven, her gaze sharp with questions. Raven ignored her.

When the mission was done, Raven and Valentina had revealed themselves only to Ms. Moretti and Asha, choosing to remain hidden from everyone else. Raven had wanted them to know she was safe, but when she realized some members of the Crimson Widow Clan were missing—including their heir—her relief turned to unease. If they had returned to the compound, it meant the security shift was already in motion. Their sudden reappearance at the wrong time would be too much of a coincidence. They needed to stay unseen.

Once she was sure Ms. Moretti and Asha had confirmed their safety, Raven and Valentina stayed in the Silent Clan's car, where Raven had stowed her weapon away. When the ceremony ended, Valentina left to join her mother. Emilia and Viper returned to the car. Emilia's eyes had burned with unspoken questions, but with Viper there, she couldn't ask.

When they returned to the academy, Raven used exhaustion as an excuse. "I'm too tired to talk," she had muttered, shutting down any interrogation. Emilia had pouted but respected her wishes. They had parted ways for the night.

Now, sitting in the cafeteria, Emilia's curiosity still burned. Raven knew it wasn't the time. They had classes to attend, and she needed to focus on transferring the information she had gathered onto blank paper later.

Raven didn't even glance up from her tray. "You can come to my room when the school day ends," she hissed. "Stop staring at me like that."

Emilia huffed but finally turned her attention to the fruit in front of her. Raven shook her head—she expected more patience from her best friend.

The seat next to Raven scraped loudly against the floor. Valentina sat down, setting her plate on the table. She gave Raven a cheerful smile. Raven smiled back, but her expression faltered when she saw Whisper approaching.

Valentina followed Raven's gaze, sighed, and leaned back in her chair. Emilia, noticing the shift in mood, watched Whisper closely as he stopped in front of them.

"Onyx says you have a thing for Emilia," Whisper blurted out.

Emilia snorted, unimpressed, and popped another piece of fruit into her mouth.

Whisper continued, voice firm. "I will not allow you to string Valentina along. You can't have them both."

Raven nearly laughed. The boy was ridiculous. Desperate. But mostly, irritating.

"I can't have anyone if they don't choose me," she said, her tone even. "And Valentina has chosen me. Not you. Not anyone else in this room. Me."

She stood up, leaning her hip against the table. "Your obsession with her is starting to irritate my soul."

Whisper glared. "And Emilia?"

Raven tilted her head slightly, considering her words. She knew exactly why Emilia had broken up with Onyx, but that wasn't her story to tell.

"She didn't want to be with someone who treats her friends like garbage," Raven said simply. "I'm sorry Onyx can't take responsibility for her own actions, and now you're here making a fool of yourself."

Whisper glanced at Emilia, who still hadn't acknowledged him. His gaze then landed on Valentina, who was watching him with an unreadable expression.

Raven took advantage of the silence. Deliberately, she reached out and brushed Valentina's hair behind her shoulder, letting her fingers rest lightly on her skin. "Valentina has already made her choice." Her voice was soft, but her eyes gleamed with challenge. "You don't want to respect that, so…" She exhaled, slow and taunting. "I'll fight you for her."

Whisper's lips curled into a smirk. This was what he wanted. A chance to prove something.

"Where?" he asked.

"Now. Outside. Training area."

Whisper nodded, the arrogant smirk never leaving his face. He turned to leave, but Raven stopped him with a sharp call.

"Hold on."

The cafeteria went silent as she raised her voice.

"Everyone," she announced, drawing every eye to her. "I encourage you to join Whisper and me outside on the training grounds as we duel for Valentina's heart. Since he refuses to take no for an answer, I think this will be… rather entertaining."

Her smile was razor-sharp.

Whisper's jaw tensed. He spun around and stormed out.

Raven chuckled. *Now, let's see if he regrets it.*

Emilia and Valentina quickly threw away their food and caught up with Raven as she made her way outside.

Emilia whispered urgently, "Do you think this is a good idea?"

Raven shrugged. She didn't care. Beating him up was her pleasure and his reality check.

Emilia didn't ask another question, and Valentina remained silent as they, along with the rest of the school, made their way outside to the training area.

The training pit was massive. Tire sheds lined the edges, weapons were racked along the borders, and scattered obstacles—blocks, tunnels, and climbing posts—offered tactical advantages.

As Raven, Valentina, and Emilia approached, the crowd parted. Students gathered along the perimeter, just behind the weapon stands, whispering amongst themselves. The prodigies stood together, watching in stoic silence.

Whisper twirled a sword in the center of the pit, bouncing lightly on his toes. Eager. Impatient. Raven smirked. She was ready to embarrass him.

"Are you going to join the other prodigies?" Emilia asked Valentina.

"No."

Before stepping into the pit, Raven glanced at Valentina, who was watching Whisper with a furrowed brow.

"Are you nervous?" Raven asked.

Valentina turned to her. "Not in the slightest."

Raven nodded, but just as she stepped forward, Valentina grabbed her arm.

"Try not to put him in a coma," Valentina murmured, her eyes still on Whisper. "He's a fool with a broken heart."

Raven hummed in agreement, and Valentina let her go.

The moment Raven stepped into the pit, silence fell. Whisper stopped bouncing, his dark brown eyes locking onto her with barely concealed disdain. It almost made her laugh.

She tilted her head, glancing at the weapons rack before strolling over and running her fingers along the spears.

"Do you always fight people over women?" Onyx sneered.

"I fight for what's mine." Raven grasped a spear, testing its weight without sparing Onyx a glance.

"Emilia doesn't belong to you," Onyx snapped.

"She belongs to me more than she belongs to anyone here." Raven spun the spear, letting its weight settle in her grip before turning to Onyx with a knowing smirk. "Would you like to join Whisper? Make this an almost even battle?"

Onyx scoffed, averting her gaze. "I'll wait for the Gauntlet to end you."

Raven chuckled. "I bet you will."

She strode back to the center and planted the spear's base into the ground, tilting her head as her smirk widened.

"Whenever you're ready, little prodigy."

Whisper let out a grunt and charged, bringing his sword down in a powerful arc.

Raven shifted the spear to her left hand, gripping closer to the head, and slammed it against the ground. The sword struck metal, sparks flying from the impact.

She knocked his blade aside, twisted the spear in her grip, and swung. Whisper ducked. Using the momentum, Raven spun the weapon around her head, tucking the shaft beneath her arm before thrusting forward.

Whisper parried and countered, his sword slicing downward.

Raven dropped the spear, rolled out of range, and kicked the side of his knee. A sharp crack echoed through the pit, followed by a strangled cry of pain.

Whisper staggered, his injured leg barely holding him up. Still, he swung wildly at her.

Raven stepped in, catching his wrist, and delivered a sharp punch to his face. His head snapped back, and before he could recover, she flipped him onto the ground. The sword clattered from his grasp.

Whisper reached for it.

Raven stepped on his hand.

She wasn't applying much pressure—just enough.

Slowly, she bent down and picked up his sword.

Whisper struggled to rise, his body trembling with the effort. The gathered prodigies watched in silence as he dragged his injured leg along. Raven's expression remained impassive as she threw a sword at his feet, her gaze never leaving him.

"I can promise you—what's about to happen next will be brutal," she said, voice steady, almost casual. "I wasn't raised here. I don't believe in mercy. If it weren't for the laws forbidding us from killing before the Shadow Gauntlet, I would strike you down where you stand. But, alas…" She tilted her head, lips curling into a mocking smirk. "I won't put you in a coma, but every time you wake up, every time you breathe, you'll remember this moment. And you'll remember how Valentina will never be yours."

The other prodigies shifted uncomfortably, their gazes darting between Whisper and Raven. She scanned their faces, searching for hesitation, doubt—fear.

"If any of you want to save your fellow prodigy," she said, voice sharp as a blade, "now's your chance."

A tense silence stretched between them. Then, movement.

One of them stepped forward. Phantom. He reached for the sword, his stance unwavering.

"Whisper is my friend," Phantom said, his voice firm. "You broke his leg. Let's keep this a fair fight."

Raven's jaw clenched, the hatred curling inside her chest. She forced her expression into one of indifference. It wasn't Phantom's fault he was born into that clan. But he knew what they'd done. He was complicit in their silence.

Slowly, she stepped forward, stopping in front of the spear she'd discarded. With a swift movement, she kicked it into her hands before walking toward the weapons rack near Valentina and Emilia.

Emilia grabbed her arm. "This fight should end," she whispered urgently.

Raven didn't reply. She only picked up two small swords, dragging the blades against each other, savoring the sound.

"Raven." Emilia's voice dropped to a plea. "I'm serious."

"I'm sure."

Emilia turned to Valentina, desperation in her eyes. "Valentina, stop her. Please."

Valentina hesitated, glancing between Emilia and Raven. She sighed. "Just remember—you can't kill them."

"Valentina!" Emilia hissed.

Raven ignored them, already turning back to face her opponents. Phantom now stood beside Whisper, both of them gripping swords. She twirled her blades, assessing them. Whisper wasn't a threat—not now, not even before his injury. Phantom was younger, untested against her, but that didn't mean he was weak.

Her smirk widened.

She lunged.

Her movement was deceptive, a feint toward Whisper. As expected, Phantom stepped in, raising his sword to intercept. She paused for half a second, watching the blade rise—just in time to see a strand of her hair slice away.

Close.

She twisted low, sweeping at his legs. Phantom leapt to dodge, but the moment his feet left the ground, she pushed off one hand and drove her foot into his stomach. He hit the ground hard.

A sharp cry came from behind her. Whisper swung down, aiming for her head.

She parried effortlessly, twisting her second blade downward—straight onto his foot.

He screamed.

With a ruthless efficiency, she yanked the sword free and kicked his legs out from under him. As he fell, she raised her sword, ready to end it—

A battle cry rang out.

Phantom.

She barely had time to roll away before his blade slashed through the space where she'd been. Standing, she brushed dust from her clothes, her expression unreadable. Then, she yawned.

Mocking. Calculated. Effective.

Phantom's face darkened. His grip on the sword tightened.

He charged.

This time, she let her weapons fall. The move startled him—his swing wavered for a fraction of a second. A fatal mistake.

She lunged, catching his wrist mid-strike, twisting it sharply.

His sword clattered to the ground.

A punch to his face.

A hard flip.

He hit the ground, gasping.

She heard the crack before she saw it. His hand. Broken.

His curse of pain barely registered. Raven wasn't looking at him anymore.

She was looking at his sigil.

Her breath hitched. Anger rose like bile in her throat.

The memories clawed their way forward. The stories her mother told her of screams, blood, and burning ruins.

His clan.

Her vision blurred. Her fingers tightened on the sword. She could end this. She should end this.

Her grip steadied.

She began to bring the blade down

"ENOUGH!"

The voice thundered through the clearing, reverberating in Raven's very core. A voice she had heard before—one that always surfaced when she lost control.

The shift in her grip was instinctive. The sword, meant for Phantom's eye, wavered at the last second, slicing down instead to graze his cheek. A thin line of crimson bloomed against his pale skin, dripping onto the steel blade.

The crowd stood frozen.

Raven looked up, her pulse steady, to see Asha standing before her, the sun framing her silhouette. Her face was obscured, but her tone made her emotions unmistakable.

"My office. Now."

Raven exhaled through her nose, pulling the blade from the tire shed and leaving it behind as she straightened. She knew what was coming. She was about to be reprimanded.

Her gaze flickered to Phantom. Fear flickered in his eyes, but she gave him nothing in return—no satisfaction of knowing what she thought or felt.

As she stepped away, she noticed Emilia exchange a look with Valentina, the latter shaking her head slightly before turning and heading off in another direction. Not surprising. Emilia, however, followed without hesitation, slipping through the crowd after them.

Asha didn't invite her. But that never stopped Emilia before.

If it involved Raven, it involved Emilia, too. Asha knew it, no matter how much it irritated her. Even if she tied Emilia to a chair and ordered her to stay, the girl would simply smile, break free, and follow anyway.

It used to annoy Raven as well. At least, that was what she let people believe. Truthfully, she had always loved it. Emilia was a constant, a force of nature that never wavered. Even as children, when Raven had scowled at her for always tagging along, she had secretly relished the loyalty.

Emilia didn't always pay attention, she just wanted to be there.

Asha or Ms. Moretti would ask her a question, and she would remain utterly absorbed in whatever she was doing—until someone hurled something at her head, forcing her to catch it. Only then would she acknowledge them. When asked why she followed Raven so insistently, Emilia would simply shrug, as if the answer was obvious.

Because Raven was Raven.

The walk to Asha's office felt shorter than usual. Too short. Raven would have preferred a few extra minutes before being lectured.

Asha held the door open, beckoning her inside. Emilia, of course, followed. Asha shot her a look.

"Emilia."

"Asha." Emilia grinned, flopping onto the couch as if she owned the place.

Raven walked over and nudged Emilia's legs. Without a word, Emilia bent her knees, opening them just enough for Raven to slip in between. She lay down, resting her head on Emilia's stomach, her feet dangling slightly off the couch's edge.

Emilia stretched her legs out again, locking Raven into place.

Asha rolled her eyes and sat down.

"Raven."

Raven hummed, eyes closed. She was comfortable.

"Raven." Asha's tone sharpened.

She cracked one eye open. "Yes?"

"Would you like to explain why you almost killed Prodigy Phantom?"

Raven sighed, shutting her eyes again. "I was never actually going to kill him."

"Weren't you?"

"I think." A pause. "I was originally fighting Whisper. He wasn't taking a hint when it came to Valentina, so I decided to put him in his place. He's weak. Phantom stepped in to play hero. Admirable, really. But unfortunately for him, I hate him and his clan."

Silence.

Asha exhaled slowly.

Raven continued, unfazed. "I wanted the Widow Clan to understand something. That when they finally learn who I really am, they won't stand a chance. Their prodigy is useless."

The weight of her words settled over the room.

No one argued. They understood Raven's anger. But understanding it didn't mean approving of it.

Asha wished she could smooth that sharp edge inside Raven. The part that knew no mercy. The part that made her the most dangerous prodigy of their time.

But that was also what made Raven unstoppable. She didn't just take risks—she calculated them. She would sacrifice millions to save one. She was no hero. And she had long made peace with that.

"Raven," Emilia's voice was softer now, her fingers idly tracing patterns along Raven's back. "You don't need to prove yourself. The other prodigies already whisper about you. They know you're stronger. That's why they hesitate to challenge you."

Raven remained still, staring past Asha.

Emilia continued. "The Shadow Blades ask me about you. As a leader. As a person. They wonder if they should follow you. If they should befriend you. They know you don't even try in your fights, yet you still dominate them."

Asha leaned back, watching Raven closely. "We don't want you getting into trouble with King Pierre."

Raven finally shifted her gaze. "I plan to kill him after I win the Shadow Gauntlet. Unless, of course, he forces me to do it sooner."

Asha's expression darkened. "You plan to kill him? Why?"

Raven explained her suspicions—theories surrounding King Pierre and his connection to her clan's demise. She had no proof. Not yet. But the last two books she sought would provide answers.

Asha sighed, rubbing her temples. "I remember when you were calm and forgiving."

Emilia laughed. "Forgiving? When was this?"

Raven smirked and bit Emilia's stomach through the fabric.

Emilia hissed, swatting the back of her head.

"Enough." Asha's voice, weary now, halted Raven's next move. "Until we have evidence, I need you to keep a low profile. Don't give them reasons to dig into your past."

Raven stood, smoothing her uniform. She met Asha's gaze, then Emilia's.

"I'll respect your wishes." A curt bow. A swift exit.

She had a book to find.

19

Raven sat in her room, meticulously copying down crucial information from *Crimson Widow* when a discreet knock interrupted her focus. Closing the book, she moved toward the door and opened it without hesitation. Valentina stood there, smiling softly.

For a week, Raven had obeyed Asha's orders—no fighting. Whisper's injuries were healing, and Phantom now bore a scar, a permanent reminder of how dangerous Raven could be. Whisper kept his distance, and he hadn't made any further attempts to approach Valentina. Since the fight, Valentina had been distant, no longer spending her free time with Raven. In class, she would brush past her, leaving only a brief kiss before disappearing. Raven had chosen not to pry, assuming Valentina would share if she wanted to. But the silence between them carried weight, filling Raven with an uneasy longing. Had she caused a rift without realizing it?

"Hi," Valentina greeted, brushing a kiss against Raven's cheek as she stepped inside.

"Hi?" Raven echoed, shutting the door. Confusion colored her tone as she turned to face Valentina, who had already settled on the bed.

"Is now a bad time?"

Raven shook her head and stepped into the center of the room. "I just didn't think you wanted to spend time with me."

Valentina frowned. "Why would you think that?"

"Because you've been gone all week."

Valentina hummed thoughtfully, her gaze drifting around Raven's room before returning to her. "Can I see your serpent birthmark?"

Raven tensed. The request caught her off guard. Her mother's warning echoed in her mind, urging caution. She'd never understood why the secrecy mattered so much. At first, she thought it was about keeping her prodigy status hidden. But then she remembered her mother's reluctance to reveal it even to Ms. Moretti and Asha.

Valentina's expression gave nothing away. Silence settled between them, stretching into an uneasy pause.

"Why do you want to see it?" Raven asked, leaning against her desk.

Valentina removed her gloves. Winding around her forearm was the serpent birthmark, its head resting on the back of her hand.

Raven stared, taking in the familiar yet mesmerizing pattern. It was only the second time she had seen it up close. When she met Valentina's gaze again, she found it clouded with contemplation.

"I cover my birthmark most of the time," Valentina admitted, flexing her fingers. "Others can hide theirs under their clothes, but mine is always visible. Everyone already knows I'm a prodigy, but this—" she gestured to the mark "—this is what sets us apart. Without it, I'd just be another assassin, a Shadow Blade. I'd grow older than eighteen, fall in love, get married." A joyless chuckle escaped her. "Sometimes, covering it makes me believe—just for a moment—that I'm normal."

Raven remained silent.

Valentina shook her head. "I know it's stupid."

"It's not."

Pushing off the desk, Raven sat beside Valentina. She stared at the door as if it might hold the answers she needed.

"My mother always told me to keep it hidden," she murmured. "Never show anyone the full marking. The head of the serpent—that was the most she'd allow. Even now, the thought of revealing it makes me nervous." She flexed her hands. "I don't know why."

"I have a theory," Valentina said after a long pause.

Raven turned to her, brows furrowed.

"That's why I asked to see your birthmark. I think it's the reason your mother wanted you to keep it hidden." Valentina gave her a soft smile before reaching for the hem of Raven's black short-sleeve shirt, the Silent Clans' sigil stitched onto the back.

Raven's heart stuttered.

"Do you trust me?" Valentina asked.

"Yes." The answer came in a whisper.

Valentina lifted Raven's shirt, her fingers brushing against her skin. Raven let her, raising her arms to make it easier. The fabric slid away, pooling beside them on the bed.

The room shifted. Raven could feel Valentina's gaze tracing the serpent's intricate design across her back, her scrutiny making Raven hyper-aware of every breath, every heartbeat. Heat curled low in her stomach.

Gentle fingertips traced the pattern, the touch sending small shivers over Raven's skin. She held still, resisting the urge to flinch.

"Find anything unusual?" she asked, voice steadier than she felt.

Valentina placed her palm against Raven's back. "Yes."

Raven's pulse quickened. She waited for an explanation, but Valentina remained silent.

"Val?"

A deep inhale. "I don't want to insult your intelligence with my next question," Valentina murmured. "I just don't know what you've been taught—what you *know*—since you've been away from us for so long."

Raven frowned. "Go on."

"What do you know about how our birthmarks came to be?"

"The origin story?" Raven repeated, a flicker of uncertainty crossing her face. "Not much. My mom barely talked about my birthmark. she just told me I was special and that I should never show it to anyone."

Valentina removed her hand from Raven's back, her gaze shifting. Something in her expression had changed. It wasn't just curiosity anymore—it was caution, as if she were afraid of saying the wrong thing.

"Tell me," Raven encouraged. "I like a good bedtime story."

Valentina offered a small smile, through her eyes held something deeper. "The serpent birthmark originates from the Serpent King himself." She took a breath before continuing. "Before the clans were separated, they were one. He was seen as a god amongst the assassin clan. Born with a unique serpent birthmark, he possessed extraordinary powers. One day, invaders sought to abduct the assassins, compelling them to become mindless soldiers. The Serpent king couldn't allow this, so he instructed his people to fight back, to defend their land and save their kin. However, some enemies managed to escape. Unable to leave the island, he sought the gods' help.

The Serpent king pleaded with the gods for a way to empower individuals within the clan. He needed trusted defenders who could be bestowed with some of his abilities, ensuring the safety of their people. The gods answered his prayers. Performing a blood ceremony with ten chosen individuals, the Serpent king saw the appearance of a serpent birthmark on their arms. These select few gained heightened senses, an ability to sense when they were being observed, silent movements regardless of the distance they fell, swifter agility than the average assassin, and increased stamina. Yet, they couldn't match the Serpent king's full range of powers. While possessing the enhanced abilities, he could also manipulate fire and summon shadows."

Valentina's voice lowered, as if sharing a dangerous secret. "When examining the birthmarks, they all realized they might have shared the same symbol, but the Serpent King's was distinct. His scales differed from the rest. Nevertheless, his prodigies possessed everything they needed to locate and eliminate the infiltrators who threatened their land, as well as anyone they disclosed the existence of Nethrala to. The brainwashed assassins who had been taken also had to be dealt with, their deaths commemorated with a burial to allow their loved ones to mourn. Once it was confirmed that their home was secure and no one knew of Nethrala's existence, life returned to normal. They carried on with their daily routines, undertook missions, and trained the next generations. As people began having children, they discovered that a select few were born with the serpent birthmark, distinct from the ones born to the original prodigies. The Serpent King, perplexed, found that even his child lacked the serpent birthmark. Seeking answers, he went to the gods, but none were given. The king observed these individuals, recognizing that they possessed the same abilities as the prodigies before them, even though they were not their descendants, yet none had the Serpent King's unique power or birthmark. Consequently, the Serpent King decided to divide the clans into ten, one for each prodigy."

Raven frowned. "But there are eleven clans?"

"There were those who chose to remain with him, loyal to him and his descendants. They believed that his offspring would one day bear the true Serpent birthmark, making them the genuine rulers," Valentina explained. "That clan became the ShadowFang clan, comprising loyal individuals whose sole purpose was to protect your bloodline and ensure the birth of the true Serpent ruler. They were correct; every century or so, the true heir is born. You keep us safe, and the prodigies' only purpose is to rule for generations as stand-ins for your rebirth."

Raven sighed and leaned back, absorbing all the information.

"I have so many questions."

Valentina chuckled lightly. "Sadly, we do not have many answers. Everything we know is what was taught to us, passed by word of mouth and text. There are a lot of questions we all wish to have answered."

A sharp breath left Raven's lips. "If I am the true queen…that means there doesn't have to be a Shadow Gauntlet?"

"Yes!" Valentina cheered, tackling Raven. "That's the best part! The true heir negates the ritual."

Raven chuckled, but her mind was still reeling. "There's just one problem."

Valentina propped herself up, brows furrowing. "What?"

"I don't have powers."

Valentina tilted her head. "When's your eighteenth birthday?"

"Two weeks."

"Then in two weeks, you will."

Raven swallowed hard, heart pounding. If the legends were true, everything was about to change.

"Do you think they know?" she murmured.

"The other prodigies?"

"No, my people." Her voice dropped lower. "And if my mother was a descendant of the Serpent King, why would King Pierre and the Widow Clan turn on us? If anyone found out, wouldn't he be tried for treason?"

Valentina ran her hands soothingly over Raven's arms. "I am not sure. None of it makes sense… unless there's something we're missing. The sooner we find the old records, the more answers we'll have."

Raven gazed up at her, heart fluttering.

"Are we allowed to have queens by our side?"

Valentina smirked. "Why? Do you have someone in mind?" She leaned closer, her lips barely brushing Raven's.

Raven closed the distance, pressing a soft kiss to her lips. "If anyone deserves to rule the clans, it's you."

Valentina's fingers traced Raven's lips. For a moment, she

hesitated. Then, forehead against forehead, eyes closed, she whispered, "I think I love you."

Raven smiled, warmth swelling within her. Love had been an abstract concept before, something distant and uncertain. But this— this felt real. She would go to great lengths for the girl before her, willing to burn down cities to keep her safe.

Valentina brought her a peace Raven had never known, as if a single touch could still all the chaos in her life. There was no hesitation, no doubt—only the quiet certainty that Valentina would stand by her through anything.

"I love you," she breathed.

Valentina opened her eyes, meeting Raven's gaze with unguarded affection.

Raven kissed her once more, lingering before gently shifting their positions. Valentina sat on the bed now, while Raven stood between her legs, hands braced on either side of her hips.

"I need to keep writing down what I know," Raven said, her voice steady despite the lingering tenderness between them. "We still have to go over the third book."

Valentina made a sound of protest and grabbed Raven's shirt from the floor, holding it up with a smirk. "Put this back on first. You're too distracting." Her gaze lingered appreciatively on the lean muscles of Raven's arms and shoulders.

Raven chuckled, taking the shirt and slipping it on with a wink. "Better?"

Valentina hummed. "Debatable."

Shaking her head in amusement, Raven returned to her desk. The moment she picked up her pen, the outside world faded. Words flowed effortlessly, pulled from the depths of her memory, driven by a relentless need to record everything before it slipped away.

Time blurred.

She didn't notice Valentina rummaging through the closet or hear her leave and return until a gentle tap on her shoulder brought her back.

Raven blinked up, startled, as Valentina held out a plate of food. "You've been at it for hours," she said with a soft smile. "I wasn't sure if you ate, so I thought you might need this."

Only then did Raven realize how tight her shoulders had become, how empty her stomach felt. She glanced at Valentina's sweater—one that bore a sigil not of her own clan but another.

"Are you allowed to wear that," Raven said, raising an eyebrow.

Valentina shrugged. "There's no written rule, but it's an unspoken thing—wearing another clan's sigil can be seen as aligning yourself with them."

"Are you not worried about what people will assume?"

Valentina smoothed a hand over the fabric. "I align myself with you. Whatever clan you fall under, that's where I stand." Her voice carried an edge of defiance. "Anyone who has a problem with it can take it up with me."

Raven let out a low chuckle, setting her plate aside. "And here I thought I was the aggressive one."

Valentina grinned. "Eat." She settled onto the floor, her own plate resting beside her. "And tell me what you wrote."

Raven took a bite, savoring the rich flavors before flipping through the stack of papers beside her. "I'm not sure yet," she admitted. "Unless I focus on recalling what I read, it's just... knowledge waiting to be revisited." She divided the pages, handing a stack to Valentina. "Here, go through this. We'll compare notes."

Valentina took the papers, glancing at Raven before setting them down. "And when we finally uncover the truth about the betrayal?"

Raven's expression darkened as she stared at the door, jaw tightening.

"They won't make it to trial."

Silence hung between them. Then Valentina let out a quiet hum of acknowledgment and took a deliberate bite of her burrito.

They lapsed into a comfortable rhythm—reading, eating,

thinking. Occasionally, Valentina snorted at the audacity of the words on the page, shaking her head in disbelief. Raven, watching her from the corner of her eye, couldn't help but smile.

Some of the delusions these so-called rulers held were beyond comprehension.

And soon, those illusions would shatter.

After scanning through countless pages, Raven finally read aloud: "Journal Entry. Councilor Magna. Date, 24th Crescent Moon, Year of the Crimson Widow.

"The whispers of destiny echo through the corridors of time, affirming that the Crimson Widow Clan is the chosen vessel for the reign of Nethrala. Within our council chambers, where the tapestries recount the ancient tales of our supremacy, I inscribe these words as a testament to the grand design guiding our every step.

"As a member of the Council, entrusted with steering the Crimson Widow Clan toward its rightful destiny, I find solace in the conviction that courses through our veins. Our pursuit of dominance over the other ten clans is not arrogance—it is divine obligation, woven into the very fabric of our existence. Nethrala is a canvas upon which our celestial prowess shall be painted; the other clans, mere actors in the grand drama unfolding under the gods' watchful gaze.

"We unravel unity among the lesser clans. Diplomacy is our silent dagger, slicing through alliances with precision. Deception is our ally, whispers the agents of our influence. The other clans, blinded by delusions of significance, fail to grasp the divine mandate propelling us forward. Our martial prowess shall be the instrument through which Nethrala is reshaped, molded into the image of the Crimson Widow's eternal rule.

"The stars align, and destiny calls. The time is near. As a member of the Council, I am honored to be an architect of this inevitable triumph. May the gods witness our ascension and bless our path to supremacy."

As Raven's voice trailed off, a silence settled between them.

Valentina had set her burrito down, elbows resting on her

knees, fingers laced beneath her chin. She exhaled slowly, eyes narrowed as she processed the words.

Raven leaned back in her chair, the pages still in hand. "They speak of ascension as though it's their birthright," she muttered. "Like the gods themselves handed them a throne."

Valentina scoffed. "There is no hierarchy among the clans. The only one respected above all was the ShadowFang Clan—for obvious reasons. I don't see what they thought they were rising to."

Raven frowned, her fingers tightening on the pages. "Widow's clan head is close with the king. Maybe that's what they meant. And now, with my clan gone, they believe they have a clear path—especially if Phantom wins the gauntlet."

Valentina chewed the inside of her lip. "Maybe. But you said King Pierre isn't going to give up his crown."

She didn't say it, but Raven caught the implication in her tone. Even if the Crimson Widows saw themselves as destined rulers, Pierre was the real power.

"A theory." Raven sighed.

Valentina echoed the words in a thoughtful whisper.

"I was told you were favored to win the gauntlet," Raven said.

Valentina hummed. "You never really know when the time comes. The weakest among us turn the most feral when their lives are on the line." She met Raven's gaze as the other woman placed her papers down. "I feel like we still have too many unanswered questions."

Raven nodded. She wasn't any closer to the truth than when she had started. If this book yielded nothing, they would have to dig deeper. And if that failed? She would have to take matters into her own hands.

The thought chilled her. Torturing Magna, revealing herself to the clans, openly challenging King Pierre—none of these aligned with the careful plan she had envisioned. She wanted them to suffer, to face justice. To bring the Crimson Widows to their knees.

These books had to give her what she needed.

"Keep reading," Raven said. "Let me know if you find anything useful. This stack is worthless." She held up a handful of pages before dropping them onto the desk.

Valentina nodded and resumed reading.

Raven watched her, memorizing every detail—how her brow furrowed in concentration, the slight tilt of her head, the way the firelight caught the edges of her hair. She knew Valentina could feel her gaze, yet she didn't shy away.

Raven exhaled, and the smallest sigh slipped past her lips.

Valentina looked up, one brow raised.

"Just admiring," Raven murmured.

Valentina smiled before turning back to the pages.

She doesn't even know. The depth of what Raven felt for her. No book could put it into words. No story could do it justice.

Valentina abruptly turned to face Raven and held out a few papers. "This is it."

Raven took the papers and let her eyes scan the passage:

Journal Entry - Councilor Magna

Date: 7th Bloodmoon, Year of Celestial Ascendancy

The council has spoken.

The Shadowfang Clan is a threat. We have suspected it for some time, but now the whispers have turned into something more— dangerous murmurs of a hidden heir. An obstacle we cannot afford.

The Widow Council has decided. There will be no war, no outright slaughter. A subtler hand is needed. I have sent emissaries under the guise of an alliance. They will guide the Shadowfang clan into a mission, where no one returns. They will march toward their own deaths, believing the mission holds purpose.

Their blood will stain the earth before they ever realize they were betrayed.

The heir, if they exist, will die with them. And the Crimson Widows will rise—unchallenged, unbroken. I do not take this lightly. Some would call it a massacre. I call it fate.

Raven read the entry again. And again. This was it.

She lifted her gaze to Valentina. "We're stealing the fourth book and going back for the third."

Valentina exhaled. "If we steal the fourth, they'll lock down the third."

"I know." Raven placed the pages down. "But we need both. If we don't have the original sources, they'll say I forged this."

Valentina met her stare. "This is dangerous."

"Everything we do is dangerous." Raven reached for Valentina's hand, threading their fingers together. "Will you keep walking this path with me? Even if it gets worse?"

"Even if it kills me," Valentina said without hesitation.

Raven brought her fingers to her lips, pressing a soft kiss to them. *No one will take you from me.*

20

The very room where Raven had first encountered Asha on her first day at school had become her refuge. The silence wrapped around her like a protective cocoon, a sanctuary where no one dared intrude unless she allowed it. Privacy was essential—especially now, as she hunted for the elusive fourth book. She couldn't risk prying eyes or inconvenient questions.

Before her, a meticulously drawn map of Nethrala sprawled across the table. The island was vast, but its terrain, surprisingly, was manageable on foot. Nature reigned over most of it, save for the bustling town that catered to assassins, providing them with food, clothing, and distractions. Clans' mansions blended into the surrounding forests, their hidden locations safeguarding the secrets of their respective factions.

Raven traced the map with her fingertips, her eyes scanning the symbols and references in the legend. She found the school's location and marked it with a swift stroke of her pencil. Then, retrieving a protractor, she leaned forward, carefully plotting the coordinates of the final book—its placement burned into her memory. When she straightened, her gaze lingered on the distance between the two points. Relief flickered through her—the school's central location made travel easier—but that relief was short-lived. The book lay atop a mountain peak.

Her fingers drummed lightly against the map as she considered the implications. Nethrala's climate was temperate, its landscapes often bathed in mist and shifting clouds. Perhaps that was the point. A book hidden atop a mountain was less a coincidence and more a calculated decision—its placement a perfect disguise, buried within nature's own illusions.

A sharp knock fractured the silence. Raven tensed, glancing toward the door. Who would come here, unannounced?

Cautiously, she cracked the door open.

"You missed class," a familiar, melodic voice teased, sending a jolt through her.

Valentina.

Raven's gaze flicked to the clock—a silent confirmation that she had, in fact, missed Asha's lecture. Not that she'd forgotten, exactly. She just hadn't cared enough to go.

Valentina tilted her head. "Are you planning to skip the rest of the day, too?"

"And lunch?" A second voice chimed in—Emilia, stepping into view. The scent of warm food drifted through the doorway as she lifted a bag.

Raven exhaled, the corner of her lips twitching. She stepped back, allowing them inside.

Valentina strode toward the table, her sharp gaze immediately locking onto the map and its markings. Emilia, more relaxed, sank into a chair and placed the bag beside her, already unpacking its contents.

"Shadows Peak," Valentina murmured, running a fingertip over the mountain's location.

Raven's brows lifted. "You know it?"

Valentina nodded.

"It's where prodigies go for their official training initiation,"

Emilia supplied, unboxing the food. "A pilgrimage. They make the journey every year."

Raven's mind sharpened. "When's the next one?"

Valentina paused, considering. "Next month, I think. It always happens a few months before the Shadow Gauntlet. A ritual of reverence, I suppose."

Raven leaned back. The timing was almost perfect. If she could blend into the pilgrimage, she could retrieve the book without drawing suspicion. No sudden disappearances. No unexplained absences. Just another prodigy participating in tradition.

She glanced at Emilia, who had gone quiet, her fingers tapping idly against the table in an unconscious rhythm.

"Emilia," Raven said, watching closely.

Her friend stilled. "Hmm?"

Raven narrowed her eyes. "What do you know about my birthmark?"

A flicker of something—guilt? Uncertainty?—crossed Emilia's face, but it was gone in an instant. "I'm not sure what you mean."

Lie.

The telltale signs were there. The tension in her jaw. The deliberate avoidance of eye contact. The tapping of her fingers, now slightly quicker.

Raven pressed forward, voice sharpening. "I've been doing some research. Turns out my birthmark is tied to something much bigger than I thought. Want to tell me why you've kept that from me?" Emilia's mask cracked. Her gaze dropped, a long exhale escaping her lips.

"Yes, my queen," she murmured.

The words hit like a slap. Raven stiffened, her mind scrambling to process them. Queen.

She wasn't just keeping secrets. She had known all along.

Raven sat back, arms folding over her chest as the weight of betrayal settled into her bones. Emilia had been her friend. Someone she trusted. And yet—

Her gaze flicked to Valentina, who had remained silent, focused on her meal. A quiet bystander to the conversation.

Raven's fingers curled into a fist.

"Does Asha and Ms. Moretti know?" she asked, voice cold.

Emilia didn't answered.

And that, more than anything, told her everything she needed to know.

Emilia finally nodded, regret shading her admission. "Your mother entrusted us with the truth, binding us to silence," she confessed. "She wanted you to forge your own path—free of expectation."

Frustration coiled within Raven, her jaw tightening. She couldn't fault Emilia for honoring her mothers wishes, but the isolation gnawed at her. She was always behind in the game of assassins , always struggling to catch up while everyone else played by rules she didn't even know.

Sensing Raven's anger, Emilia rose, crossing the room to kneel beside her. She took Raven's hand, her touch soothing.

"Il mia grazioso uccello," Emilia murmured. "You bear enough burdens—fighting for your clan, seeking justice, navigating alliances. The weight of your birthright is just another layer of chaos in an already turbulent world."

Raven sighed and pressed her forehead against Emilia's, her anger dissolving into something softer. A longing for simpler times.

"I miss when we were kids," she admitted.

Emilia chuckled, a bittersweet sound. "Ah, yes. Not a care in the world. Which is why we got into so much trouble."

Raven smirked. "You got us into trouble." She reached for Valentina's hand, grounding herself in their shared presence. "I love you both. This mission is dangerous—promise me you'll stay by my side. I can't lose either of you."

Valentina squeezed her hand in silent affirmation, while Emilia pressed a kiss to her brow.

Raven pulled away and turned her attention to the map spread across the table. "By the time we reach Shadows Peak, my powers will have fully manifested. Whatever they are, I need to be ready."

"Do you really think you can master the power of the serpent in a month?" Valentina's skepticism was clear.

Raven's lips curled in a knowing smile. "I could've bested you when I was five."

Valentina laughed, easing the tension between them. "Very well. Let's see what gifts you've been given. We'll train relentlessly until Shadows Peak."

Raven nodded, determination steady in her veins.

As they ate, their conversation turned to the Widow Clan's message. Raven favored a bold, public declaration, rallying the assassin community. Emilia preferred a quieter, more strategic approach—spreading their influence subtly. Valentina proposed a grand display, an announcement to all of Nethrala.

Their debate circled with no clear resolution. Frustration built, but before they could push further, Emilia stood. "I have to go. Onyx awaits our rendezvous."

Raven's expression tightened. She didn't trust Onyx, but she wouldn't voice her concerns. It wasn't her place to dictate Emilia's choices—only to be there when the consequences came.

Emilia met her gaze briefly, then slipped out the door.

Raven exhaled, shoving her unease aside.

Valentina lingered in the doorway, watching her.

"Waiting for me?" Raven asked, an edge of playfulness in her voice.

Valentina smiled, warmth flickering in her green eyes. Their hands found each other effortlessly, and she pulled Raven close.
Their lips met—soft, grounding, familiar. A promise without words.

"Sleepover tonight?" Raven asked, her voice quieter now.

Valentina's eyes gleamed. "Only if you tell me more about your childhood. You and Emilia have quite the history."

Raven hummed in thought. "Emilia taught me the importance

of connection. Of embracing vulnerability instead of fearing it. Without her, I might never have acknowledged my feelings for you."

Valentina tilted her head. "So, I'm your weakness?"

A slow smile spread across Raven's face. "You're my strength. And my greatest vulnerability."

Valentina brushed her fingers along Raven's cheek, her touch featherlight. "I refuse to lose you."

Raven's grip on her tightened. "I would fight wars for you. Set the world ablaze if I had to." Her voice wavered, but her conviction did not.

Valentina's lips curled into a knowing smile. "I'm grateful our love burns just as fiercely. I would love to sleep over."

The next day, Raven stood before her professors, stoic as ever. Their voices droned with disappointment, yet she offered only a carefully composed expression—shoulders square, chin high, contrition sketched across her face like a mask she'd worn a thousand times before. But beneath the surface, defiance simmered. She didn't regret skipping class.

By lunch, the tension of the morning had faded. The cafeteria buzzed with noise, but at their table, it felt like a time capsule—just the three of them, locked in laughter and memories.

"I used to idolize you both," Emilia said between giggles, wiping at tears that spilled freely now. "You were like superheroes. With your abilities and everything, I thought you could do anything."

"And the serpent drawing Emilia wore was legendary," Valentina added with a grin, eyes flicking to Raven. "I always wondered what possessed her to flaunt it like that."

Raven laughed, the sound warm and free, her hands raised in mock surrender. "Guilty. It was a terrible idea, but… it made sense back then."

It had been her idea. A mark to make her feel less alone, to turn make-believe into belonging. Emilia had gone along with it without hesitation, drawing that serpent birthmark on herself with all the pride and love a child could muster. It had been more than a game—it was a bond.

"People thought I was weird for it," Emilia mused, sipping her drink, eyes distant. "But some admired my courage. Even if the prodigies hated it."

Valentina gave a dry laugh, her voice softer now. "I didn't hate you. I envied you. You could wipe your mark away. We couldn't. Ours was permanent—our fate tattooed into our skin."

Wordlessly, Raven reached for her hand, peeling back the glove Valentina wore like armor. There it was. The mark that tied all prodigies together. Her thumb brushed the serpent's curve.

"I admire you," Raven said quietly. "For bearing this. For still being kind. Still being you."

For a moment, the world narrowed to just the two of them. Raven realized then—truly realized—Valentina would stand beside her, no matter what came next.

Valentina's smile was faint, but it reached her eyes. "Funny how things turn out. I kind of like having it now. Can't risk anyone mistaking me for Emilia."

"Hey!" Emilia scoffed, tossing a piece of fruit at her. Valentina dodged easily, laughing.

"I have skills, you know," Emilia huffed. "Who do you think trained Raven before she got all elite?"

"She's not wrong," Raven admitted with a smirk. "Emilia taught me most of what I know. I spent years kicking her butt."

"Until Asha got involved," Emilia added proudly. "But yeah, I was the first. And she always picked stuff up in two tries. Two! Do you know how annoying that is?"

"It's a gift," Raven said simply.

"It's theft," Emilia shot back.

"Two tries?" Valentina arched a brow. "I expected better."

Raven's smirk widened. "I have to stay humble."

"I would've nailed it on the first try."

Raven turned to her, brows raised. "Are you challenging me, my love?"

Valentina flushed. "I'm just saying. You talk a big game."

Raven's eyes glittered. "You did land a hit on me. But let's not pretend I didn't let you."

Valentina narrowed her eyes, a playful warning in her smile.

She leaned in. "Training room. Five minutes."

She stood, slipping on her glove with quiet precision, and walked away—leaving Raven grinning at her retreating form.

Emilia snorted. "You're in trouble."

"You think she can beat me?"

"That's not the point," Emilia said, rising from her chair. "It's not about who can win. It's about you respecting her strength."

Raven blinked. "I respect her strength."

"You just said you let her hit you."

"Because I did."

Emilia groaned. "Raven. Sometimes it's not what you say—it's how you say it."

Raven rolled her eyes. "Should I really be taking advice from you? Your last relationship was a disaster."

"I hate you," Emilia muttered, walking ahead.

"You could never hate me," Raven teased, slinging an arm around her shoulder.

Emilia didn't answer. But the smirk tugging at her lips said enough. "I hope she gives you a run for your money," Emilia teased, her voice carrying a hint of playful challenge.

Raven only smirked, ignoring the quick thrum of anticipation in her chest as they stepped into the training room.

They didn't expect anyone else to be there. But Asha was already waiting, lounging on a bench as if she had all the time in the world. She looked completely at ease, one leg crossed over the other, eyes sharp and unreadable.

Valentina stood a few paces away, deep in quiet conversation with her. But the moment Raven entered, Valentina turned—and her gaze locked onto Raven's with a look that made something flutter warm and unsteady in her chest.

"I didn't think you'd actually show," Valentina called, a slow smile curving across her lips.

Raven arched a brow, letting her grin match Valentina's. "And miss the chance to remind you who's the dominant one in this relationship?" she countered, her tone light but threaded with a spark of challenge.

Valentina rolled her eyes, though a flush crept up her neck. "You're impossible," she muttered, but she was already turning, her steps steady as she strode to the sparring area.

There was nothing fancy about it—just a wide space outlined with a single length of rope. No markers, no elaborate boundaries. Raven liked it that way. Simple. Honest.

Valentina paused at the weapons rack, her hand hovering over the array laid out in precise rows. She didn't look back when she spoke, but her voice was soft, almost thoughtful.

"Weapons or no weapons?"

Raven hesitated, just for a moment. The idea of striking Valentina—of feeling the impact of her own strength against her— made something tighten in her throat.

"Weapons," she decided quietly. She needed the distance they offered. Something to stand between them if the fight got too close, too real.

Valentina nodded once, silent as she chose her blade. Each movement was deliberate, methodical—like she was giving the choice the respect it deserved.

Raven turned away, needing something else to look at. She found Asha watching her, Emilia at her side. For a second, Raven thought she saw something almost like worry in Asha's eyes.

"What brings you here?" Raven asked, trying to sound casual.

Asha tilted her head, her expression unreadable. "It is my

classroom," she said simply, gesturing to the empty space around them.

Emilia made a small, disgruntled noise under her breath. "One of many," she muttered, not quite loud enough to be a real challenge but not soft enough to be ignored either.

Asha's gaze flicked to Emilia, a quick, measuring glance, before settling back on Raven. Her expression didn't change—calm, composed, impossible to read.

"Why are you fighting Valentina?" she asked, her voice deceptively mild. "And do you ever get tired of fighting?"

Raven's answer came without hesitation, her tone edged with something sharp. "We're sparring," she said flatly. "And no." She let the word hang between them, defiant.

But something restless stirred in her chest, something that made her add—almost without thinking—"Maybe it has something to do with me being the true heir."

The flicker in Asha's eyes was there and gone in a heartbeat, but Raven saw it. The tiny pulse of panic. The way her arms folded tighter across her chest.

Raven felt a cold satisfaction curl through her. She let it show in the smile that ghosted across her lips—small, humorless.

"We'll talk about this later," she said, her voice low, steady. "And I expect the truth. My birthday's in two weeks. I don't know what you had planned for that day, but if I'm going to wake up throwing fire from my hands, I'd appreciate a little warning."

Her gaze shifted to Emilia, who hadn't looked up. She stood motionless, staring at the floor as if it might swallow her whole.

"All of you," Raven added, her voice softening into disappointment. "Have left much to be desired."

She turned on her heel before anyone could answer. Each step toward the weapons rack landed with quiet finality.

Raven chose a faux sword, testing its weight in her hand. Familiar. Solid. Something she could control when everything else felt like it was slipping out of reach.

When she turned back, Valentina was waiting inside the ring, her posture loose but her eyes bright, alive with the same restless energy that thrummed under Raven's skin.

Raven crossed the rope line and slowed, taking her in—the way the light framed her, the unguarded warmth in her expression, the effortless grace she never seemed aware of.

"You're beautiful," Raven murmured, her voice so low it was meant for Valentina alone. The words slipped out, unplanned and too honest to swallow back.

Valentina stilled as Raven approached, her bouncing energy quieting to something softer. She met Raven halfway, reaching up to tuck a stray curl behind her ear. Then she leaned in, pressing a gentle kiss to Raven's mouth—just a brush of lips, light as a promise, but it left Raven's heart skittering against her ribs.

When Raven opened her eyes, she was smiling, warmth curling in her chest despite the anticipation thrumming in her veins. "That kiss won't save you," she teased, her voice low but bright with challenge.

Valentina's laugh rang out, clear and effortless. "I'd never expect it to," she said, her grin lingering as she turned away, her steps smooth as water.

But the moment she pivoted back, the softness was gone. She moved with assassin's precision—silent, sudden. Her sword arched down in a clean strike that would have landed square across Raven's shoulder.

Raven's reflexes snapped into place. She blocked the blow, their blades colliding with a force that sent Valentina sliding back several feet.

Valentina didn't hesitate. She caught her balance in one fluid motion, her laughter low and exhilarated as she lunged again.

Steel clashed in a flurry of strikes—each one faster, sharper. They moved like two halves of the same thought, neither yielding, neither breaking the rhythm. It wasn't just sparring. It was something older and deeper—a language they both understood without ever needing to speak it.

The ring echoed with each impact, the sound a steady percussion to the heat building in Raven's chest.

And then—

A shift.

Something inside her uncoiled, huge and electric, surging through her like a tide she couldn't hold back.

Raven tried to shake it off. She gripped her sword tighter, lunging forward, determined to ground herself in the familiarity of movement.

But as Valentina sidestepped and turned to counter, the world fell away.

Darkness swallowed her whole.

One heartbeat she was there, blade raised— The next, nothing.

No light. No sound. Just a void so complete it pressed against her skin like cold hands.

"Raven!"

Her name reached her, distant, echoing off invisible walls. She spun in place, breath ragged, heart hammering.

"Valentina?" she called out, but her voice dissolved into the black.

Panic rising, Raven lifted a hand, hoping to touch—anything. The floor. The rope. Another person.

Her fingers closed on emptiness.

Again, she heard her name—this time sharper, edged with urgency.

Asha's voice.

Raven's breath hitched, something fierce and determined cutting through the panic. She turned toward the sound, her first steps slow, hesitant. Then faster.

She broke into a sprint, chasing that flicker of light in the endless dark.

Her heartbeat thundered as she ran, her feet striking ground she couldn't see, until finally—

She broke through.

The darkness fell away in an instant. She hit the floor hard, landing in a tangle of limbs at Valentina's feet.

"Raven!"

Valentina was there in a heartbeat, dropping to her knees. Her hands framed Raven's face, gentle but searching.

"Are you okay?" she asked, voice raw with worry.

Raven dragged in a shaky breath, her chest tight, tears blurring her vision. "What…what just happened?" Her gaze darted to Emilia, then Asha, searching for something—answers, reassurance, anything to make sense of it.

The three exchanged a look—something heavy and unspoken passing between them—before Valentina leaned closer, her thumb brushing a tear from Raven's cheek.

"I think your powers came early," she said softly, as if speaking too loudly might shatter what was left of Raven's composure. There was awe in her voice. And something like fear.

Raven's frown deepened, her pulse skittering. "Powers?" she echoed, her voice rising. "I was—there was nothing. No light, no sound. It was like being swallowed whole. What kind of power does that?"

Asha stepped forward, her face solemn.

"Shadows," she said quietly. Her eyes searched Raven's, as if trying to gauge how much she understood. "It's a gift that hasn't appeared since the time of the first Serpent King."

Raven's breath caught. For a second, she thought she'd misheard.

"What does that mean?" she asked, her voice barely above a whisper. Instinctively, she reached for Valentina, grounding herself in the warm press of her hand.

Asha held her gaze, her own steady but shadowed.

"It means," she said, each word deliberate, "that we have no idea how to help you control it."

21

Raven sat cross-legged on the floor, the weight of solitude pressing against her like an invisible force. Valentina and Emilia had given her space, sensing that their presence would do little to ease her turmoil. She appreciated their restraint, though their absence only deepened the silence she could not escape.

Before her lay an ancient tome, its brittle pages whispering of the enigmatic Serpent King. She scanned the text, searching for insight, but the words blurred into the same tired myths Valentina had already told her. With a frustrated exhale, she snapped the book shut. Nothing.

"I bet my clan could have provided answers," she muttered, her voice tight with resentment. A sharp pang bloomed in her chest, a mix of anger and longing threatening to spill as tears welled in her eyes. She clenched her fists, swallowing the ache that clawed at her throat. If only her mother were here. If only her clan had not been taken from her.

She inhaled deeply, closing her eyes. Breathe. She willed

herself into meditation, seeking the calm beneath the storm. But the silence was not a refuge—it was a reminder. Of everything she had lost. Of everything she had never even had the chance to know.

"Please, help me find my way," she whispered, her plea vanishing into the still air.

Time passed, though she barely noticed. The world beyond her mind faded, replaced by the quiet hum of her own existence. She reached inward, searching for that elusive spark—the power she had felt flicker inside her earlier that day. But the harder she grasped for it, the farther it slipped from reach.

Frustration surged. With a sigh, she opened her eyes, stretching her arms. As she did, something shifted. A sudden jolt pulsed through her body—a crackle of energy that leapt from her fingertips in jagged, electric arcs.

Raven gasped.

The air around her shimmered as tendrils of electricity danced across her skin. It should have felt foreign. But instead, it was… familiar. As though it had always been there, waiting for her to notice.

She flexed her fingers, testing the current. It obeyed. Effortlessly. Without the strain, without the concentration her other ability demanded. As if it were an extension of her very being.

Her lips curled into a slow smile. This… this, she could work with.

Asha would help her master it—of that, she was certain.

For the first time in what felt like forever, Raven felt something stir within her. Not just power. Hope.

Eager to share her discovery, Raven sprang to her feet, a surge of excitement propelling her toward the door. The dimly lit hallway stretched before her, shadows clinging to the walls like silent sentinels. The academy grounds were treacherous at night, but that didn't matter. Not now. Not when she had uncovered something that could change everything.

Her footsteps echoed softly against the polished floor as she stole a glance at the clock. A quarter past ten. A flicker of hesitation gnawed at her resolve. Was it wise to disturb Valentina at this hour? Would she even be awake?

The thought lingered as she stepped beyond the reach of the flickering torchlight, surrendering herself to the waiting darkness.

And then—

Everything shifted.

The walls that should have enclosed her were gone. The familiar corridor had unraveled into an abyss, a vast nothingness stretching in every direction.

Her breath hitched. No floor. No ceiling. No guiding landmarks.

Panic clawed at the edges of her mind, but she wrestled it into submission. Fear was a luxury she couldn't afford. Instead, she let the emptiness settle around her, mirroring the void she carried within herself.

She moved forward, careful, deliberate. Her thoughts drifted to Valentina, to the warmth of her presence, to the way she could anchor Raven even in the most uncertain moments. Maybe she was asleep. Maybe this could wait. But the need to see her, to share what she had discovered, was stronger than reason.

Then—

A sharp impact. A sudden jolt as her body pitched forward.

She hit the ground hard, the breath knocked from her lungs. Before she could recover, an unseen weight pressed down on her, pinning her in place. Cold metal kissed her throat.

A blade.

The realization sent a pulse of alarm through her, but she forced herself to remain still. *Stay calm. Don't startle her.*

"Val—" The whisper barely left her lips before the grip on the weapon tightened.

Through the haze of dim light, Valentina's face loomed above her, eyes stormy, unreadable. Her breath came in sharp bursts, fingers trembling against the hilt of the knife.

Then, something shifted. Recognition flickered across her

features. The blade clattered to the floor, the metallic clang slicing through the silence.

With a sharp movement, she turned away, retreating toward the bathroom without a word.

Raven exhaled shakily, pressing a hand to her throat. A thin bead of warmth trickled down her skin. Not deep. Just enough to remind her how close she had come to something irreversible.

As the overhead lights flared to life, she blinked against the sudden brightness. The room unfolded before her, its every detail impossibly sharp, impossibly vivid.

The floating bed draped in silken pillows. The bookshelves entwined with delicate vines. The circular rug that burned like a captured sunrise beneath her.

And the bean bag chairs—the ones she had tripped over.

Realization settled over her like a slow-moving storm.

She had walked through shadows. Through space. Through something she couldn't yet comprehend.

And she had no idea how to find her way back.

Returning with a damp towel in hand, Valentina approached Raven with careful precision, her touch featherlight as she wiped away the trickle of blood marring Raven's porcelain skin. "I'm so sorry," she murmured, voice hushed with guilt.

Raven offered a small smile, meant to reassure. "It's okay," she said, her gaze meeting Valentina's with sincerity. "I would've reacted the same way."

Yet, despite her words, doubt lingered in Valentina's dark eyes, a shadow that Raven couldn't quite dispel.

Eager to shift the mood, Raven glanced around. "Your room is really warm and welcoming," she noted, her admiration genuine.

A faint smile softened Valentina's features. She discarded the towel and turned back to Raven. "I'm glad you like it," she murmured, almost shyly. Taking Raven's hand, she led them to the window seat, where moonlight bathed the cushions in silver light. With a gentle tug, she urged Raven to sit beside her.

Raven's gaze drifted beyond the glass, drawn to the courtyard below. The soft lamplights cast long shadows over the pathways, their golden glow lending an air of serenity. The silence of the night wrapped around them like a cocoon.

Beside her, Valentina studied her intently. The weight of her scrutiny pulled Raven from her thoughts.

"Is something wrong?" Raven asked, brow furrowing.

Valentina hesitated, her expression unreadable. "I feel like I should be asking you that."

Raven blinked. "Why would you think that?"

A wry smile tugged at Valentina's lips. She leaned in slightly, searching Raven's face. "Because you've never come to my room before. Especially not in the middle of the night."

Raven let out a soft laugh. "Well, I only got here two weeks ago." She glanced at the window, then back at Valentina. "And it's not the middle of the night. It's barely ten."

Valentina arched a brow. "Try one in the morning."

Surprised, Raven looked at the slim watch on Valentina's wrist. Sure enough, the hour hand had crept past one. A quiet hum left her lips.

"One in the morning," she echoed. That... didn't feel right. Hadn't she only been in her room for a little while? The realization settled uneasily in her stomach.

"Raven," Valentina's voice pulled her back.

She forced a reassuring smile. "Do you want me to go?"

A faint flush colored Valentina's cheeks. She looked down, fidgeting with her fingers. "No," she admitted, then exhaled a soft chuckle. "I'm just worried."

Raven covered Valentina's hands with her own, their warmth steadying. "I'm fine," she assured her. "Actually, I came because I wanted to tell you—I discovered something."

Valentina perked up. "What is it?"

Raven nodded, excitement lighting her features. "Another power. I was in my room, trying to figure out the whole shadow thing, and—"

A sharp crackle snapped between their hands.

Valentina yelped, jerking away, her fingers tingling. "What the hell?" She rubbed her palm, staring at Raven with wide eyes.

Raven's heart pounded. She stared at her own hand, where faint sparks still danced along her fingertips.

"I am so sorry," Raven apologized, her voice tight with genuine contrition. "I didn't mean to do that."

Valentina flexed her fingers, placing her hand on her lap with a reassuring smile. "It's okay, it didn't actually hurt. It just caught me off guard."

Raven studied Valentina's expression intently, searching for any hint of deception. But Valentina met her gaze with unwavering honesty.

Raven exhaled and lifted her hands, turning them so her palms faced upward. Electricity crackled along her skin, the faint blue light dancing across her fingers. "I have some sort of electrical power," she murmured, her tone laced with both excitement and uncertainty. "I'm not sure what that means yet, but I can control it—at least, to an extent. It travels up my arms, and I can make it appear when I want." As if to demonstrate, she let the energy fade, the crackling sparks vanishing into nothing.

Valentina nodded, her expression thoughtful. "There were two true heirs before you who had electrical powers," she mused. "But their abilities didn't work the way yours do."

Raven frowned. "Do you think they just had different limitations, or does power manifest differently for each heir?"

Valentina's gaze drifted toward the courtyard window, her brow furrowing in contemplation. "That's a good question," she admitted, her voice laced with curiosity. Then, with a teasing glint in her eyes, she turned back to Raven. "Do you believe you'll wield all their abilities and more?"

Raven straightened, determination flashing in her gaze. "I think I can do whatever I put my mind to. And I refuse to be weak."

Valentina's lips parted, as if to respond, but something in her expression shifted. A flicker of confusion. A pause. Then she abruptly stood. Without a word, she strode to the door, gripping the handle firmly—only to find it wouldn't budge.

Raven arched an eyebrow. "What's wrong?"

Valentina turned slowly, confusion etched into her features. "Raven," she said carefully, "how did you get in here?"

Raven hesitated. "I... I'm not sure," she admitted, a frown tugging at her lips. "I was in the hallway, thinking about telling you about my powers. Then suddenly, I was in the void. I got nervous and started thinking about what I should do. Next thing I knew, I tripped— and I landed here."

Valentina's fingers tightened around the door handle. "That's not possible."

Raven's brow furrowed. "What do you mean?"

Valentina exhaled sharply and let go of the handle. "Did this happen around ten?"

Raven blinked. "Yeah. Why?"

Valentina crossed the room and perched beside her on the window seat. "That means you were in the void for hours. But it only felt like a few minutes to you?"

Raven exhaled in frustration. "The shadow thing is frustrating. I don't understand how time, or anything, works there."

Valentina chuckled softly, shaking her head. "You've had your powers for less than twenty-four hours. Be patient."

Raven playfully rolled her eyes and stretched. "I should go."

Valentina stood, warmth shining in her eyes. "Stay," she murmured.

Raven smiled softly, shaking her head. "I shouldn't. You have classes tomorrow."

A flicker of disappointment crossed Valentina's features, her lower lip caught between her teeth. "Sleep with me tonight," she whispered. "You've never stayed in my room before. I want to wake up with you here."

Raven's breath hitched at the quiet sincerity in Valentina's voice. The request wasn't about desire—it was about comfort, connection. Warmth bloomed in her chest, and she nodded. "Okay."

A radiant smile spread across Valentina's face. She hurried to close the drapes, then led Raven to the bed. The air between them hummed with something unspoken—not urgency, but understanding.

Valentina slipped under the blankets beside her, and Raven felt the warmth of her arms encircle her. The moment felt fragile, yet infinitely strong.

"I love you," Valentina whispered against Raven's hair.

Raven sighed, her heart settling into an easy rhythm. "I love you too."

22

aven's mind drifted in a haze, her fingers searching blindly for Valentina, only to find the bed empty. Confusion gnawed at her senses, her heart picking up speed as she grasped blindly for the cool sheets beneath her fingertips.

A sudden jolt of awareness surged through her, her breath catching as her eyes snapped open. The familiar warmth of Valentina's room was gone. Instead, rough grass pressed against her palms, damp with morning dew.

Raven sat up abruptly, blinking against the sharp light filtering through the towering tree above her. The distant clang of metal rang through the air—swords clashing, students calling out commands, Asha's authoritative voice cutting through the training session.

Her heart pounded as she took in the training ground, the organized chaos unfolding around her. How had she gotten here? She was still in her sleepwear—shorts and a loose shirt—but she had no memory of leaving the bed.

"Professor Zion," she called out, her voice urgent. No one

reacted. Her pulse quickened.

Nearby, Asha paced through the training ground, her sharp gaze monitoring the students' movements. Just then, Valentina appeared, weaving through the crowd with purpose. Raven exhaled in relief at the sight of her, but her sense of unease remained.

Valentina reached Asha's side, her voice hushed as she whispered something into the older woman's ear. Asha's reaction was immediate—her sharp eyes flickered around, scanning the area as if searching for unseen threats. Asha's eyes landed on Raven.

Raven stepped forward, but something made her pause. Asha wasn't looking at her. They were looking past her, through her.

The realization sent a chill down her spine. Asha couldn't see her.

Moving on instinct, she reached out just as Valentina turned to leave. Her fingers curled around Valentina's wrist, stopping her mid-step.

Valentina spun in a flash, her blade unsheathed and ready to strike. But Raven was faster. She caught Valentina's arm, twisting just enough to disarm her.

A sharp breath passed between them.

"I don't think I can take another cut, my love," Raven murmured, drawing Valentina into the shade of the tree.

At the sound of her voice, Valentina stilled. The tension bled from her body as she exhaled, allowing herself to sink into Raven's embrace.

"You disappeared this morning," Valentina whispered, her voice unsteady. "I've been searching for you."

Raven rested her forehead against Valentina's shoulder, trying to steady herself. "I woke up here. I don't know how or why. My powers must be acting on their own again. I need to get back to my room."

Valentina pulled back just enough to scan her, her gaze flicking over Raven's sleepwear before a teasing smile touched her lips. "You do realize you can't walk around school dressed like that, right?"

Before Raven could respond, Asha approached, her expression unreadable. She studied them both before speaking.

"I thought you were talking to yourself," she remarked to Valentina, though her eyes remained locked on Raven. "I didn't see you at all."

Raven crossed her arms. "I called out to you. You didn't hear me either."

Asha nodded, thoughtful. "I suspect it's your shadow powers. No one else sees you, which means if you step out of the shade, there's a chance they will. That will lead to confusion—and whispers."

Raven let out a frustrated sigh, and began pacing. "So, what am I supposed to do? Hide here until midnight?"

Before either of them could answer, the world shifted.

The scent of grass and steel faded. Darkness wrapped around her like a cocoon, swallowing her whole.

Then, just as suddenly, she was somewhere else.

The familiar scent of her belongings filled her senses. Blinking, she realized she was in the confined space of her closet.

What the—?

She pushed the door open, stepping out just as Emilia— lounging on her bed—leapt up in alarm. A dagger flew through the air, aimed straight for Raven's head.

Without thinking, Raven caught it mid-flight, twirling the blade in her fingers before tossing it back.

Emilia caught the dagger and narrowed her eyes. "Were you in the closet this whole time?"

Raven flopped onto the bed, exhausted. "No. I just… ended up there."

Emilia studied her for a long moment. "Are you being sarcastic?"

Raven stared at the ceiling. "No."

Silence stretched between them before Emilia sighed and sheathed the dagger.

"Fine. Doesn't matter how you got here. What matters is that we figure out your powers before this gets worse," she said, moving to stand beside the bed.

Raven closed her eyes. "I can't research this. If anyone sees me looking into shadow abilities, they'll start asking questions."

Emilia huffed in frustration. "Then I'll do it."

Raven shook her head. "You're too close to me. If they suspect anything, they'll monitor you."

Emilia groaned. "Then how the hell am I supposed to help you?"

A slow smile curved Raven's lips as she patted the space next to her. "I have an idea."

Emilia settled beside Raven, mirroring her posture.

"I'm going to need you to find me," Raven said, her voice soft but resolute.

Emilia furrowed her brow. "Find you?"

Raven nodded. With each disappearance, she had begun to understand her powers—whenever she vanished into the shadows, she either reappeared elsewhere or found herself adrift in an enigmatic void. The mechanics were still a mystery, but one thing was certain: she couldn't control where she ended up.

"I need to keep testing my limits," Raven explained. "I don't know how long it'll take to figure this out, but until I do, I might wake up in strange places. I need someone I trust to find me and pull me out of danger if necessary."

Emilia considered her words. "Why not ask Valentina?"

Raven let out a dry chuckle. "Because depending on the situation, I might need someone who can talk me out of trouble, not someone who will start a war in my defense. Valentina is protective, but you? You know how to de-escalate. I don't want bodies piling up just because I got lost in the wrong place."

Emilia laughed. "She is crazy about you. Rightfully so." Then, with a playful nod, she added, "Fine. I'll be your finder. When do I start?"

Raven's lips curled into a smirk. "Oh, honey, you already have."

Throughout the week, Raven's disappearances became routine. Some days, she reappeared in darkened corners of classrooms, invisible to the naked eye. Emilia, keeping her promise, would find clever ways to clear the area—convincing teachers to move lessons outside or creating distractions long enough for Raven to slip away.

Other times, Raven materialized in forgotten alcoves or abandoned corridors, where the dust suggested no one had stepped foot in years. There, she practiced, pulling the shadows around her, trying to bend them to her will.

With time, she stopped fearing the void. What once felt like an abyss of nothingness now revealed itself as a network of passageways—an unseen web connecting the school's darkest places. She learned to listen to the rhythm of the shadows, sensing the hidden doors within them. Her movements became smoother, her transitions faster. The void wasn't a trap. It was a pathway.

Meanwhile, Asha crafted an excuse for her absences, spreading the rumor that Raven had fallen seriously ill. It was a cover that granted Raven the freedom to train. And under Asha's guidance, she learned to wield electricity as effortlessly as a seasoned warrior wields their blade. Each day, she grew stronger.

One evening, as they gathered in Valentina's room, the scent of chicken mein noodles filled the air.

Raven set her chopsticks down. "Change of plans. This weekend, I go after the last book."

Emilia and Valentina exchanged a look, their hesitation obvious.

"Why not wait until the prodigies leave on their trip?" Emilia asked.

"Because King Pierre is coming with them," Raven explained. "He'll have eyes everywhere. If I disappear for too long, they'll notice. And if the other prodigies are watching me, they might piece things together."

Valentina studied her carefully. "You said 'I'—as in, you're planning to go alone?"

Raven nodded. "It'll be faster and safer that way."

"You don't even know where it is," Valentina pointed out.

Raven smirked. "The mountain or the book?"

"Both," Valentina shot back.

Raven shrugged. "I can read a map. That part's easy. As for the book—" She leaned back, confidence gleaming in her eyes. "I'll figure it out."

23

Raven gestured behind her, impatience edging her voice. "Isn't the mountain that way?"

"Yup." Valentina's reply was casual, her gaze fixed ahead, as though Raven's question had no real bearing on their direction.

Raven shot her a look, but Valentina remained unfazed.

They had left the academy the moment classes ended. Asha had suggested traveling in secrecy, though she hadn't explained why. Still, she'd seemed oddly satisfied with the look of disapproval on Ravens face when Valentina had said she would lead Raven on this particular journey.

Now, they trekked through the thick forest, the shadows stretching long in the fading afternoon light. The air was warm but crisp, a welcome contrast to the humidity that sometimes hung over Nethrala. Sunlight filtered through the canopy, dappling the ground with shifting patches of gold and green.

Raven kept a steady pace behind Valentina, watching as she moved effortlessly through the terrain, her hiking pack barely slowing her down. The gear Valentina had packed was enough for a full expedition—extra clothes, survival tools, provisions, even weapons. It was overkill for a simple trip, but Raven had learned not to question Valentina's methods.

What had puzzled her more was Valentina's insistence that she wear something specific for the trip—a compression tank top and shorts that matched Valentina's sleek black attire. When Raven had raised an eyebrow at the choice, Valentina had only grinned and said, *"Trust me. You'll thank me later."*

That was an hour ago.

Now, as Valentina veered away from the mountain path, Raven's curiosity finally won out.

"Where are we actually going?" she asked, adjusting the strap of her pack.

Valentina didn't turn around. "You'll see."

Raven sighed but followed without protest. There was something about Valentina's energy—excited, almost mischievous—that made it hard to argue.

Fifteen minutes later, Valentina finally slowed, stopping near a low-hanging tree. She turned toward Raven with a knowing smile.

"Almost there," she said, reaching out.

Raven hesitated for a second before taking her hand. Valentina pushed aside the curtain of leaves, revealing the hidden clearing beyond.

Raven stepped through—and inhaled sharply.

The forest opened into a secluded meadow, the grass lush and speckled with wildflowers, their colors vivid against the deep green. And nestled against the far side of the clearing was a cave. It was beautiful. Tranquil. As if it existed outside of time.

Valentina turned to her, squeezing her hand. "This is where we're staying for the night. Tomorrow, we head for the mountain."

Raven exhaled slowly, taking it all in. "And until then?"

Valentina smirked. "We set up camp, gather firewood—then we go for a swim."

Raven arched an eyebrow. "A swim?"

The sound of rushing water reached her ears as they neared the cave, confirming Valentina's words before she could question them. She glanced toward the cave, suddenly eager to see what lay inside. Without waiting for an answer, she released Valentina's hand and hurried forward, slipping into the dim interior.

Inside, the cave was bathed in the soft glow of the setting sun, the light streaming in from the entrance, casting warm hues over the smooth rock. The far side, was shrouded in shadow, save for the shimmering reflection of water that flowed gently across the cave floor. The air was cool, thick with the scent of fresh water. She was behind a waterfall.

Raven stepped closer.

Beyond the waterfall, the pool stretched deep into the rock, its surface reflecting the light like liquid silver. She could already imagine how it would feel—the crisp water, the weightlessness of being submerged.

Then, suddenly, something shifted inside her. A memory, sharp and unexpected.

Her breath hitched. The cave blurred.

She swayed.

"Whoa." Valentina was beside her in an instant, an arm wrapping around her waist. "Hey—are you okay?"

Raven blinked, grounding herself in the warmth of Valentina's touch.

"Yeah," she murmured, though her voice was quieter than she intended. "I just... I wasn't expecting this."

Valentina studied her for a moment, then tightened her hold, a silent reassurance.

"Well," she said lightly, "you're here now. And I plan on making sure you enjoy every second of it."

Raven let out a small laugh, the tension easing from her shoulders.

Maybe this detour wasn't such a bad idea after all.

Raven could only manage a nod in response, her throat tight with emotion, her breath caught between silence and tears. She didn't trust her voice to hold the weight of everything she felt.

"Let's set up the tents first, and then we can explore," Valentina suggested gently, her voice an anchor in Raven's turbulent thoughts.

Raven hesitated, then turned fully into Valentina's embrace, wrapping her arms around her neck and burying her face against her shoulder. Tears slipped silently down her cheeks, dampening Valentina's shirt. She didn't sob—there was no shuddering breath, no broken cries—just the quiet surrender to the comfort Valentina offered.

Valentina held her without a word, her hand tracing slow, soothing circles along Raven's back.

When Raven finally pulled away with a soft sigh, Valentina reached up, brushing the lingering tears from her cheeks. Without a second thought, she pressed a kiss to her thumb, still damp with Raven's tears.

Something inside Raven twisted at the tenderness of the gesture. Without thinking, she leaned in, capturing Valentina's lips in a kiss. She tasted the salt of her own tears between them—a silent promise exchanged in the space where words felt inadequate. *I will love you even in your weakest moments.*

Valentina smiled against her lips when they finally parted, fingers lacing through Raven's. "Shall we start setting up?" she asked, voice warm with quiet amusement.

A chuckle escaped Raven. She nodded.

They turned to their bags, unpacking the one-person tents the academy had issued them for long missions. As Raven brushed the dirt off her clothes, she glanced at Valentina. "I'll gather some rocks and sticks for the fire."

Valentina gave a small nod, already sifting through their supplies. "Be careful."

Just as Raven stepped outside the cave, Valentina called out to her.

"Take a dagger, just in case." She held up a blade, offering it to Raven. Though she stood in the shadows near the cave's entrance, Valentina was still as clear to Raven as if she were bathed in moonlight—a gifted effect from her shadows.

Raven arched a brow. "Throw it."

Valentina frowned. "I don't like the idea of hurling sharp objects at you."

Raven smirked. "Says the girl who swung a sword at me last week?"

Valentina pressed her lips together, but amusement flickered in her eyes. "I don't recall," she deadpanned before flicking the dagger toward Raven.

It landed inches from her feet, the blade sinking cleanly into the soil.

Raven bent to retrieve it, twirling it between her fingers as she turned toward the open meadow.

As she walked, her thoughts wandered. Had her mother ever crossed these woods before her? Had she known what it was to steal a moment with someone special?

She had never known her father, and her mother never spoke of him. Maybe it was too painful. Maybe it was a wound that time refused to mend.

She pictured Ms. Moretti, Asha, and her mother, once young, laughing, whispering secrets under the stars. They had shared something she always longed for. Maybe that's what had drawn her and Emilia together.

A quiet longing settled in her chest.

She gave the dagger another twirl and walked on.

Raven halted abruptly at the sound of rustling nearby, her senses sharpening. Though she saw nothing and felt no prying eyes, instinct warned her—something lingered, unseen.

She stood motionless, her breath shallow, scanning her surroundings. Then, a flicker beneath a bush—a small shadow, called her attention. She extended her senses, calling the shadow toward her until it brushed her boot. A presence. A disturbance.

Murmurs drifted through the shadows. Moving seamlessly through the void, she melted into the nearest shadow, emerging unseen above the clearing. Below, two assassins dragged a slain animal through the woods, their hushed voices carrying a weight that demanded attention.

"Prodigy Valentina was favored to win, but I still think she has a chance," said a woman, adjusting her grip on the carcass.

The man beside her grunted. "Perhaps. But have you noticed how the clan heads whisper about Prodigy Raven? The way the other contenders watched her? She isn't just another competitor. She's a threat."

The woman hesitated. "True. But Prodigy Valentina didn't seem intimidated by her."

A knowing chuckle. "Intimidated? No. In love? Definitely. Did you see how she looked at Raven during the ceremony? As if Raven had the power to shape the world itself."

"What does that mean for the gauntlet."

Raven didn't hear the rest of the conversation. Their voices faded as they drifted farther away.

She remained still, hidden within the embrace of the shadow.

Then—

A vibration.

Faint, but unmistakable.

Without hesitation, Raven moved.

She slipped through the void, letting it swallow her, guide her, toward the next shadow.

When she emerged, Valentina was waiting, her expression lined with worry. "You were gone longer than I expected," she said. "I couldn't find you among all the vegetation."

"Sorry." Raven reached for some of the supplies Valentina carried. "I heard something. Went to check it out."

"What was it?"

"Just a pair of assassins hunting," she reassured. "Nothing concerning."

Satisfied, Valentina nodded. "Good. Now, let's head back. I'm dying for a swim."

The transition into the cave was easy, natural. Firewood stacked, makeshift bedding arranged. Valentina stood, stretching, her smile soft and teasing.

"Alright, camp's set. Now, time to swim."

Raven arched an eye brow. "And what exactly are we wearing?"

Valentina's grin turned mischievous as she peeled off her shirt. Raven's breath caught, her gaze tracing the sculpted lines of Valentina's abdomen. Heat coiled in her chest, and she closed her eyes, inhaling sharply.

"Look at me," Valentina whispered, her voice soft enough to be carried away by the sound of rushing water.

Raven hesitated, breath caught somewhere between nerves and longing. Slowly, she opened her eyes.

Valentina was already shedding her shorts, calm and unhurried, holding Raven's gaze the entire time.

"You can look," she said with a teasing lilt, one brow arched in mock challenge.

Raven's lips twitched. She didn't smile—not quite—but her eyes roamed with quiet reverence. Every line of Valentina's frame was familiar and yet brand new in this light. Muscle and scar, strength and grace.

She stood, fingers working at the hem of her shirt. Her heart pounded, but she didn't look away.

Valentina took a step closer, a soft hum of approval slipping from her lips. She brushed a kiss against Raven's cheek, light and reverent. "Beautiful."

The word landed like a stone in a still pond.

Flushed, Raven gently nudged her back—not with rejection, but with a shyness that felt almost foreign to her. Valentina laughed, low and warm, the sound echoing around the rocks.

"There should be extra sports bras and boy shorts in our bags," she said, casually nodding toward the bag. "We can change into dry clothes after."

"Noted," Raven murmured. She reached for Valentina's hand, lacing their fingers together, and tugged her forward toward the water.

The roar of the waterfall grew louder as they stepped beneath its veil, cool mist clinging to their skin. When they emerged on the other side, they found themselves on a narrow, rocky ledge.

Valentina let go of her hand and, without a word, began scaling the stone face with practiced ease. Raven watched her go, heart full and aching, the way light scattered across her damp skin, how her strength lived in every step.

The path branched on either side, both winding up to where the falls emptied into a broad, crystalline pool. Raven's eyes lingered there, caught by its quiet beauty. She wondered where the water ran off—some hidden spring, tucked deep in the woods.

Then—

A splash.

The stillness shattered.

Raven blinked and turned, searching the rippling surface. Valentina had disappeared beneath it.

She waited, listening to the silence stretch between seconds, until at last—

Valentina broke the surface, water cascading from her hair as she flipped it back and glanced over.

"Well?" she called, lips curled in a smile. "Are you coming in or just planning to admire me from the edge all day?"

Raven tilted her head, a mischievous glint in her eyes. "Actually, I was thinking I'd race you."

Valentina floated on her back, amusement flickering across her face. "Race me?" she echoed, a teasing challenge dancing in her tone.

"Yes. You take that side, I'll take this one. First to the top, then jump." Excitement laced Raven's voice.

Valentina emerged from the water, meeting Raven's gaze with a knowing smirk. "And what do I get when I win?"

Raven scoffed. "When?" she teased, shaking her head. "Alright, what would you like?"

Valentina's reply was swift. "Half of your food."

Raven blinked, momentarily caught off guard.

"I get hungry often," Valentina added with a shrug, though Raven wasn't convinced.

A slow grin spread across her face. "I feel like you just want it because it's mine."

Valentina's smirk deepened, neither confirming nor denying the accusation.

"Fine." Raven stepped back, rolling her shoulders. "Ready. Set—"

"Wait!" Valentina cut in, and Raven straightened impatiently.

"What?"

"I'm assuming you can actually swim."

Raven shot her a deadpan look.

"Yes, well, I had to make sure," Valentina said, eyes twinkling with mock innocence. "Such attitude." Then, her expression turned serious. "You should know—there's a current under the lake. It's light on the surface, but if you dive too deep, it gets stronger. The runoff flows underground for a mile before resurfacing. If you get pulled into it, unless you can hold your breath that long… well." She let the warning linger. "I say this now so you're prepared. When you hit the water, be ready for the pull."

Raven nodded. "Thanks for the warning. Now stop stalling."

Valentina rolled her eyes. "Start your countdown, Falcon."

Raven gasped in mock offense. "Oh, now we have issues." She crouched. "Get ready. Get set. Go!"

They both surged upward, scaling the rocks. Raven moved with speed and confidence, but Valentina had the advantage of familiarity. The realization that Valentina was pulling ahead sent frustration bubbling in Raven's chest.

By the time she reached the final stretch, Valentina was already at the summit, standing at the edge of the waterfall with a smug expression. She would officially win once she jumped, but her lingering gaze was a silent taunt.

Raven huffed, pushing through the last few feet. The moment she crested the top, Valentina winked at her—then, with effortless grace, plummeted backward off the edge.

Raven rushed forward, just in time to see Valentina execute a flawless backflip before slicing into the water below.

She rolled her eyes. "And people think I'm secretly cocky," she muttered before launching herself off, flipping forward into a precise dive.

As she hit the water, the current yanked at her limbs. Just as Valentina had warned. Raven kicked hard, muscles straining against the pull. Years of training in rivers and lakes had prepared her for this. She sliced through the resistance, emerging at the surface with a triumphant breath.

On the rocky ledge, Valentina kicked her feet lazily in the water. "Took you long enough."

Raven swam closer, narrowing her eyes. "I feel like you cheated somehow."

Valentina spread her legs slightly, offering Raven a space to rest between them. "No," she countered smoothly. "I just had motivation."

Raven rested her arms against the ledge. "My food?"

"Your safety." Valentina's voice softened. "I was nervous the current might sweep you away. I know you're skilled, but everyone has vulnerabilities."

Raven swam around, hoisting herself onto the rock beside her. "And what's your weakness, my love?"

Valentina hesitated. Then, she exhaled. "Besides you?" A faint blush dusted her cheeks.

Raven smiled. "Besides me."

A shiver ran through Valentina as Raven leaned closer for warmth. "I'm claustrophobic," she admitted, eyes fixed on the rippling water. "During my prodigy training, I was buried alive. I was twelve." Her fingers fidgeted against the damp stone. "I thought I was going to die down there."

Raven stilled. The pieces clicked together. "Is that why you had a panic attack during our first fight?"

Valentina gave a tight nod. "The sensation of suffocation... it brought everything back."

Raven reached for her hand, cradling it in her lap. "You are my weakness," she murmured, fingers tracing delicate patterns along Valentina's skin.

Valentina glanced up, eyes searching. "Really?"

Raven's grip tightened slightly. "Yes." A quiet confession. "You challenge every ounce of control instilled in me. I would face the world ablaze if it meant keeping you safe. Maybe that's selfish. Maybe that's not what a future queen should say." She exhaled, her thumb brushing Valentina's knuckles. "But I'd do it anyway."

Silence stretched between them, weighted with things unspoken.

Then, Valentina turned her hand over, lacing their fingers together. "I think," she said softly, "I'd be selfish too."

24

Raven stirred, her head nestled against Valentina's chest, their limbs entwined in a comfortable embrace. One arm draped over Valentina's stomach, while Valentina's arm encircled her waist. Though the fire had long since died out in the middle of the night, their shared warmth was enough.

Tents had been forgotten after their meal. Instead, they had chosen to lay together, speaking deep into the night—exchanging stories, fears, and desires until words gave way to something deeper. Their bond, now sealed, felt unshakable.

As Raven sat up and stretched, a light touch along her spine made her shiver. She tensed, then relaxed as Valentina traced a slow, deliberate line down her back.

"Good morning," Valentina murmured, her voice thick with sleep.

"Morning," Raven replied, pressing a soft kiss to her lips. "Time to go?"

Valentina nodded. They dressed quickly, slipping into fresh clothes identical to the ones from the day before. After brushing their teeth and gathering their now-dry clothes, they dismantled their tents and scanned the area, ensuring they left no trace behind—a habit ingrained in them through years of assassin training.

Raven slung her backpack over her shoulders. "Alright, mission time. Let's move fast, get what we need, and get out."

Valentina mirrored her, adjusting her straps before setting off at a jog. Raven followed close behind as they tore through the forest, weaving around fallen logs and thick underbrush. The sun bore down on them, sweat gathering on Raven's brow, but exhaustion never came. Their training had honed their endurance beyond that of most assassins.

They reached the mountain's base in record time. Raven planted her hands on her hips and stared up. The summit loomed high above, sharp against the bright afternoon sky.

"Free climb?" she mused.

Valentina pulled a face. "What do you think we are, ninjas? There's a path right over there."

Raven smirked, nudging her playfully. "Lead the way, then."

Their ascent took two hours. When they finally reached the summit, they dropped their packs onto the wide stone plateau. Sigils of all eleven clans adorned its surface—a testament to its significance.

Raven pulled out her daggers, spinning them between her fingers. "The book is here, either hidden within the mountain or somewhere on this plateau." She glanced at Valentina. "I'll scout below. You stay here and keep watch."

Valentina nodded. "Be careful."

"Always," Raven said with a wink before jogging back down the trail.

She scanned the mountainside for anything out of place, but the terrain revealed nothing—no hidden entrances, no unnatural formations. The Crimson Widow Clan wouldn't simply leave a book in the open, but how could they conceal it within solid rock?

Raven frowned, retracing her steps. The coordinates they had were precise—too precise. They led directly to the summit. Her gaze shifted upward, thoughts racing. *If the book wasn't on top the mountain, then maybe… it was inside it.*

When she reached the plateau, Valentina stood at the edge, daggers in hand.

"Find anything?" she asked.

"No." Raven's gaze drifted to the smooth stone beneath their feet. "When was this flooring put here?"

Valentina shrugged. "I think they said it was laid down about eighteen years ago."

Raven's pulse quickened. Eighteen years. That was worth investigating.

"How often do people come here?" she asked, kneeling to inspect the stone more closely.

"Rarely, if ever. It's always for a special occasion," Valentina replied.

"Are there any places you're told not to go or touch?"

Valentina furrowed her brow, aware of Raven's intense gaze. A small smile tugged at her lips. She walked over to a section of the stone floor, where a thin crack marred its otherwise seamless surface.

"We were warned to steer clear of this area because the stone is unstable. One wrong step, and we'd fall to our deaths."

Raven nodded, stepping closer. With cautious deliberation, she pressed her foot against the crack, expecting resistance or some shift in the fracture. Instead, the stone felt hollow. She exerted more weight. A faint hiss of air escaped, and the ground trembled beneath her.

The stone gave way.

As she descended on the precarious platform, Raven looked up and met Valentina's wide eyes.

"Stay calm, Val. I'll be fine. Keep watch."

Valentina swallowed hard and nodded, though her concern was evident.

Raven landed in a cavernous space beneath the stone floor. Instinct kicked in. She dropped into a defensive stance, scanning her surroundings. The chamber was silent, the air thick with dust and the scent of damp earth.

A single object stood out: a book resting atop a boulder at the far end of the chamber.

Between her and the book, sixteen large stone tiles stretched across the floor, each engraved with unique symbols arranged in four rows of four. The formation struck her as deliberate, a pattern with a hidden purpose.

Raven's instincts flared. The Crimson Widow clan wouldn't rely on a simple cracked floor to guard something valuable. There had to be more.

She stepped onto the first tile. Nothing happened.

Another step. Still nothing.

She narrowed her eyes. *It's never this easy.*

The moment her full weight settled onto the next tile, the stone dropped beneath her feet.

A rush of adrenaline shot through her as she launched herself backward, barely escaping the pit of jagged spikes that had been waiting beneath. The tile reset, as if nothing had happened.

A humorless chuckle escaped her lips. *Of course.*

Assessing her options, Raven realized she had only two paths forward—left or right. She calculated her odds. The left seemed less treacherous.

With a controlled leap, she landed on the adjacent tile. It held. She exhaled.

Now came the true challenge. *Continue forward or shift to another row?*

She eyed the tile ahead. It sat directly beside the one that had nearly killed her. Logically, it should be safe.

Bracing herself, she stepped forward—

And the floor collapsed beneath her.

Reacting on instinct, she lunged forward, her fingers scrambling for purchase. Her daggers slipped from her grip, clattering against the stone as she clung to the edge. Below her, a writhing mass of serpents coiled in the pit, their bodies shifting over one another in a sickening dance.

With a sharp intake of breath, Raven hoisted herself back onto solid ground. Her pulse pounded in her ears as she steadied herself. One thing was certain.

She had to rethink her approach.

Raven moved along the final row with measured steps, every muscle taut with focus. She hovered at the edge, then cautiously stepped onto the next square, her breath held tight in her chest.

Solid.

She allowed herself a small exhale—just enough to steady her nerves—before setting her sights on the final tile.

The book sat just ahead, untouched, gleaming faintly in the low light.

Her pulse quickened.

One last step.

Raven pushed forward, her foot landing with a quiet thud as she crossed the final square. Her fingers closed around the spine of the book, the leather cool beneath her touch. A rush of triumph surged through her—sharp and fleeting.

Got it.

She turned without hesitation, retracing her path with urgent precision. Each step back felt more certain than the last, the strain in her shoulders loosening as she neared the cracked stone floor.

The trembling beneath her boots slowed.

The platform began to rise.

Raven let out a breath she hadn't realized she'd been holding, the adrenaline ebbing slowly from her veins. She had done it. Passed their twisted test. But the taste of victory was bitter on her tongue.

The Crimson Widow Clan had made a game of danger— risking someones life like it meant nothing. The resentment simmered deep, coiling tighter with every beat of her heart.

Then she surfaced.

And the world stopped.

Raven stepped out of the mountain's maw and froze.

Before her stood a man—an assassin, Crimson Widow crest emblazoned on his chest. His blade rested against Valentina's throat. She knelt at his feet, still and silent.

Rage bloomed like wildfire.

But Raven didn't move. Not yet. She took in the scene with a soldier's calm, her eyes scanning the mountaintop.

Bodies littered the stone.

Nine dead.

Three more still breathing—barely.

Valentina had fought them all. And she had nearly won.

Raven's fingers tightened around the book.

The assassin's eyes locked on hers. His voice cut through the stillness.

"Hand over the book, Prodigy Raven," he said, each word dipped in menace.

Raven's voice cut through the stillness like a blade. Cold. Steady.

"Nightfall approaches."

The words hung in the air, quiet but heavy—like a promise.

The assassin blinked, confusion flaring across his face. He glanced at his remaining comrades, the masked ones still holding formation nearby. Unease passed between them, a silent current beneath their menace.

But the threat remained.

He yanked Valentina's head back by the hair, forcing the blade tighter against her throat.

She flinched, a hiss slipping past her lips—but that was all. Her body stayed firm, her eyes sharp. Unbroken.

Raven's nails dug into her palms.

The fury was rising—low and hot and impossible to contain.

With one breath, she let it in.

The energy surged through her, wild and electric, filling her limbs with raw, thrumming power. Her heart pounded like war drums.

She needed speed. She needed a weapon.

And her body listened.

The book slipped from her hand, forgotten.

She moved.

In a single, blistering blur, Raven closed the distance. One heartbeat, she stood still. The next, she was already there—

Her hand collided with the assassin's chest, a crack of electricity exploding outward.

He flew back, weapon forgotten, his body arching through the air like a puppet cut from its strings.

The book hit the ground with a dull thud.

The assassin dropped without a sound.

His body hit the ground in a heap of finality, the gaping hole in his chest still crackling faintly with residual electricity.

Raven stared at him for a moment, the weight of the kill settling into her bones. There was no triumph. Only silence.

Behind her, Valentina pushed to her feet, one hand moving to rub the back of her neck with a wince. She was bleeding—bruised, worn—but still standing.

"New skill?" she asked, her voice strained but curious.

Raven turned to her, stepping close, her eyes tracing every inch of Valentina with barely disguised worry. She placed a hand gently on her back, grounding them both.

"I can only cover short distances," Raven murmured, her fingers brushing Valentina's shoulder like she was afraid she might disappear. "It's fast. Better suited for close-range combat."

Valentina gave a small nod. They didn't need to say more. The look they exchanged spoke volumes. A silent pact, unshaken by blood or battle.

"Are you alright?" Raven asked, her voice quiet now. Her gaze dropped to the crimson stain spreading across Valentina's side.

Before Valentina could answer, one of the remaining assassins took a hesitant step forward.

"How did you…" he began, but the words faltered, lost in the haze of fear.

Raven looked up, meeting his eyes with tired patience. She had no energy left for mercy.

"Darkness," she whispered.

She lifted her hand.

The shadows obeyed.

They slithered across the stone like living smoke, curling around the two remaining assassins, drowning the world in black.

They screamed.

Twisted and raw.

Clutching their heads, they dropped to their knees, gasping like the air had been stolen from their lungs. Inside the illusion, they were alone—surrounded by every fear they had ever buried.

Their blades came up.

Raven didn't flinch.

Steel met steel in a frenzy of panic.

Two strikes. Two gasps.

And then—

Silence.

The assassins collapsed, swords buried in each other's chests, their final expressions frozen in terror.

Raven lowered her hand. The shadows dissipated like mist, leaving behind nothing but bodies.

Raven turned to Valentina, her concern written plainly across her face.

"Can you walk?" she asked softly, her hand never leaving Valentina's back. Ready to steady her. Ready to carry her if it came to that.

Valentina winced, her palm pressed against the wound at her side. Blood had soaked through the fabric, but her eyes burned with resolve.

"Yes," she said through gritted teeth. "Let's get out of here before more show up."

Without another word, Raven moved. She bent to retrieve the

fallen book, slipping it carefully into her backpack before slinging it over one shoulder. Then she gathered Valentina's bag and hoisted it onto her other shoulder, adjusting the weight with practiced ease.

When she returned to Valentina's side, her hand was already outstretched.

"It's night now," Raven said, voice low and sure. "The shadows are stronger. I can move faster in them, and I'm not leaving you to limp through the woods like a target."

Valentina hesitated, eyes narrowing with a mix of curiosity and unease.

"You can bring someone with you… through that?"

Raven paused.

She hadn't thought about it before—not really. But the answer emerged without hesitation, borne on instinct and trust.

"I've never tried," she admitted, her fingers twitching ever so slightly in the air between them. "But you'll be my first."

Valentina blinked, a soft flush coloring her cheeks. She didn't speak for a second, but her hand lifted—steady, brave.

"I trust you," she said, threading her fingers into Raven's without hesitation.

And that was all Raven needed.

25

Valentina lay on Raven's floor, her wound carefully bandaged. Across the room, Raven sat at her desk, her fingers tracing the edges of an old, leather-bound book. She had instructed Valentina to rest while she scoured its contents, searching for evidence against the Crimson Widow clan.

Valentina complied, her exhaustion evident in the sluggish rise and fall of her chest. But Raven couldn't rest—not now. The truth had to be uncovered.

As she reached the midpoint of the book, her pulse quickened. Her eyes skimmed over the same passage again. And again.

No.

No, this couldn't be right.

Her hands trembled as she clenched the book tighter. A sharp pang tore through her chest, sorrow twisting its cruel fingers around her heart. Her breath came in quick, uneven gasps, tears threatening to spill.

With a sudden surge of emotion, she shot up from her chair, the abrupt movement sending it scraping against the wooden floor.

Valentina startled awake, her body jerking upright before a sharp wince cut through her features.

"Are you alright?" she asked, her concern immediate despite her injury.

Raven hesitated, her rage flickering as she took in Valentina's pained expression. Guilt pricked at her. "I'm sorry," she murmured, forcing herself to calm down. "I didn't mean to wake you. Are you okay?"

Valentina exhaled, shaking off the discomfort. "I'll live," she said, though the tightness in her voice betrayed the effort it took. Her sharp gaze flicked to the book clutched in Raven's hands. "What is it? What did you find?"

Wordlessly, Raven turned the book toward her, her finger pressing against the damning passage. "Read it," she said, voice hollow.

Valentina's eyes scanned the words. Her expression shifted—from confusion to dawning horror.

"Is this—"

"Yes," Raven interjected, her voice breaking. She swallowed, fists tightening at her sides. "I need to find Emilia. Now."

Valentina started to rise. "I'll go with you."

Raven shook her head. "No. You need to heal. I don't know how this will go down, and I won't risk you getting hurt again."

Valentina hesitated but relented. She lay back against the floor, exhaling in frustration.

Raven turned away, staring at the book in her hands, the inked words branding themselves into her mind. She shut her eyes and inhaled deeply. When she exhaled, it was with a quiet resolve.

She crossed the room to her closet and pulled open the door. Shadows curled inside, waiting. With a whispered command, they wrapped around her like a second skin, and the world dissolved into darkness.

Raven stepped from the shadows into Emilia's dimly lit room.

Emilia sat cross-legged on her bed, a book resting in her lap.

She glanced up at Raven's sudden arrival, unfazed. She had gotten used to Raven's shadow entrances— no longer flinging knives at her every time she appeared unannounced.

"Raven," Emilia greeted, a small smile tugging at her lips. But then she caught the look in Raven's eyes. The warmth faded. "What's wrong?"

Raven hesitated. She had trusted Emilia with everything. More than a friend, Emilia was family. The person who had helped her survive grief. The one who had been by her side when her mother—

Her throat tightened.

Instead of speaking, she extended the book.

Emilia frowned but took it, eyes scanning the passage. The further she read, the deeper her frown became. Her grip on the book tightened.

Silence stretched between them, thick with unspoken turmoil.

Then Raven asked, voice barely above a whisper, "Did you know?"

Emilia's head snapped up.

A flicker of something—hesitation, doubt—crossed her face.

"Did you know?" Raven repeated, this time more insistent.

Emilia exhaled sharply. "No!" Her voice cracked, the word sharp as a blade. With a sudden, violent motion, she flung the book across the room. It hit the wall with a heavy thud.

"This has to be a lie." She gestured wildly, her breaths coming in ragged bursts. "She wouldn't—she couldn't—"

"But she did." Raven's voice was quiet, but firm.

Emilia pressed a hand to her forehead, as if trying to hold herself together. "You're just going to believe what's in that book?" she demanded. "Turn your back on her, just like that?"

Raven inhaled sharply. "Emilia, my entire plan hinges on the widow clan books holding the truth. You know that." She gestured toward the discarded book. "I can't just ignore it because it hurts."

Emilia shook her head. "If this is true, she betrayed the

Serpent Kings Clan. Valentina's father. Your mom. Asha." Her voice cracked. "She betrayed everyone."

Tears streaked her face now, but she barely seemed to notice. "She loved your mom. They were best friends. My mother wouldn't—" Her voice broke completely.

A sob shuddered through Emilia. She clenched her fists, breathing hard, as if trying to force down the reality unraveling around her.

Watching Emilia's distress, Raven felt her heart twist with empathy. Anger flared at the betrayal, but beneath it pulsed a deeper sorrow—for the loss of innocence, for the illusions now broken. Seeing Emilia's world fall apart was a painful reminder of how treachery never ended with just one wound.

Kneeling beside her, Raven rested a gentle hand on Emilia's shoulder. "Emilia," she murmured, her voice a soothing balm against the storm of emotions.

Emilia flinched at the touch, shaking her head and pushing Raven's hand away. "I don't deserve your kindness," she muttered, her voice thick with self-reproach. "I should have seen it. I should have known."

Regret lined her face as she paced, her movements restless. "I left you all those years ago because she said it was to protect you, but what if it wasn't? Then your mother dies, and we're not even there for you. She never spoke of you, not even in private. She claimed to be her best friend, yet she only mourned her during the ceremonies." Bitterness sharpened her words, her pacing mirroring the churn of her thoughts.

Raven remained kneeling, watching Emilia with concern. The weight of betrayal pressed heavily between them.

"I just don't understand," Emilia whispered, turning away, her back to Raven.

The question burned in Raven's mind, but she hesitated before voicing it. "Emilia, tell me you weren't a part of this."

Emilia stiffened, and for a fleeting moment, indignation

flashed across her face. But as their eyes met, the facade crumbled, revealing the raw vulnerability beneath. "I would never betray you. My heart wouldn't allow it," she said, her voice barely above a whisper. Yet her gaze faltered, guilt flickering in her eyes.

Raven swallowed hard, forcing her voice to remain steady. "Your mother is a traitor, Emilia. She cannot live. When we expose the Widow Clan—when we expose her…" She faltered, the weight of her words sinking in.

"I understand, my queen," Emilia responded, bowing before Raven.

The title pierced through Raven like a dagger. She never thought hearing it from Emilia would wound her so deeply. Without another word, she gathered the book and withdrew into the shadows, the burden of Emilia's quiet acceptance pressing down on her.

Seated at the foot of Asha's bed, Raven watched her mentor pace. The revelation sat heavy between them, an unspoken storm brewing in the silence.

"I told Emilia," Raven finally said.

Asha stopped pacing. "And?"

"She's struggling. Maybe in denial." Raven exhaled, her exhaustion palpable. "I fear I've lost my best friend."

Asha waved off the concern. "Emilia will stand by you. No matter what." Her confidence was unwavering, but her expression darkened. "But we can't ignore the risk. Alexanderia knows about your powers. She hasn't acted yet, but that doesn't mean she won't."

Raven nodded, frustration simmering beneath her calm exterior. "It doesn't make sense," she muttered. "What did they promise her? What does she stand to gain?"

The passage she had uncovered confirmed Ms. Moretti's involvement, but it left more questions than answers. Betrayal from a mother figure stung deeper than she cared to admit.

Asha crossed her arms. "How do you plan to get the third book? The fourth was stolen, the Widow Clan's assassins are dead, and their guard will be higher than ever. Entering through the same route is too risky. Especially if Alexanderia suspects that you're onto her."

Raven met Asha's gaze evenly. "I'll infiltrate the Widow Clan's territory using the shadows. Once underground, I'll find a path through them. After securing the book, I'll return, transcribe its contents, and distribute them through the schools. You can ensure the clan heads receive them."

Asha nodded in agreement, satisfied with the plan's outline for now. The finer details would need addressing later, but at least they had a course of action.

Raven rose to leave, exhaustion settling in after the day's events. But before she could take a step, Asha's voice cut through the quiet.

"Raven." The firmness in her tone made Raven pause. "Under no circumstances should you contact or meet with Alexandria. Cutting ties with her is imperative for our safety moving forward."

Raven's response was barely a whisper. "Emilia."

"I'll handle it," Asha assured her.

Raven gave a slow nod. The weight of the night pressed against her shoulders, but she turned toward the door, intent on slipping away.

"You're not going to use the door, are you?" Asha's dry remark carried a familiar exasperation.

A faint smile played at Raven's lips, though any real joy felt distant in the wake of the night's revelations. She remembered the early days, when Asha used to startle every time she flicked on the lights and found Raven waiting in the shadows. But familiarity had dulled the shock, replacing it with nothing more than a resigned groan or a pointed glare.

"You know me better than that," Raven murmured.

Asha sighed, shaking her head. "Goodnight, Raven."

Raven melted into the shadows, the room fading into darkness as she shifted through the unseen spaces between worlds. When she reappeared, she was in her own room, stepping silently out of the closet.

Valentina lay curled in bed, her breathing slow and steady. She had left the lights on, except for the one nearest the closet—an unspoken invitation, a small gesture of understanding.

Raven exhaled softly, tension slipping from her frame as she watched Valentina sleep. Despite the storm of anger and grief raging within her, Valentina was an anchor, an unspoken promise of something worth holding onto.

With practiced ease, Raven extinguished the lights and tucked away the book in its hidden place. Then, sliding into bed, she wrapped an arm around Valentina's waist, pulling her close. Their bodies fit together effortlessly, like two halves of a whole.

Raven pressed a kiss to the back of Valentina's shoulder and let her eyes drift shut. For now, in this quiet space, she allowed herself to rest.

26

Raven woke to the rhythmic rise and fall of Valentina's chest, the steady breath a quiet reassurance. The early morning light filtered through the curtains, casting a soft glow over the room. She slipped out of bed carefully, mindful not to disturb Valentina's much-needed rest. It was Sunday, which meant they had another day before facing anyone's scrutiny.

Asha's skill had ensured Valentina's wound wasn't severe, but it still needed time to heal. It would take only one wrong move for it to reopen.

Raven moved to the closet, instinctively reaching for one of her black hoodies. Her hand hovered over the fabric as she caught sight of the Silent Clan sigil emblazoned on it—a stark reminder of Ms. Moretti. The sight left a bitter taste in her mouth. She didn't want any connection to that woman, not anymore.

Glancing at Valentina one last time, she stepped into the closet and let the shadows pull her into the other room. The darkness obeyed her, depositing her seamlessly into Valentina's space. She scanned the clothes and settled on a black sweatshirt bearing the Nightshade

Syndicate sigil, pairing it with matching sweatpants that bore the same emblem.

A quiet sense of finality settled over her as she put them on. A clean break. A choice she had made.

Emerging from the closet once more, Raven left her room and headed toward the cafeteria. Valentina often brought her breakfast when she could—today, Raven would return the favor.

The cafeteria was buzzing with morning chatter, but Raven barely registered the noise. Her eyes, however, flicked toward Emilia and Onyx at one of the tables. Laughter. It sounded sharp, grating.

Raven forced her gaze away, suppressing the unease that settled in her stomach. She trusted Emilia, but that didn't erase the betrayal she had experienced with Ms. Moretti. Trust wasn't something she could easily rebuild.

She grabbed two to-go containers, each filled with loaded omelets and crispy bacon, tucking two bottles of orange juice alongside them. But as she turned, she was met with an obstacle.

Onyx.

The smug tilt of her lips was deliberate, a challenge waiting to be acknowledged.

"Hello, Raven," Onyx greeted, voice laced with artificial sweeteners.

Raven's gaze flicked past her to Emilia, who stood silent, eyes lowered.

"Onyx," Raven replied evenly, keeping her tone void of emotion. "Always a pleasure."

Onyx's eyes raked over her, amusement flickering in their depths. "Betraying your clan, are you?" she mused. "You may be new to our world, but even a prodigy should know better than to wear another clan's sigil."

Raven barely blinked. "If it weren't for the rule against killing prodigies before the Gauntlet, I would've slit your throat the first time we met. Be thankful for the rules I do choose to follow."

Onyx faltered, only for a fraction of a second, but Raven

caught it.

"Is violence your answer to everything?" Onyx asked, regaining her composure.

"Yes." Raven didn't hesitate. She brushed past Onyx, intent on leaving, but the next words stopped her in her tracks.

"I told the same thing to Valentina."

Raven didn't turn, but her muscles coiled, bracing for impact.

"The day she came out wearing your hoodie," Onyx continued, voice edged with disdain. "I told her she was a traitor. That she was letting her love for you tarnish the respect everyone had for her."

The room fell into a hushed silence, all eyes fixated on them.

Raven clenched her jaw, every nerve alight with restrained fury. She had spent years mastering control, but Valentina was the one person who could shatter her restraint with a mere thought.

"Emilia," she said at last, her voice low, dangerous.

A shift behind her. A silent acknowledgement.

"Tell your whore that if she speaks about Valentina again, or even looks at her the wrong way, I will kill her."

A sharp, collective inhale. Even Onyx, who thrived on conflict, seemed momentarily stunned into silence.

Raven didn't wait for a reply as she strode out of the cafeteria, leaving behind only the weight of her promise.

Back at her bedroom door, Raven took slow, deliberate breaths, forcing her heartbeat to steady. She could still feel the fury simmering beneath her skin, hot and consuming. She couldn't let it control her—not when Valentina needed her.

She pushed the door open to find Valentina sitting by the window, bathed in soft morning light.

The sight alone was enough to ease some of the tension gripping her chest.

"Hi," Valentina whispered, a gentle smile touching her lips.

"Hi," Raven breathed, shutting the door behind her.

She crossed the room and settled beside Valentina at the

window seat.

"I got us breakfast," she said, pulling the containers from the bag. "Thought we could spend the day relaxing while you heal."

Valentina leaned in, pressing a kiss against Raven's lips before pulling back slightly. "You're amazing." Then, with a teasing smile, she added, "And you look great in my clothes."

Heat crept up Raven's neck at the comment, but she covered it with a smirk. "Didn't feel right wearing the Silent Clan's sigil anymore." She handed Valentina her food. "But Onyx had plenty to say about my choice."

Valentina rolled her eyes, stabbing at her omelet with her fork. "Onyx always has something to say."

Raven exhaled. "Why didn't you tell me she confronted you about my hoodie?"

Valentina shrugged, chewing thoughtfully. After swallowing, she said, "I can handle myself. And I didn't want you getting into trouble for going after her."

Raven chuckled. "Funny. I just told Emilia I keep things from you for the same reason."

Valentina's eyes twinkled with amusement. "Some might say we're unhinged."

"Oh, we definitely are," Raven smirked. "But it's okay—because it's all fueled by love."

Raven and Valentina spent most of the day in Raven's room, wrapped in each other's company, sharing laughter and quiet moments. As the afternoon approached, Raven finished reading the last book from the Widow Clan, leaving her in a somber mood. Valentina, sensing its weight on her, suggested a distraction— something she knew would take Raven's mind off the book.

After losing themselves in each other for hours, they dressed and ventured outside. Valentina longed to feel the warmth of the sun against her skin, especially atop the hill, where they could stay until sunset.

As they strolled through the academy grounds, they passed the outdoor training area, where Onyx and Emilia were engaged in an intense sparring session.

Valentina leaned in, whispering, "When did they get close again?"

They didn't slow their stride, but Raven's gaze lingered, watching Emilia's fierce aggression and Onyx's struggle to keep up.

Raven shrugged, a knowing look crossing her features. Her confrontation with Emilia had likely played a role. Emilia's closest companion—besides Raven—had always been Onyx. Their years of dating had forged a bond not easily broken, even with Emilia's loyalty to Raven. Raven could empathize with Onyx's position. She couldn't imagine what she'd do if someone from Valentina's past suddenly reappeared, demanding Valentina's attention and loyalty.

Still, any sympathy she might have felt was overshadowed by something deeper—disdain. What had once been playful teasing, an annoyance born from Emilia's relationship with Onyx, had turned into something more venomous. Onyx's hostility toward Valentina had stripped away any patience Raven once had. If anything, she would be content to see Onyx's head on a spike.

A sharp grunt pulled her from her thoughts. Emilia hit the ground—not in pain, but in sheer exhaustion. She lay there, staring up at the sky while Onyx rushed to her side, brushing damp strands of hair from Emilia's forehead. Raven observed the interaction with an unreadable expression.

She had never seen Onyx in such a tender, caring light. It might have been heartwarming. If it weren't Onyx.

Atop the hill, Raven and Valentina settled into the grass. Valentina lay her head on Raven's lap, absently playing with the drawstrings of Raven's hoodie.

"Does it hurt?" Valentina's voice was soft, nearly lost in the wind.

Raven hesitated, uncertain of the question's meaning.

Valentina didn't wait for an answer. "Not being able to talk to your best friend because you aren't sure if you can really trust her?"

Raven felt a pang in her chest.

Valentina continued, her voice thoughtful. "I don't want to tell you how to feel. And you can tell me to shut up for my unsolicited advice. But we live in a world of betrayal and death. We tell ourselves we're better than others because we hold onto loyalty, but there's a hierarchy to that loyalty—blood, clan, the assassin world, and then love and friendship."

Raven attempted to lighten the mood with a smirk. "Is this your way of telling me to be wary of you?"

Valentina stopped playing with the hoodie string and instead reached up, fingers threading through Raven's hair. Her gaze was unwavering.

"I would die before I betray you," she said. "My loyalties are secure."

A sad smile flickered across her lips as her gaze drifted back to the training ground below.

"As are Emilia's," Valentina added. "Her training tells her that blood and clan come before everything, but her love for you outweighs that. And it's tearing her apart. Imagine if you had to choose between your best friend and your mother—your clan, your blood, and someone who has your heart. Someone who understands you. Someone you love—not because you have to, but because you chose to."

Valentina's words settled in Raven's mind, like ink sinking into parchment.

"She's grieving the loss of a mother who is still alive," Valentina finished softly. "She needs you. Don't blame her for her mother's sins."

Raven wrestled with the impulse to push her thoughts away. But Valentina's insight had carved through the silence, forcing her to confront the truth.

"I just need time," Raven admitted.

Below them, Emilia and Onyx began making their way back toward the academy.

They sat in silence, letting the weight of the conversation settle between them. Eventually, Raven shifted them so she could lie back against Valentina's stomach.

"What's wrong?" Valentina asked, eyes closed as she soaked in the sunlight.

Raven hesitated. She wanted to protect Valentina from the weight of her worries.

"What makes you think something's wrong?" she deflected.

Valentina smirked. "I can feel it. You're nervous about something."

Raven let out a soft chuckle. "So you know me that well, huh?"

"Every part of you," Valentina teased.

Warmth bloomed in Raven's chest at the words, memories of their earlier time together washing over her.

"Is that all it took for you to understand me?" Raven asked.

"No," Valentina drawled. "But it solidified the fact that I know you better than anyone. Though I think Emilia still has me beat. I'll have to change that."

Raven laughed, conceding the truth in that statement. "Good luck. Emilia could read me before I could read myself."

She sat up, her expression turning serious. "I'm going after the third book alone," she announced, cutting off any protest before it could form. "I can get in and out using the shadows. I can avoid a full-out war."

Valentina's mouth opened, but before she could argue, an announcement blared through the academy's outdoor speakers.

"All assassins to the auditorium. All assassins to the auditorium."

King Pierre's voice carried a weight of urgency.

Raven and Valentina exchanged a glance. A flicker of unease passed through Valentina's eyes.

"Do you think…?" she began, trailing off as the implications settled in.

If they were being summoned, it meant everyone had returned from their weekend away.

Raven stood, offering a hand to Valentina. Valentina took it without hesitation, their connection unspoken but understood.

"Let's go see," Raven said.

Together, they made their way to the auditorium.

27

King Pierre's voice reverberated through the vast auditorium. "There has been an attack," he announced. The polished wood floors gleamed under the overhead lights, reflecting the sigils of every clan that adorned the walls. He paced the center, his gaze sweeping the room, ensuring every assassin heard him.

Around him, the bleachers were filled with masked figures from various clans—some revealing their faces, others keeping their expressions hidden. Near the entrance, where no seats were placed, the Elders stood with their hands clasped, their faces unreadable, carved from stone.

In front of the bleachers, the prodigies stood in pairs, posture rigid, masks concealing their expressions. The hierarchy was clear. Raven stood beside Prodigy Viper, her stance disciplined. Across the room, Valentina stood next to Nikolai, the youngest prodigy. Their eyes met briefly, a silent tether anchoring them in the growing unease.

"The time has come for us to unite," King Pierre continued, his voice even but charged. "We must stand together against this threat."

He let the words settle before delivering the blow.

"Twelve members of the Crimson Widow Clan were found dead atop Shadows Peak." His voice echoed through the silence. "There was no sign of struggle, no evidence left behind. The perpetrators were precise and methodical. To take on twelve highly trained Widow members, it is clear that it wasn't the work of one person—it was a team. We are sweeping the island to ensure no outsiders have infiltrated our sanctuary."

He paused, scanning the faces before him. "If we find no outsiders… then it means our own did this."

A ripple of tension spread through the room.

"We do not know if the killings will continue. Or why they started." He let his words sink in. "Be vigilant. Watch those around you. Remember what we taught you."

No one spoke. The weight of the king's words pressed against them.

"Effective immediately, a curfew will be enforced," King Pierre continued. "No one is allowed to leave the academy on weekends. Patrols will monitor the borders and the academy grounds. Our future is at stake."

The assassins didn't protest, but Raven could feel their unease crackling in the air. The restrictions would not be welcomed. But defiance had its consequences.

"Thank you for listening," King Pierre concluded. "Concerns or questions should be directed to the Elders or the prodigies. They will ensure I receive them. You are dismissed. Elders, prodigies, and professors—stay."

As the majority of the assassins filed out, their murmurs hushed, Raven held her gaze on Valentina. A flicker of unease passed through Valentina's green eyes before she looked away.

When the doors closed, the remaining figures took their seats. The prodigies occupied the first row, the elders the second, and the professors the third. Raven sat beside Valentina, their legs barely touching, an unspoken reassurance between them.

"The curfew does not apply to you," King Pierre said, "but no one leaves. I cannot risk the lives of the prodigies, nor my trusted advisors and professors, this close to the gauntlet."

Raven caught Valentina's subtle reaction—a tightening of her jaw, the briefest twitch of her fingers. The irony was clear. They worried about their safety now, but when the gauntlet arrived, their survival was left to fate.

"I know your skills," King Pierre continued. "But until we know the scope of this threat, I won't take risks."

No one argued. It was not their place to speak.

"Professors," King Pierre addressed the third row. "Pay attention in your classes. Listen carefully. If it were one of our own, someone knows something. The precision of the kills was no accident."

His voice dropped. "Valentina. Raven. Stay. Everyone else, dismissed."

As the others filed out, King Pierre leaned toward the Elders, whispering. Raven glanced at Valentina. There was something in her expression—worry, uncertainty—that made Raven's chest tighten.

Then, King Pierre turned his attention back to them.

"I heard you two went out this weekend. You didn't return to your clan homes, and several people saw you with camping packs." His tone was level, but there was steel beneath it. "So, where were you going?"

Raven met his gaze, then pulled down her mask, revealing her face. "Do you actually want an answer, or are you just accusing us?"

Valentina sucked in a breath. "Raven," she warned.

To their surprise, King Pierre smiled. "I'd prefer not to accuse, especially since Valentina is my protégé. But I can't ignore the obvious. So... where were you going?"

Raven exhaled, her voice low. "Valentina wanted to take a couple's trip. I've never been to the island, and she thought it might be good to show me around. We just... wanted to spend time together.

As much as we could." She glanced away. "Considering one of us might be dead in a few months."

King Pierre nodded slowly, his boot dragging along the floor, absently tracing the edge of a sigil etched into the stone.

"Or both of you," he said flatly.

Raven scoffed, folding her arms. "Not against these amateurs."

"Raven," Valentina warned under her breath, her tone a quiet reprimand.

The King's eyes flicked to Valentina, then back to Raven with cool curiosity.

"So, what did the lovebirds do on this little getaway? Where'd you go?"

"To Fallen Clove," Valentina answered, stepping in smoothly—drawing his attention away from Raven like a protective barrier.

Pierre tilted his head. "That's not far from Shadows Peak."

"Yes," Valentina said, pulling her mask down. She met the King's gaze directly, her voice steady. "No one goes near it because of the undertow beneath the water. It's isolated. Private. I thought it'd be a good place for us to have time alone."

Pierre didn't let up. He crossed his arms, eyes narrowing. "There are other private places on the island. Why that one?"

Valentina didn't flinch.

"The waterfall drowns out sound. And the cave is hidden, even from above. Nowhere else on the island offers both."

King Pierre tilted his head, gaze sharp. "And why were you so determined for that type of privacy?"

Silence settled like fog over the auditorium.

Valentina didn't flinch, but Raven could see it—the shift in the King's eyes. The doubt. The slow tilt toward suspicion. He was starting to see Valentina not just as a soldier, but as someone hiding something.

Before the moment could stretch too long, Raven spoke.

"We had sex."

The words dropped flat, emotionless. Calm as a weather report.

But inside, Raven was panicking.

King Pierre blinked. Once. Twice. Then his hands shot up like he could physically block out the sentence.

"Nope. We don't need to continue this conversation," he muttered, waving his hands as though trying to erase the air between them. His gaze darted toward the door, full of desperate longing, but his posture stayed upright, kingly. Barely.

"I hope you understand why I had to ask," he added stiffly. "I can't afford to leave any stone unturned."

"Of course, my King."

Valentina stood and bowed, perfectly composed.

Raven managed not to roll her eyes. Barely.

"As wise rulers do," she said, standing and offering a quick bow of her own.

King Pierre nodded and gestured to the doors. "Dismissed."

They left the hall together, the air finally clearing once they stepped into the corridor. But they didn't get far.

A cluster of prodigies stood waiting. Some leaned against the walls, others loitered in anxious silence. Their eyes sharpened when they saw the two girls approaching.

"Is everything okay?" Prodigy Viper asked.

Before Raven could answer, Valentina stepped forward, positioning herself between Raven and the others. Shielding her.

Raven appreciated it. She never cared for the prodigies' curiosity, didn't trust most of them. But Viper... Viper was different. She still remembered their first fight—brutal, honest. There'd been something real in it. A strange kind of respect.

"Yes," Valentina said evenly. "Raven and I were on a date near where the incident happened. King Pierre wanted details. We explained our location, our timing, and he was satisfied."

"I'm glad it wasn't anything serious," Prodigy Nikolai said, his voice genuinely relieved.

"We should sharpen our skills. Train harder," Prodigy Phantom said, stepping forward. His voice was steady, but there was an urgency behind it. "The gauntlet's coming, yeah—but if someone from the guild is a traitor, who knows how many they've got backing them? What if they're planning to wipe us out and take over?"

Raven watched him carefully. His words sounded sincere, but she didn't buy it.

Not from him.

Phantom belonged to the very clan she intended to dismantle. He wore their colors like a badge of honor. And she couldn't shake the thought—what if they suspected her?

What if the assassins on the mountain hadn't been surprised to see her because they expected it? Because they already knew?

Then again… maybe it was just Valentina they'd recognized, and knew Raven would be with her.

"I agree," Valentina said, calm and composed as ever. "Rest up. I have a feeling it's going to be a long week."

The prodigies nodded, the tension softening—but only slightly—as she and Raven began to leave.

They barely made it a few steps.

"Being in love with her is making you look weak."

The words came from Onyx.

Every prodigy stilled.

Raven's jaw locked. She was already pivoting, her body tense and ready, but before she could take a single step, Valentina's hand found hers.

Fingers intertwined, firm. A silent tether.

Valentina turned back with the sweetest smile Raven had ever seen her fake. Her head tilted just slightly, almost curiously.

"Onyx," she said softly, like she was starting a lullaby. "I can't keep saving your life."

The smile didn't reach her eyes.

"You talk big for someone who couldn't touch Raven on her

worst day. I've known you since we were kids, so maybe I've been generous. But you speak to her—and about her—like she shares that same history with you."

Her voice cooled, each word sharper than the last.

"She hasn't. In her mind, none of you matter. Not yet. Which means your lives? Already forfeit."

A beat.

"This is your last warning. Watch your mouth. Or next time, I won't stop her from gutting you where you stand."

The air went still.

Onyx clenched her jaw, arms crossing over her chest. But she didn't speak. Didn't dare.

Valentina's eyes swept over the others, pausing briefly on Whisper. She expected him to say something—but he didn't. Still recovering. Still smart enough to stay quiet.

Her smile returned, brighter now, but with an edge. She turned, pulling Raven with her.

"Train hard," she called over her shoulder. "Stay vigilant. We may have traitors among us."

28

The week unfolded just as Raven had anticipated. The entire island remained on high alert, bracing for an imminent attack. She and Valentina kept their heads down, blending in by pretending to be just as vigilant as the others.

Raven avoided meeting with Asha, knowing that too many eyes were watching. But she couldn't delay much longer—she needed a solid plan to retrieve the last book. Even with her abilities, going in blind felt too risky.

She sat up in bed and glanced at the glowing time display on her wall. A little past midnight. Should she risk seeking out Asha? The patrols would be out, and Asha was sometimes among them. Was she walking the grounds now, or was she in her room?

A knock on the door pulled her from her thoughts.

Raven slipped out of bed and opened the door to find Valentina standing there, holding a cake and beaming.

"Happy birthday!" Valentina announced, stepping into the room.

Raven shut the door, chuckling. "I didn't know you could bake."

Valentina eyed the cake warily. "Neither did I. But I wanted to make you one, so I put my heart and soul into it. They say if you make something with love, it'll turn out amazing." She set the cake on Raven's desk and handed her a fork.

Raven accepted it and prepared to dig in, but Valentina placed a hand on her shoulder.

Raven arched a brow. "What?"

"I mean, I say that," Valentina admitted, her gaze flicking toward the cake. "But also…I've never cooked or baked in my life. So if you die, it wasn't intentional. I swear."

Raven laughed. "I'll remember that." She took a bite, chewing slowly. Then, setting the fork down, she turned to Valentina, who was leaning against the desk—pointedly avoiding the cake. "It's very good."

Valentina studied Raven's face. "You're lying."

Raven tilted her head. "You think I'd lie to you?"

Valentina stepped closer, their bodies nearly touching, and plucked the fork from Raven's hand. Their eyes remained locked as Valentina took a bite of her own creation.

Raven suppressed a smile, watching as Valentina's expression cycled from confidence to uncertainty—then to outright horror.

"That is awful," Valentina declared.

"Absolutely terrible," Raven agreed.

Before Valentina could react, Raven leaned in, pressing a quick kiss to her lips. Then she took the fork from Valentina's hand and set it beside the cake.

"But I appreciate your kindness," she murmured.

Raven turned back to face Valentina, taking one of her hands between her own. "This is my first birthday without my mother, and it's supposed to be my biggest one." She sighed, eyes lowering to their joined hands, her thumb gently rubbing over Valentina's knuckles. "I know I can't bring her back, and I know I'm going to feel down all day, but I'm thankful for you. I don't want you to think I don't appreciate what you've done for me." A soft chuckle escaped her lips. "That cake… was awful."

Valentina laughed. "Yeah, it was."

Raven smiled, the warmth in Valentina's voice easing the weight in her chest. "But you thought of me. You put the time in to learn how to bake it, and that means everything."

"I'd do anything to make you happy."

Raven looked into her eyes and felt a wave of sincerity so strong it tightened her throat. Tears welled up against her will.

"Hey," Valentina cooed, cupping her face gently. "I felt empty for so many years. I hated who I was, the life I had to live. But after meeting you, spending time with you, loving you… I've never been happier to be myself. Being a prodigy means I'm connected to you— it means I can protect you, fight for you. And if making you awful cakes for the rest of my life makes you happy, I will."

A quiet laugh slipped from Raven, but tears still fell. Valentina wiped them away with her thumb. Raven placed her hands over Valentina's, resting their foreheads together.

"I love you," Raven whispered. "I'm not good with words, but you bring me peace. You distract me from my pain. When I'm with you, I know everything will be okay, no matter what happens. Thank you for being here. For making sure I'm not alone."

Valentina kissed her forehead. "We can throw out the cake when the sun comes up in a few hours. Let's get some sleep."

Raven bit the inside of her lip. It was one in the morning. She should sleep.

But she couldn't.

"I need to see Asha before bed," she admitted, voice lower now. "I need to finalize a plan and go for the book. I wish we'd just taken it earlier."

Valentina shook her head. "If we had, the fourth book would be too heavily guarded by now. We needed to know if this was worth the risk." She leaned back on her hands, sighing. "At least now we know. Asha has guided you well. Everything has worked out so far."

Raven exhaled, knowing she was right.

"Go," Valentina said, patting the bed beside her. "See if she's in her room. I'll wait for you to get back."

Raven lingered for a moment before walking to the light switch. She turned off the lights, her voice softer. "I'll see you soon. Get some rest."

She watched as Valentina got comfortable in bed before she melted into the shadows.

The cool darkness enveloped her as she traveled, the familiar pull of the void guiding her to Asha's room. When she stepped out, she found Asha standing at the foot of her bed, back turned.

Something felt... off.

Raven took a cautious step forward, reaching for her.

Asha turned.

A gust of wind hit Raven hard—too fast to react.

Her vision blurred.

The world tilted.

Her body crumpled before she could even register what was happening. The last thing she saw was Asha's wide, confused eyes, rushing toward her.

Then—nothing.

Raven groaned, the pounding in her head relentless, unlike any pain she had ever known. A dull ache settled behind her eyes as she attempted to open them, only to be met with blinding light. She shut them tight, breathing through the discomfort. Slowly, she tried again, blinking until the brightness became tolerable.

Her body felt foreign. Heavy. When she tried to move, she couldn't. Panic shot through her as she realized her arms were restrained, wrists bound tightly behind her. She shifted, but her legs were also secured.

A chair. Water pooled beneath her feet, though she couldn't feel its cold touch.

Someone cleared their throat.

She turned toward the sound, and suddenly, every light in the room flared to life. The brightness was suffocating, illuminating every shadow.

Asha stood inches away.

"Asha."

The name left her lips before she fully understood what was happening. Her mind was still foggy, disoriented from whatever had knocked her out.

Then—

"Let her go!"

The familiar voice cut through Raven's confusion. Her head snapped toward the sound.

Ms. Moretti.

Bound. Bloody. Helpless.

Raven's breath caught in her throat. What was happening? Why was Ms. Moretti here?

Asha barely acknowledged her. Instead, she tilted her head and smiled. "Happy birthday, pretty bird."

Raven struggled to steady herself, her mind catching up to her body. Asha. Ms. Moretti. The restraints. The water. This wasn't just a kidnapping. This was a setup.

"Raven, baby, are you okay?" Moretti's voice was laced with concern.

"She's fine." Asha's gaze remained fixed on Raven, her tone mockingly affectionate. "She is the true heir, after all."

Silence settled between them before Raven let out a low, hollow chuckle. Her lips curled, though there was no humor in her expression.

"Do you really think you can keep me here, Asha?"

Asha met her stare, but instead of answering, she moved

behind Ms. Moretti, her fingers pressing into the woman's bruised shoulders.

Ms. Moretti jerked forward, trying to shake her off, but Asha's grip tightened.

"My dear Alexandria." Asha's voice was smooth, controlled. "Guess whose powers have shown themselves early."

Ms. Moretti's gaze snapped back to Raven.

"You've discovered your powers, my love?" Ms. Moretti's bruised face softened with a smile.

Asha scoffed. "Love." She said it like an insult. "Did you know Raven was ready to kill you?"

Ms. Moretti's face twisted in confusion.

"Thanks to me," Asha continued. "I had the Widow Clan plant your name in their book years ago. A failsafe. I'd almost forgotten about it, but when Raven brought it up, I let her believe you were a traitor." Asha tilted her head. "If she had killed you, it would've been rather poetic. I would have been rid of you both in one move."

Ms. Moretti exhaled sharply, shaking her head. "And now?"

"Now?" Asha smiled. "Now, I speed up the process. Raven's pursuit of the third book took too long, and I can't risk the Guild discovering the truth." She gestured vaguely toward Raven. "Who she really is."

Ms. Moretti scoffed. "You plan to kill us both?"

"That's the idea." Asha stepped back, keeping a safe distance. "But first, I have other loose ends to tie up. I can't risk Emilia or Valentina searching for you."

Raven narrowed her eyes. "King Pierre isn't working with you?"

Asha laughed, genuinely amused. "That imbecile? No. It's ridiculous that a birthmark and combat skills entitle someone to rule. That ends with me."

Ms. Moretti spoke before Raven could. "And what do you plan to replace it with?"

Asha squatted, dragging a fingertip through the water. "A new system. One without prodigies. One where no one is born to rule."

Ms. Moretti frowned. "You can't just erase generations of bloodlines—"

"We can." Asha wiped her finger dry. "We let this generation kill each other in the gauntlet. The winner dies before they can take power. The rest? We ensure no new heirs are born, and if they are. Well. We kill them. Their first breath into this world will also be their last ."

The casual cruelty in her voice sent a chill down Raven's spine.

The door creaked open.

"Asha, we need to leave."

A hooded figure stood at the entrance.

Asha hummed. "Right." She turned back to Raven, her expression unreadable. "Mind the water, pretty bird. You wouldn't want to fry Alexandria."

Raven's breath hitched.

Asha flipped a switch, flooding the room with even more light. No shadows.

She paused at the door. "I'll inform Valentina you went after the book. And don't worry—I'll take care of her, too."

She turned to Ms. Moretti.

"As for Emilia… she's in my hands now."

Ms. Moretti screamed.

The door slammed shut.

29

Ms. Moretti's voice was thick with sorrow. "I am so sorry. My job was to protect you and I failed," she whispered. Raven shook her head. "It wasn't your job."

"Yes, it was. The moment your mother was no longer with us, you became my responsibility. I promised her I would watch over you when she was gone. I would protect you. I would love you." Tears slid down her cheeks, unchecked.

A lump formed in Raven's throat. She had spent so much time pretending she didn't need anyone that she could handle everything on her own. Yet here was Ms. Moretti, still standing, still loving her, even after everything.

She forced a small, teasing smile. "I'm still alive, so technically, you're doing a great job."

Ms. Moretti let out a shaky laugh, though it was brittle, broken. "Well then, feel free to sing my praises."

Raven studied the woman who had been a constant in her life, who had loved her mother just as fiercely. Guilt twisted inside her. "I'm sorry."

Ms. Moretti met her gaze, eyes filled with quiet understanding. "What could you possibly be apologizing for, my love?"

Raven looked away. "I thought you betrayed us. I was hurt and angry. I resented you. I told Emilia you would have to pay for your supposed treachery, and I feared she might be a traitor too. I might have driven her away from both of us." Her throat tightened. "I don't know if she'll ever forgive me."

Ms. Moretti exhaled, the sound carrying both sympathy and restrained frustration. "Oh, sweetie. That was Asha's plan all along—to turn us against each other. You have no idea the things I've imagined doing to her. She took my best friend, shattered our lives, and hurt you. She won't live to see tomorrow." Her voice was steel now. "We need to find a way out of here."

Raven scanned the room, searching for anything that could aid their escape. Every assassin learned how to break free from bindings—but they also learned how to restrain effectively. Asha had trained her personally. She would know exactly what Raven could and couldn't do.

The realization sent a fresh wave of anger rolling through her. Damn her.

"What powers do you have?" Ms. Moretti asked.

"Shadows and electricity."

Ms. Moretti tilted her head. "Shadow manipulation is rare—powerful. Electricity is a gift reserved for the greatest heirs in our history." She studied Raven for a long moment. Then, with quiet certainty, she said, "Hold your breath."

Raven frowned. "Uh, okay?"

She inhaled deeply and held it.

Ms. Moretti simply watched her.

After several moments, Raven exhaled. "Was I supposed to do something? You didn't say anything."

Ms. Moretti rocked her chair slightly, shifting its balance. "Hold your breath again."

Raven did.

Ms. Moretti froze mid-rock.

The realization hit Raven like a jolt of lightning.

"You froze."

Ms. Moretti's lips curved into a knowing smile. "You have the ability to stop time for as long as you can hold your breath."

Raven's pulse quickened. "How did you know?"

Ms. Moretti shrugged. "Historically, the strongest heirs possess multiple abilities. The power to manipulate time was revered in our original serpent king. I wasn't sure if you had it, but given your talents, I was willing to bet on it. If not this, then perhaps super healing or enhanced strength."

Raven sighed. "Super healing would've been useful. Super strength too. Stopping time doesn't seem all that helpful right now."

Ms. Moretti chuckled. "Maybe. But let's focus on what we do have. How far along were you with your electricity training?"

Raven clenched her jaw at the memory of training under Asha's watchful gaze. "I made considerable progress, but the way she bound my hands prevents me from using it properly."

Ms. Moretti nodded, deep in thought. "And your control over shadows?"

A small, sad smile flickered across Raven's face. "Exceptional. Emilia helped me master it." Her chest ached. Emilia.

"Then summon a shadow to aid your escape. Use your electricity to break the bindings and free me."

Raven shook her head. "I can't. There are no shadows. She flooded the room with light. I'm useless right now."

Ms. Moretti's voice softened. "It's your birthday, Raven. Today, your powers should be at their peak. Shadows are always there, even in the light. You just have to find them."

Raven closed her eyes. Reached out.

Nothing.

She opened them, shaking her head. "I can't."

Ms. Moretti's expression hardened. "Raven, if you don't,

Asha will hurt Emilia. She'll hurt Valentina."

A shiver ran down Raven's spine.

No. I won't let that happen.

She took a slow, steady breath, and this time, she reached deeper.

And in the smallest sliver of space—beneath the chair's legs—she felt it.

The darkness.

Waiting.

Raven took a deep breath, willing the shadows to heed her command. The sliver of darkness slithered toward her feet, responding to her desperation. It was all she needed. Without hesitation, she stepped into the void, where she held dominion.

Inside the darkness, she focused her energy, shaping crackling electricity into a serpent-like form. It coiled around her wrist restraints, its edges sharpening with her will. With a flicker of concentration, she transformed it into a dagger and severed the bindings, freeing herself from the chair.

The moment her feet hit the ground, she re-emerged at her mentor's side. She reached for one of the daggers strapped to Ms. Moretti's assassin attire, working quickly to slice through the ropes.

As soon as Ms. Moretti was free, she rubbed her wrists and stood. Her smile was warm and genuine. "Happy Birthday, my pretty bird," she murmured, pulling Raven into a tight embrace and pressing a kiss to her forehead.

Raven sighed, melting into the embrace. Ms. Moretti had become the closest thing to a mother she had. Doubting her loyalty had been a mistake.

Ms. Moretti scanned their surroundings, her expression tightening. "We need to get out of here. We have to reach King Pierre and tell him what's happening."

Raven shook her head. "Not yet. I need the third book first. If we go to him without solid evidence, they'll turn this on us. As an outsider, he'll be more inclined to believe them."

Ms. Moretti hesitated, her brows knitting in concern.

"I'll take you home, to the safety of your clan," Raven continued. "Then I'll find Emilia and Valentina, bring them to you, and go after the book."

A flicker of protest crossed Ms. Moretti's face, but Raven pressed on. "You need to prepare your clan for war. Or at the very least, safeguard Emilia. Please. I need that book to expose the truth." She softened her tone. "I need you by my side."

Ms. Moretti exhaled and brushed a stray strand of hair from Raven's face. "I've always been on your side. Just as I was on your mother's." Her lips curled into a wistful smile. "You look just like her, you know."

A lump formed in Raven's throat, but she pushed down the emotion. There was no time for sentimentality.

"Fine," Ms. Moretti relented. "But you'd better be back before the day ends. If you die on your birthday, your mother will have my head in the afterlife."

Raven smirked and clasped her mentor's hand, pulling her into the shadows. Ms. Moretti shivered, glancing around as if trying to understand the void surrounding them.

"Are these all openings?" she asked in wonder.

Raven nodded. "Every shadow is an entry and exit point for me. I can see what lies beyond before stepping through it. No one can see me until I fully emerge."

Ms. Moretti hummed in awe as Raven focused on the image of her mentor's home. The shadows shifted, revealing the exit.

They stepped through. Light flooded Ms. Moretti's office, forcing her to blink against the sudden brightness. She turned, spotting the sliver of shadow in the corner, and smiled.

"You truly are skilled," she praised.

"Thank you," Raven said, scanning the room. "Keep a shadow near you at all times. If you do, I can always find you."

Ms. Moretti nodded in understanding.

Raven inhaled deeply. "I'll be back soon."

Ms. Moretti hesitated. Then, softly, she said, "I love you."

Raven paused at the threshold of the shadows, glancing back. "I love you too," she whispered before vanishing into the void.

She needed to find Valentina and Emilia—but first, she had to change.

The shadows twisted, guiding her to the nearest exit. She stepped out, opening the door to her room

Her breath hitched.

Blood stained the floor. Her belongings lay in ruins, torn and broken. The remnants of her birthday cake smeared across the surface like a cruel joke. And worst of all—

Three bodies. Lifeless.

A cold chill ran through her. Valentina had been here before she left to see Asha.

Her heartbeat hammered in her ears, but she forced herself into motion. She tore off her clothes, slipping into her black mission uniform—no insignia, no ties to any clan. She strapped her sword to her back and checked her pouches, ensuring she had everything she needed.

As she stepped over one of the bodies, a hand clamped around her ankle.

Raven whirled, drawing her sword, its edge stopping mere inches from the man's throat. He coughed weakly.

She grabbed his collar and yanked him up. "Why were you here?" she demanded.

The man wheezed. "The book. We came for the book. We didn't know she was here."

"She? As in Prodigy Valentina?"

The man nodded. "She claimed she didn't know what we were talking about. The others didn't believe her. They tried to search the room. Then… something in her snapped. She attacked. We never stood a chance." His gaze shifted toward his fallen companions. "I don't know what happened after that. I blacked out."

Raven turned, lifting the floorboard where she had hidden the book. Empty.

Maybe Valentina had taken it. Maybe she had escaped.

She crouched beside the man again, studying him. "Why betray the guild?" she asked. "Do you truly believe all prodigies should die? That the true heir should be eradicated?"

His lips parted, his expression conflicted. "I believe we deserve a chance to lead," he said. "They have too much power."

Raven hummed softly, pressing a hand against his chest. Electricity crackled beneath her fingertips. His eyes widened.

"As the true heir," she whispered, "I condemn you to death."

A surge of power jolted through him. His body spasmed. Then, he was still.

Raven pulled back, exhaling slowly.

Her gaze flickered to the chaos around her.

"Where are you, my love?" she murmured into the silence.

30

Raven took in the scene before her. Valentina stood bloodied but unyielding, her sword drawn as she faced off against the assassins. Three already lay dead at her feet, yet she remained unfazed. The flickering torchlight illuminated her features, revealing a fierce determination in her sharp eyes.

Bound to a pole, Emilia struggled in vain against her restraints.

One of the remaining assassins stepped forward. Clad in nondescript mission uniforms, their affiliation was concealed, but Raven recognized the telltale signs of the Widow Clan—the same assassins who had been hunting her for years.

"Put the sword down, Prodigy Valentina," the assassin demanded. "We just want the book."

Valentina's lips curled into a cruel smile. She adjusted her grip on her sword, gaze flicking over her opponents. "Tell me where Raven is, and I'll tell you where the book is."

The assassin tilted his head, feigning consideration. "Raven is safe."

Valentina snorted, making air quotes with her fingers. "If she were truly safe, she'd be here with me."

"Enough of this," another assassin snapped. "Give us the book or die."

Valentina twirled her sword with a confident flourish, lowering into a fighting stance. Raven felt a shudder of anticipation—this was Valentina in her element, a warrior bred for battle.

But Raven wasn't one to sit back and watch.

Electricity crackled along her arms, illuminating the shadows curling at her feet. With a flick of her wrist, she summoned them closer, shrouding the assassins in darkness. In a single, fluid motion, she moved—her electrified hands and dagger a blur as she struck.

One. Two. Three.

Before they could react, the assassins dropped silently to the ground, throats slit.

Valentina blinked. "Uh."

Emilia stared at the bodies, wide-eyed. "Did you see that?"

Valentina straightened, still in shock. "I think?"

Emilia struggled more urgently against her restraints. "Well, get me out of here before whatever that was kills me too!"

Raven rolled her eyes and stepped out of the shadows. "Always so dramatic."

At the sound of her voice, Valentina and Emilia's heads snapped toward her. Raven barely had time to react before Valentina rushed forward, wrapping her in a tight embrace.

"I thought something bad happened to you," Valentina whispered into Raven's shoulder.

Raven's arms circled around her, rubbing her back. "Something bad did happen. But it'll be handled. I'm okay."

Valentina pulled back just enough to wipe the tears from her eyes. Then, without hesitation, she pressed a fierce, searing kiss against Raven's lips.

Raven melted into it, tasting the salt of Valentina's tears.

A loud throat-clearing shattered the moment.

Emilia.

Raven pulled away, exhaling as she turned to her best friend. She quickly moved to cut the bindings at Emilia's wrists. Emilia rubbed her skin, frowning as she avoided Raven's eyes.

"I'm glad you're okay," Emilia muttered. Then, softer, she added, "Happy birthday."

A pang of guilt struck Raven's chest. She reached for Emilia, pulling her into a tight hug. At first, Emilia stiffened, but then she slowly relaxed, her grip tightening on the back of Raven's shirt.

"I'm sorry," Raven whispered.

Emilia shook her head. "No. If your mom was the reason my mom is dead—after I trusted her—I would be upset too. I would question everything."

Raven pulled back, gently touching Emilia's cheek. "But your mom didn't betray me. Asha set her up as a fail-safe."

Valentina, standing nearby, stiffened at the name. "Asha?"

Raven sighed. "Yes. She's been behind this all along. I don't know why she's working with the Widow Clan, but she said she killed my clan to stop the heir from being born. If I die—if my bloodline ends—then the prodigies will cease to exist. No one with our abilities will stand in their way."

Valentina clenched her fists, her entire body vibrating with rage. She began pacing.

Emilia frowned. "What did my mom have to do with this?"

Raven exhaled slowly. "Asha made sure your mom's name was written in the book as a fail-safe. They were best friends, but Ms. Moretti wouldn't have let Asha live if she knew the truth. The safest option for Asha was to get rid of her."

Raven's fingers curled into fists. "She said she forgot about the fail-safe—until I confronted her. Then she decided it would be poetic to let me kill Ms. Moretti before she got rid of me. Two birds, one stone."

Emilia's eyes darkened with rage.

Raven's voice wavered. "Your mom was tied up with me. She forgave me. She told me it wasn't my fault, that Asha had planned this all along. I will never forgive myself for doubting her." She swallowed hard. "I'm sorry, Emilia."

Emilia stared at her, emotions warring in her eyes. "I want to be mad. I want to scream at you for ever doubting her."

Raven lowered her head in shame.

"But…" Emilia sighed, her expression softening. "It's not your fault. You did what you thought was right. You were manipulated. And my heart loves you too deeply to let this break us."

She lifted a hand to Raven's chin, forcing their eyes to meet.

"You will always be my best friend. So stop beating yourself up." Her lips twisted into a cold smirk. "Instead, let's make Asha pay."

Raven tilted her head until her forehead rested against Emilia's. Closing her eyes, she took a deep breath. She was ready for justice.

She turned to Valentina, who approached with the book in hand.

"Where do we put this?" Valentina asked.

Relief flooded Raven as she took the book and flipped through its pages. "We need to start making copies," she said, handing it back. Without waiting for a response, she extended her hands toward Valentina and Emilia. Without hesitation, they grasped them.

Calling on the shadows, Raven enveloped them in darkness. Emilia and Valentina shivered slightly.

"Are you cold?" Raven asked.

"It's freezing in here," Emilia replied. Her teeth weren't chattering, and the shivering was barely noticeable—a testament to their cold-weather assassin training. Valentina said nothing, but her grip on Raven's hand tightened occasionally.

Raven sifted through the shadow pathways, searching until she found the one leading to Ms. Moretti's office. They stepped through.

The moment they emerged, Ms. Moretti reacted on instinct, flinging a knife toward Valentina. Raven caught it midair; Valentina didn't even flinch.

Ms. Moretti shot to her feet. "I am so sorry. Reflex. I just threw it at the first person I saw."

Raven twirled the knife once before flipping it in her hand and offering the handle back to Ms. Moretti. With an apologetic smile, she accepted it.

"It's okay," Valentina said, waving off the near-fatal mistake.

"I threw so many at Raven at first," Emilia grinned, stepping forward to embrace her mother.

Ms. Moretti hugged Emilia tightly, pressing a kiss to the top of her head. "I'm so glad you're safe, love. I was worried."

Emilia pulled back, studying her mother's face. The blood was gone, and she looked slightly better than the last time Raven had seen her—but the exhaustion in her eyes spoke volumes.

"You were worried about me? Look at you," Emilia frowned.

"Wow, thank you so much," Ms. Moretti said dryly before turning to Valentina and Raven. She eyed Valentina. "How are you holding up?"

Valentina shrugged. "Irritated. Confused. Angry."

Ms. Moretti nodded. She understood. So did Raven.

"Okay," Raven said, pulling up her hood. "Make copies of those pages, destroy the false accusations against Ms. Moretti, and be ready for me when I return with the third book."

Ms. Moretti and Emilia nodded. Valentina, however, didn't move.

Raven raised an eyebrow. "Yes?"

Valentina set the book on Ms. Moretti's desk and stepped toward her. "I'm coming with you."

"Absolutely no—"

"I am going with you," Valentina said, her voice steely.

Raven turned fully to face her, arms crossing. "No. I'm not risking you getting hurt. I can't lose you, and if someone hurts you..."

Her throat tightened. She had always known being an assassin meant danger, but the thought of Valentina injured—or worse, dead—sent a sharp, visceral pain through her chest.

"How do you think I feel?" Valentina's voice rose, making Raven flinch. Valentina never raised her voice. Not at her.

"I worry, Raven. You don't know how I felt when you didn't come back, and assassins entered your room. I wondered if you were okay or if they had killed you. I worried the entire time. Then they touched your desk. It was just a stupid desk, but it was yours, and I felt rage. Rage because they dared enter your space, as if they had the right. Rage because you could've been captive somewhere, bleeding out on the floor, and I wouldn't know. Rage because I should have gone with you.

"We are a team. We agreed. I can't be left behind on these missions anymore. I can't stand being somewhere else, helpless. We protect each other, and when we're together, I don't have to worry. We can take on anything."

She grabbed Raven's hand and gave a teasing smile. "We're the top two prodigies, after all."

Raven's resolve wavered.

"Okay," she relented.

Valentina beamed.

Raven reached out, pulling Valentina's hood up over her head. The blood on it smeared against her fingers. "But you stay close. I need to do this correctly, and if anything happens to you, my logic goes out the window."

Valentina nodded, stepping forward to place a quick kiss on Raven's lips. Heat crept up Raven's face as she remembered their audience. When she turned, both Ms. Moretti and Emilia wore knowing smiles.

It didn't take Raven and Valentina long to reach the forest surrounding the Crimson Widow Clan house. What surprised them, however, were the figures lurking in the trees and around the home—mercenaries.

Clad in black and armed with guns, they stood out starkly against the backdrop of assassins who traditionally shunned firearms on the island.

Raven exchanged a glance with Valentina. Two mercenaries stood just feet away, oblivious to their presence in the shadows.

How? Raven's mind raced. King Pierre was always alert, the clans were constantly patrolling—so how had these mercenaries infiltrated without raising alarms? The only explanation was an inside collaborator. And only one name fit.

Asha.

Raven squeezed Valentina's hand, silently asking: *Do we strike now or keep moving?*

Valentina flicked her gaze back to the mercenaries before tilting her head toward the void. Raven nodded. They slipped back into the darkness, vanishing completely.

Valentina let out a frustrated breath. "This doesn't make sense. How did they get on the island? How did no one see them? Where the hell is King Pierre?"

Raven remained silent, her thoughts echoing the same questions.

She refocused, gripping Valentina's hand tightly as she envisioned the book's hiding place. She knew there would be guards inside. But down here—in the cave where light couldn't reach—she had the advantage.

Especially now.

Her newfound ability to freeze time while holding her breath is useful, but there were still gaps in her understanding. What would happen if she miscalculated? If she ran out of air mid-action? The thought unsettled her.

The shadowy entrance to the book's resting place loomed

ahead. Raven's sharp vision scanned the space, spotting the mercenaries posted inside—too many. Just as she prepared to step forward, Valentina yanked her back.

Raven stumbled into her. "What—"

"Trap," Valentina whispered.

Raven crouched, following Valentina's pointing finger. A metal device, hidden within the shadows, gleamed faintly. It resembled a bear trap—smaller, deadlier. Raven's jaw clenched.

Asha...

For a split second, anger tightened her chest. If Asha had truly betrayed them, if she had set this, it meant she was willing to kill Raven.

Raven took a slow breath and pulled Valentina upright.

"They've set it up so we can't just take them out from the shadows," she murmured. "We'll have to fight."

She searched Valentina's eyes for hesitation. There was none.

"You'll have to leap past the trap," Raven instructed. "I'll pull the shadows back the second we disconnect. You'll be exposed first, but I'll be right behind you."

Valentina gave a sharp nod, green eyes flickering with determination. "I love you."

Raven's heart clenched at the quiet intensity of her words. "I love you too."

They moved in tandem, Raven gripping Valentina's shirt and throwing her forward. Valentina hit the ground, rolling smoothly as she drew her sword. Raven collapsed the shadows immediately. Valentina's blade sliced through two mercenaries' wrists, sending their guns clattering.

Raven landed beside her, unsheathing her own sword. Lightning crackled at her feet as she propelled herself forward, cutting through the remaining mercenaries before they could fire. By the time she halted, the bodies lay still, weapons discarded.

Valentina huffed, wiping sweat from her brow. "I don't think I'll ever get used to your lightning."

Raven smirked. "Then this will really impress you." She lifted her hand, summoning electricity into her palm before flicking it outward. Bolts surged into the shadows, triggering every hidden trap, disarming them in a single motion.

Valentina let out a slow clap. "Well done."

Raven chuckled and went for the book.

The moment Raven touched the book, a deafening siren exploded through the cavern.

Both she and Valentina winced in agony, hands flying to their ears. Valentina collapsed to her knees, while Raven stood frozen, teeth clenched against the onslaught of sound.

The wail of the alarm echoed through the cave like a living thing, vibrating through stone, making the very shadows quake.

Raven didn't need confirmation—she knew.

The mercenaries were coming.

She turned toward Valentina, reached for her—

But the second her hand left her ear, the noise intensified tenfold. It felt like knives driving into her skull.

Raven blinked through the blur of pain, just in time to see the first wave of mercenaries pour into the tunnel. They wore earplugs. Smirking. Armed.

A second entrance opened behind them, and more followed, surrounding them with surgical precision.

Their weapons rose.

And Raven knew.

These weren't orders to capture. They were orders to kill.

Did Asha give the command before she escaped? Did Asha even know she was gone?

Raven's gaze dropped to Valentina.

She lay curled in on herself, blood trickling from her nose, her body trembling.

Something snapped.

A violent heat surged through Raven's spine—up across her left shoulder, collarbone, right shoulder, the back of her kneck, and up her left cheek. It stopped at her left brow, just as her left eye sharpened.

Suddenly, she saw everything.

Every flicker of movement. Every glint of sweat on the mercenaries' faces.

And she felt nothing but rage.

"Enough," she said.

The word wasn't hers. Or maybe it was—just no longer human.

She inhaled, held her breath—

And the world stopped.

Time froze.

The pulses in the mercenaries' necks ceased. Their grins stilled.

Silence swallowed the cave.

The siren vanished.

Raven lowered her hands, letting the ringing in one ear fade into the background.

Electricity coiled through her limbs as she knelt, pressing her palm to the ground. A surge shot outward in every direction, deadly and precise. She curved the current away from Valentina, her control razor-sharp.

Then—

She summoned the shadows.

They slithered across the floor like snakes, wrapping around the mercenaries' weapons, locking them down—ensuring not a single shot could be fired.

And she let time resume.

The mercenaries screamed.

Their bodies convulsed violently, caught in the current's grip.

Valentina didn't move.

One ear still ringing, Raven gritted her teeth and pushed harder. The voltage increased.

One by one, the mercenaries dropped.

Dead.

Raven inhaled shakily, trying to ignore the ringing in her ears. She grabbed the book, crouched, and touched Valentina's trembling form.

She wrapped them both in shadows, vanishing into the void.

31

This time, Raven felt untouchable.

She didn't drift through the shadows. She didn't guide Valentina across the void like before.

She simply moved.

From the darkness of the cave to the shadows in Ms. Moretti's office—effortlessly, instantly.

But with power came risk.

She hadn't checked if the room was clear.

So when she and Valentina emerged from the shadows, there stood Prodigy Viper directly in front of them.

Raven's hand snapped to her dagger, the blade drawn before she could blink. Her body angled in front of Valentina, ready to strike.

But Viper dropped to one knee.

"Your Majesty," she said, her arm resting across her bent knee, head bowed low.

Raven kept her hand on Valentina, dagger raised, her gaze still locked on Viper in suspicion—until Ms. Moretti's voice cut through the moment.

"She's with us, Raven. Loyal to her clan—and to you."

Raven let out a slow breath, then sheathed the blade. "Stand, Viper."

Viper rose smoothly, but her eyes lingered on Raven's face. There was something in her expression—uncertainty, maybe even awe.

Raven narrowed her eyes. "What?"

"You've fully awakened," Emilia said, stepping forward. Her gaze swept over Raven's face with quiet intensity. "Look in the mirror. See who you really are."

Raven didn't respond. She looked down instead, at Valentina, still unconscious on the floor. Carefully, she brushed a strand of hair from her face.

"Help me," she said quietly, voice soft and laced with worry. "Lay her on the couch."

Without hesitation, Viper moved to assist. Together, they lifted Valentina with care and settled her onto the nearby couch.

Emilia was already there, draping a blanket gently over her.

Raven lingered, watching the steady rise and fall of Valentina's chest. She scanned her face, searching for any flicker of pain, any sign that the siren had done more than just knock her unconscious.

But Valentina looked peaceful.

Resting.

Safe.

Only then did Raven turn away.

She crossed the room slowly and stepped in front of the mirror.

Raven stared into the mirror—and gasped.

Her hand flew to her face.

It felt the same beneath her fingers, but her reflection told a different story.

The serpent birthmark had changed.

What once lay hidden along her spine now curled upward—

slithering across her collarbone, wrapping around her neck, and climbing the left side of her face. It settled there, bold and permanent.

The burning she'd felt earlier—now it made sense. The mark had been moving.

Transforming.

Her eyes—

She leaned closer. Her left eye, once a deep warm brown, now shimmered with silver. Not just glowing—alive. A storm behind glass.

Power hummed beneath her skin.

It surged through her veins like wildfire, pulsing with such intensity she swore she could command the island with a single thought.

But she didn't have time to drown in it.

Not yet.

Raven inhaled sharply and summoned her will, focusing on the serpent. Slowly, the mark began to recede, flowing down her face, uncoiling from her neck, sliding back into place along her spine. The warmth faded with it, replaced by a steady calm.

She stepped back.

Her reflection stared back at her—disheveled, blood-streaked, clothes torn and scorched from the electrical discharge, hair tangled from the fight.

She looked like a storm that had survived its own wrath.

And she had.

Turning away from the mirror, Raven met the eyes watching her. Emilia. Viper. Ms. Moretti. All silent.

All waiting.

Valentina lay motionless on the couch, untouched by the moment.

Raven pointed to the book now in Emilia's hands—the one she must have picked up while Raven stood at the mirror.

"Have you made copies of the fourth book?" Raven asked, voice cool and steady, despite the fire still lingering beneath her skin.

Ms. Moretti nodded. "It's done. Distribution's already underway. And another set of copies of the third book is en route."

Raven gave a single nod.

Smart. Secure. No single point of failure.

"Then finish it," she said. "Make the final copies. Spread them far and wide."

She let the weight of her next words settle.

"Then we confront Asha. And we burn the Crimson Widow Clan to the ground."

Viper stepped forward, hesitation in her posture. "Um… Your Majesty," she said, her voice careful, reverent but unsure.

Raven met her gaze, waiting.

"Will you… announce yourself?" Viper continued. "Let everyone know who you really are? End the charade?"

Raven opened her mouth to respond, but Viper rushed on, her words tumbling.

"Not that I'm not honored to serve you—as a prodigy, as a part of you, I just…" Her voice faltered, fingers twitching at her sides.

Raven gave her a gentle smile. "You just want to live."

Viper blinked.

Raven stepped forward, voice steady and resolute. "I will announce myself. I will fulfill my role as the true heir. I will bring peace—to you, to all the prodigies, and to those who come after us. And when my final breath comes, the next heir will rise. The cycle will continue."

Her gaze drifted to Valentina, unconscious but safe, and her tone softened.

"You deserve more than survival. You deserve joy. You deserve love."

A hush fell over the room.

Ms. Moretti and Emilia exchanged a quiet look—one of relief, and maybe, hope.

Viper nodded, emotion welling behind her eyes. A single tear slipped down her cheek.

"Thank you," she whispered, swiping it away quickly, her expression hardening once more into something focused. "I'll handle the preparations," she said, taking the book from Emilia's hands. "You rest. We'll find something to help Valentina recover."

Raven nodded, gratitude flickering in her eyes as she watched Viper disappear through the door.

She returned to Valentina's side and gently lifted her head, settling it in her lap. Her fingers threaded through Valentina's hair, slow and careful.

Raven looked up.

Across the room, Ms. Moretti sat at her desk, lost in thought. Emilia stood nearby, arms folded, brow furrowed—both quiet, but alert.

"Shall we address the elephant in the room?" she asked, her voice calm, but edged with steel. "What should be Asha's fate?"

Ms. Moretti looked away, her composure fracturing as her eyes fell to the desk.

Emilia didn't speak right away, but Raven saw the tight clench of her jaw—the storm brewing just beneath the surface. Anger. Hurt. Betrayal.

Raven felt it too.

She remembered the warmth in Asha's voice, the quiet strength in her mentorship. The way she'd once looked at Raven like she believed in her. Like she cared.

And now, all of it twisted into something hollow.

Had it all been a lie?

A carefully constructed facade to erase the last thread of her family's legacy?

The thought made Raven's chest ache.

"She should stand trial," Emilia said at last, her voice sharp with conviction. "Just like the Crimson Widow Clan. She betrayed us, and betrayal demands justice. Not vengeance."

"Death," Ms. Moretti said, her voice cold and final.

Emilia turned sharply, pushing off from the desk and walking toward the couch. She perched on its arm, directly across from her mother, eyes burning.

"She was your best friend," Emilia snapped. "How can you say that so easily?"

Ms. Moretti didn't flinch. "Exactly. She was my best friend. Nova's best friend. And despite that, she chose betrayal. That makes it worse, not better."

Her voice was hard, but Raven could hear the pain in it, buried deep.

"She doesn't deserve a trial. She deserves to face me. And her fate."

Emilia's hands curled tightly against the couch frame.

"But she didn't kill us. She had so many chances—to take out Raven, to eliminate Ms. Norris—and she didn't. That means something. Maybe she couldn't go through with it, even if she wanted to."

Ms. Moretti's gaze sharpened, her tone low and fierce.

"You think that makes her noble?"

"No," Emilia replied. "But it makes her human."

Ms. Moretti stood still, but her words carried the full weight of leadership.

"As future head of this clan, you'll need to learn—friendship doesn't excuse treason. She helped wipe out Raven's entire bloodline. She orchestrated Nova's death. And she still wants Raven gone. That mercy you think she showed? It doesn't erase what she's already done. Or what she is currently doing."

Her voice trembled, just slightly.

"I won't let her take Nova's daughter, too."

Then, colder.

"I'm done listening to her excuses. Her actions were her verdict."

A breath.

"She dies."

Emilia opened her mouth to protest, but Raven spoke first.

"Very well," she said, her tone calm. Unshaken.

Emilia turned toward her, eyes wide in disbelief. "Raven—"

But Raven met her gaze head-on.

"Ms. Moretti will deliver justice to Asha," she continued. "In a final duel. Asha will have the chance to fight for her life. If she wins, she's banished. If she loses... she dies."

Emilia's frown deepened. "If she wins... that means my mother is dead."

Raven gave a small nod. "You can't have it both ways. You wanted her to have a trial. Ms. Moretti wants her dead. This is the only way to honor both without compromising either."

Ms. Moretti's voice was quiet, but firm. "That seems fair. A wise decision, Your Majesty."

Raven resisted a smirk. "Please. Save your pleasantries for when we have an audience."

A dry chuckle escaped Ms. Moretti's lips, but it faded quickly. She leaned back in her chair, gaze drifting upward, lost in a memory Raven couldn't see.

Raven thought she caught the faint whisper of a name—her mother's name—but the moment was gone before she could say anything.

A soft sound tugged her attention back.

Valentina stirred.

Raven's fingers paused, still tangled gently in her lover's hair, as green eyes slowly fluttered open.

Their gazes met.

"Hi," Valentina whispered, a sleepy smile curving her lips.

"Hi," Raven murmured, her thumb brushing lightly along her temple.

Valentina sighed, closing her eyes again for a breath. "My head is pounding."

"That's from the ear-splitting siren. How do your ears feel?" Raven asked gently.

Valentina lifted a hand, touching her ear with delicate care. A frown formed between her brows.

"They're okay. But I don't want to hear anything that loud ever again."

Raven smiled. "Noted. We'll avoid death traps labeled siren caves moving forward."

Valentina chuckled softly, her eyes opening once more. Raven felt the warmth flood her chest as their gazes locked again.

"You're so kind, my queen," Valentina whispered.

Raven laughed quietly. "Viper's bringing something to help you feel better."

As Valentina pushed herself up, Raven let her hand fall away. Valentina shifted beside her, curling close and resting her head against Raven's shoulder. Their fingers intertwined naturally.

"I feel okay… mostly." She tilted her face up. "When does the final mission begin?"

"Soon," Raven said, voice even. "Once Viper returns, Ms. Moretti will distribute the final copies. Once they're in the hands of every clan, I'll step forward. I'll reveal myself, call for the arrest of every Widow Clan member tied to the betrayal—Asha included—and the trial will begin."

"And if they resist?" Valentina asked quietly.

Raven didn't hesitate.

"Then they die."

The room was silent, but the agreement was clear—etched in every nod, every look.

There would be no more mercy for those who cloaked betrayal in loyalty.

32

veryone in the Silent Clan gathered around Raven, forming a tight circle. Valentina stood beside Viper, Ms. Moretti, and Emilia. Raven turned slowly, meeting the gaze of as many clan members as possible. She had chosen not to clean up—the blood of her enemies still stained her clothes and face. Her hood was pulled back, revealing herself fully.

Ms. Moretti had briefed the clan about the coming war and the presence of traitors within the guild. But Raven knew that words alone weren't enough. They needed to see her—know her—to trust her. The Silent Clan would replace the ShadowFang Clan in protecting her bloodline.

"Thank you all for gathering and for aiding Ms. Moretti in distributing crucial information. I'm here to provide clarity," Raven began, her voice steady, commanding. "I've deceived you all. The story I told to join this clan was a fabrication."

A ripple of tension passed through the crowd.

"I chose the Silent Clan because of Ms. Moretti and Emilia. I've known them my entire life, and with my mother gone, I wanted to be among people I trusted. People I felt safe with.”

She felt the weight of their uncertainty but pressed on.

“My mother is Nova Norris, former head of the ShadowFang Clan, a descendant of the Serpent King. And I am Raven Norris, rightful heir to the ShadowFang Clan, the true heir of the Guild.”

Gasps rippled through the clan. She willed her birthmark to reveal itself, her skin tingling as the mark of her bloodline flared to life. A stunned silence followed.

“I am the true heir, and this war is about restoring justice and order to the guild,” she declared. “The Crimson Widow Clan orchestrated the massacre of my people, luring them into a deadly trap. My mother, pregnant with me at the time, survived with the aid of Ms. Moretti and Professor Zion.”

She hesitated. The name alone sent a knife of betrayal through her.

“They raised me, trained me, loved me. Emilia, born shortly after, became my best friend. She taught me about all of you, about the academy, about social interaction—some might argue I still have much to learn.” A few smiles flickered across familiar faces, those who had been at the academy with her.

Raven exhaled, her fingers tightening at her sides.

“My mother passed not long ago, and I spent time alone before coming to the Academy. At first, I only wanted to expose the Crimson Widow Clan. I knew I was a prodigy, but I didn’t know about my connection to the Serpent King. That changed when I uncovered the Widows’ secrets—their admissions of guilt.”

She let the words settle before she delivered the real blow.

“What you all may not know is that Professor Zion, Asha, was the mastermind behind it all.”

A sharp intake of breath spread through the clan. She could see the disbelief in their eyes. The Widow Clan’s corruption was one thing—but Asha? A beloved mentor? The foundation of their trust cracked beneath them.

“I understand it’s hard to believe,” Raven continued, meeting their eyes with unwavering resolve. "Believe me, I struggled to accept it myself. She was one of the four people I loved deeply—a mentor, a companion on countless training exercises, someone my mother trusted until her dying breath. Discovering her betrayal felt like a dagger in my heart. But I won't let emotions cloud my judgment."

She forced herself to look at Valentina, drawn into her gaze for a moment before refocusing.

"Asha revealed her true intentions to me and Ms. Moretti. She held us captive, threatened to kill me and every prodigy until the mark of the Serpent King was wiped from existence. She wants to reshape the guild under her rule."

Silence stretched between them.

Raven let the moment sink in, her gaze sweeping across the clan. Then, she spoke the words that could change everything.

"The ShadowFang Clan is no more. The Silent Clan is my chosen family. The one I stand with now." She let the conviction in her voice carry through the room. "Will you stand with me in this war? Will you bring justice to the traitors and protect my bloodline from this day forward?"

The room was thick with uncertainty. A moment stretched— too long, too heavy. Would they follow her? Or would she stand alone?

"I'm in."

The voice came from a younger clan member. "I've seen what you can do in combat. You never seem to break a sweat. I'm curious to see what you're capable of when you go all out."

Raven allowed a small smile.

"Are your powers fully activated?" an older clan member asked.

Raven nodded. With a thought, she let electricity crackle over her skin. Gasps echoed around her as the energy danced along her arms.

"I can also manipulate shadows and stop time," she added.

The older man studied her with quiet reverence. "Powers akin to those not seen since the Serpent King himself. But electricity… we have known only great kings and queens with that ability." He inclined his head. "I will fight alongside you."

Raven exhaled, relief washing over her. "Thank you."

One by one, others followed. But they didn't just agree. They dropped to one knee. A wave of devotion swept through the room as heads bowed in allegiance.

Raven's throat tightened. She bit her lip, forcing back the flood of emotions.

She hoped her mother could see this moment. Hoped she would be proud of the leader she had become.

"Stand," Raven commanded.

The room obeyed in unison, a collective energy pulsing as warriors straightened, their eyes locked on her.

"It's time."

They moved swiftly, pulling up their hoods and gathering their provisions for the impending battle. Raven wove through the controlled chaos, halting before the towering windows that framed the darkened forest beyond.

She worried about the unknown. Would the clans support her? Did Asha have allies beyond the Crimson Widow Clan? Had others been tempted by the promise of a different future? Every possibility carried weight, and the war could end in swift bloodshed or drag on as a brutal conflict. The uncertainty gnawed at her.

Strong arms wrapped around her waist, grounding her. She leaned back into Valentina's warmth, her gaze never leaving the treeline.

"What are you thinking about?" Valentina's voice was soft, as she rested her head on Ravens shoulder.

Raven exhaled slowly, resting her cheek against Valentina's head. "How this war might unfold."

A beat of silence. She could feel Valentina thinking.

"If I die—"

Raven stiffened, twisting in Valentina's arms so quickly that

Valentina stumbled back a step, though her hands remained firm on Raven's waist.

"Don't." Raven's voice was sharp, urgent.

Valentina's lips curved in a sad smile. "We have to consider all possibilities, Raven."

Raven shook her head, the thought of losing Valentina leaving a bitter taste in her mouth. "Please," she whispered, dropping her gaze to the floor. She had lost too much already.

Valentina understood. She pulled Raven into a tight embrace, murmuring against her hair, "Okay, I won't say it. Just promise me you'll always do right by our people. Do right by yourself. And love."

Raven clung to her. "I love you. There will be no other."

Valentina rubbed soothing circles on her back. "I want you to be happy."

"Then fight like hell," Raven said, stepping back. "Because I won't lose you. I won't lose anyone."

A voice called her name.

She turned to see Emilia approaching, Onyx at her side. Raven's gaze locked onto Onyx, reading every flicker of her expression.

"Onyx has something to say," Emilia announced.

Onyx stepped forward, then—shockingly—dropped to one knee, head bowed.

"I am here to fight for you, my Queen." Her voice was steady. "Please forgive my past actions. I act impulsively when emotions cloud my judgment. But I pledge my loyalty. I will dedicate my life to yours."

Raven's tense stance eased. She flicked a glance at Emilia, who frowned but said nothing.

Raven chuckled. "I assume the last part didn't sit well with you?"

Emilia rolled her eyes. "We're all here, ready to lay down our lives for you. It's just..."

"I understand," Raven replied. She met Valentina's gaze

briefly before turning back to Onyx. "Rise, Prodigy Onyx. You are not my enemy. I forgive you."

Onyx stood, pushing back her hood. "Do we have a plan?"

Raven was about to respond when she felt something shift in the shadows. Instinct prickled at her. Dipping into the nearest shadow, she vanished. The darkness carried her forward, and within moments, she was in front of them, though they did not know that. Figures approached the mansion, hoods concealing their faces, their weapons and uniforms unmarked. Were they reinforcements? Enemies? Too many unknowns. She went back.

She reappeared in front of the others.

Onyx's eyes widened, seeing shadow manipulation for the first time.

"We've got company. I couldn't make out their faces, but they're moving fast. Stay alert."

Everyone tensed, shifting into position. Raven maintained her connection to the shadows, sensing the movements and gaging the proximity.

"Thirty seconds," she murmured, hand resting on her sword but resisting the urge to draw it.

A knock.

Raven arched a brow. That was unexpected.

Ms. Moretti stepped forward. Raven started to protest, but Emilia's grip on her arm stopped her.

"They might be allies," Emilia whispered.

Raven hesitated, then gave a small nod. Ms. Moretti opened the door.

The figures entered cautiously, eyes scanning the room before settling on Raven's group. Valentina stepped forward, sword drawn.

"Identify yourselves," she ordered.

The group exchanged glances before pulling down their hoods one by one.

Raven's gaze swept over them—prodigies and clan heirs. But she lingered on one face.

Prodigy Phantom.

"We've heard the news," Prodigy Frost announced. "We're here to assist the Silent Clan in bringing justice to the Widow Clan."

Raven's group turned to her for a response, but her gaze remained locked on Prodigy Phantom. Her expression was unreadable, yet her silence carried weight.

Valentina took the lead. "Prodigy Phantom, your clan stands accused of treachery. Why have you come here?"

Phantom met Raven's eyes briefly before lowering his gaze. A flicker of hesitation crossed his face, but when he spoke, his voice held firm conviction. "I know what my clan has done. I don't condone their actions, and I won't stand by while they destroy everything we stand for. I had to make a choice.

"Choosing to protect our world means confronting traitors to our way of life, even when they are family," he added, lifting his gaze to meet Valentina's without flinching.

Raven studied him, noting the pain buried beneath his composed exterior. His words rang with sincerity. Without addressing him directly, she reached out and placed a hand on Valentina's arm, a silent signal of acceptance.

Valentina relaxed slightly but remained positioned in front of Raven.

Scanning the gathered group, Raven quickly noticed two familiar faces missing. Her stomach tightened, though she forced her voice to remain steady.

"Where are Prodigy Seraph and Whisper?"

A heavy silence settled over the group. Eventually, Prodigy Tariq stepped forward. "Prodigy Seraph and Prodigy Whisper have sided with the traitors."

Raven feigned surprise, though inwardly, she had anticipated this. Seraph was of Asha's clan, and Whisper… she had never trusted him. His heart carried old wounds, ones that could easily drive him toward vengeance. If given the opportunity, he would likely align himself against her—if only to settle an old score.

Pushing aside personal thoughts, Raven turned to Luna, the heir to the Death Lotus clan.

"Your clan's prodigy chose the traitors, yet you stand with us?"

Luna's jaw tightened, her voice carrying the weight of divided loyalties. "Our clan has splintered. Half followed Professor Zion, believing in her wisdom. The rest, including my father and me, remained loyal to the guild. We are only fifteen now."

Raven absorbed this information before shifting her attention. "And Whisper's clan? The Ghost Orchids?"

Luna shook her head. "From what I've gathered, they did not side with him. Every other clan has aligned against the Widows and Asha. Only my clan fractured, with some joining the Widows and Asha's cause."

Raven's mind whirred. With the clans united behind her, she commanded four hundred and fifteen assassins. Asha had only one hundred and seventeen. On numbers alone, victory seemed certain. But numbers weren't everything. Asha had something far more dangerous—firearms. A single well-placed bullet could take down even the most skilled assassin.

Viper, ever observant, broke the silence. "What's on your mind, Your Majesty?"

"That we have the advantage in numbers, but they have superior firepower," Raven admitted, her gaze dark with contemplation. "We can't rely on sheer force. Strategy will determine who wins this war."

A voice interrupted her thoughts.

"Apologies," Prodigy Nikolai spoke, drawing everyone's attention. "Why did you call Prodigy Raven 'Your Majesty'?"
The question hung in the air.

Raven hesitated. She had known this moment would come, but now that it was here, she felt the weight of it. She could explain—but words would not suffice. Instead, she let her power speak for itself.

A familiar energy coursed through her, her presence shifting as she felt her birthmark move and settle around her like an unseen mantle. The very air seemed to acknowledge her authority.

Gasps echoed through the room. The prodigies, recognizing the truth in her transformation, dropped to their knees in unison.

"Rise," she commanded, and they obeyed immediately, their expressions a mix of awe, understanding, and—most importantly—relief.

With formalities out of the way, she turned back to the matter at hand. "Now that we know our numbers, our enemy's strength, and our weaknesses, we must act. We will seize control of the academy grounds and convene in the auditorium. It's the only space large enough for all clans to coordinate strategy."

"What if they attempt to infiltrate or eavesdrop?" a clan member asked.

"The prodigies will be vigilant, and my own senses are heightened beyond theirs. But as an added measure, I will set shadow traps around the auditorium," Raven stated firmly. "Anyone who dares trespass through them will be swallowed by the darkness."

She turned to the assembled prodigies. "I will escort you back to your respective clans through the shadows for safety. Deliver the message. We will reconvene in thirty minutes."

A synchronized nod followed.

Pulling up her hood, Raven reached for the shadows, letting them rise around her.

It was time to prepare for war.

33

Murmurs rippled through the auditorium. All the clans had assembled, but they remained in tight clusters, avoiding intermingling. Tension hung thick in the air.

At the center of it all stood King Pierre, surrounded by the council. Every member was present except for Counselor Magna. Her absence was no surprise, given her ties to the traitors' clan.

Meanwhile, Prodigy Phantom, still without a clan of his own, had sought refuge with Prodigy Frost's people.

King Pierre raised a hand. The murmuring quieted at once. He turned to Ms. Moretti.

"We received your message," he said, his tone measured. "We've learned of the deceit and betrayal. But how did you find the books? How did you obtain them? Our summons gave little information beyond the instruction to assemble here. Due to the urgency, I assume you had no time to explain. Please, elaborate."

Ms. Moretti rose gracefully, a quiet authority radiating from her. She gestured toward Raven.

"Forgive me, but this is the Serpent Queen's story to tell."

A fresh wave of murmurs surged through the clans. Confusion flickered across King Pierre's face. But before the whispers could escalate, Raven stepped forward, moving past him to stand at the center. Pierre exhaled slowly, then took a seat among his people.

Raven spoke without embellishment, recounting everything—from her birth to these final moments. When she finished, she summoned her elevated form.

Gasps echoed through the hall.

Then, one by one, the clans bowed—even King Pierre himself.

Raven held their awe in silence before speaking again.

"Thank you for your acceptance and willingness to fight. I will not let Asha get away with this. I will not let her endanger us all. I know some among you have kin who sided with her. If you change your mind about standing with us, speak now. If not, we must strategize."

The clans rose from their bows and returned to their seats. Not a single voice spoke against her.

King Pierre approached, his expression unreadable. Then, he removed the crown from his head and bowed, extending it toward Raven.

"There is usually a formal ceremony to place a ruler on the throne," he said, "but as the Serpent Queen, you ascend naturally—ceremony or not. "Here, before the clans and the council as your witnesses, accept this crown and your rightful place as ruler."

Raven hesitated. She glanced at Ms. Moretti, who smiled reassuringly. Then her gaze found Emilia, who grinned widely, and finally Valentina, who gave the faintest bow, her forest eyes shining with pride.

She looked back at the crown in Pierre's hands.

"If I accept this now, do I still get a ceremony?"

Pierre's lips twitched at the question, though his head remained bowed. "Is it important to you?"

Raven glanced at Valentina once more before returning her

gaze to Pierre.

"If it means I get to dance and crown a Queen Consort, then yes."

Pierre nodded. "Then your wish is my command, my Queen."

Raven smiled, inhaling slowly as the weight of the moment settled around her.

She wished her clan could see her now.

Wished her mother were standing beside her, proud.

And—strangely, painfully—she wished Asha were here, too. Not as an enemy, but as the woman who once guided her.

As someone who might've stood at her side to witness this.

Raven reached for the crown and placed it on her head.

Applause thundered through the auditorium.

She raised a hand. The room fell silent.

"It's time to make a plan," she began, her voice steady, strong. "We have the numbers. Asha has the weapons."

She paced slowly, gaze sweeping across the room.

"She's likely set traps in the shadows again—hoping to catch anyone foolish enough to use them." A pause. "Unfortunately for her, shadows are everywhere. And I can access them all."

Her silver eye caught the light.

"In this form, I am strongest. And at night—I am a nightmare."

A ripple of tension moved through the room. Not fear. Respect.

"I'll use the shadows to take out their weapons. You'll move through them too, like you've been trained."

She stopped in the center of the room.

"When I'm done, you'll see an explosion in the sky. Electricity. That's your signal to emerge and strike full-force."

A beat.

"I want them alive. I want them on trial. But if they resist…"

Another pause.

"You do what you must."

There was no hesitation in the nods that followed.

They understood. These were assassins. Professionals.

Raven glanced at the clock. Midday. Still hours before sunset—before the shadows turned against the traitors.

"This place is well guarded," she continued. "No one can enter or leaves until I lower my shadow traps."

She looked to the crowd.

"Rest. Rotate shifts. Stay alert. I need you at your best. I'll scout their positions and map our ground before nightfall."

"You cannot go alone," Counselor Zephyr said.

Raven tilted her head, unsure if it was a command or concern. She offered a faint smile.

"No," she replied. "Which is why I'm taking Valentina."

Counselor Lyra frowned. "She's the strongest prodigy we have. Shouldn't she stay, just in case?"

Raven shrugged, gesturing casually toward Valentina. "Sure. Would you like to tell her that?"

Valentina was already standing. Frowning.

"You've got eight prodigies here," she said. "They're trained. And like the Queen said, the auditorium is surrounded by shadow traps. If anything happens, Raven will know—and we'll be back before anyone can draw a blade."

She took Raven's hand, giving it a firm, silent squeeze.

Raven nodded. "Pierre, you're in charge until we return."

Then she called to the shadows. And with Valentina at her side, they disappeared into the void.

They walked in silence at first, hand in hand, the hush of the void comforting in its weightlessness.

But then Valentina stopped.

Raven stopped with her, turning with a questioning tilt of her head.

Valentina's voice was soft. Honest.

"I'm really proud of you," she whispered. "And I'm so in love with you."

Raven's heart fluttered at the words—at the way Valentina said them like they were sacred.

But then her voice grew uncertain.

"Still… do you think it's wise for me to be your queen consort?"

She looked down at their joined hands.

"We're not married. We haven't even been together a year. What if… you grow tired of me someday? What if you don't want me anymore?"

Raven didn't hesitate.

She tugged Valentina forward by their joined hands, wrapping her arms firmly around her waist.

Valentina melted into the embrace, her arms slipping around Raven's neck as she rested her forehead against hers.

"Valentina," Raven said softly, her voice barely above a breath. "I could never grow tired of you."

She cupped Valentina's face gently, her thumb brushing along her cheekbone.

"You are my strength. My heart. Our bond is deeper than time, deeper than blood." Her eyes glistened with emotion. "I don't need a ceremony or a crown to know you're my queen consort."

A beat passed. Then, quietly—

"I am madly in love with you," Raven whispered. Her voice cracked just slightly. "When you're near, everything is easier. Lighter. I feel like myself, but safer, freer. I don't know how to exist without you anymore. And I don't want to."

She closed her eyes briefly, steadying the storm behind her ribs.

"I'll love you until my last breath."

When Raven opened them again, her gaze was full of quiet ache.

"You would have won the gauntlet, you know," she said, her tone bittersweet. "If I weren't the true heir of the Serpent King."

She swallowed.

"I would've taken my own life before ever raising a blade against you. You would've been a great ruler."

She pulled the crown from her head with slow reverence and gently placed it atop Valentina's. Then, taking her hands, Raven dropped to one knee.

"I chose you as Queen Consort not just because I love you," she said, bowing her head, "but because it should have been you."

She pressed her forehead to the back of Valentina's hand.

"You are the true Queen in my eyes. And I will always follow you."

Valentina's voice was quiet, but firm.

"Get up."

Raven rose.

Valentina didn't hesitate—she pulled her into a kiss, fierce and full of fire.

Raven melted into her arms, the world falling away. She deepened the kiss, feeling the surge of energy swell through her chest, not from magic, but from the simple truth of this.

This was her anchor. Her home.

Her breath stilled, and for just a second, Raven called on her elevated form.

She thought of war. Of the Widow Clan. Of fire and vengeance.

But then Valentina's lips pulled her back.

And Raven smiled into the kiss.

Valentina held her closer.

When they finally broke apart, Raven chuckled breathlessly. "We have a war to prepare for."

Valentina hummed, brushing her fingers gently along the left side of Raven's face.

Her thumb traced the serpent mark curling up her cheek.

"So beautiful," she whispered.

Raven took the hand Valentina had used to trace her face and placed a soft kiss on its knuckles. Releasing Valentina's other hand, she pulled her out of the void and into the shadows.

Valentina blinked, taking in the scene before her. "How did you find them so fast?" she asked, admiration shining in her eyes.

Raven shrugged, a faint smile playing on her lips. "I asked the shadows, and they did the work for me. When I'm in this form, it's like my powers aren't just a part of me—they are me. It's as easy as breathing. I feel like I could take on the world. It's terrifying, but exhilarating."

Valentina squeezed Raven's hand and pointed toward a set of mercenaries in the distance. They shifted seamlessly into the next shadow, moving undetected. Raven studied their weapons, her teeth sinking into her lower lip thoughtfully.

"We need to find the armory from this location," she said, her voice edged with determination.

Valentina surveyed the area before pointing to the east. "Widow Armory. Get us two hundred meters that way. We should end up in the same location we were last time when we accessed it."

Raven nodded, pulling Valentina closer before slipping them into the shadows again.

They reappeared in Widow territory, the air thick with tension. The security was tight, but no mercenaries patrolled the immediate area. That was telling. Had the Widow Clan grown distrustful of the mercenaries after the battle in the cave? Raven's gaze darted between the assassins, noting how they moved through the trees like ghosts, near-invisible if one didn't know where to look.

"Where's the main armory?" she asked.

"Attic," Valentina murmured, her eyes locking onto something in the distance.

Raven followed her gaze and immediately spotted Prodigy Whisper.

"We should pull that traitor into the shadows and watch him suffer," Valentina muttered.

Raven studied her carefully. "Does it hurt you that he changed sides?"

A long pause. Then, "Yes. He was my best friend. My boyfriend, once. Even after we ended things, he was still one of the people I trusted most." Her voice tightened. "I never thought me falling in love with you would break him. I never thought he would fight against me."

Raven didn't reply, only watching Whisper in the distance.

Valentina exhaled. "I don't regret falling for you," she said quietly, as if to reassure Raven. "I just wish I could've kept my friend."

"I understand," Raven admitted. "I won't insult him or call him a fool, because if I were in his place, I might feel the same. Seeing you love someone else—knowing you were giving yourself to another—I would rather burn this world down."

Valentina turned, her expression unreadable.

"But," Raven continued, her voice firm, "if it meant hurting you, I wouldn't go through with it. I would leave."

A silence stretched between them before Valentina brushed a light kiss against Raven's cheek. "I'm not going anywhere," she whispered. "Now, take us through the house."

Raven obeyed, shifting them through the shadows until they reached the attic. She had doubted Valentina's claim that an armory could be housed in such a space—but now, standing in the dim glow of blue-lit walls, she realized she should have known better.

Weapons lined the walls in meticulous order, organized by combat type. Yet, despite the arsenal, no guards patrolled the room. Overconfidence.

"Traps?" Raven asked, glancing at Valentina.

"None," Valentina said. "They think they're untouchable."

Raven scoffed. "Bold for a clan that's been infiltrated three times."

Valentina chuckled, stepping forward to examine the armory. "They have changed some things."

Raven trailed her fingers along a row of guns, a spark of electricity dancing at her fingertips. A surge spread across the weapons, frying their circuits. "How so?" she asked, satisfied as the last gun short-circuited.

"More weapons," Valentina answered. "We need to hit the other armory too."

"The one in the shed?"

Valentina nodded.

Raven extended her hand, and Valentina took it without hesitation. A light blush dusted her cheeks.

"What?" Raven asked.

Valentina shook her head. "Nothing. It's just... the pull you have on me is terrifying. You could lead me to my death, and I'd follow without hesitation."

Raven smiled. "Good thing I have no plans to live in this world without you."

With that, they disappeared into the shadows.

34

Once Raven and Valentina had finished moving through the shadows, neutralizing every weapon—including those held by unaware mercenaries—they returned to the auditorium.

The sun hovered on the horizon, casting golden streaks across the dimming sky. The assassins stirred, rising to their feet, stretching, and meticulously inspecting their weapons. Despite the weariness of waiting, anticipation thickened the air.

"My Queen," a shadow blade intoned, his voice reverent. A ripple of acknowledgment spread through the room as others bowed.

Raven inclined her head, her grip tightening as the crown Valentina had returned to her just moments ago slipped from her head and landed in her palm.

"Gather around," she commanded.

The entire auditorium obeyed, forming a disciplined semicircle before her.

Raven studied them, absorbing the silent vow in their gazes. They had chosen her, accepted her leadership despite knowing her only briefly. These assassins, bound not by blood but by shared purpose, had handed over the crown to her not out of obligation, but recognition. These were her people now, and by this time tomorrow, some of them would be gone.

She swallowed hard.

"Thank you." Her voice carried through the space, firm yet tinged with emotion. "Thank you for standing with me. For fighting for me. For upholding the legacy of the Serpents. Tomorrow, some of you may not be with us, but your courage will not be forgotten. Your sacrifice will not be in vain." She paused, scanning their faces. "I wish I could promise to see you all on the other side, but I know that's a promise I cannot keep."

A hush settled over the room.

Raven inhaled deeply, centering herself. "I have disabled their weapons—they do not know this yet because they have not needed to use them. We have the advantage. You are trained, and they are not. The mercenaries are expendable; they fight for coin, not cause. The Widows, however, will be harder to defeat." She let that sink in before continuing. "Try to incapacitate them first. If you can force them into the shadows, I will take care of the rest. But if capture is too dangerous, do not hesitate. Justice is our goal, but I will not sacrifice you for traitors."

Her gaze lingered on Emilia, Ms. Moretti, and Valentina. Committing their faces to memory.

"It's time," she said. "They will try to ambush us at the school. We must leave now and position ourselves beyond their expected attack zone. Trust your instincts. Use your training. I will be in the shadows, guiding you." She exhaled. "Good luck."

With a final bow, the assassins dispersed. Raven lifted the shadow barriers at the entrance, ensuring a safe exit.

Her focus remained fixed on Emilia.

Emilia stepped forward, closing the distance between them until their foreheads touched. A lump formed in Raven's throat.

"Be careful," Raven murmured.

Emilia smiled softly. "Always, il mia grazioso uccello." She pressed a kiss to Raven's forehead before turning to embrace her mother. Then, with Onyx at her side, she vanished into the night.

Ms. Moretti approached next, her eyes glistening. "God, your mother would be so proud of you," she said, her voice thick with emotion. "I am so proud of you."

Raven leaned into her embrace, allowing herself a fleeting moment of solace.

"Be careful, my sweet girl," Ms. Moretti whispered. "I love you."

"I love you too," Raven murmured, holding onto the warmth of the moment before letting go. Ms. Moretti pressed a gentle kiss to her forehead, then departed.

Only Valentina remained.

A bittersweet smile touched Valentina's lips as she approached. "I guess this is where we part ways—for now."

Raven lifted a hand, tucking a stray strand of hair behind Valentina's ear. "It seems that way," she murmured.

They had agreed on this. It was safer for Raven to move through the shadows alone, unencumbered by the risk of losing Valentina to their depths.

Valentina placed her hand over Raven's. "I love you," she whispered, the words filled with quiet resolve.

"And I love you." Raven's voice was steady, though her heart ached. "If you ever need me, step into the shadows. I'll be there."

Valentina smirked as she pulled up her hood, adjusting her mask. "You'll get that kiss when this is all over."

Raven chuckled. "I'll be counting on it."

With a final lingering glance, Valentina turned and disappeared through the doors.

Raven exhaled slowly, summoning the shadows to her. The familiar warmth of her power wrapped around her like a second skin. She pulled up her hood and mask, then stepped into the darkness, vanishing into the night.

By the time the widows and mercenaries launched their attack, darkness had fully descended. Raven's electricity crackled through the sky. The clans had anticipated the assault and shifted their positions, catching their enemies off guard. What began as a swift, calculated strike quickly devolved into brutal, close-quarters combat.

Raven had counted on the growing shadows at sunset to enhance her mobility. Yet, in her elevated form, she realized she no longer needed natural darkness—she was the darkness, slipping unseen between fights like a specter.

When one of her assassins was outnumbered, Raven intervened without hesitation. The mercenaries fell swiftly to her blade, their bodies crumpling to the blood-soaked ground. Though her warriors never saw her directly, they felt her presence, offering silent bows before returning to the fray.

She moved tirelessly, ensuring the safety of her clans, eliminating threats before they could strike. Then, movement caught her eye.

Valentina stood with her sword drawn, its edge gleaming with fresh blood. Opposite her, Whisper pulled back his hood, revealing dark, wind-tousled hair. They circled each other like predators.

"Where is Raven, Valentina?" Whisper's voice was steady, but his eyes searched hers.

Valentina raised an eyebrow. "Do you really think I would tell you?"

Whisper exhaled slowly. "I don't want to hurt you. I care about you."

"Care?" Valentina scoffed. "Is that what you call siding with traitors? Helping them hunt the woman I love?"

Whisper's jaw clenched. "She's not one of us."

Valentina tilted her head, studying him. Then she moved—

fast. Her blade struck with deadly precision, forcing Whisper onto the defensive. He blocked her strikes, but barely.

"She's better than us," Valentina spat, landing a fierce kick to his chest. Whisper staggered backward, colliding with a tree. He barely had time to react before Valentina's sword sliced toward his throat. He rolled away just in time, dirt and leaves scattering beneath him.

He pushed himself to his feet, panting. "Did you ever love me?"

Valentina hesitated, and for a moment, the battle between them disappeared.

"I did," she admitted softly. "We grew up together. You were my best friend. Even after we chose different paths, you still mattered to me."

"But you weren't in love with me," Whisper said. It wasn't a question—it was a quiet acceptance.

Valentina met his gaze without hesitation. "No."

Whisper's eyes darkened. "But you love her?"

Valentina lifted her chin. "If I were dying of thirst and she needed water, I would give her my last drop—just to see her smile one last time before I died."

Silence stretched between them. Then, Whisper exhaled sharply, pulling his hood back up. "Then there's nothing more to say." He turned to flee into the woods.

Valentina was faster.

Her kunai flew, burying itself in his calf. Whisper collapsed with a sharp cry of pain.

"Over my dead body," Valentina whispered, stepping forward. She didn't hesitate this time. Her blade found his heart, and as blood bubbled from his lips, she watched the life leave his eyes.

Raven chose that moment to step from the shadows, her presence soft but unmistakable.

Valentina looked up, their eyes meeting in the dark.

Raven's gaze drifted down to Whisper's still body. Silent.

Then back to Valentina.

"What would you like to do with him?" Raven asked quietly.

Valentina stared at Whisper for a long moment before straightening. Her voice was steady when she finally spoke.

"Take him," she said. "He was a boy with a broken heart."

Her breath hitched, but her composure held.

"Maybe if I hadn't fallen in love with you… he wouldn't have turned against us."

Raven nodded, understanding the weight of what went unsaid.

"There's no maybe about it," she said gently. "He would've stood beside you. That much was always certain."

She lifted her hand. The shadows responded, curling around Whisper's body with eerie grace, cradling him like a fallen soldier.

"We'll bury him where he belongs," Raven murmured, her voice low, resolute. "Among the prodigies who came before him."

Valentina's voice dropped to a whisper. "Thank you."

Raven turned back to her, searching her eyes—not for guilt, but for grief.

There was no anger. No resentment. Only sorrow, worn quietly like a veil.

Raven felt a wave of relief settle through her chest.

"I'll see you soon," she said softly, placing a soft kiss on Valentina's cheek.

Valentina nodded, solemn and sure, as Raven vanished into the night once more.

Moving swiftly through the dark, Raven let the shadows guide her—watching from the trees, the rooftops, the quiet corners of the battlefield.

Her clans were winning.

The battlefield quieted. The widows surrendered, the mercenaries fell. Victory was near.

But then—a shift in the darkness.

Raven felt it before she saw it. The sharp, unnatural wrongness. She moved instantly, shadows swallowing her whole.

Raven materialized in a rush of shadows—
and froze.

The air was thick with the copper scent of blood.

Emilia lay on the ground, crimson blooming beneath her, pooling from the corner of her mouth like a whispered secret.

For a moment, Raven couldn't move.

Couldn't breathe.

Then the world snapped into focus.

She ran.

Dropping to her knees, Raven pulled Emilia into her lap, cradling her like something sacred and broken all at once.

"Em," she choked out, her voice cracking as tears blurred her vision.

There was no one else around. Just them.

Emilia looked up at her through glazed, pain-filled eyes and gave a sad, bloodstained smile.

"Hi, il mia grazioso uccello," she whispered.

Raven's heart clenched at the familiar endearment.

"What happened?" she asked, gently pressing her hand over the wound at Emilia's side.

"I… saw Asha," Emilia rasped, coughing, her body wracked with pain. Her hand reached up to Raven's face, trembling. "I was angry. I needed her to look me in the eyes. To admit the lies. To stop pretending."

Her fingers slipped away, too weak to hold.

"She did," Emilia whispered. "She finally did. And I thought I could be the one to end it. To bring her in. It should've been one of us."

A bitter, broken laugh escaped her lips, followed by a sharp wince.

"But I wasn't strong enough."

Raven's jaw clenched. "She did this to you?"

Emilia gave a faint nod, eyes shining with sorrow. But her gaze stayed on Raven—soft, unwavering.

"I'm glad I met you."

The words hit like a blade.

Raven's breath caught. "Em… please." Her voice trembled. "You can't leave me."

Emilia hummed faintly, and with the last of her strength, her hand returned to Raven's cheek.

"I was in love with you," she said, so quietly that Raven barely heard it. "You were everything I ever wanted. But I was scared. I didn't know how to tell you… So I chose to be your friend."

Raven's eyes widened. Pain rippled through her chest like lightning through bone.

"No," she whispered. "Emilia—"

Emilia's hand fell away.

Her eyes began to close.

"Emilia," Raven called, desperation lacing every syllable.

No answer.

"Emilia," she whispered again, her voice cracking into broken glass.

Then—

With her final breath, Emilia whispered, "Be the ruler you were meant to be, il mia grazioso uccello."

Raven stared at her.

Still.

Gone.

The weight of it hit like a tidal wave.

Tears streamed down her face, unstoppable, her body shaking with the force of it.

She clutched Emilia to her chest, her fingers digging into blood-soaked fabric, as if holding her tighter could undo the inevitable.

Her breath fractured into sobs.

And then—

The grief erupted.

A raw, anguished scream tore from Raven's throat—violent,

guttural, endless.

A sound that shook the trees. That made the shadows recoil. That carved a wound into the night sky.

35

(Valentina's POV)

 wiped the blood from my clothes—a futile gesture, but one that momentarily lightened my spirit. Cleaning my sword on the grass, I sheathed it and moved through the woods toward where the clans were gathering prisoners.

"Prodigy Valentina!"

I turned at the familiar voice and saw Nikolai rushing toward me. My heart ached for him. He was the youngest of us, yet he had seen more battle and bloodshed than any child should. It was why I was grateful for Raven—she was forging a future where prodigies wouldn't have to grow up under constant threat of death.

Throwing an arm over his shoulder, I tousled his hair. "I'm glad you made it through, youngster."

Nikolai squirmed out of my hold, fixing his already-messy hair. "Yeah," he said, puffing out his chest. "You guys underestimate me. I'm really fast and talented. One day, I'll prove it to all of you. I'm just glad it isn't in the Gauntlet."

I smiled at that. I had always seen Nikolai as a younger brother, and the thought of ever having to face him in mortal combat tore at my soul.

His expression turned serious. "Anyway, did you find Prodigy Whisper?"

I had. And I had killed him.

A part of me still struggled with the weight of that decision. Whisper had been my friend, my confidant. But love is not something that can be controlled. He had tried to take Raven from me, and if he had succeeded—if she had suffered at his hands—I would have razed everything he held dear.

"I found him," I admitted. "He was resolute in his choice, so I ended him myself." My voice was steady, but my stomach twisted at the memory. "Raven suggested we give him a proper funeral. Lay him to rest with the prodigies who came before."

Nikolai nodded, thoughtful. "Our queen seems… compassionate."

I raised an eyebrow. Compassionate wasn't a word typically associated with Raven.

He chuckled. "I may not know her personally, but from what I've seen in the past month, she's fair. A good ruler."

He wasn't wrong. Even in war, Raven made calculated decisions. There was steel in her, but there was also something more. Something only a few had the privilege of seeing.

Nikolai gave me a quick grin before sprinting off toward the others.

I scanned the gathering. Most of our forces were accounted for. The guild maintained its usual stoic facade, but I knew better. Even the strongest warriors felt the ache of loss, the weight of those who would never return.

Ms. Moretti caught my eye. Before I could speak, she pulled me into an unexpected embrace.

"I'm so relieved you're safe," she murmured. "Raven couldn't bear losing you. She's already endured so much."

The words settled deep in my chest. I loved Raven—fiercely, endlessly. Knowing she felt the same gave me something to hold onto in all this bloodshed.

I pulled away, concern flickering in my eyes. "Is Emilia back yet?"

Ms. Moretti shook her head. "No, but I saw her in battle. She was holding her own. She's probably rounding up captives."

I nodded, reassured but still uneasy. "She's going to be a great leader when she takes over."

"She already is," Ms. Moretti said warmly. "She has the clan's loyalty. The young ones adore her. And she broke through to Raven's heart—no small feat."

That was true. At first, I had been jealous, unsure of the bond between them. But the more I learned, the more I understood. Emilia had been there for Raven in ways I never could, and for that, I was grateful.

"I should go find Pie—"

A blood-curdling scream shattered the air.

Raven.

My heart stopped.

Without a second thought, I sprinted toward the sound, panic surging through me. The edges of the world blurred as I reached the tree line.

Then, darkness.

Ky'erra Sylva

The Shadow Sigils

Glossary

Prodigies: Assassins born with serpent birthmarks, their abilities traced to the ancient bloodlines of the Serpent Heir. The birthmarks — unique in shape and placement — can appear anywhere on the body. Gifted with slightly heightened sense compared to the Shadowblades, they can hear better, see better in the dark, and move with preternatural speed and strength. Their landings, even from great heights, are soundless. They are stand in rulers for the true serpent heir.

Shadowblades: The name of all the assassins who do not bear the serpent birthmark.

Serpent Birthmark: It is a recessive gene that randomly appears every generation. The only birthmark that stays in the family is the true heirs.

Clans: Bound by code and secrecy, yet independent in blood and purpose. All walk the path of shadows, but no two clans are the same—each guided by its own creed, forged through centuries of tradition, belief, and war. Marriage between clans demands allegiance; one must choose which banner they will bear, there are no divided loyalties. Every clan bears a distinct insignia.

Clan Heads: The sovereign rulers and living embodiment of their clan's will. Each Clan Head serves as both leader and voice— upholding the ancient codes, commanding loyalty, and deciding the fate of those beneath their banner. Their word carries the weight of law, their judgment the balance between honor and execution. To defy a Clan Head is to defy the clan itself.

Clan Heirs: The blood-born successors of the Clan Heads. Trained from childhood in the arts, laws, and secrets of their lineage, Clan Heirs embody the future of their people. In them, the clan's strength, pride, and survival converge.

King/Queen: The reigning Prodigy—the last survivor of the Shadow Gauntlet—who stands as ruler over all clans. They are the living law, unmatched in skill and authority, the embodiment of the assassin guild's power and unity. They command every mission and pass judgment upon all who dwell in the shadows. Yet their reign is not eternal; they serve as sovereigns in waiting, temporary stewards of power until the birth of the True Serpent Heir.

True Serpent Heir: The destined successor born from the sacred bloodline of the Serpent King. Unlike the Prodigies who fought through death and darkness to claim the throne, the True Serpent Heir inherits their crown by birthright. Marked by ancient power and gifted with abilities unseen in generations, their arrival signifies the end of bloodshed. The Heir is both ruler and omen—a living embodiment of balance, unity, and peace within the assassin guild.

The Shadow Gauntlet: A brutal trial of survival where all living Prodigies are forced to fight to the death, bound by ancient law and watched by the clans they represent. The Gauntlet determines the next ruler of the assassin guild—the last one standing ascends as King or Queen.

Assassin Guild: The united body of all assassin clans—an empire of shadows bound by shared law, secrecy, and blood. Though divided by creed and insignia, every clan answers to the Guild's authority, its hierarchy upheld by the reigning King or Queen.

About the Author

Ky'erra Sylva, gifted name "Wolf", is a fantasy author captivated by the shadows between vengeance and love. With a degree in criminology and training in six combat sports, Wolf crafts emotionally intense, action-driven narratives that explore power, identity, and destiny. Their stories feature morally complex heroines, ancient powers, and high-stakes worlds. When not writing, Wolf can be found reading fantasy novels, refining fight techniques, or exploring the symbolic layers of myth. Their current work-in-progress is a sapphic assassin fantasy set in an elite academy where loyalty is lethal and shadows hold ancient secrets.

Acknowledgments

First and foremost, I want to thank one of my best friends, **Sydney**. From the very beginning, she's been one of my biggest supporters—constantly asking about my book, giving feedback, and staying involved every step of the way. She inspired the character **Emilia**, though I may have added a few dramatic twists here and there (which I'm sure Syd will find hilarious).

To my other best friend, **Jenna**, who was often randomly forced to give her opinion on the book covers, ideas, a scene, or a line with absolutely no context of the story—you handled it like a pro. I love your honesty, your patience, and your delicacy in telling me when something wasn't working.

To my friends who have been endlessly excited for this book—thank you for your encouragement, and for bullying me just enough to make sure I actually finished it whenever my "short breaks" turned into month-long disappearances.

A special thank you to **Whitney**, my amazing beta reader. If she hadn't liked the book, I probably would have scrapped the entire thing and started over from page one.

And to **Walker**—I take time out of my day just to mess with you, but you've always had my back. You really helped me push this book out into the world. I'd write something sweet, but since this will be public forever, I can't have any evidence. You're alright.

To all my friends—you've been my foundation through this entire writing process. Your laughter, your patience, and your belief in me have meant everything. I am forever grateful.